KRESLEY COLE

sweet ruin

**SIMON &
SCHUSTER**

London · New York · Sydney · Toronto · New Delhi

A CBS COMPANY

First published in the USA by Gallery, an imprint of Simon & Schuster, Inc., 2015
First published in Great Britain by Simon & Schuster UK Ltd., 2015
A CBS COMPANY

This paperback edition, 2016

1 3 5 7 9 10 8 6 4 2

Simon & Schuster UK Ltd
1st Floor
222 Gray's Inn Road
London WC1X 8HB

www.simonandschuster.co.uk

Simon & Schuster Australia, Sydney
Simon & Schuster India, New Delhi

A CIP catalogue record for this book
is available from the British Library

Paperback ISBN: 978-1-4711-1368-0
eBook ISBN: 978-1-4711-1369-7

Printed and bound by CPI Group (UK) Ltd, Croydon, CR0 4YY

MIX
Paper from
responsible sources
FSC® C020471

Simon & Schuster UK Ltd are committed to sourcing paper
that is made from wood grown in sustainable forests and support the Forest
Stewardship Council, the leading international forest certification organisation.
Our books displaying the FSC logo are printed on FSC certified paper.

Dedicated with much gratitude to Nancy Tonik, production genius.

You always help me build a better book.

EXCERPTED FROM
THE LIVING BOOK OF LORE . . .

The Lore

". . . and those sentient creatures that are not human shall be united in one stratum, coexisting with, yet secret from, man's."

- Most are immortal and can regenerate from injuries, killed only by mystical fire or beheading.

Primordial

"The mightiest of them all; filled with power, magicks, and majesty."

- The firstborn—or the oldest generation—of a species.

The Møriør

"In the tongue of the Elserealms, Møriør can mean both 'The Dozen' and 'Soul's Doom.'"

- An alliance of otherworldly beings led by Orion the Undoing.
- Have seized control of most planes of existence.

The Noble Fey of Grimm Dominion

"A warrior nobility who ruled over all the demon serfs in their realm."

- Were *féodals*, an ancient term for feudal overlords, which became shortened to *fey*.
- Their source dimension is Draiksulia, their empire the Grimm Dominion.

The Dark Fey

"Offspring between darkness and light. Cursed banes on the fey."

- Halflings born of a fey and a demon.
- Their black blood is poisonous, known as baneblood.

The Demonarchies

"The demons are as varied as the bands of man. . . ."

- A collection of demon dynasties.
- Most demon breeds can teleport or trace to places they've previously been.
- A demon must have intercourse with a potential mate to ascertain if she's truly his—a process known as *attempting*.

The Accession

"And a time shall come to pass when all immortal beings in the Lore, from the Valkyries, vampire, Lykae, and demon factions to the witches, shifters, fey, and sirens . . . must fight and destroy each other."

- A kind of mystical checks-and-balances system for an ever-growing population of immortals.
- Occurs every five hundred years. Or right now . . .

sweet
ruin

Those who oppose us will know their doom.

—Rune Darklight (a.k.a. Rune the Baneblood
and Rune the Insatiable),
assassin and secrets master of the Møriør

When in doubt, squeeze till something breaks.

—Josephine Doe (a.k.a. Lady Shady)

ONE

Houston County, Texas
Fourteen years ago

Jo woke to the taste of copper.

She smacked her lips, moving her tongue. *Something's in my mouth?*

Her eyes flashed open. She bolted upright, and spat two pieces of crumpled metal. *What the hell are those?*

Clutching her aching head, she gazed around, wrinkling her nose at the antiseptic smell. *Where am I?* Her vision was blurry, the light dim. She thought the room was tiled.

Shit, was she in a hospital? No good. That'd mean she and Thaddie were back in the foster system and off the streets. Which meant she'd be breaking him out yet again.

Where was he? Why couldn't she remember what happened?

Think, Jo. THINK! What's the last thing you remember?

Slowly images of the day began to surface. . . .

It's getting too hot to stay here.

Closing in on the library, Jo scanned the streets for the gang lord's

Monte Carlo. She thought she heard its newly replaced engine rumbling a couple of blocks over.

The streets of this hood were a maze, the Monte Carlo a dragon. She was a plucky superhero, carrying her trusty sidekick on her back.

But last night hadn't been a game.

She craned her head around to ask Thaddie, "What do you think?" His little body was secured in the Thadpack—the stolen backpack she'd modified, cutting out holes for his legs. "We lost 'em, didn't we?"

"Loss 'em!" He waved his single toy, his Spider-Man doll, to celebrate.

She and Thaddie needed to get scarce, maybe head to Florida, making a new start in Key West.

She eyed their surroundings one last time, then slipped through the library's back door, left open for her by Mrs. Brayden, part-time librarian/full-time busybody, a.k.a. MizB.

The woman was in the lounge, already setting up the high chair. Her picnic basket was full.

Do I smell fried chicken?

"Hope you two are hungry." Her dark-brown shoulder-length hair had a touch of gray. Her eyes were light brown behind her boxy glasses. As usual, she wore some lame pantsuit.

Don't look too eager for chicken. "Whatever." Jo freed Thaddie from the pack, then took a seat, adjusting him in her lap. "Guess we could eat." She propped her combat boots on the table.

MizB sighed at Jo's outfit: ratty jeans, a stained T-shirt, and a black hoodie. The woman had offered to do laundry for them, as if Jo and Thaddie had a wardrobe of other stuff to change into while they waited.

"We need to talk, Jo." She sat, but didn't unload the basket.

"Uh-oh, Thaddie, it looks like we're about to get a lecture." Jo winked at him. "What do we say to MizB when she lectures us?"

He grinned at the woman, his adorable face dimpling, then yelled, "Fuggoff fuggoff fuggoff!"

Jo laughed, but MizB was unamused. "Excellent, Josephine. Now he has a potty mouth because of you."

"He hasn't reached his full potential of potty. Oh, but he will. Because my baby bro is brilliant!" Two and a half years old, and he was a boy genius.

At least, that's how old she thought he was. Thirty months ago, she'd been found wandering the outskirts of Houston, wearing black robes and speaking "gibberish." She'd clutched Thaddie in her arms, hissing at anyone who tried to take him from her. Before that day, she had no memories.

The docs had put him as a newborn and her age at eight. They'd figured head trauma had caused her memory loss.

No parents had come to claim them. *Fuckers.*

Sensing the drop in her mood, Thaddie made his Spidey doll kiss Jo's cheek. "Mwah!" He smiled again. The kid loved showing off his new teeth.

Whereas Jo would just as soon sneer at someone, he babbled greetings to everyone, inviting them to play with his toy. If she'd ever owned a toy of her own, she never would've *shared* it with people who weren't Thaddie.

"Be fwends?" he'd ask anyone, blinking his big hazel eyes at them, and "awws" would follow.

Folks fell in love with him as deeply as they fell in hate with Jo and her "sullen attitude," "sickly looks," and "pinched expression."

"He needs a checkup," MizB said. "And vaccinations. You both do."

"If Thaddie didn't like you so much, I would've popped you in the mouth by now. You realize that, don't you?" She swiped her sleeve under his running nose. "He's fine. We're doing fine." Jo had never meant to get so dependent on the woman.

A year ago, the tiny library had seemed like a good hideout for the day. She'd planned to steal some comics and wash herself and Thaddie in the bathroom like the rest of the homeless did.

MizB had set out food for Jo and Thaddie, then backed away, as if she were luring feral cats.

Fuck if it hadn't worked. Woman made a mean tuna-fish sandwich.

They'd dropped by the next day, and the next, until Jo actually trusted her enough to leave Thaddie for an hour now and then.

Whenever Jo had to do battle against villains.

Sometimes doing battle got dangerous. She glanced at the window. *Way too hot to stay here.* She'd need bus fare. MizB would watch Thaddie, and Jo could go roll some tourists. Doing her part to make their vacation more eventful.

"So are we gonna get to lunch, or what?" A full meal for the road wouldn't be bad.

"In time." MizB was holding out till she'd said her piece.

That chicken smelled like deep-fried crack. MizB was a sorceress! One the heroine and plucky sidekick must resist!

As much as Jo liked the food, she hated the way Thaddie gulped it down, like he knew he was only getting gas station chow until the next basket. Made her feel like shit.

So what was Jo going to do when they ditched this town? Who'd baby-sit Thaddie? Who'd feed them every day?

"You might be doing okay," MizB said. "But you'd do better with me and Mr. B." Her husband was a ruddy-faced dude whose laugh sounded like it came out of a barrel. He picked his wife up from the library and dropped her off every day, walking her to the door as if she were precious cargo. He clearly didn't like her working in one of the worst hoods in Texas.

When the two of them thought no one was looking, they linked pinkies. 'Cause they were tools. MizB smelled like cinnamon and sun, Mr. B. like motor oil and sun.

Jo had no urges to do lasting violence to them—her highest measure of approval.

MizB continued, "But we can't adopt you two unless you get back into the system."

With no sign of parents, Jo and Thaddie were adoptable. The Braydens were okayed for adoption.

Jo didn't trust the system. "And what happens if you and Mr. B. don't get us? Did I ever tell you about my first foster 'father'? Night one, dickwad shoved his hand down my pants—before the freaking *Late Show* came on."

"Digwad!" Thad echoed.

MizB pursed her lips. "That man is the exception to the rule. And you should've reported him. Other children might get sent to him."

"No. No chance of that." Jo had set dickwad's house on fire, using the silver Zippo she'd already stolen from him—before the freaking evening news had come on.

The look on his face as he watched his place burn still made her chuckle. From their spot in the bushes, Thaddie had clapped his little hands. Fires were free fun. *Just ask that gang lord . . .*

"Do I even want to know?" MizB asked.

"Nope." There'd be no system for them. If the Braydens didn't land the Doe siblings, Jo and Thaddie would be separated.

Docs had diagnosed her with scary-sounding disorders and disabilities; Thaddie was in the ninety-ninth percentile of everything good.

Her eyes and skin were jaundiced. Thaddie was pink-cheeked and bright-eyed. Every time she pulled down her hoodie, more of her hair would fall out. His was curling down.

Inside and out, she was as bad and defective as Thad was good and perfect. The only thing the siblings had in common was the color of their eyes—hazel irises with blue flecks.

"If you come to our house, it would be *for good*." MizB looked fiercer than Jo had ever seen her. "We'd never let anyone take the two of you from us. We'd be a family."

Jo's opinion of the woman rose a notch. Still she said, "Are we done yet? For fuck's sake, woman, feed us."

MizB glared, but she did unpack the basket. "You need to be in school."

"It didn't take." Jo couldn't read. Kids caught on. Her awkward attempts to make friends had turned into scrapping, a pastime she preferred to do outside of a structured environment.

Jo had Thaddie; nothing else mattered.

In a kiddie bowl, MizB mixed pieces of chicken with mashed potatoes. Thaddie grew still, eyes locked on the grub. His stomach growled; Jo's chin jutted. *Mental note: Steal more gas station chow between baskets.*

Wait . . . When they left for the Keys, there'd be no more baskets.

He was clambering for the high chair before the woman had even sprinkled cornbread crumbles on top of the chicken mash. She wouldn't hand it over till he'd accepted a kiddie spoon from her.

"Like we taught you, Thaddeus."

"We?" Jo snorted. "Two hands, ten fingers. What's he need a spoon for?"

Once Thaddie was shoveling food into his piehole, MizB started back up again. "Mr. B. and I lie awake at night worrying about you two out here." She and her hubby lived in the burbs. Ginormous yard. The woman had shown Jo on a map, then withheld barbecue until Jo could recite the address.

If MizB knew a fraction of what went on in these streets . . .

But Jo saw all.

The local gang lord was the worst. The street people called him the Wall because of his steroidal build, but also because he liked to screw his prostitutes from behind; in other words, your back was always up against him. Jo nicknamed him Wally.

He hung with a pair of brothers named TJ and JT. *Because cleverness.* The hookers named the older brother Knuckle behind his back since his dick was the length of a finger from knuckle to knuckle. The younger brother didn't even merit a body-part nickname. The fourth crony was called Nobody. In other words: "Who did it?" "Nobody."

Girls went into Wally's crib one way, and after screams sounded, they stumbled out different. Whatever those four were doing in that house took the fight out of girls. Which was unforgivable.

Jo worshipped fighting. She dreamed about being a comic-book superheroine—just so she'd have an excuse to mess people up. With no superpowers on the horizon, she'd launched a one-girl guerrilla war, kicking the ant mound and running.

She'd started out small. Stick of butter underneath the door handle of Wally's car. A little breaking and entering to slather his toilet seat with superglue. Then sand in the Monte Carlo's gas tank.

She could stomach the risks, but she had a kid to think about. So why couldn't she stop herself? It was as if some instinct was *forcing* her to target prey, stalk it, then hurt it.

She'd struck a much bigger blow last night, putting a stop to Wally's revolving door of bad. She grinned.

When a car rumbled down a nearby side street, her grin faded. *Waaaay too hot.* She could feel the dragon's breath.

"Come stay with us, Josephine. Just try it out," MizB said. "There are only so many times I can watch you leave here before I do something."

Jo went motionless. She gave the woman the same scary stare she'd given that dickwad foster dad, the look that got him to yank his hand away and back off. "You report us, and I'll bust Thaddie out just like I always do, and I'll take him so far away you'll never see him again. We clear?" *You're already gonna do that, Jo.*

How would MizB react? It'd probably break her. Which Jo didn't care about. At all. Jo's job was looking out for number one.

"I have no doubt. That's why I stop my fingers from dialing Child Protective Services every day."

"*I* am his mom," Jo said, even as Thaddie shoveled the woman's grub into his mouth.

MizB softly said, "A mother would want better for her son."

She sounded reasonable, but here was the thing: Jo *was* feral. There'd be no living under someone else's roof and following someone else's rules. Rules didn't apply to Jo and never had.

There'd be no sharing Thaddie with a woman who desperately wanted to be his mother.

He's mine, not hers. He was Jo's number one.

But a tiny part of her said, *Thaddie's not feral. Not yet.* Sometimes Jo had dreams about him with the Braydens. The three of them as a family.

Those dreams weirded her out, because she wasn't in them.

Done with this, Jo snagged a chicken leg and stood. "I gotta blaze. Be back in an hour or so." She swooped in to kiss Thaddie. "Mwah!" Then she whispered to him, "Bitch tries anything, you tit-punch her."

He nodded happily. Smacking cornbread, he said, "Bye-bye, JoJo."

MizB walked her to the door. "Out to pick pockets again?"

"Yeah, you want me to grab you anything while I'm out?"

But the woman grew really serious. "How can you touch a child so innocent and good when your hands aren't clean?"

Jo shoved the chicken leg in her mouth, raising both hands. Around the drumstick, she said, "Clean as they'll ever be."

"That's not true, Josephine. I think you've forgotten you're just a little girl."

"Little girl? I've been a lot of things, but that ain't one of them. . . ."

Out on the street, Jo mimicked, "How can you touch him? Meh meh MEH meh meh." She snatched a bite of chicken, hating how good it was.

She turned the corner. Stopped in her tracks and swallowed hard. The chicken fell from her limp fingers.

A gun barrel was pointed at her face.

Wally.

Behind him stood his trio of asshole friends. They all looked spaced-out, eyes crazy bloodshot.

Wally's long, stringy hair had been singed, and sweat poured down his blistered face. "People been saying the creepy pale girl's always fucking with me." His words were slurred, and the gun shook in his bandaged hand. "People been saying she was sneaking around my place last night. So I'm gonna ask the creepy pale girl once: why'd my goddamned house catch on fire last night—with us in it?"

Oh. Shit. "You left your teakettle on again?"

"Wrong answer, bitch." He squeezed the trigger, and all the world went dark.

Wally had shot Jo in the face! So how had she lived? And where was she? Damn, her scalp was itching like crazy. She scratched—

A crumpled piece of metal was sprouting . . . sprouting from her forehead! She stifled a cry as she scraped it out. Immediately her vision cleared.

She pinched the thing between her fingers. Recognition. A spent bullet had just come out of her skull!

She found others caught in her hair. Shed from her head too? She collected them with the two that had been in her mouth. In her cupped palms she held six slugs.

But I'm alive. I'm . . . bulletproof?

I AM a superhero. (Secretly she'd always known it!)

She pocketed the slugs, narrowing her eyes. It was payback time. She hopped down from the table, or tried to. She floated to her feet—feet that *weren't touching the ground.*

She gaped down at her body. She was wearing her same clothes, but her faint outline flickered. She glanced at the table. Atop it, a zipped-up body bag lay flat. This was a morgue? Other bodies in bags were lined up on tables, waiting for whatever happened in fucking morgues.

Realization sank in.

I was in that empty bag.

Because I died.

I'm a . . . ghost.

Her gaze darted. How the hell was she going to care for Thaddie? Surely MizB had taken him home after the shooting.

Jo's shooting.

Wally and his crew killed me! Those pricks! She squeezed her fists and screamed. The lights above shattered, glass raining down.

She'd haunt Wally until he went insane, would drive them all crazy! She needed to hurt them—NOW!

Suddenly she felt herself moving, as if she were being sucked into the air. She blinked; her surroundings had disappeared, replaced with the hood. She was standing in front of Wally's still smoking house.

She'd . . . teleported here? Of course! Because she was *supposed* to get revenge. That's what ghosts did. Once she'd finished with that, she'd go snag Thaddie; they'd find a spooky deserted mansion somewhere. Live happily ever after and all that shit.

First step: get a bead on Wally. She started walking/floating over cracks in the sidewalk. Why did this movement seem so familiar? Why was her ghostness not freaking her out?

There was something so right about her new form, as if she should've been freaking out about her existence *all the years before.*

Homeless kids and runaways, other street rats like her, peeked out from lean-tos and abandoned cars. Gasps sounded as she made her way along the street.

So ghosts were visible to people. Would she meet other ghosts?

She heard the kids' whispers. They all knew Wally had killed her. Some had watched her body get bagged.

A prostitute on the corner didn't see her coming and backed right into—or *through*—Jo. Their bodies got tangled, and suddenly Jo was inside her, sharing her movements as the woman shuddered.

It was as if Jo was a hermit crab in a hooker-shaped shell. She couldn't feel anything through the woman's skin, but she could make her move. *Awesome!*

When Jo backed out of the shell, disentangling herself, the woman turned around with a terrified look on her face.

A moment passed before she registered what she was seeing. "Oh God!" She stumbled back, making the sign of the cross. "You died! The Wall shot you."

"It didn't take." Jo's voice sounded ghostly and hollow. "Where's Wally staying now?"

The woman sputtered, "F-few houses down from his old crib."

Jo float-walked back in that direction. Others followed her at a distance, wide-eyed, as if they couldn't help themselves.

She found the digs—with the dragon guarding the lair. Voices sounded from inside, Wally's among them.

Her nails lengthened and sharpened. They were *black*, and they ached. *Ghosts have claws?*

She tried to teleport into the house, but her body didn't move, so she float-walked up to the porch, stopping at the front door. Could she knock? They probably wouldn't open for her. Maybe she could "ghost" into the house, as she had the hooker shell.

With a shrug, Jo floated forward—and passed right through the door. Score! *Breaking and entering* would now simply be *entering*.

In the den, packets of smack and guns topped the coffee table. They'd already replaced all the weapons and drugs. Bags of new clothes were strewn around the house.

These dickwads had set up a few doors down. Burning down his pad had done jack.

Jo clenched her fists. She'd only come here to scare the gang, to moan *woo-woo* and send them running. But rage took hold of her.

Her claws ached to slash someone.

When the lights flickered, Knuckle and the two others glanced up. Saw Jo. Their mouths moved wordlessly—

They lunged for the guns.

With a shriek, she flew at Knuckle. "You gonna shoot me?" She slashed out with her claws. She half-expected her fingers to pass through his torso—yet four deep gashes appeared on his belly.

She gasped. Her claws dripped with his blood. She could become solid when she wanted to?

He clutched his bloody stomach, but guts slithered out between his fingers like eels. His knees met the blood-wetted carpet, and then he collapsed.

I just dropped a dude! Superheroes didn't kill people. Not even bad people.

She should be screaming, yet all this felt natural. *This is me. I ghost. I hurt bad guys.*

No, I hunt *them.*

Realization struck her. She'd always been *hunting.*

Been waiting for this. All. My. Life.

JT and Nobody scrambled toward the door, barely got it open. She flew after them, catching them on the porch. She easily dragged both men back inside. She winked at the kids gathering across the street, then kicked the door shut.

The pair screamed as she attacked. Red covered her vision, some kind of animal instinct taking over. As she slashed, blood splattered; her head spun.

Then she realized neither of them was moving. *I've dropped* three *dudes.*

Her ears twitched, and she heard a low moan from a back room. Wally. *Let's make it an even four.* He must've peeked out and seen Jo offing his posse.

She ghosted through the door into another room. "Oh, Wall-ee . . ." Muffled breaths sounded from under the bed.

She floated downward until she was directly in line with him. "Psst!"

He jerked his head around and yelled with horror. Like a rat, he scurried out on the other side of the bed.

She floated upright, taking her time. He pointed another huge gun at her and fired away, unloading bullets. When they passed through her into the wall, he pissed himself.

She wanted to meet his eyes, to make him understand what he'd done. She felt herself moving, disappearing and reappearing right in front of him. *Handy.* She floated higher to catch his gaze. "You shouldn't have shot me."

"N-never do it again," he said, blubbering.

"Wrong answer, dick. I'll see you in hell." She would. No one could enjoy hunting as much as she did and not wind up there—

He swung a bat he'd concealed behind his back; her hand shot out in reflex, striking.

Blood spurted from his throat. The bat fell as he clamped his neck. Gushes of crimson escaped to spray over her.

Her feet touched the ground, her body solidifying, as if to catch the shower. Her appetite leapt. Her teeth ached. She could swear they were sharper. As he watched in glassy-eyed shock, she raised her face with curiosity and parted her lips.

The first drop hit her tongue. Delicious! Her eyes rolled as blood filled her mouth.

She swallowed with a gulp. *I'm drinking Wally's blood.* Part of her was grossed out, but as warmth slid down her throat, power flooded her.

Her senses came to life, her eyes picking up new colors, as if she had comic-book infrared vision. The hum of distant streetlights buzzed in her ears. She could smell baitfish down by the bay.

As Wally collapsed, she heard his last heartbeat.

She gave a cry when her hoodie began stretching across her chest, her zipper ripping open. The waist of her jeans cut into her sides. *What's happening to me?* She rushed into the bathroom, clawing away her strangling clothes. She was burning up. From the blood?

She reached into the shower and twisted the tap on, as cold as she could get it. When she scrubbed away the gang's remains, her palms glided over her skin. It'd grown soft as silk, the jaundiced color fading.

She gaped down at her body. She'd filled out, no longer sickly thin! No bones jutted. Even better, she had tons of energy! She exited the shower and crossed to the basin with a spring in her step.

She stared at her reflection. An eerily pretty girl with gleaming black eyes and a blacker heart stared back.

Dark smudges highlighted her gaze like heavy eyeliner and hollowed her cheeks. Her full lips were blood red.

For kicks, she tried to return to her "ghost" form. She went completely invisible, then dialed it back a notch to *faint-ish*. Worked! The circles around her eyes deepened and her lips turned pale, yet even that appearance was pretty.

To look and feel like this, all she had to do was steal others' lifeblood?

She'd awakened a ghost; now she was a blood-drinker too. A vampire.

No, she wasn't a *superhero*.

Jo flashed a fang at the mirror. *I'm a fucking villain*.

Her heart soared. This was her origin story. She was going to be a legend (Secretly she'd known that too)!

Then her heart sank. Thaddie. *Gotta get to him*. Shit, she needed clothes. She scrounged through those bags until she found JT's smaller threads. She slipped on a pair of sweats, rolling them up and tying them tight, then snagged a jersey.

With her revenge done, the urgency to find her brother overwhelmed her. Could she teleport to him as well?

She pictured him with MizB in some burbs house. Nothing. Jo strained to teleport. Didn't move an inch. *Do this the old-fashioned way*. She tore out of the house, running toward the neighborhood MizB had shown her on a library map. Past the interstate, past the tower, past the pond . . .

Right when Jo thought she'd maxed her speed, she increased it. Trees and houses zoomed by. She was like a rocket!

In minutes, she'd reached the outskirts of the neighborhood. She raised her face to scent the wind.

Thaddie. Close. She followed his trail to a fancy house. Outside, she leapt into a tree, peering in windows. Spotted him! He was asleep in what looked like a guest bedroom. She imagined sitting beside him on that bed; suddenly, she was.

Adult voices murmured just beyond the door. The Braydens.

God, Thaddie looked so small and vulnerable under the covers, his Spidey doll clutched in his tiny hand. What if he'd been in the Thadpack when Wally had struck? What if he'd . . . died?

The more emotional Jo got, the more she wavered between ghost and body. She had to get Thaddie out of here before the Braydens saw her. "Wake up, baby bro," she whispered.

He blinked open his eyes, sitting up in bed.

"We gotta go, Thaddie."

His brows drew together. She heard his heartbeat race. "You're not JoJo."

She couldn't look *that* different. "It's me, kid."

"Not JoJo, not JoJo," he repeated as he scrambled back from her.

"It's me. Spidey knows me." She reached for the doll, to get a kiss on her cheek.

Thad yanked it from her, yelling, "You're not JoJo! Not JoJo! NOT JOJO!"

She shot back in confusion, her palms raised; the door burst open. The Braydens.

MizB gasped at Jo, then lunged for Thaddie on the bed. Mr. B. shoved them behind him, his strong arm protecting them.

From me?

"Oh, dear God," MizB murmured, as Thaddie squeezed her like a lifeline. "You d-died."

Jo nodded.

"You need to pass on." Mr. B. swallowed. "Or s-something."

The three of them looked like . . . a family.

Jo's voice cracked as she said, "Thaddie?"

He wouldn't look at her, burying his face against MizB's neck. Jo reached for him, but her fingers passed right through him. Grasping, grasping for her little boy.

The Braydens shielded him, MizB screaming, "Get away from him, you, you ghost or . . . or demon! Go back to hell where you came from!"

No, Thaddie's mine! When he wailed as if in pain, Jo's eyes watered. She told the Braydens, "I'm gonna get this figured out. But I will be coming back for him."

MizB whispered, *"Don't."*

Jo floated forward, yearning for one last stroke of Thaddie's curls . . . but she felt nothing. She couldn't touch him, couldn't hug him. Her Thaddie. A sob burst from her lips. *I did die after all.*

And this *is hell.*

TWO

TEN MONTHS LATER

I t was finally time to collect her boy.

Jo ghosted to the Brayden house and stood outside a window, scanning for him among the people crowding the rooms. They were all dressed in black, talking in hushed voices.

She was busting Thaddie out tonight, couldn't stand the separation anymore without tearing her hair out. . . .

For the first couple of months, she'd ghosted around the household, hovering over him as the Braydens spoiled him with tons of toys and a puppy and all the things Jo had wanted to give him. His washed Spidey doll sat on his toy shelf, buried among all the others.

If Thaddie called out for her, Jo had been there in an instant, never quite showing herself. Yet at the same time, her presence had seemed to upset him.

She'd found the Thadpack in a closet and had stolen it back—would hug it like an idiot.

For the next couple of months, she'd tried to back off, watching over him from a distance. Other kids came over to play, and he was always so psyched, finally having the "fwends" he'd longed for. They ran around in the Braydens' perfect backyard with the puppy on their heels.

Her baby brother called out for her less.

While Thaddie grew like a weed and laughed more and more, Jo had been doing her worst, no closer to figuring herself out or controlling her on-again, off-again ghosting. Sure, she could float right into his bedroom, but how could she nab him when she was just air?

Determined to get to the bottom of her transformation, she'd returned to town. The hospital's blood bank had drawn her. After gorging on bags, she'd gotten her body back, growing solid.

She guessed that was what vampires did. Though she did wonder why she could still go out in the sun.

Stronger from drinking, she'd practiced switching from ghost-mode to body and back. In time, she could ghost *things*. Anything she carried turned to air like her, but returned to solid as soon as she let go: purses from cars, clothes from stores, a wigged-out cat.

She'd worked hard at it until she felt confident she could steal Thaddie.

But deep down, she knew he was better off with two parents and his treasured puppy. So she'd strung together the filed bullet slugs from her "death" to make a necklace. If tempted to return, she touched the bullets, reminding herself she wasn't right.

MizB had banished Jo for a reason. And the woman didn't even know Jo was a killer ghost/vampire.

So she'd hung out at the morgue, hoping for someone like her to float out of a body bag, but it'd never happened.

She'd tried so hard to stay away. . . .

Then last week, she'd seen the coroner working on a corpse.

It was Mr. B.

Killed in a work accident. He never rose, just stayed dead.

It was a *sign* for Jo to return. Surely?

No longer were the Braydens better than Jo just 'cause there were two of them, and MizB would be in no shape to raise a kid on her own. Jo was sorry the woman would lose her husband and Thaddie all at the same time, but she couldn't take this any longer.

She'd decided to let Thaddie attend Mr. B's wake today, but then she was done. Once MizB put him to bed, Jo would go to him. She had the Thadpack with her and everything.

She could be just as good a mom as MizB. She could protect Thaddie, was strong enough to lift a freaking car. Rolling folks for money had never been easier, so she could buy him toys. And she hadn't killed a single person since that first night. In self-defense, she sometimes squashed guys' balls like grapes—but zero murders!

She craned her head. Where was he? The sun would soon set. There! He was scampering into the room, dressed in a little black suit with tufts of dog fur on the pants.

Looking from the pack to Thaddie, she realized he'd never fit. Maybe she could stuff the dog in there.

She'd take Thaddie's hand, and the three of them would all ghost away together.

He crawled up to sit in an older woman's lap. Jo had seen the lady visit before. She was MizB's mom, Thaddie's . . . "Gram." The old chick was explaining to him that she would live there from now on and help out around the house.

Isn't that swell? Jo squeezed the pack. *He's mine!* Her necklace felt cold and heavy around her throat.

Storm clouds gathered, thunder rumbling. Jo glared at the sky. Unlike her, Thaddie shouldn't be out in the rain.

MizB came into the room, her eyes all puffy. She must feel like crap rolled over, but she wasn't crying, and her dress and hair were neat.

Thaddie crawled from the old woman's lap to MizB's. Gazing up at her with those big hazel eyes, he asked, "Mama, where did Daddy go?"

Jo swayed, her breath knocked from her lungs. *Mama?* Tears welled and spilled. He hadn't even called Jo that.

If she took him today, Thaddie would lose a father *and* a mother. Would that mess him up beyond hope?

The clouds opened up, rain falling as fast as her tears. Drops streamed through her; she must've gone into ghost-mode without noticing.

MizB wrapped her arms around him. Jealousy clawed at Jo when he curled up against the woman with so much trust. Jo found herself clutching the Thadpack to her chest.

Keeping a stiff upper lip, MizB answered, "Oh, sweetheart, remember? Daddy's gone to heaven to be with JoJo."

Knife in gut. Knife in gut. Knife in gut.

Jo stood in the worsening storm, heart shriveling—because she'd reached a conclusion about Thaddie's future.

I won't be in it.

She pressed her palm to the window. Though no imprint showed, she willed him to turn in her direction, to *see* her.

But he didn't.

Tears pouring, she hugged the Thadpack tighter. Between sobs, she whispered, "Bye-bye, Thaddie." She turned away, with no idea where to go.

As night fell, she ghosted down the lonely highway with only the storm as her companion. . . .

THREE

The dimension of Tenebrous,
Perdishian Castle, capital of the Elserealms

Beings of power stirred in the echoing stronghold as Rune Darklight made his way through the immense black castle.

He was the sole Møriør who'd stayed awake for the last five centuries and was tasked with rousing the others when Tenebrous had ground through time and space to near its destination: Gaia.

Also known as Earth. Rune had sounded the telepathic call moments ago.

Boots clicking across the ancient stone floor, he entered the war room—a chamber with a massive star-shaped table and a wall made of blast-proof glass.

Outside the glass, against a slate of black nothingness, images of worlds flashed by, as if from a film projector.

He took one of the twelve empty seats at the table, propping his boots up on the gold surface as he awaited his allies. Or at least, he awaited five of them. Two seats remained vacant, and four Møriør would slumber on; considering their natures, waiting to unleash them on Gaia was for the best.

Abyssian Infernas, prince of Pandemonia, was the first to join Rune. Sian, as his compatriots called him, was over seven feet tall and muscled, with long black hair. He wore leather bands over his broad chest and dark trews.

Rune could admit the prince of hells was as wickedly handsome as the devil who'd sired him.

Sian turned his green eyes toward the glass wall. "Good, we're still a few days out. Gives us time to prepare." He took his seat at the table. "I haven't been to Earth in ages."

"Much has changed. As you'll soon see." Rune had been the others' eyes and ears over the last five centuries, documenting every realm he'd visited. Once his allies had convened, they would delve into his memories, updating their speech and learning about these new times in which they would war.

They were in for some graphic scenes; Rune had spent most of his years plowing slick nymph flesh.

Out of habit, he slid an arrow from the quiver strapped to his calf. He tapped his forefinger on the arrowhead, collecting some of his black blood to draw symbols on the shaft. With those demonic runes, he could focus his fey magicks, amplifying a regular arrow into one of power.

Allixta, the Overlady of Witches and the newest Møriør, entered, sauntering toward the table. How she walked in such a skintight dress baffled Rune. A question for the ages. "Are we finally here?" Curses, her familiar, trailed her. The creature was an Elserealm breed of panther, so large its whiskers brushed her shoulders.

"Close enough to wake," Rune answered.

Adjusting the brim of her oversize witch's hat, she sank into her chair. Curses hopped atop the table, reclined its gigantic frame, then hissed at Rune.

Rune hissed back, baring his demon fangs.

"This is what I wake to, baneblood?" Allixta glared at his arrow. "Why spill your disgusting poison in the presence of others? Do you intend to cause offense?"

Rune paused his drawing. As a dark fey, he had poisonous black blood, fatal even to immortals. "My dearest Allixta, if I've caused offense, it was unwittingly done—but a welcome development."

Blace, the oldest vampire, suddenly appeared in his seat at the table, goblet of blood mead in hand. His dark-brown hair was tied back into a neat queue, and he wore an impeccable suit, though the shirt, cravat, doublet, and breeches were centuries outdated.

"Good awakening, friend," Rune said. He liked the vampire. Blace provided welcome counsel. He was sparing with it, and usually dead-on.

Blace swigged his libation. "I wonder what sights your mind will show us this time."

Darach Lyka, the first werewolf, entered the chamber, still transforming from his wolven form. The primordial wolf wore only trews and carried a wadded-up tunic in one fist. Rune had little in common with the quietly intense Darach—other than a mutual loathing of Allixta—but Rune respected him.

The best tracker in the worlds, Darach had proven invaluable in locating magickal objects. And on the few occasions when he'd mastered his beast and was able to communicate more easily, he'd shared keen insights, demonstrating a surprising cynicism for a man who'd risen from the dead.

Now Darach struggled to reclaim his human body, compacting his nine-foot-tall werewolf frame. Fangs grinding, he clenched his fists tighter, his bones cracking into place.

Each transition grew more difficult. One day Darach would transform into a beast and never return. Unless he found a way to keep his human form. Perhaps in the Gaia realm?

In addition to the Møriør's overarching aims, each of them coveted something from Earth and its connected planes, had traveled across the universe to collect.

Most thought Rune wanted the throne of his home world. No, his desires ran much darker than that. As dark as his unnatural black blood. . . .

Their liege, Orion—the Undoing—was the last to convene. He was a being of unknown descent, but Rune believed he was at least a demigod. Perhaps a full deity, or even an overdeity.

Orion's appearance and scent had changed; he altered them regularly. Today he was a tall blond demon. At their last meeting, he'd been a black-haired giant.

He moved to the glass wall without saying a word. He could remain silent for a decade. Before him, that line of ever-changing planets floated by as the stronghold passed one after another.

Now that all the awakened Møriør had assembled, the others began digging into Rune's mind. Their mental link was so strong, they could even speak to each other telepathically.

He opened his memories wide for them, offering access to almost everything, at least after the first millennium of his life. He worked to conceal that earlier time of betrayals and violation.

Within a few moments, Blace raised an approving brow. "A dozen nymphs in one night?"

Rune grinned. He'd bedded thousands of them, was a favorite of Nymphae coveys far and wide. They were excellent sources of information. "That was merely the first round. The real debauchery started a day later."

Blace shook his head ruefully. "Ah, the vigor of the young." Rune was seven millennia old—young compared to Blace. "You come by your trailing name honestly."

Rune the Insatiable. He buffed his black claws. "Wringing orgasms and breaking hearts for eons."

Sian said, "Gods pity any female who loses her heart to you. I could almost feel sorry for your bedmates."

"If one of my tarts is stupid enough to want more, then she deserves all the heartache in the worlds." He made no secret of his detachment during sex. He felt physical pleasure but no connection, no immediacy—no emotions. Outside of bedsport, he did. He knew amusement; he grew excited about upcoming battles. He experienced kinship with the Møriør. But during sex . . . nothing.

Which was unsettling, since he spent a good deal of his life tupping.

"Tarts?" Allixta sneered. "You are such a whore."

A former slave, he'd known his share of insults; most didn't bother him. Now his claws sharpened as he remembered his queen's words from so long ago: *You possess the smoldering sensuality of the fey and the sexual intensity of a demon. . . . I have a use for you after all.*

Old frustrations made his tone sharp: "On the subject of whores, did I ever get around to swiving *you*, witch? For the life of me I just can't remember."

Darach bit back a roughened laugh as he pulled on his tunic.

Allixta leveled her green gaze on the wolf. "Something to say, mongrel?" Then she turned to Rune. "Trust me, baneblood, if I could stomach your befouled body long enough to bed you, you'd never forget it."

Befouled. Rune loathed his blood. Worse, she *knew* how deeply he did. Some things in his mind were too prominent to disguise from prying eyes.

He reached into his pocket, seeking the talisman he always kept near. Carved from a demon ancestor's horn and inscribed with runes even he couldn't decipher, it always helped him focus, reminding him to look toward the future—

Suddenly Sian's head jerked up. "My brother is dead?" Sian's twin, the Father of Terrors, had been as hideous as Sian was physically flawless.

Rune nodded. "Killed in a blood sport contest. Murdered in front of cheering crowds."

Blace shook his head. "Impossible. A primordial like the Father of Terrors can't be killed."

"He was slain—by a mere immortal," Rune said. "These days in the Gaia realms, they no longer fight one species against another; they've *allied* into armies. And more, these immortals don't just take down primordials. They assassinate gods."

Allixta smirked. "Perhaps your dirty blood has finally rotted your brain. Deities can't be assassinated by immortals."

He turned from her and addressed the others: "Several gods have perished, all in the last year. Including one of the witch divinities." While

Allixta sputtered, Rune reeled off names of old deities, extinguished for-ever. He studied the set of Orion's shoulders for signs of tension.

How would a god feel about the deaths of his kind?

Orion just stared at the worlds flickering past.

"Why do you trust this information from your . . . nymphs?" Allixta demanded of Rune.

"Because I pay them well in their favorite currency: stiff fuckings with a stout cock. It just so happens I'm rich beyond measure."

Before she could launch into a scathing response, Blace said, "These assassinations have occurred. Read his thoughts, Allixta. The information is there."

"They seem connected," Sian said. "It's as if someone is trying to at-tract our notice. Our very presence. Who would dare?"

"A Valkyrie named Nïx the Ever-Knowing," Rune answered. "The pri-mordial of her species." According to the nymphs, Nïx had orchestrated these killings. "She's a soothsayer and a wish giver. Close to goddesshood."

Orion often made allies of enemies—he had with Blace, Allixta, and two of the sleeping Mørïør. Would the god enlist the primordial Valkyrie?

Orion raised his flattened palm. The projections slowed, then stopped on an image of a crimson planet. He tilted his head, perceiving things no one else could.

Weaknesses.

He could see vulnerabilities in a man, a castle, an army. An entire world.

The Undoing slowly curled his fingers to make a fist. The planet began to lose shape, crumbling, as if he wadded up parchment.

Was Orion mimicking the destruction? Or *causing* it?

The world dwindled and dwindled, until it . . . disappeared. A whole realm—gone. The inhabitants dead.

Orion turned to face the others. His expression was contemplative, but his eyes . . . dark and chilling, like the abyss Sian hailed from. His fathom-less gaze fell on Rune. "Bring me the head of the Valkyrie, archer."

No enlistment. Just death. Why not attempt to sway Nïx? Two seats remained at the table, and a soothsayer was always an asset. Lore held that she was one of the most powerful oracles ever to live.

Too bad she couldn't see her own future.

Rune shrugged off his curiosity. He had no love for Valkyries anyway. They were staunch allies to the fey, a colonizing species of slavers and rapists.

Judged by the company you keep, Nix.

Rune knew she prowled the streets of a specific mortal city—a place of ready sin—from sundown to sunup. There was a large covey of water nymphs nearby. Tree nymphs as well.

They had eyes and ears in every pond, oak, and puddle.

In the name of duty, I'll pump them for information. As Rune had answered so many times over the millennia: "It is done, my liege."

FOUR

New Orleans
PRESENT DAY

*O*h, gods, Rune, so close! Pleasepleasepleaseohgods, yes, yes, YESSSSSS!"

When Jo's super-hearing picked up a third woman screaming her way to ecstasy—from the same location—her curiosity got piqued.

Time to finish up with the guy she was strangling.

She'd pinned him up against a brick wall, unmoved as he squirmed. He'd come into her territory, carrying a pimp cane?

In Jo's mind, *pimp cane* signaled *open season*. Then the fucker had *used* it on a prostitute, a girl younger than Jo. The chick huddled on the curb, cheek swelling as she watched Jo delivering punishment.

"You gonna come back here?" Jo asked, though he couldn't answer. She squeezed till things broke; this guy's windpipe was crushed. "Huh?"

Staring at her eyes, he tried to shake his head.

"You do. You die. Get me?" He attempted a nod. "And if you ever hit a woman again, I'll come for you. You'll wake up with me hovering over you in your bed, your very own nightmare." She flashed her fangs and hissed.

He started to urinate—occupational hazard—so she tossed him across the adjoining parking lot.

The girl gazed up at Jo. "Thanks, Lady Shady."

My moniker. Somehow Jo's alter ego had morphed into some weird-ass villain protector of prostitutes. Could be worse. "Yeah. S'cool."

As Jo dusted off her hands, she heard another scream. *"Rune! Rune! YES!"*

All three ecstatic women had called out that Rune guy's name. *This I gotta see.*

Though the girl was watching her, Jo went into ghost-mode. Invisible and intangible, she headed down Bourbon Street toward the screams, her feet never touching the ground.

Since she'd arrived in the city a few months ago, she'd been doing a lot of spying. The uncanny things—and beings—she'd witnessed here had lit a hope in her she hadn't felt in years.

No longer did she gaze at the stars, losing herself in dreams of having her brother back with her. No longer did she pass endless days and nights, zoning out with comics or TV.

Jo was zoning *in.*

A wasted pedestrian stumbled through her, and shuddered. So did she. Tourists were rank. They sweated like crazy, gorged on mudbugs and garlic bread, and boozed to kingdom come, like pre-detonated puke grenades.

Would she puke if she drank from them?

She'd never bitten anybody. The smell—of whatever the guy had eaten for dinner, or the starch from his collar, or the slobbery pets he'd cuddled—warded her off. Or worse, he'd reek of cologne.

Axe cologne.

How could she put her tongue on skin saturated with that crap? Until someone invented a fang condom, she'd continue stealing from the blood bank.

A few blocks off Bourbon, she came upon a high-walled courtyard. A water fountain splashed within. The woman was screaming even louder; the sound of slapping skin quickened.

Hmm. Maybe Jo could possess one of the participants, live vicariously through her. Aside from an initial shudder, the "shells" never knew she was inside.

Or Jo could pick their pockets. Her rent-by-the-week motel room was filled with loot. She pretended each stolen prize was a gift to her—a bridge to get to know someone better—just as she pretended each possession was a visit.

A connection.

Having never made a friend before, how could she know the difference?

Her compulsions to steal and to possess others had grown worse lately. Maybe she needed a real connection. She'd had so little real interaction she wondered if she'd been resurrected at all.

Sometimes, she had nightmares about floating away. Who would even notice her absence?

As Jo eased toward the entry of the courtyard, a *fourth* woman's voice sounded: "It's so good, Rune! My gods in heavens! YES! Never stop, never stop! *Never, NEVER!*"

Jo floated to the cracked-open wooden gate, peeking around to see a wicked scene.

A half-dressed blonde was pressed against the ivy-covered courtyard wall by a tall dark-haired man with his pants at his thighs. The woman's lithe legs wrapped around his waist as he bounced her.

Must be *Rune*. What kind of name was that?

Three other stunning women were sprawled naked on a lounge sofa, heavy-lidded as they watched him pounding the fourth.

This guy had just screwed them all? Line 'em up and knock 'em down? *Ugh.* Forget possessing any of them.

Jo floated to the side to see him better. He looked to be in his late twenties or early thirties, and apparently he had serious stamina. He was attractive, she supposed. His eyes were nice, the color of dark plums, and she liked his thick black hair. It was carelessly cut and longish, with random small braids. But he had rough-hewn features—a fighter's crooked nose and a too-wide jaw.

His long, lean body, however, was smoking hot. He must be nearing seven feet tall, would tower over her five and a half feet, and every inch of him was ripped. A thin shirt highlighted his broad chest and chiseled arms. His bared ass was rock-hard. His powerful thighs would nicely fill out those black leather pants bunched above his knees.

He had a bow slung over his back and a quiver strapped to his calf. A knife holster was clipped to his wide-open belt.

She shrugged; she'd witnessed weirder things on Bourbon Street. If he pulled out a little more, she'd be able to see his dick—

Whoa. Brow-raising. The brow-raising-est she'd ever seen.

How could he last this long? He wasn't even out of breath. Maybe she'd have more sex if other guys had his staying power. Her handful of quick-draw hookups hadn't been worth the admission price of a condom.

As she watched this tall stranger working his body—sometimes stirring his lean hips, other times withdrawing to the tip to slam back in—she wondered what his tanned, smooth skin would feel like. Smell like. When Jo was in ghost-mode, her super-keen sense of smell was weakened.

She'd bet Rune didn't wear Axe.

Her gaze locked on the pulse point in his neck. The slow, steady rhythm was hypnotic.

Beat . . . beat . . . beat . . .

Amazingly, the tempo wasn't speeding up.

How would he react if she pierced that pulse point with a fang? What would he taste like?

And still he was going. His stamina had to be supernatural. Plus, the women were almost too pretty. Jo suspected these people were otherworldly.

What she called *freaks.*

From her hidden vantages along New Orleans streets, she'd spied paranormal people doing inhuman deeds. Which made her wonder— what if she wasn't some kind of abomination who'd been resurrected from hell? She might be one among many.

She reached for her necklace, fingering the string of misshapen bullets. She never took it off, still kept it as a token of the night she'd risen from the dead.

But her discovery of other freaks had made her start rethinking herself, her world.

Her decision to remain away from Thad.

She'd approached some of these strange beings with questions on her lips: *What am I? How did I come to be? Are there others like me?* Yet they'd fled her.

She had a feeling this male wouldn't. She could talk to him once he got finished! She'd be on guard, of course, ready to bare her claws and fangs if things went sideways. . . . Jo supposed she *still* was like a feral cat.

Appearing lost, the blonde leaned up to kiss him, but he averted his face. Interesting.

The other three whispered to each other:

"I forget myself sometimes too."

"Can you imagine what he could do with that mouth? If only . . ."

"Why'd he have to be a bane?"

The man must be able to hear their soft voices. He narrowed his eyes, his lips thinning with irritation, even midthrust. Jo felt sorry for him.

"Have you ever seen his black blood?"

"His cock isn't poisonous, and that's all that really matters."

Poisonous? Black blood? He was definitely a freak!

The bouncing blonde cupped his craggy face. "MORE! I'm so close! Don't stop, Rune, *don't stop!*"

He stopped.

"Noooo!" the woman wailed.

"You want more? I won't disappoint you, dove." His deep voice had an unusual accent Jo couldn't place. "But you can't disappoint me. Promise me you'll do as I've asked."

He was using sex to manipulate the chick? What an asshole. Strike feeling sorry for him.

The woman's expression grew frantic. "I will! I swear, SWEAR! Just *pleasepleaseplease* keep going!"

Rune chucked her under the chin and grinned at her; she seemed to dissolve. "Good girls get rewards, don't they?"

Jo would laugh in his face if he talked to her like that. The blonde nodded helplessly.

He resumed with a harsh shove. The woman convulsed on his big dick, babbling between cries.

"This is what you want, dove?" he demanded. "My cock's all that really matters, is it not? You can't live without it, can you?" So arrogant!

The blonde whimpered, shaking her head. The other women gazed at him as if he were a god.

Jo's plan to ask him stuff grew less appetizing by the second. Would he make her beg for information, or toy with her? But she stayed. She wanted to see him get off. To watch as he lost his iron control.

To see him vulnerable.

Her gaze returned to that pulse point. Would his blood truly be black? She fantasized about it coursing through his veins, all over that gorgeous body.

Her fangs sharpened. Her heart began to thud, her spectral breaths shallowing. She struggled for control. As ever, heightened emotions affected her ghosting, making it harder to stay intangible. If she materialized even a little, these freaks might be able to sense her presence.

Her body started to float downward like a weighted balloon. *No, not yet.* He probably wouldn't be keen to talk if he discovered she'd spied on his orgy. She'd have to leave before she materialized, then "run into" him later.

The blonde began screaming in ecstasy. Though Rune was pummeling her, and she was orgasming all over him, he smiled and calmly purred, "I'm coming."

The woman gazed up at him in moaning awe.

He briefly froze. Then his hips pistoned. *Thrust, thrust, thrust, THRUST, THRUST.*

With a smirk, he stilled. He was done? He'd just come! Jo had risked staying for that? If she'd blinked, she might've missed it.

When her gaze dipped to his ass and her breaths shallowed even more, she made for the exit. Over her shoulder, she took one last glance at his pulse point.

Its beat had never sped up.

FIVE

Meadowberries mixed with warm rain.

Another female was nearby—and, gods almighty, her sweet scent was mouthwatering.

Rune had just finished securing his last informant and was already envisioning the search for his Valkyrie target. Yet when he detected the new female's scent, he found himself stiffening once more inside the nymph.

She believed his reaction was for her and cast him a smug smile.

Unacceptable. A male should never lose control of his body during sex. He pulled out abruptly, making her gasp, then set her down. While he dressed, she stumbled over to join her friends. They would likely carry on without him.

And there they go. What male could leave a tangle of wanton nymphs?

He could. This was a nightly occurrence for him.

Besides, the faceless meadowberry female awaited investigation. He could tell she'd been *in* the courtyard—a voyeur?—but she'd put distance between them.

If she looked half as good as she smelled . . .

He fastened his heavy belt. Without glancing back, he told the nymphs,

"I'm off, doves. Contact me as soon as Nïx goes to ground. And keep an eye out for a lock of hair."

Between moans, one nymph asked, "Why are you wanting past the wraiths?"

Those ghastly beings defended Val Hall, the Valkyries' lair, with a guard that was impenetrable, even for a Møriør like him. But tonight he'd learned—through swiving—that there was a key of sorts; if one tendered Valkyrie hair to the wraiths, those creatures would allow entry.

The nymphs would be on the lookout for a lock. In the meantime, they would conceal themselves in Val Hall's oaks to spy, alerting Rune when Nïx returned.

Until then, he would search the streets for the soothsayer. *After* he tracked this scent.

Another nymph asked him, "You wouldn't hurt Nïxie, right?"

She'll never feel a thing. He turned to smile at his bevy. His grin, he well knew, was as crooked as his morals, and held a hint of snide; females creamed when they saw it.

Another question for the ages.

"Hurt Nïx?" he scoffed. "I merely want to make a conquest. What male doesn't want to lay a Valkyrie?"

He already had, of course. Huge disappointment. She'd clung afterward, and the pointed ears—such a feylike feature—had been a turnoff. He despised the fey, hating that his own ears were pointed as well. The nymphs had them too, but at least they were up for a good time with no strings attached.

Conquest was something the nymphs understood. The first one he'd pleasured tonight said, "Nïx might be out in the Quarter even now. At least until sunrise. Good luck!"

He left them sighing at his grin as he stormed from the courtyard. He needed to be scouring this city for his target. So why was he hurrying after the voyeur?

Out on the street, drunken pedestrians milled around him. Bleary-eyed females regarded him with desire.

Though half fey/half demon, he could pass for a—very large—

human. His hair concealed his ears, and he'd etched runes into the bow and quiver he wore to camouflage them from mortal eyes.

Among the humans were other immortals. Most mistook him for a rough-around-the-edges fey—as long as he didn't bare the fangs he'd inherited from his demon mother.

Though his sense of smell wasn't nearly as keen as Darach's, Rune was able to lock on the voyeur some distance ahead. His gaze zoomed in on a short black miniskirt and an impossibly hot ass.

Her thighs were shapely but taut. Made to close around a male's waist. *Or his pointed ears.*

Not that a poisonous male like Rune could pleasure her in such a manner.

A long mane of dark brown curls swayed down her back, looking as silky as mink. Her cropped black tank top revealed a tiny waist. She wore combat boots, and she knew how to walk in them.

If her tits were as gravity-defying as that pert ass . . . As though on command, she turned back in his direction, giving him a view of the front.

First thought: *I wish I could eat her up.*

Her skin was the palest alabaster, her wide eyes hazel and heavily shaded with kohl. She had high cheekbones and a haunting airiness about her face. But her red lips were full and carnal.

She wore a strange necklace made of uneven hunks of metal. Appearing lost in thought, she rubbed one chunk across her chin.

His gaze dipped, and he nearly groaned. *Those tits.* They were generous; she was braless. *Good girl.* He watched those mounds rise and fall with her confident steps—a glorious sight.

Even better, her nipples were straining against her shirt. He'd bet his performance had caused that response.

He inhaled more deeply. Oh yes, he'd affected her. When he scented her arousal, his muscles tensed, his body strung tight as his bow.

Her navel was pierced, with a dainty chain dangling from a ring. He would nuzzle that. Without going farther south. If he tongued her, she'd know pleasure for an instant, then convulse with agony.

His bodily fluids were as toxic as his black blood. His fangs and claws as well.

The only thing he hated worse than the fey was his poison. If he killed another, it should be by his choice—not because of some anomaly of nature. . . .

He leaned against a lamppost, studying the female. Ghostly makeup, black clothes, combat boots. What did mortals term this style? Ah, she was a *Goth*. Why anyone would harken to that human age perplexed him.

But with ethereal looks like hers, she had to be an immortal. Perhaps another nymph? No, too edgy.

Maybe a succubus? If so, she would crave semen, which he couldn't give, even if he weren't poisonous. Still, not a deal killer. Rune had seduced his share of seed feeders, promising them a teeth-clattering ride. He'd always delivered.

Even those tarts had wanted more of him. After just one bedding, non-nymph females uniformly grew attached to him, becoming jealous and possessive.

Over his lifetime, thousands had sought monogamy from him. He shuddered. The concept was incomprehensible to him.

The voyeur possessed no secrets he wanted, and he risked her attachment. So why was he inhaling for more of her scent?

What is she? He had a healthy measure of fey curiosity in him, and it demanded an answer.

Only twenty feet separated them.

If she was a halfling like him, then had he never in all his years and travels scented her combination? That didn't make sense.

Ten feet away. He moved to block her.

She raised her face, blinking in surprise.

"Hello, dove. Were you wanting to join the party in the courtyard, then?" He backed her to a wall, and, naturally, she let him. "The nymphs would've been happy to share me. And there's *plenty* to go around."

Her surprise faded. She craned her head up to cast him a measured look.

"You were watching, no?" The thought of those spellbinding eyes taking in his action hardened his cock even more. Would she deny it?

"I did watch." His voyeur's voice was sultry, with not an ounce of shame.

Phenomenal looks. Sexy voice. Would she have curved or pointed ears? He prayed for the former. "I know you enjoyed the show."

"You *know*, huh?" She tilted her head, sending glossy curls cascading over one shoulder. "You were passable."

The scent of her hair struck him like a blow. Meadowberries. They'd grown in the highlands of his home world, far above the sweltering fens he'd worked as a half-starved young slave. Their scent had tantalized him to distraction.

Wait . . . "Did you say *passable*? I assure you that word has never been applied to my performance." He watched in fascination as her lips curled. The bottom one had a little dip in the center he wanted to tongue. But never could.

" 'Performance.' " Her vivid eyes flashed. "Exactly how I'd describe it."

Damn it, what was she? Then his brows drew together at her comment. Over the last several millennia, he might have consolidated his sexual . . . repertoire. His poison limited his options. But *performance*? "I get zero complaints."

She shrugged, and her breasts bobbed in her tank. He'd licked his lips before he caught himself.

"You want my honest opinion?"

As if he cared what she thought! Yet his mouth was saying, "Tell me."

"You showed hints of game at times, but nothing I'd strip for."

Game? "Then you didn't watch the scene I partook in."

She gave him an exaggerated frown. "My honesty hurt your feelings. It wasn't *all* bad. How about this: there's a live-sex club right around the corner—I bet you could place in their amateur-night competition."

He leaned in. "Ah, dove, if you're the expert to my novice, I'd appreciate any hands-on instruction."

"Here's a tip. Maybe settle in enough to take off your boots. Or, hey, how 'bout removing your bow and arrows?"

"Sound advice, but I never know when I might need my weapons. Even when I fuck, I still listen for enemies."

"You must have a lot of them. What kind?"

"All kinds. Untold numbers of them. In any case, I'm leery of removing my bow; it was a priceless gift." Ages ago, Orion had loosed Darach into a foreign realm with scant guidance: *Find the Darklight bow with a black moon and white sun etched above the hand grip.* A week later, Darach had returned, wild-eyed, bow in hand. Orion had given it to Rune, saying, "Your new weapon, archer. . . ."

"Priceless?" The voyeur's gaze flickered over his bow with a touch too much interest. "Sure would hate for it to get stolen."

"Never." Why had he bragged to her about his weapon? Information flowed *to* him, not *from* him.

He could talk for hours and never say a meaningful thing.

Yet something about her had made him boast? He'd taken prettier women. He'd had demigoddesses beneath him. Why did he find her so captivating?

Maybe her disdain toward you, Rune?

"Are you a good archer?" she asked.

"I'm the best in all the worlds." Crowing again? Though it was true.

Initially, Rune had resisted taking up a weapon favored by the fey. Orion's answer: *Even when you'll be more lethal with it than all of them combined?*

"Worlds, is it? Where are you from?"

"Very, very far away." He wondered what she'd think if he told her his primary home was in a dimension that moved. That he lived in a mystical castle filled with primordials and monsters.

"Who taught you to shoot?"

"I taught myself." Determined to be worthy of Orion's notice, Rune had practiced till his bowstring was stained black from his bleeding fingers.

"If your performance is gonna be predictable, at least you're good at archery." She nibbled that dip in her bottom lip, and his cock twitched in his pants.

She needed that mouth kissed until her vision went blurry. And he couldn't be the male to do it! His hands fisted, and he grated, "You can talk all you like about my *performance*, but it got you wet. I can scent it."

"You got a woodie; I got a wettie. Doesn't mean mine was for yours."

She was terse, borderline aggressive. *I want her.* "Are we going to do this or not? The courtyard awaits, and I'm on a clock." He didn't have time for this! His target might be roaming these very streets. "Or we can meet later."

"No dice," she told him. "I like a guy with passion. When you finished back there, I couldn't tell if you'd gotten your nut or muffled a sneeze."

His eyes narrowed. "I have to keep a rein on myself. I'm half demon/ half fey, a dark fey through and through"—he pulled his hair back to reveal his pointed ear—"and if I lose control, I might harm partners."

Though true, he was in no danger of losing control. *There's nothing within me to bridle. No fire to contain.*

In any case, he'd learned to restrain himself for other reasons as well. He'd realized at an early age that the power dynamic shifted between bedmates when one surrendered to the throes.

Power was everything during fucking.

"You really can't kiss?" she asked. "I heard them say you're poisonous."

He shrugged, as if this limitation were trifling. "To all but my own kind." His first kill had been with a lethal kiss.

Reminded of his past, he gritted his fangs and shoved this female's hand to his dick. "Anything you think you might miss? I'd make up for it with size."

She gave him a light squeeze, then withdrew her hand—as if she'd deigned to *acknowledge* his cock, and only because he'd been gauche enough to put it out there. Her disdain could put the old fey queen's to shame.

"Some cavemen carry big sticks. Doesn't mean I want to get clubbed with one."

Inner shake. "I have other tricks in my bag." He was good with his hands. Once he retracted his poisonous claws, he could use his fingers to get a purr out of her. "Meet me back in the courtyard at midnight, and I'll make you see stars." He cast her his grin, awaiting the reaction he always garnered.

The wench covered a yawn.

His grin faded.

"I might meet you," she said, "if you agreed to talk with me over coffee."

As a prelude to sex? What the hells could he discuss with her, a woman he planned to bed? He got tunnel-visioned at that point.

She added, "I'm not a big coffee drinker myself, but isn't that what people do?"

Her desire to talk must be a ploy of some kind. Otherwise, this would mean a female wanted something of him . . . *other than sex*? No, that made zero sense. "What would we discuss?" He laid his palm against the wall over her head. "You'll tell me your truth, and I'll tell you a lie?"

A shadow crossed her face. "All my truths are lies."

Curiosity flooded him. Bloody fascinating female. He reached forward to brush her hair over her shoulder. Her little ear was blessedly rounded on top. Two small rings decorated the helix, highlighting the perfect curve.

He bit back a groan. To a male like him, that couldn't be sexier. He wanted to kiss her ears, nuzzle and nip them. "Look at those piercings. Any hidden ones on your body?"

"Yes." A single word. Succinct. No additional explanation.

Just enough to send his imagination into overdrive. His claws dug into the brick wall. "If I meet you, I'll seduce you to do more than talk."

She exhaled as if she'd reached the end of her patience with him. Which, again, made zero sense. Rune elicited many responses from females: lust, possessiveness, obsession. Never *exasperation*.

"You've gotta be satisfied after four babes."

"Those nymphs were a warm-up. I'm called Rune the Insatiable for a reason. I'm never satisfied," he told her honestly, as if this were a good thing. He jested with his compatriots, but in reality, his existence could get exhausting. Always seeking the next conquest, the next secret . . .

He'd considered hibernating after this Accession.

Then he'd remembered he would need at least five hundred years to savor his victories.

He leaned down to rasp at her lovely ear, "Maybe you'll be the one to sate me at last." If it hadn't happened in millennia, he didn't expect it to now, but tarts ate that line up. He dangled the prospect because Lore females liked challenges.

This one pressed her hot palms to his chest, digging in her black nails. "You wanna know a truth?" She held his gaze. Her eyes were mesmerizing, her hazel irises flecked with brilliant blue and amber.

Finally they were getting somewhere! "I do."

In a breathy whisper, she said, "Maybe I wouldn't give a good goddamn if you were sated or not."

Sexiest voice. *Bitchy* words. "What *are* you?"

"You really don't know?"

He shook his head, but she was already looking past him, her interest turned off in an instant.

"I'm done here." She patted his chest, then sidled under his arm. "Later, Rune."

"Wait, I didn't catch your name."

She walked backward, flashing him a dazzling smile. "Because I didn't toss it, sport. Only good boys get rewards." She pivoted to saunter away from him.

His lips parted in disbelief as she strutted down the street. She turned every head, leaving mortal males agog. Rune's muscles tensed to pursue her, but he ruthlessly quelled the urge.

He'd become the master of his impulses. For the first hellish centuries of his life, his body and his mind had been commanded by another.

No longer.

But the damage had been done. He'd grown so detached during his early abuse that he'd felt like two separate beings. *And one was dead.*

Rune had stifled the fire within himself for so long, he'd extinguished it. And yet his heart thundered in his ears as he watched his voyeur melt into the crowd.

SIX

J o could still feel Rune's gaze on her back, so she kept up her casual
pace down the street.

She'd just met another freak! Had talked to one!

But even he hadn't known what she was. So she'd ended her encounter
with the womanizing *dark fey*, the dogged one obsessed with sex. He truly
would have lined her up like those others, making Jo fifth of the night (if
not more).

Now that she knew what to look for, she would find other
paranormal-type people, more *knowledgeable* ones.

Despite his arrogance, she burned to glance back. Were all male freaks
that conceited? Were they all so seductive?

The more she'd talked with him, the more attractive he'd grown. She'd
watched that calm, steady pulse point of his beating faster and faster as
they'd bantered. And she'd dug the hints of tattoos peeking up from his
collar and the ancient-looking silver bands he wore on most of his fingers.
When he'd lifted his hair to reveal one slightly pointed ear (which was
badass), she'd seen that the sides of his head were partially shaved (also
badass).

And, good God, that man could wear leather. His powerful, lean legs had stretched his pants just right, as had his huge cock—which he'd put her freaking hand on! The temptation to keep rubbing it had almost won out.

Even if she hadn't witnessed him in action, she'd deem his look: *bad-boy lady-killer with a big, swinging dick.*

His grin had been so sexy she'd had to cover her gasp with a feigned yawn.

Yet more than just his appearance attracted her. Beneath the smell of sex and *nymphs*, his innate scent was irresistible. Like leather and evergreen.

After one hit of that, she'd had the urge to kiss him, despite his poison. She could've reached up and fisted his cool hair, yanking him down to kiss until her fangs sliced his tongue.

Whoa. Sharing blood through a kiss? Stutter-step. She'd never fantasized about that before. Her fangs had always remained dormant during hook-ups.

Damn, that image was filthy hot. Instant wettie.

She needed to get hold of herself. Just as her emotions could make her embody, she could accidentally ghost as well, and Rune might still be watching her.

The lady-killer had wanted to know her name. He'd wanted to screw her, lining her up and knocking her down like the nymphs. He'd wanted a connection to her, however brief.

She'd craved a connection too.

So she'd stolen the contents of his pocket, one rectangular object. When she turned the corner, she opened her palm, peeking at her take. It was some kind of etched bone.

How weird. He must value it for some reason. Not as good as the "priceless" bow she'd eyed, but she'd have to make do.

Would he notice his empty pocket soon? She grinned. How pissed would he be that a *dove* had rolled him?

Her grin faded. Aside from her name and her body, he'd wanted her *truth.*

I could contact my little brother at any time, barging into his can't-possibly-get-better life, and he'd welcome me with open arms. No damage done to my boy at all. For now, I'm fine. I'm not slowly dying of loneliness. I don't fear I'll float away. I don't regret that no one will even know I'm gone.

Her truths *were* all lies.

She reached for her necklace. *You can never go back for him.*

Never. Never. Never.

So why did she continue to look for excuses to do just that?

She was antsy, not ready to return "home" to her dingy room at the Big Easy Sleeps motel (known to regulars as the Big Sleazy Weeps).

She needed a hit of her favorite drug. Just a little one. Her eyes darted. Suppliers. She needed suppliers—

There! A middle-aged couple strolling hand-in-hand.

Perfect. She ghosted into the woman, relaxing to flow with her. Boneless. Effortless. Like floating in water.

Jo imagined she could feel the man's rough hand, the warmth coming off his body. She pretended she was the one he loved.

The two walked along in silence, but the vibes between them weren't awkward or strained, just . . . peaceful.

She inwardly sighed. People took the wonder of hand holding for granted.

Down by the river, the couple sat on a bench. Stars twinkled above, a half moon low over the water. Strains of jazz carried on the breeze.

The man took his hand away. *No*—

Only to wrap his arm around his woman. He tugged her close. *Bliss.* They murmured in a foreign language, but Jo didn't need to understand it. Whatever he said made the woman rest her head on his shoulder, as she'd probably done a thousand times before. They leaned back and gazed at the stars.

Jo's past was a mystery, and she sometimes sensed the stars held the answers. She loved to stargaze. Well, she did for the first ten or so minutes. Then the realization of her friendlessness would steal over her. Stargazing for one had to be the loneliest hobby.

Now she had company. This couple.

For what might have been hours, they remained like that, lost in their own little world as a mist rolled in from the Mississippi.

No one had ever cherished Jo. No parents, no boyfriend. All on her own, she'd discovered how much she craved this: an unbreakable bond between two people.

Love and a future she could count on.

She was a killer with blood on her hands, but she wanted to give her heart away. As these two had. They were partners, two halves of a greater whole. Jo yearned for her other half with all the desperation of someone who'd always known something was missing.

She soaked up the feelings between these two like a sponge. Maybe she was a love junkie.

Yet pretending wasn't as good as the real thing.

Recalling the warmth of Rune's body affected her. When she imagined sharing a blood kiss with him, she feared she'd solidify inside the woman, killing her. She swiftly disentangled.

As Jo looked on, the woman shivered, so her man drew her closer.

Jo sighed. If she had someone real of her own, he would hold her like that. He'd own her heart, and that would anchor her to him.

He'd never let her float away.

SEVEN

Expectancy.

As Rune hunted for Nïx along the most decadent street in the town of New Orleans, anticipation thrummed inside him, seeming to grow like the thickening fog.

Why? He was on a routine mission, one among thousands.

For hours he'd searched, questioning low creatures and staring down alphas of other species.

Maybe he craved a fight. He hadn't been raised as a frontline warrior, but he'd come to enjoy a good battle with his fellow Møriør.

They warred seamlessly together. Sian would charge into the fray to massacre troops with his mighty battle-ax. Blace would use his great-sword and unmatched skill to behead waves of warriors.

Rune's "bonedeath" arrow would explode into reverberations so violent the bones of their foes would disintegrate, never to be healed.

Darach would already have sped behind the army to track down and maul any who fled.

Allixta created shields and neutralized others' magicks. Rune supposed her talent would be helpful if the Møriør ever faced a worthy adversary. For now, the tart looked decent in a hat.

Orion amplified all their strengths and directed them to their enemies' vulnerabilities.

The Møriør who still slept? Well, the weakest one could consume a city.

When Orion and the Møriør offered opposition the chance to surrender, they accepted. Or died. . . .

This anticipation Rune felt could *not* be about the voyeur. She'd held his interest only because she was a rarity—no, a singularity.

The one woman he hadn't been able to seduce.

Which was saying something, as his professions had always involved sex. He'd started young in the fey kingdom of Sylvan, because his queen had discovered uses for Rune, her husband's halfling bastard.

Queen Magh the Canny had forced Rune to become an assassin.

With malice in her gleaming blue eyes, she'd explained, "Many of my foes could be tempted by a sensual creature like you. My assassins fail to get past sentinels, yet you would seduce your way into a place where no guards attend: the bedroom. Even if divested of your weapons, you'd carry death in your very blood. Your escapes would be easier still. With some help, you could pass as a full-blooded fey; who would suspect you can teleport like a demon?"

Keeping secret his potential for magicks and knowledge of runes, he'd learned fey ways and customs. He'd tapped into his demon side, learning to trace. The combination had made him unstoppable.

He'd had such success as a hitman that Magh had expanded his duties to become Sylvan's secrets master, spying and interrogating—while still killing of course.

For all three pursuits, he'd used sex as a weapon, callously exploiting his targets' weaknesses or perversions. There'd been little challenge.

He narrowed his eyes, scanning the streets for his voyeur. Maybe Lore females weren't the only ones who liked a challenge.

Midnight neared. If he decided to show in that courtyard, would she be there? Perhaps she still had hopes of meeting him. His lips thinned. For *coffee*.

No. He refused to chase after her like some slavering lad. Captivation was as involuntary as captivity.

Remember how far you've come, from such humble beginnings.

With Orion's help, he'd turned his life around. The Undoing wasn't Rune's friend, nor a father figure (as some supposed). Orion was . . . an idea. A feeling.

He represented *triumph*—something Rune hadn't known until he'd sworn fealty to Orion.

Soon Rune would prove to be Sylvan's undoing. How would that realm fare when he assassinated their present king, along with their entire line of succession . . . ?

Seeking focus, he reached for his most cherished possession, his talisman, a last gift from his mother. She'd been a Runic demon, one among a breed that could harness magicks through symbols. The talisman had been accompanied by a note that had raised more questions than answers. The runes themselves presented a puzzle he often contemplated.

He dug into his pocket.

Gone.

Gone? He froze. He would never have left it anywhere; had never in all these eons lost it. The nymphs wouldn't have dared to steal it.

Realization. Only one other person had gotten close enough to him.

Under his breath, he muttered, "That beautiful little wench." The voyeur had picked his pocket! Oh, she was good. He'd been hard as rock, stretching his trews taut—yet he'd never perceived her hand dipping beside his dick.

What a surprise.

What a bad girl.

He turned toward the courtyard. Bad girls got punished.

If she'd stolen anything but his most prized belonging, he could have grinned.

Back at her rundown motel room, Jo set Rune's bone thingy among her other mementos. They lined the top of a picnic table she'd teleported from a park.

She'd stolen most of these items from her shells. Though she couldn't feel through any of the people, for the most part Jo got to *be* them.

She'd inhabited a cellist during her concert and had received a standing ovation. She'd served coffee at Café Du Monde (and later she'd punished patrons who'd grabbed "her" ass). She'd crashed a bachelorette party and laughed with other girls, pretending they were old friends from camp.

At a grand southern wedding, she'd been a bride for a day. She'd danced in a candlelit ballroom and had given away her garter as her new husband gazed on with adoration. Later, violins had played into the night as her groom had made love to his bride. He'd looked into her eyes so intently, Jo had pretended he could see *her*.

Which meant she existed.

That groom's voice had cracked when he'd made vows to her. *I would die for you. I'll love you alone for the rest of my life. You are everything.*

Jo reverently traced her fingers over the dried roses from her stellar concert performance. With those, she could pretend she'd once been admired. With the tiara from that bachelorette party, she could pretend she'd belonged. A dollar-bill tip from Café Du Monde allowed Jo to believe she'd once been just a normal girl.

She straightened the cuff links stolen from her romantic groom. They were her favorites. She could rub her thumbs over them and pretend she'd once been beloved.

With a wistful exhalation, she scuffed across the worn carpet of her room. She would've liked to stay somewhere less shitty, but she didn't have an ID, could never get one.

Because she couldn't read the application form.

She turned to the banged-up set of drawers. One was filled with Thad memorabilia—scrapbooks and the Thadpack. She opened the drawer, brushing her fingertips over the nylon material. At times, her three years with Thaddie felt like a dream, as if it were just as imaginary as the rest of her life experiences.

She drew out her most recent scrapbook, filled with pictures of him holding up trophies or Eagle Scout badges or community service awards.

Wherever she'd ended up in the Southeast (she couldn't stray too far from him) she had descended upon the closest library for a computer. Using the text-to-speech feature, she'd learned about his sports, charity work, and honor-roll grades.

She knew when his football team was going to the playoffs and when his . . . *mom* had won a pecan pie cook-off.

Jo stalked his social media so much she could tell when he was nervous about a big game, or even when he had a crush. Through his online yearbook photos, she'd watched him grow into a handsome seventeen-year-old with an easy grin that said, *All is right with the world.*

He was tall and strong, a world away from the tiny boy she'd carried everywhere.

Fourteen years ago, she'd made a heartrending choice, but obviously it'd been the right one. Every day Jo stayed away, his life seemed to get better and better.

Yet to spare Thad from grief, she'd suffered, willing each minute of her lonely existence to hurry by. She only slept for about four hours a night, so she had twenty hours each day to kill.

At least in New Orleans, there was the prospect of other freaks!

A knock on the door sounded.

She hissed with irritation. Few dared to disturb her.

When she'd first moved here, she'd been one of the motel's only guests. After a month of her hunting—crushing testicles and "disappearing" rapists and fight-stealing pimps—the rooms had filled up with women, mostly prostitutes, many with kids.

Another knock. Jo traced to the door, removing the brace—she usually ghosted past it—and opened up.

The smarmy motel owner. He was always leering at the women here. Automatic probation. *One strike, and he's out.*

His expression was a mix of fear and lust, his attention dipping to her body.

As long as she consumed blood, Jo retained a ballin' figure. Without it, she turned all sickly again.

"What do you want?" she demanded. Even this guy wasn't *seeing* her; he damn sure wasn't looking into her eyes.

He asked her tits: "I was wondering if you, uh, wanted to go get a cup of coffee with me?"

Coffee must be the theme of the night. She could drink java if she had to, but it tasted awful and made her pee. She liked never having to go to the bathroom.

Vampirism did have benefits. No running out of toilet tissue, no flu, no periods.

When she didn't answer, he finally met her gaze. She leaned in until they were nose to nose. The shadows around her eyes weirded people out; he was no exception. She told him, "Trying to drum up reasons not to kill you; comin' up short."

He swallowed thickly. "Oh." Axe would be an improvement on his smell.

She wrinkled her nose, her mind drifting to Rune's skin. So tempting. But even if Jo wanted to, she couldn't drink the poisonous dark fey.

The man cleared his throat. "Do you, uh, happen to have the money you owe me?"

Jo had tons of cash, piled up in the corner next to her comic books, and she could get more whenever.

"If not, maybe we could . . . work something out," the owner added.

Just for that crack he'd get nothing out of her. *Lucky to be alive, little man.*

She gave him her standard answer: "With your flayed skin, I'll be able to finish my man quilt." She slammed the door in his face.

One of these days she was going to have to start that quilt, or she'd just be a no good liar. . . .

She floated to the mini fridge to snag a bag of blood. It smelled dank and plastic-y. If Rune was toxic, then why had his flesh smelled so enticing? Even now her fangs were sharpening. *Aching.*

She'd sensed power in him, there for the taking. That pulse point had called to her as little else in her life ever had.

Just because he was poisonous to others didn't mean he would be to her.

When had rules ever applied to Jo?

Her gaze fell on his bone thingy again. Why did he keep it? For years to come, she would imagine scenarios for it.

Unless she met him for their date and simply asked him.

EIGHT

Y ou're good, female, I'll give you that," Rune said as he entered the courtyard.

The voyeur was sitting on the edge of the fountain, skimming her delicate fingers across the water's surface, her black nails glinting. "Be specific. Good at lots."

The mere sight of her made heat rush through him, pooling in his groin. When he'd scented her a couple of blocks away, he'd had to force himself to slow his steps. "Where did you learn to steal like that?"

She quirked an eyebrow. "Practice."

"I never felt you near my . . . pocket. Are you a thief by trade?"

"I guess you could say I'm between jobs." Her lips curled, like that was an inside joke. "You showed; does this mean you'll join me for coffee?"

"Return my belonging," he said as he closed in on her, "and I might only spank you."

"And that's a hard no on java." She rose and squared her shoulders—as if they were about to spar.

How strange. Aside from Allixta, no females opposed him. They were too busy trying to land him. "What could you want with such a useless trinket?"

The voyeur reached into her skirt pocket, then held up the talisman. "I want it, because *you* obviously want it."

His gaze locked on the piece. "It's of no value." It meant *everything*. "I'll have it back simply because it's my belonging."

"See, here's the thing—this is now my belonging. I stole it fair and square. What's it for, anyway?"

"It's not *for* anything. As I said, it has no value." *It's merely the thing I care most about in all the worlds.* The nerve of this bitch!

"What do the symbols mean?"

"That's not your concern." He didn't know!

Captured and enslaved young, his dam had only remembered a limited number of runes to teach her son. That talisman had been the sole possession she'd had on her, yet even she couldn't read it.

Unless Orion could help him decipher the markings, Rune would *never* know—because his mother's breed of demon had gone extinct, their lore lost.

All Orion had told him was that the answer lay in Gaia.

The voyeur pocketed the talisman again. "I might consider returning it if you answer some of my questions."

His ire was at the ready. "You do *not* make the rules."

"I do if you want your 'trinket' back." She gave him a sardonic wink.

Her defiance was so unfamiliar, he felt his cock stirring. "Brazen little thing, aren't you?"

"Brazen is when you can't back it up."

She couldn't know he was a Møriør, but she should still fear him as a much larger male. He stood well over a foot taller than she, and easily had a hundred and fifty pounds over her. "You dig your own grave. Unless . . ." His gaze fell to her lips. "Perhaps your mouth can yet convince me not to whip that pert ass of yours raw."

She laughed at him.

He leaned forward, feeling the overwhelming need to shut her up—with his mouth over hers. *Kiss her quiet.*

How quiet would she be screaming in agony? Frustration simmered.

In a drawling voice, she said, "I suppose retreating is another choice for you. Turn around and walk away. Perhaps the sight of your ass can yet convince me not to whip it raw."

He stalked closer. "Are you a mad one then?" Older immortals often fell prey to insanity.

"Sure." Again, she seemed amused. "Why not?"

"You're going to give me my belonging." He bared his fangs at her. "Or I will make you suffer."

"Suffer? Oh, sport"—she rolled her neck to pop a crick—"I love a good fight."

"Such defiance against a male—"

She swung a fist at his face.

He caught it effortlessly, but hadn't expected another immediate hit. She punched him in the stomach with surprising force.

When he squeezed her fist in his grip, she grabbed his arm with her free hand. Her black nails had lengthened and sharpened into claws. Was she a demoness? A succubus?

She sank her claws into his arm. She was strong for a female. Still, nothing he couldn't shake off.

"Careful, girl. If you break my skin, you'll draw my dirty blood." Baneblood. Old angers seethed. He shoved her against the wall, knocking the breath from her lungs.

He took the opportunity to reclaim the talisman from her pocket, his hand a blur as it dipped.

Shock registered on her face. "You're fast too!"

"Fast as the fey. You're no match for me."

She thrashed against his hold. "No?" Her head shot forward, her forehead connecting with his.

"The hells!" That hit should have cracked her skull like an egg. He felt blood—from an actual injury—trickling down his forehead. How long had it been since someone had landed a blow?

"You've loosed my poison, wench. Playtime is over."

Her gaze locked on the blood. "Look at it flowing." She began to pant, her breasts pressing against his chest. He could feel her nipples stiffening into tight points.

He swiped a sleeve over his face, clearing away the blood. It wasn't poisonous to the touch—wouldn't harm her unless it got into her system—but he'd take no chances.

She muttered, "Rules don't apply. . . ."

"What rules?" he absently asked. Her irises had wavered in color from hazel to onyx—as black as night. "Damn you, tell me what you are." He stared down at her finely boned face, and again that unfamiliar need to kiss rioted inside him.

"I'm *thirsty*." She clambered against him.

Pain in his neck. Fangs? Vampire! "The FUCK are you doing?" He fisted her hair to fling her away. "You *want* to die—"

She sucked at her bite.

Pleasure seared him like a lightning bolt, wrenching a yell from his lungs. *"AHHHHH!"* His cock shot harder, twitching to come. "Ah, gods!" A vampire was feeding from him—from *him*—and it was unimaginable. "You drink your death."

"Ummm." Her ruby lips kissed his flesh. When her tongue darted for more of his taste, his eyes rolled back in his head.

Never . . . so much . . . pleasure . . .

Nigh mindless, he let her sink her claws into him, let her coil her limbs around him as she made him her prey. *Poison should've hit her.* Somehow she wasn't weakening; her body grew stronger and stronger, her moans louder.

She rocked her hips against his torso, grinding her sex. The scent of her arousal filled his senses.

Figure the rest out later. He used his grip on her hair to shove her against his neck. "Then suck me like you mean it, you little bitch."

She did, piercing him deeper, moaning into his flesh.

With her every draw, he grew more light-headed. *Hold out.* His balls tightened, his breaths heaving. *Hold out!* "You're going to make me come like this!" *Inside her . . . need inside her. She'll be so wet.*

He tore open his weapon belt. He struggled to remember power dynamics and control—only managed to attack his fly. *Need inside!*

He yelled when his engorged cock sprang free. Trews at his thighs, he bucked his hips, sending his shaft between their bodies. He'd threaded it into her lace panties. He felt her soft, bare mons against his rod—just as she gave a wanton suck.

She can't get enough of my baneblood.

At the realization, he shuddered against her, staggered. He was about to come—without deciding to.

NINE

Rune's black wine hit her veins, carrying fire throughout every inch of her. It drugged her, made her head spin, her flesh burn! Blood drunk. Lust drunk.

How had she gone so long without biting another? Her pierced nipples tightened. Her clitoris throbbed. Her thong was soaked.

Heat poured off his body as he thrust his dick over her. His groans vibrated her aching fangs. He was about to come! She wasn't far behind. She ground against him for more friction.

When her skirt bunched up at her waist, he gripped her ass, claws digging into her skin. "Fuck, fuck, FUCK!" His cock pulsed against her. "Can't hold on much longer!"

She moaned, pawing at his back to get closer.

"Drain me of it, then!" His heart thundered, pumping dark wine for her. "Take. More."

Before, she'd sampled him lightly, unsure how to drink. Now instinct ruled her. She drew from him. *Hard.*

"Uhhhnnn!" Every muscle in his body strained. "Yes, suck me! Feels like my cock'll explode!" He grunted, groaned, shoving his hips. *"Fuckyes-sogoodsogood."*

Crazed, he pinned her against the wall, thrusting in a frenzy, shoving his dick between their grinding bodies. On the brink, she writhed to meet him.

"Can't hold back . . . can't hold out!" Between his ragged breaths, words from a foreign language spilled from his tongue. He was finishing! No, too soon!

"*Ahhh, gods!*" His hips surged between her thighs. "I'm . . . I'm . . . COMING!" His big body jerked. He threw his head back to yell.

His throat muscles milked her fangs as he bellowed to the sky again and again. . . .

When his hips gradually slowed and he gave a low groan of satisfaction, the sound of his yells was still echoing through the night. The *city*.

She remained on fire, subtly rocking on him, wanting this bite never to end. She'd done it, had drunk from another! And his tanned skin had been the cherry on top of his luscious blood. The act had been like sex—except this had been good. Like the best sex she'd ever imagined.

With that bite, she'd known the connection she'd dreamed about.

He released her hair, so she reluctantly withdrew her fangs with a last greedy lick that made him moan.

Catching his breath, he pressed both hands against the wall. He didn't need to hold her; Jo's claws were sunk into his back, her limbs coiled around him. The side of her face rested against his.

Moments passed like this. *What do I do? Say?* She hoped they weren't fighting anymore. The trinket had been a good trade for his blood.

She wanted to get off with him, and then drink again. Or both at the same time!

He pulled his head back to stare down at her, astonishment in every line of his face. His magenta irises had darkened, and fissures of black forked out from them. Was that typical for a dark fey? Very cool.

In a hoarse voice, he said, "You made me come so hard I thought I would spill seed."

He hadn't? His dick still pulsed against her belly, but her skin was dry.

As if in a trance, he raised his hand to her mouth. He rubbed his ringed thumb along her bottom lip, collecting drops of blood she'd spilled. He offered them back to her.

She daubed her tongue to his thumb. Delectable.

Had he ruined her for other blood?

"Suck it," he commanded her.

When she drew his thumb into her mouth, his lids went heavy. "So damned beautiful. I don't know how this is possible, female. But the plans I have for you . . . I'm going to eat you alive."

Earlier, she'd considered him somewhat attractive. Now that she knew what he tasted like, his craggy features took on a whole new aspect. Not to mention that he was supernaturally strong and fast.

Like me.

Plus, he was digging her hard. She admitted to herself she was digging him back. Understandable, since his big dick was still in her panties and he was gazing down at her with an enthralled look.

After the wedding night she'd spent with the romantic groom, she'd had no interest in casual hookups. Now she felt changed again.

She couldn't live without the connection she'd just experienced with Rune. There was no going back for her.

"Did you pick my pocket to lure me here? So you could feed?"

She released his thumb. "No, I hadn't planned this. I just wanted something of yours."

"Why?"

"I guess to know you." She'd *known* him in unforeseen ways. Her gaze flitted from his eyes to her bite mark.

His hand rubbed along her outer thigh. She shivered when his fingers traced the back of her thong. "You took my forbidden blood, and you drank it down. Instead of dying in pain, you're blooming. Did you use some kind of spell?"

She'd known his blood was poisonous but not *lethal*. At least to others. Just as she'd suspected—rules didn't apply to Jo. "Don't know any spells. I survived probably because I'm wicked strong and all."

"That you are." He tilted his head, and a black lock tumbled forward.

She wanted to fist his hair and kiss him till their lips hurt. "Nobody's ever bitten you before?"

"No other vampire would dare."

Other vampire. More existed. *I'm one of them.*

How had she become one? Did all ghosts become vampires? She was parting her lips to question him when he said, "I still can't believe this happened, and little should surprise an immortal my age."

Immortal? "How old are you?"

"Seven millennia."

Holy shit! Would she live to be that old? Her mind couldn't wrap around that number.

"You must be old as well to be this strong." *Nope.* "Strange you don't have a vampire's scent."

"What do you think vampires smell like?"

"Aggression and blood." He leaned his forehead to hers. "Were you very hungry, or did you enjoy my taste?" His tone was gruff, almost vulnerable. "How do I . . . how does my blood compare to others?"

"It's amazing."

The corners of his lips curled into that cocky, slanted grin. "What we just did is wicked. Loreans would consider it a taboo."

Loreans? "Okay. Whatever."

"Whatever," he repeated in a rasp. "You not only don't give a shit, you're looking at my neck like you want seconds."

"And thirds and fourths."

His brows drew together suspiciously. "Have you drunk another of my kind?"

"No, never."

"Then why did you do it? I warned you I was poisonous."

She shrugged. "You smelled . . . right."

"Right?" He said the word as though he were testing it, trying it on. "If you prick me with those fangs again, I'll penetrate you with this." He thrust, rubbing his dick over her mound. "Just so we understand each other."

"Ah! S-seems fair." She wasn't the only one who likened her bite to sex.

His sigh-worthy grin deepened. "Tell me your name."

In a breathless tone, she said, "Josephine." She'd just given him her name? Her *real* name.

"The pleasure's mine, Josephine." He ripped her panties clean off her body. Then he pocketed them.

Something to remember her by? Because he was going to nail and bail her? As with those other females, he still hadn't taken off his bow. Ooh, wouldn't he still have nymph funk on him? And she didn't have protection. Not that she could get pregnant—no periods—but still . . .

"Now it's your turn to come," he informed her. "I'm going to demonstrate that I've got more than *hints* of game. In fact, I believe I promised you I'd make you see stars."

"I like stars," she murmured.

He leaned in. To kiss her? "My bag of tricks just got far more extensive. I'm eager to explore this with you."

Explore. That sounded less nail-and-bail-y. *Maybe give him a shot.* She eased closer to meet him—

Giggling sounded from the courtyard gate. Rune drew back.

Two women in skimpy party dresses whistled at them. A blonde and a redhead. Like the four she'd seen earlier, this pair appeared too flawless to be human.

"Ah, water nymphs," he said.

"We heard you across town, Rune!" the blonde said. "It sounded like you lost your ever-loving mind."

His wide jaw clenched. Well, he didn't like that comment at all. In a nonchalant tone, he said, "When it's good, it's good."

Good? *Dick, please.* Her ears were still ringing from his yells.

The redhead added, "If you're in such a desirous mood, we can tag out with her."

Hello? He was obviously taken. Clue one: she was panties-less, with her legs wrapped around him. *Not a chance, freaks.*

"Of course, doves. Later."

He did not *just say "later."*

"We'll find you after some trysts," the redhead called. "We've got something we know you'll like."

"Come back at sunrise," he told them.

Four nymphs at sunset. One vampire at midnight. A couple more nymphs at dawn?

They blew him kisses and sashayed away.

He returned his attention to Jo. "Nymphs: can't live with them . . ."

She'd just gotten this guy off—his dick was still wedged between them—and he was making a date with other women! With . . . with nymphs! *Asshole!*

Why would he do that? He'd reacted to her far more strongly than he had to those others.

Even more confusing? His expression toward Jo was tender. She could almost pretend he was *seeing* her. Except for the fact that he was planning to see others.

"Now, where were we?"

"You were just arranging a couple of hookups for later." Her claws sharpened.

He cast her a disappointed look. "Jealousy? You're already possessive of me." He too was coming out of a lust haze, seeming to wake up. "I don't do *jealousy*. Great gods, vampire, I've known you for a total of fifteen minutes." He dragged his hips back, then all but dropped her. "I haven't even swived you yet." He yanked up his pants, dressing so fast his movements were a blur.

She swatted her skirt down. "Possessive? As if I'd want you for my own." *I'd kind of wanted you for my own. I want* someone *for my own!* "You're just a blood bag in a big-dicked package. Who didn't last long enough to get me off." Story of her life! Her lips drew back from her fangs.

With a growl, he pressed her against the wall again. "You're baring your fangs at me? Defying me again? You have no idea what I could do to you!"

"Do to me? Other than leave me hanging?"

"I fed you, did I not?" He trailed his fingers over her bite mark, and a look of realization dawned on his face. "You *bit* me, drinking my blood straight from my flesh. Something I have never had to worry about. Blood-taking has consequences, female. Which you well know."

No, she didn't!

For the briefest moment, his expression morphed into one of intent. Deadly intent. "Such plans . . ."

Then he flashed her that grin, even as his free hand discreetly inched toward his blade. Shock radiated through her. He was going to knife her because she'd taken blood from his neck?

Lady-killer, literal.

Dickwad!

Too bad he could never hold her.

"Oh, well. What's done is done." His words were light, but the timbre of his voice had changed.

As hers did when she was about to kill someone.

TEN

Rune inwardly cursed. A vampire had drunk from his flesh, taking his blood—and possibly his memories.

After all these years of protecting the secrets of the Møriør, he'd allowed a security breach.

Of epic proportions.

Eliminating the breach was the only alternative. He knew this, and yet he hesitated, his desires warring with his duties. Josephine had given him the most blistering pleasure he'd ever experienced.

She'd somehow tolerated his poisoned blood. It had pleasured them both, and nourished her.

Naturally he wanted to investigate this, at least until he'd tired of her—or discovered another who could drink him. If one such creature existed . . .

It only took seven thousand years to find this one, baneblood.

And even if he came across another, no such female could trump Josephine's attractiveness. Right now, he had trouble coming up with *any* female who could.

No matter what, beheading this woman seemed such a waste. His hand paused at his blade. "Do you dream the memories of those you drink?" Maybe she didn't possess that ability; some vampires didn't.

"I've definitely never done that."

He was tempted to believe her. "You're not a *coşaş*? A reader of blood-borne memories?"

"No."

Natural-born vampires were incapable of lying. When attempting to voice a falsehood, they experienced severe pain.

Of course, in the world of the immortals, every rule had an exception.

Perhaps he should force Josephine back to his lair and monitor her. In addition to his opulent rooms at Perdishian Castle, he had a second home in the realm of Tortua. The outer walls were warded, escape-proofed.

He would keep her for a while, making certain she posed no threat.

Yet what if a *coşaş* drank *her*, then what would happen? Though unable to read memories, she still could have harvested them.

Rune could never let her go free into the worlds. A *permanent* female capture? In his private sanctuary?

Unless he disposed of her.

Damn it, he didn't have time for this! His dick had led him straight into trouble, and he was no closer to killing Nïx.

He would secure the vampire, debate his options, then return to search for his target until sunrise.

He looped his arm around Josephine, crushing her against him. "I'm going to imprison you, female. Regrettably for both of us, you'll remain my captive for the rest of your life, however short a time that might be. The longer you keep me interested, the longer you'll live."

She thrashed against him. "Let me go, freak!"

He sighed with irritation. "I'm far too powerful for you to break free. Not even a millennia-old demon can trace from my hold." A proven fact.

"Trace?"

"Don't play ignorant, little girl."

Her widened eyes narrowed to slits. "*Little girl?* I've *never* been a little girl."

When she stilled, his irritation turned to bafflement, because she began dematerializing—like tracing, but slower. "Impossible." Somehow she was evading his viselike grip.

Face gone even paler, eyes even darker, she smirked at his disbelief.

He'd never known a vampire who could control their tracing to this degree.

"I'm more powerful than I look, *little boy*," she purred. "I'll remember you planned to imprison me—at best—and gut me at worst. Guard your back, because I'll be watching you." Then she disappeared.

Jo had heard of coffee dates gone wrong, but *seriously*? What a prick!

After ghosting from his hold, she'd gone fully invisible, settling into the opposite wall of the courtyard.

She meant what she'd said; she intended to monitor his every move. Tonight she would discover more about his world.

About my world.

This dude was old—holy shit, was he old!—so he would have answers.

Already she'd learned she was a vampire, and there were others. Dark fey and nymphs and demons existed.

On an abomination scale, a mortal turned vampire would have to be better than a demon, right? *Hey, Thaddie, I'm a vampire, but luckily—phew— not a demon.*

Again she wondered if she would live to be thousands of years old. The thought depressed her.

Rune spun in place, his face a mask of rage. He bit out words in that weird language he'd used earlier, then adjusted his bow over his shoulder. He gazed up at the sky, as if to gauge time, then started away.

To find me.

She followed, ghosting from one lamppost to another. . . .

For hours, she watched as he checked every backstreet, pausing, and then seeming to track down stray scents. They'd gone far afield from the Quarter but were almost back at the courtyard where this night had started.

At one point, he'd launched his fist into the brick wall of an abandoned building. The force hurtled the two-story structure onto its side, as if he'd knocked it off its feet. Without a look back, he'd stormed away, his hand unharmed, his strength unbelievable.

Studying Rune raised even more questions. Was it this important to imprison her? Were his memories that valuable? And for that matter, *could* she dream them as a *cosaş*?

She never had. But then, she'd never taken blood "straight from the flesh."

Now she only wanted to do it again! To have skin closing around her aching fangs. To feel muscles working beneath her claws as she secured her prey.

From her spot in a lamppost, she noticed a handsome blond stumbling along the street with his friends, each wearing a graduation cap. They were trashed, and their shirts all read the same thing, but she couldn't decipher the words.

Maybe they were graduating from Tulane. Since arriving in New Orleans, she'd often visited the campus. She'd watched students reading, as if that talent was no big deal.

The blond tripped over his own feet, and his hand shot out to the lamppost she occupied. His attractive fingers grasped it right above her tits. *Well, hello there.*

His skin was smooth, his teeth white. What would it be like to drink him? Would she gain memories of college parties and classes?

She tapped her tongue to a fang, but it remained dormant. Her heart sank. She could *not* imagine drinking this male. Nor any of his friends.

Besides, even in ghost form she could smell the Axe.

She sighed. She tried to tell herself she was full. If she got hungry enough . . . But she knew the truth: nothing could compare to Rune's black blood. How could she ever go back to the bags in her refrigerator?

Rune, that bastard, *had* ruined her. Rune was ruin.

How fitting. It'd be his new name. She hissed in his direction, making the blond jerk back.

In drunkenish, he said, "Dihyaguyz hearat? Pose histat me." With shrugs, they lurched on.

Closing in on the courtyard, Rune scrubbed a hand over his face, seeming to curse the rising sun.

ELEVEN

Josephine had disappeared. He'd scoured the streets for both her and Nïx, expanding his search into the heart of the city, but he'd never caught scent of either.

Maybe his tracking had grown rusty since the last Accession. Wallowing in nymph flesh could do that to a male.

He tried to recall his last marathon session at a covey or pleasure den, yet all he kept seeing was Josephine's haughty smile.

He knew what was happening. Female vampires were notoriously hypnotic, as entrancing as succubae. It was a survival mechanism, a hunting tool—because both species depended on the bodies of other beings for sustenance.

Tonight he'd been used for food. He should be outraged, but replaying her bite got his cock so hard he feared for his trews.

Those nymphs were right; he had lost his ever-loving mind.

No, no, Josephine had mesmerized him. And with her thong in his pocket—a constant reminder of her scent, her *arousal*—he was primed for her. In time, he'd shake this.

He'd stop thinking about taking her lips.

Because he *could* take them. Dear gods, he finally could without killing. An added bonus: he'd never craved a female's kiss more than Josephine's—and that had been *before* he'd known he could have it.

Dawn neared. Nïx was rumored to go out only at night. The light would drive the vampire to ground. He would find neither today.

Though Josephine could have traced anywhere in the universe, she'd be back.

He reached into his pocket. Beside her ripped thong was the necklace he'd stolen, the one she'd been touching to her lip when he'd first come upon her. He pulled it out, turning it in his hands. He'd taken the necklace for turnabout—his fingers were just as sticky as hers—but also because he'd suspected the piece would have meaning.

Those bits of metal were spent bullets.

Oh, yes, she'd be back. He had the bait; how to trap her? Evidently, his hold wouldn't be enough.

When Rune had set out from Tenebrous, he'd outfitted himself to *kill* a Valkyrie, not to *keep* a vampire. He had no traceproof manacles with him, nor in his sanctuary at Tortua.

The nymphs had told him of a Lore shop in town. If he found a pair of cuffs there, he'd lure the vampire close with the necklace, then snare her.

Once she was his captive, he would do all the forbidden things he'd fantasized about.

Clawing, sucking, tonguing.

Kissing.

One of his most heated fantasies was the simplest: to take a woman's mouth and make her moan—with pleasure instead of pain.

The last time he'd tasted another's lips had been a kiss of death. Whenever he pictured kissing, he recalled that night.

Rune yearned for a kiss to erase his last.

Earlier, when one of the nymphs had forgotten herself and sought his lips, he'd grown sickened to remember, but he'd kept fucking. . . .

He pocketed the necklace, his fingers drawn to Josephine's silk thong as if magnetized. With his other hand, he traced her bite mark, almost healed.

For all he knew, Nïx had dispatched the vampire as a spy. The Møriør's weaknesses were few, but they could be exploited by a clever strategist. Just as Orion did to his enemies.

Rune stroked the silk again. Tonight he'd come harder than he ever had, and yet touching her panties had his balls so blue every footfall pained him. Maybe he should release some of the pressure, so he could *think*.

A pair of water nymphs at dawn would do the trick. He headed toward the courtyard. He'd just entered when the nymphs strolled in right behind him.

Exactly what he needed, a palate cleanser! A blonde and a redhead—ideal for getting past a brunette. He thought the blonde was named Dew, the redhead Brook. They looked well-tumbled.

What would Josephine look like when well-pleasured? He hadn't seen to her at all, as she'd pointed out. *But she moaned lustily enough when feeding from me!*

He pulled his collar over his bite mark. "Did you two rush through your other trysts to meet me?" Of course they had.

They nodded. The blonde said, "We know tricks to speed things up, you see."

He'd been forced to learn those same tricks as well. A memory arose of Queen Magh telling him, *Please your customers, cur. Or perish.*

Through a wave of revulsion, Rune flashed the nymphs a practiced grin. "May you never use those tricks on me. . . ." He trailed off, his ears twitching. He glanced around, sensing the vampire's nearness. But he would've scented her if she were close.

Damn it, why couldn't he stop thinking about her? Could her mesmerizing still have a hold of him if she wasn't even here?

"We've got some info for you," Brook said. "Will you pay us *handsomely* for it?"

"Indeed." He was the Møriør's secrets master now, and nymphs knew much.

"It's about the female you were with earlier," Dew said with a shrewd look. "The one we heard rocking your world."

Brook added, "The whole parish heard it."

He didn't bother with a denial. "Continue."

"What do you know about her?" Dew asked.

"Very little. Tell me."

"We think"— Brook lowered her voice—"we think she's a vampire."

"What gives you that impression?" he asked, feigning ignorance. "She doesn't smell like one."

"We've seen her in a fight." Brook shivered. "She hissed, she had fangs, and her eyes turned black. It's why we've never tried to seduce her." Few species would harm a nymph, but some vampires craved drinking them dry.

What if they *had* seduced Josephine? He pictured her sleeping with them—and, of course, himself—at the same time. Imagining any combination of attractive tarts servicing him and each other would normally be a pleasant musing.

This one filled him with irritation. He would be plenty for Josephine to handle. Nymphs would just muddy the waters. He pointed out to them, "Black eyes and fangs could mean demon."

Brook smoothed her hair behind a pointed ear. "But she doesn't have horns or wings."

Dew nodded. "We've gone our whole lives without seeing a female vampire, and now the streets seem to be teeming with them. There's a Valkyrie halfling one, and a Dacian one, but she's sick with vampire plague—"

"Do you know where mine resides?" *Mine.* He almost laughed. That was a word he would never apply to a female.

"I think somewhere in the city," Dew said. "She comes to the Quarter to pick pockets. She's a klepto. One time I saw her wandering around in the pouring rain, seeming sad. She looked desperate to steal from someone."

Josephine had said she'd stolen from him because she wanted to *know* him. Apparently, she knew *many*. The little wench could make a man feel cheap. If he let her.

And what in the hells would she have to be sad about? She was a beautiful, powerful immortal.

Dew smiled slyly. "You want a repeat with your vampire, don't you?"

A repeat? Josephine's fangs piercing his neck again? While she pressed her taut nipples into his chest and clawed him . . .

He shrugged, even as his cock jerked in his pants. "I seek her for business only." Once she returned for her necklace, all would be well. *Time to cleanse my palate.* He swooped Brook into his arms.

She squealed. "Someone's already raring to go."

They didn't need to know his erection wasn't for them. "When am I not?"

"Rune, your neck!" She stared wide-eyed at it. "You have . . . she *bit* you?"

Dew pawed him. "Let me see!" Her jaw dropped at the bite mark. "That's so filthy. And hot."

Gods, it was.

Brook said, "She couldn't drink your baneblood, though, right?"

"Of course not. Just nipped me with her fangs."

Dew said, "Still, a bite! She's a gutsy one for piercing your skin. And you're a dirty dog for letting her! We knew you walked on the wilder side, but that's wicked! Can we watch next time?"

"Maybe." He cast them his crooked grin. "But only if you're *very* good girls."

TWELVE

What. A. Skank.

Jo gaped from her spot inside the courtyard wall. This guy was the biggest manwhore she'd ever seen.

And a thief to boot. The bastard had lifted her most prized possession—from her freaking neck—and she'd never noticed! When she'd seen her necklace in his hands, she'd almost attacked. But she couldn't risk a capture, and she didn't know what other stunts he was capable of.

She would be forced to wait here until he got so caught up with those nymphs that he didn't perceive her own thievery. Wouldn't take long. The females were climbing him like a rock wall.

They thought it wicked for a vampire to bite a dark fey. *They* thought *her* pervy.

Her stomach clenched when he pulled Brook up into his arms and the woman wrapped her legs around his waist.

Jo decided then and there to get more sexual experience. If she'd been around the block, this wouldn't sting as much. Those nymphs didn't suffer jealousy. Rune had said "jealousy" like it was a dirty word.

But Jo *was* jealous. The connection she'd thought she'd experienced with him had been one-sided.

What was new?

He palmed the back of the nymph's head and drew her to his neck, to the unmarked side. "Here, dove, give us a nip. You won't break my skin."

Jo straightened. What the hell?

He leaned away, his hair falling to one side, revealing the shaved part of his head and his pointed ear.

Brook said, "You want to fantasize like I'm the vampire?"

Dew giggled.

"Just so," he baldly admitted. "And it'd help if you two quieted down."

The nerve of this asshole! Did those nymphs have *no* pride? And why would he be fantasizing about Jo when he'd been so quick to pass her over?

To contemplate her murder?

God, this man confused her!

While Dew struggled to unfasten his belt, Brook bit his neck.

Rune commanded, "Harder, dove."

Yes, Jo had seen weird things in the course of her voyeurism, but this male trying to relive her own bite was bizarre. Despite herself, her fangs sharpened into points.

"I said harder," he grated.

I would bite him till he howled for mercy.

With a mouthful of his skin, the nymph mumbled, "I'm 'iting as 'ard as I 'an!"

"It's no good." He made a sound of frustration. "Leave off, Dew."

Brook released his neck and jerked her thumb at the other nymph. "She's Dew."

That nymph had finally managed to unfasten his belt and was reaching for his fly.

"Whatever." Rune flexed his claws. "Draw back. I'm about to bleed."

"So freaking hot," Brook breathed, but she leaned far back.

He stuck two claw tips into the remnants of Jo's bite. Piercing his own neck, he gave a mindless groan and his eyes slid closed.

With a whimper, Dew fumbled to get his pants undone.

As his throat worked, blood trickled down his neck. It *was* so freaking hot. That dark, rich blood of his. *To have just one more taste . . .*

Ruined.

But unlike the nymphs, Jo did have pride. She wanted him only for the things he'd taken—and now was the time to strike.

Her scent.

Rune's eyes shot wide when he caught that lush thread of meadowberry. Was he imagining it?

No, Josephine was materializing right in front of him. "Oh, Ruin . . ." Her shoulders were back, her chin raised. Her hazel eyes glittered.

He dropped Brook. Without a glance down, he shoved Dew's hand from his fly.

Had the vampire seen his attempts to mimic her bite? His fantasizing about her as he used two stand-in nymphs? At least he hadn't yet brought out her thong.

"Poor Ruin. I'm often imitated." She gestured to the nymphs. "And *never* duplicated."

Why did he feel guilty about the females, as if he'd been disloyal?

He was ever loyal to those that mattered. Josephine meant nothing to him. Nothing more than a mystery to be solved—and a liability to be handled.

A liability with the most exquisite bite.

In a whiskey voice, she said, "If you hadn't decided to capture me, I would've fang-fucked your neck till you screamed."

Filthy, wicked girl. *I want her NOW.*

She smiled, flashing those sharp little fangs, and his mind went blank. As if his legs knew better than he did, they stumbled toward her. *"Josephine."*

When she held up her ripped thong, his steps faltered. She'd rolled him again? He'd never felt her. Never scented her until now.

How? *How?*

Next she waved to her necklace—which was back around her slim, pale neck.

He swallowed hard. They both knew what else had been in his pockets.

For the second time tonight, she raised his talisman with a mean smile.

Bluff her. He shrugged. "Still just a trinket, vampire."

"Are you a liar on top of everything else, Ruin?"

"It's pronounced *Roon*," he said absently. "Not *Roo-in*."

"Of course, *Roo-in*. Enjoy the rest of your evening." She nodded at the nymphs. "Ladies." She began to disappear.

He vaulted forward, arms outstretched, but the only thing left of her was her echoing laughter.

THIRTEEN

Hours into the morning, Jo tossed and turned in bed, determined not to think about the dark fey's blood. Or anything else about him.

Like his grin—slanted, a touch sneering.

Or his scent—leather and evergreen.

Definitely not his body—long, tall, with rippling muscles she wanted to bite.

She'd already gotten off in the shower to fantasies of him, had even sunk her fangs into her own wrist. When she'd tasted his blood mixed with hers, she'd come over and over, until she'd dropped to her knees in the tub. . . .

Now she glared at his trinket, sitting on her bedside table. "Dickwad." She punched her pillow.

At the beginning of the night, he'd been unemotional with that blond nymph, like a robot. He'd coldly informed her, "I'm coming." He'd all but yawned as he'd gotten his nut.

With Jo, he'd bellowed so loud the whole city had heard it. Why would he want to be with others when he'd liked her best?

They'd been good together.

Briefly. Before he'd decided to kill her and all.

When would it be *her* turn to find a partner to hold her hand? She pined for her own groom, one who'd gaze into her eyes and tell her, *"You are everything."*

But pining was a problem. Whenever she was filled with yearning like this and she did manage to doze off, she risked her own type of sleep-walking.

Sleep-ghosting.

She would go intangible, sinking through her bed, through the floor, and then into the ground. Nothing could awaken her before she opened her eyes to total blackness, shrieking and scrabbling for the surface.

If she ever solidified underground, she could die—already entombed.

Worse, what if she didn't sink? What if she floated? The stars seemed to beckon her. . . .

Finally Jo relaxed enough to drift off, and the strangest dream arose. She was in a boggy field, toiling under a scorching sun. She wiped her gritty forearm over her sweat-drenched face.

No, not *her* arm. Not *her* face.

Rune's? Somehow she was seeing a scene from his point of view.

The castle's bells tolled. His head whipped toward the sound. My father is dead. *The mortality curse that had befallen Sylvan's leader had ended even a regent's immortal existence.*

Serves you right for trying to colonize the Wiccae realm, old king. *Rune felt no sympathy for the distant sire who'd spared his life but had never graced his bastard with a spoken word.*

The demon slaves who worked these fens shoulder to shoulder with Rune turned away. To them, a baneblood like him was already dead, and good riddance. They feared his poison. They wondered why he hadn't been stoned to death as an infant like all the other dark fey halflings.

Perhaps that would have been a mercy.

Because with the king's death comes mine.

For all his fifteen years, he'd known his days were numbered. But when the king had fallen in battle, bespelled by a warlock general, Rune had thought he'd have at least a few weeks more to plan.

Now panic filled him. How to escape? The queen's demon guards would soon come for him.

For his head.

His eyes darted. Crossing the fens with no food or fresh water would be suicide. He bared a claw, drawing blood to ink an invisibility spell on his forearm. His powers were undeveloped. Maybe this time the combinations of runes would work.

As his black blood spilled, laborers swooped up their young and fled, cursing him to the hells.

Frustration boiled inside him, and he yelled, "I never wanted to be like this!"

Concentrate. *Another carefully crafted symbol. Just as his dam had taught him. Only one more left—*

Royal guards traced into the fields, seizing him.

He fought wildly, but the guards' armor repelled his claws and fangs. The demons had already transitioned into full immortality, were massive brutes. They bound his hands to prevent his clawing. They muzzled him to prevent his bites.

Taking me to the executioner.

Yet once they'd beaten him down into the mud, they made no journey to the block. They hauled him to a bathhouse, stripping him and scrubbing his skin like an animal's.

As he'd thought daily since he could remember: Gods give me the power to destroy Sylvan's royal house. *His colonizing, slaving, rapist father had succumbed, but what of the rest of his execrable line? The now-widowed queen and her spawn, Rune's half siblings.*

The guards dressed him in fine breeches, a billowing shirt, and shoes that pinched his feet. Leaving his hand bindings, they removed the muzzle, then traced him into an echoing chamber.

Unused to teleporting, Rune wobbled on his feet. Was this . . . the royal court? They must've taken him to the capital, to the Forest of Three Bridges. He gawked at the riches around him.

A single female awaited him: Magh the Canny, the queen who loathed him, begrudged his very life.

A mere scratch across her neck would bring her to her knees. But he could do nothing with his hands bound. The guards would block him before he could get his fangs into her.

She was seated upon her elaborate throne, her cutting blue eyes studying him. "You refuse to bow before your regent?" *Her crown was a circlet of polished gold, and it rested far too comfortably atop her regal blond head.*

Seething, Rune forced himself to bow.

"How old are you?" *she asked.*

"I've survived the fens for fifteen years." *He was strong and hardened, could do the work of two adult demons.*

"Such bravado, cur."

"My name is Rune."

Her eyes gleamed at his challenge. "Your face isn't handsome. And yet I understand you've made many conquests among the highborn females of this kingdom."

Reminded of his success, he drew on the patience he'd learned when seducing empty-headed, thrill-seeking féodals. "Yes, my queen, they have honored me so." *Rune had slept with all those highborns to uncover his dam's fate after she'd been taken from him. But none had been able to help him.*

"Ah, you can be glib of tongue. You must be to convince them to risk your toxins." *She canted her head.* "I suppose you must abstain from certain acts."

Kissing and kissing below. If only he could find a female dark fey to enjoy. Another halfling who'd been spared.

The queen continued, "But what of your leavings? Are you demonic in that manner? Have you a demon's mystical seal over your member?"

He scarcely believed he was discussing his seed *with the queen.* "I do." *A demon could know the pleasure of a climax but couldn't spill semen. Not until he was inside his destined female and his seal disappeared.*

In other words, never for me.

"I doubt abominations like you get a mate, especially since we've exterminated your ilk in Sylvan."

His claws ached to rend her flesh. But Rune had feared the same. How many times had he heard that dark fey were creations never meant to be, outcasts from the reach of destiny?

"I wanted my husband to obey convention and dispose of you as well. To allow such a lethal being to remain alive, even enslaved, seemed a tremendous folly."

Gods give me the power . . .

"But now I see more in you, and I can almost comprehend why those idiotic females risk your poison. You have the smoldering sensuality of the fey and the sexual intensity of a demon." She gazed past him. *"It appears I have a use for you after all."*

Chills skittered up his spine, and again he wondered if a stoning mightn't have been a mercy. . . .

Jo's eyes flashed open.

That hadn't been a simple dream—it was a memory of Rune's! She'd witnessed it as if from his eyes. She'd known his thoughts and language as if they'd been her own.

He'd suspected Jo would read memories from his blood. She must be—what'd he call it?—a *cosaş* vampire!

What memory would he kill to prevent her from seeing? Surely not scenes like the ones she'd just experienced.

She burned to find out what that heartless queen had wanted from him. What use would Magh have for sensuality and intensity?

Jo found it baffling that the arrogant Rune had once been a slave. She felt unwelcome sympathy for him. How he hated the fey! And he despised his blood. He'd longed for a female of his own species as much as she'd longed for a partner.

No wonder he hadn't spilled semen on Jo. No wonder he'd been so stunned when she'd fed from him. He could do to her everything he'd dreamed of.

And yet he'd decided to kill her.

She pulled her knees to her chest, reeling from everything she'd learned. Entire worlds of freaks existed.

Fey and Wiccae kingdoms. Immortal dimensions with intrigues and wars.

Demons could teleport, or *trace*. Jo supposed she should get the lingo down. Tracing was disappearing and reappearing, traveling over distances.

So what did they call it when they ghosted or dematerialized or hung out in walls?

Could they?

If a fey world existed, then was there a place for creatures like her? Maybe her shooting hadn't turned her. Maybe neither she nor Thaddie had ever been human. What if they'd crossed over from some fantastical realm—perhaps from a nation of ghost vampires?

Seventeen years ago, the docs had blamed her memory loss on a head injury. That could be why she'd forgotten her birthplace.

She shot upright in bed. If she could find out for certain, she'd *have* to go to Thaddie, to explain their origin and their powers and this entire weird world! She ghosted with happiness; then embodied with a frown.

Right now she didn't have much to explain.

Rune might return to the Quarter tonight. Information for the taking.

An unwelcome realization arose: Rune the Insatiable Asshat might be the key to her reuniting with Thaddie.

FOURTEEN

A vampire has my bloody talisman.

Rune would rather have forfeited the Darklight bow. All day he'd stormed down New Orleans streets, seeking any Lorean to question about Josephine. Most took one look at his expression and fled. Even the nymphs had retreated into the trees or the river.

No one stole from him. No one was fast enough, crafty enough. It simply didn't happen.

Yet the vampire had.

Twice.

After she'd disappeared—taking her necklace, his bait—he'd interrogated the nymphs for any detail he might have missed, then he'd used those clues to try to unearth her lair. He'd been tempted to fetch Darach for the wolf's tracking abilities, but Rune didn't want to explain his new target. Besides, time moved differently in Tenebrous; tracing there and back would take several Earth days.

Damn that leech!

He found himself touching her bite mark yet again. A day later, he remained astounded that she'd not only bitten him, but fed.

A vampire consumed my befouled blood.

He pierced the remnants of her bite with his claw tips, seeking to re-create a fraction of the pleasure—only to fail.

He'd reacted like a madman, couldn't even remember what he'd said to her. He thought he'd spoken to her in Demonish. He knew he'd bellowed so loud his throat had stung.

Part of him was glad of his response. Hardly that of a deadened man whose fire had been extinguished! Rune had *felt* with Josephine. Some buried cinder must have lingered deep within him, because it was . . . sparking.

His reaction to her—and hers to him—made him ponder the most asinine and far-fetched possibility.

What if she was his mate?

What were the odds he would meet a female whose scent put him to his knees—and who also happened to be immune to his poison? She'd told him, *You smelled right.*

No, no, there'd be no *mate* for Rune. Thousands of years ago, he'd con-cluded his kind didn't get a fated one, were cursed to be alone.

He'd never met a mated dark fey, had never heard of a second genera-tion of his species. His own solitary years had cemented the idea in his mind.

Even if he got a mate, Josephine the vampire wouldn't be his. He'd re-acted so violently to her and her bite because she'd mesmerized him.

Her scent enticed him more than anyone else's simply because she had the most alluring scent. Other men on the street had responded with just as much heat.

None of the other Møriør had a mate. To take on such a glaring vul-nerability would have to affect Rune's standing. He'd be damned to the hells before he relinquished his spot at their table.

Plenty of immortals would sell their soul to take his place. . . .

By late afternoon, Rune headed to the Lore shop the nymphs had mentioned. It was a ramshackle store with a symbol of the Lore in the window. The shingle read: *Loa's Emporium*

Perhaps he could find manacles here. He could definitely pry for information.

Unshaven and wearing last night's clothes, he strode inside. A bell jingled above the door. Mortal wares crowded the shelves. A Lorean market must be concealed in the back.

A woman sat behind the counter, engrossed in a book. Her nearly sheer white dress clung to her dark skin, revealing a voluptuous figure. Loa, the proprietress?

He raised his brows. *Well, then, this customer will be sure to return.*

His response was yet more evidence he had no mate. If he'd found his fated female, then he wouldn't be planning to bed this buxom shopkeeper at his earliest convenience! He asked her, "Where can I find handcuffs, dove?"

She didn't look up from her book. "Back room. Aisles are marked."

"I don't suppose you've met a Lorean named Josephine? Brunette about five and a half feet tall." *Unbelievable body, whiskey voice.* "Fairly blunt." *Bit of a bitch.* "Wears combat boots and has piercings." *Even secret ones.*

The woman licked her thumb and turned a page.

"She lives in the city and prowls the Quarter. But she's species closeted." Josephine wasn't the only one. When he recognized what Loa was, he hid a grin. He'd bet she wouldn't want that known.

Without taking her eyes off the book—a tome on neuroscience—Loa said, "Too many beings to keep track of this time of the millennium. Accession calls them close. Ask the low creatures." Her accent was lyrical and drawling. Josephine's accent had been drawling as well, but in a different way.

"Among your wares, do you happen to have a lock of Valkyrie hair?" The nymphs had promised to be on the lookout for one, but he didn't hold out much hope. Information from them in the heat of the moment was one thing . . .

"You'd have better luck orderin' a Valkyrie head," Loa said.

He hadn't thought it would be easy. "Do you sell information?"

She finally glanced up. "By the looks of you, I'm thinkin' you can't afford the information I have in my catalog."

No? His wealth was so vast it was incalculable. He smiled at her, picturing all the relics he'd amassed over the ages, the ones that filled his private collection. Ah, the secrets he kept.

He found himself wondering how Josephine would react to his treasures. No doubt pure astonishment. How could she not be impressed? "Perhaps you're right," he told Loa, turning toward the back. He located the concealed doorway and entered.

Scents overwhelmed him. Every manner of Lore creature must have shopped here recently. Signs papered the walls: *"Accession Savings!" "Fire Sale!" "Mass Death = Estate Sales!"*

Affecting every immortal in the Gaia realms, the Accession was a mystical event that occurred roughly every five centuries, bringing Loreans into contact with each other—for better or worse. Some immortals would bond; others would war. Usually most of the factions fought against each other.

Nïx was attempting to change the rules of the game, transforming what should be a drawn-out war of attrition into a great Lorewide battle between immortal alliances.

The Møriør—a brotherhood of killers with very few weaknesses—would prevail. They always did. To their enemies, they were the Bringers of Doom.

He headed farther inside. The aisles were marked CONTRACEPTION, GLAMOURS, CONJURINGS. . . . He raised a brow at APOCALYPSE PREPARATION. They were already planning on it? He turned down the BONDAGE aisle, then selected a pair of cuffs with a tag that read:

Mystically reinforced and trace-proofed by The House of Witches

Est. 937

1st-Class Curses, Hexes, Spells, and Potions

We Won't Be Undersold!

info@houseofwitches.com

Member LBBB

Those witches were a proud bunch, considering they'd never received permission from their overlady to start this colony on Gaia—and considering they'd never paid taxes to Akelarre, their source dimension.

Most Loreans would rather face a vengeful deity than a bureaucratic tax collector.

In the year of 937, you lot bollixed up. Allixta arrives forthwith.

He examined the cuffs, assessing the magick in them. Not bad. He could customize them with his own runes, magnifying and steering the power, just as he did with his arrows.

Yes, if the little leech returned tonight, he'd capture her. Once he had her in his keeping, then maybe he could tear his thoughts from her and focus on his mission.

At the counter, he stowed the cuffs in a back pocket, then proffered gold coins. He'd made exchanges for these newer coins in the Elserealms, but they were still old. No choice but to use them.

As he tendered payment, his ears twitched. Something large was moving beneath the old floorboards of this shop, something . . . slithering. He despised snakes. He inwardly shuddered at the memory of the serpent shifter he'd been forced to pleasure. "Loa, do you keep a snake down there?"

She narrowed her amber gaze. "For dark fey askin' too many questions."

"I pass for pure-blooded fey. How'd you know?"

"Your canines. Touch too long. Says demon blood to me."

"Ah, but I could be half vampire."

"Plum-colored eyes."

He grinned down at her. "Keen observations. And here I thought you were studiously ignoring me."

"No threats escape Loa's notice."

She must possess a wealth of knowledge about her customers. Secrets for the taking. "How did you know about the eyes? You couldn't have met many of us."

The few dark fey he'd encountered had each been born of a different combination of fey and demon. Rage demon/ice fey, forest fey/smoke demon, and so on . . .

Their characteristics and level of toxicity had varied. But all of them had possessed plum-colored eyes.

Loa's mien turned calculating. "Perhaps I've been seein' a dark fey female in this very city. Perhaps she's pretty to look upon."

He straightened, quickly asking, "How much to buy a lead on her?" For some reason, Josephine's ethereal face flashed in his mind.

"Why should I transact with you?" Loa asked.

Rune rested his forearms on the counter, leaning in. Catching her gaze, he raked one of his fangs over his bottom lip. "Why *shouldn't* you want to do more with me, dove?"

Her pupils dilated as she focused on his mouth, her breaths shallowing. She blinked several times, then glared. "You're a baneblood—with a healing *vampire bite* on his neck—who's buyin' *restraints* with too-old gold. What could possibly be troublin' there?" Despite this, she was definitely interested.

"It's a funny story." *Which I will never tell you.* "We should have dinner."

An arched brow. "Should we, then?"

He lowered his voice to a murmur, "Yes, and while we're there, I'll convince you to *transact* with me. Over and over."

Loa crossed her arms over her ample breasts. "I don't think—"

"Ah-ah, dove. I know females, and I'm gazing at one who needs more than just coin. . . ." He trailed off, muscles tensing.

Over all the other smells of this shop, he caught a scent.

Valkyrie.

FIFTEEN

Maybe I don't have more pride than the nymphs, Jo thought as she gazed into the mirror at her new dress.

A scarlet sheath. Strapless. Micromini length.

When she'd decided to return to the Quarter to confront Rune, she'd surveyed her clothes rack of vintage threads, but she'd found nothing as sexy as what the nymphs had worn.

Unacceptable.

So she'd dashed to a second-hand boutique for a bit of shopping. Or more accurately, for a bit of shop*lifting*. Then she'd heated a mug of blood to drink while getting ready. She frowned. The mug was untouched, the blood cold. It'd smelled off anyway.

As long as she didn't expend too much energy, she could miss a meal.

She turned in the mirror, then back. She'd opted for a strapless push-up bra that concealed her nipple piercings and lifted her boobs almost to her chin. She'd blown her hair out into big curls and defined her eyes with smoky liner. Clear glitter nail polish made her black claws sparkle. After nibbling her lips till they were blood red, she'd slipped on strappy stilettos.

Her bullet necklace dipped toward her cleavage. A silver bangle circled one bare arm above her elbow. She'd chosen chandelier earrings to dangle from her lobes and her customary helix rings at the tops of her ears.

Jo had enjoyed all her piercings, even the one below the belt. Each bite of pain had proved she was of the earth, *incarnated*, or something. Her jewelry helped remind her of that.

Plus, any guy she'd been with had lost his shit when he saw them. It was a given that a tongue would make contact directly.

She smoothed her hair one last time and eked out a smile for the mirror. She didn't expect Rune to take one look at her and think, *How could I have passed up that ass? Maybe I ought not to murder her?* But she hoped he would have a qualm or two.

Her gaze flitted to his bone thingy beside her bed. The one thing she knew for certain? It was anything but a *trinket*.

She had no pockets to store it, but was leery of leaving it behind. If other freaks had senses like hers, they could sniff out a hiding place. With a shrug, she tucked the piece into the safest place she could think of—the snug cleavage between her pushed-up breasts.

Because she'd never give Rune access to it.

As ready as she'd ever be, Jo "traced" to the Quarter, heading straight for the courtyard. Did she really want to see Rune up to his eyebrows in nymph? Maybe he'd still be trying to relive her bite, and then she could laugh at him.

Nearing the gate, she made herself invisible, but the courtyard was empty. After a survey of the surrounding area, she traced to a rooftop overlooking Bourbon. It was a busy Saturday night in the Quarter, but then, every night brought something different here: tour groups, bands, warnings to repent.

In time, a couple strolling arm-in-arm below drew her attention. The short, black-haired woman wore only one shoe. What looked like a *bat* clung to the back of her peasant blouse, peeking over a shoulder. The woman's face was captivating, her golden eyes seeming to glow.

Definitely not human. Freaks were coming out of the woodwork!

Aside from the woman's oddness, something about her put Jo on guard. Simply because she was paranormal?

Jo turned her attention to the tall man with her, but his cowboy hat blocked Jo's view of his face. He wore shit-kicker boots and had a rolling, confident gait.

The female asked him, "Have you ever been bait? Well, besides jailbait. *Rowr.*"

"I can't say that I have, ma'am." Texan accent?

Jo cocked her head at his voice, at the grin in his tone. The couple turned the corner onto an empty side street.

In ghost-mode, she traced to another rooftop to get a better look at him. When she caught sight of his face, Jo's mouth went dry.

Thaddie!

Brother!

He appeared older than the last clipping she'd taped into her scrapbook, but it was him!

All grown up. No longer the little boy who'd ridden around in the Thadpack and worshipped Spidey.

She clutched her chest at the sharp ache.

Why was he in New Orleans? Maybe a sports playoff had brought him to the city. Or maybe he was a tourist, visiting with his high school friends.

So what was he doing with a nonhuman? *Associating with freaks is* not *acceptable, Thaddeus.*

If he was going to just . . . *hang out* with them, then had Jo sacrificed a life with him for nothing?

No, she'd get him away from that woman. And out of this town. An enemy might discover Jo's connection to Thad. An enemy like—

Movement out of the corner of her eye.

Rune. On the roof of the neighboring building.

His towering, lean frame was crouched like a predator's, his body seeming to thrum with readiness. For what? Black forked out across his eyes.

She glanced from Thad back to Rune. *Threat.* She needed to lure the dark fey away from her brother.

She was about to trace to Rune when his hand dropped to his quiver. He fingered the flights of his arrows, as if choosing among them. With blinding speed, he slipped his bow off his back and into place, nocking a black arrow.

Her eyes shot wide. He was aiming at Thaddie!

She focused on a spot in the sky above Rune, tracing to it. She rotated in the air, diving headfirst for him, materializing on her way.

She'd take the dark fey from the roof down to the goddamned basement—and bury him there.

SIXTEEN

About to end thousands of years of life, Rune locked on his target and drew his bowstring.

He'd chosen his favorite arrow. Sian laughingly called it "one-and-done." Shot into the neck of a target, the arrow would sever the head cleanly.

Rune took an even breath. He was on the verge of relaxing his string fingers when he caught Josephine's scent.

From *above* him?

A split second later, he heard her incensed scream.

She was coming at him like a rocket, her eyes black with rage. An ally of Nïx's? A protective one! Out of habit, he shifted his bow toward the new threat.

Damn it!

He only had time to pop his arrow off the string—

Josephine slammed into him.

The force was like a meteor, shoving him back. *BOOM.* In an explosion of shingles and wood, the roof cracked open beneath him.

She clawed his throat, holding him in place as she pummeled his face. He took the furious hits, scrambling to secure his bow in his fist.

They plummeted into an attic. She kept hitting. They crashed through the attic floor into an apartment below.

Nothing could pry Rune's bow from his grip. Which left him with only one hand to defend himself, much less reach the cuffs. Yet he couldn't bring himself to coldcock her.

As the next floor ruptured, he caught sight of a stunned family at a dinner table, forks hovering over plates.

CRASH. Down he and Josephine plunged to a lower story. In that apartment, a guy was pile-driving a girl, the stereo blaring. Never looked up.

Enviable. Rune was getting his ass kicked by a female he couldn't seem to hurt.

BOOM. Another story breached. Their momentum should be slowing, but with a wild look in her eyes, she traced them, accelerating the velocity. She meant to put him into the ground?

"Stop this, vampire! If I trace against you, you'll go flying—"

She popped him in the mouth.

They tore through a last story, rupturing a web of water lines. Rune's back slammed into the basement floor, cracking the foundation wide open. She landed atop him.

The impact punched the air from his lungs. He sucked in a breath of cement dust and mist, coughing beneath her.

She eased upright, sitting astride him, seeming to gauge how much she'd injured him.

The building groaned and wobbled. They both froze. A second passed. Then another. It stood fast.

"What the hells, female?" Josephine had surely spooked his target with her scream, much less when the entire building had shimmied. He strained to detect the Valkyrie's scent. Nothing. "Gods damn it!" Though Nïx couldn't foresee her own destiny, she might have the ability to start clocking *his* future. Had she gotten a look at his face?

If so, she could predict where he would strike every time.

But this situation was salvageable. Josephine was in league with Nïx, which meant he could use his new prisoner to get to the Valkyrie. Perhaps Nïx would bargain for Josephine's release.

Not to mention the information he could squeeze from the vampire. Yet another excuse to capture her. Those cuffs in his back pocket awaited.

Once he'd secured her, he'd force her to return his talisman, then utilize one of his particular talents.

Interrogation. "You're going to pay for this move, vampire."

She drew back for another punch. With his speed, he caught her fist. As he squeezed, he registered her appearance. Mist from the water lines had dampened her porcelain skin—her short dress revealed a lot of it. The scarlet sheath barely contained her plump breasts and rode high on her thighs.

She wore jewelry, makeup, and fuck-me heels, dressing like a man-eater. *Dressing like?* Josephine the vampire was the very definition of a man-eater.

Blood rushed to his cock at the thought: *She made a meal of me last night.*

When he hardened beneath her, she squirmed with outrage, and that micro hem exposed a fruitful view.

His man-eater had left her panties at home, revealing her smooth pussy.

Fuck. Me.

At the sight, a haze covered his vision. Burning for her kiss, he grasped her nape, pulling her in—

Wham! Another jab to the mouth. "Naturally you're thinking about sex!"

"After all this foreplay? Of course I am!"

"Foreplay? In your dreams!"

His gaze dipped between her thighs and back up. "Only the sweetest reveries."

"You are such a . . ." She trailed off, her shimmering eyes locked on his bottom lip.

He daubed his tongue, tasting blood. He smirked with triumph when she dreamily licked a fang. "Does my vampire thirst for baneblood? Ah, she thinks me delicious." Her craving made his chest bow and his cock swell even more. "No need to get violent, female. All you have to do is ask me real nice to feed you. A beauty like you could coax me to do just about anything in the name of pleasure."

She shook her head hard, but her breaths had shallowed, those creamy breasts rising and falling before his rapt gaze.

She clearly struggled for control. Which meant he could take it. She leaned over him, gripping his shoulders, her dress slipping higher.

The scent of her arousal swept him up, blanking his mind. His target was forgotten, his mission. Liabilities, vulnerabilities, gods, wars—none of it mattered at that moment.

Her claws dug into his shoulders. The vampire was pinning her prey? This prey was going *nowhere*.

He released his bow to slip his hand between her thighs and cup her soft pussy. He groaned when his palm met hot, giving flesh. "Female, I'm going to make you come till you can't walk."

She blinked. "Rune?"

Just his name on her tongue made him shudder. "Give me your lips, Josephine." Gods, he needed her kiss—

She snatched his hand away then launched a haymaker at his face. "Don't you dare!"

"The hells, woman!" He seized her wrists. "Dare? Because I'm a dark fey?" And damn if he wasn't leaning up to do it again, pulling on her wrists. "Any barrier between us disappeared when you drank me down."

With her hands captured, she defended herself with her legs, squeezing her thighs around his waist, shoving her knees into his sides.

His plan to take her mouth and slip his cock inside her wasn't happening—for now—so he snagged the cuffs. Quick as a blur, he bound one of her wrists to his own.

She gasped with realization, attempting to teleport. She even did that slow tracing thing again, but she wasn't going anywhere. The metal would hold her. Earlier, as he'd been running down Nïx's scent, he'd hastily etched runes into those cuffs, directing the power only to one. Josephine couldn't trace—but he could.

As she thrashed to get free, he caught a glimpse of white between her breasts. "And there's my treasure." He reached for the talisman, but couldn't resist a grope. He groaned. *A perfect handful.*

She slapped at him till he reluctantly released her, collecting the talisman. Back into his pocket where it belonged.

"Take this cuff off, Ruin!"

He laughed at her. "Not a chance, dove." He yanked on the chain, forcing her closer. "And it's *Rune.*"

Still she fought him. "What are you doing?"

"Exactly what I said last night."

Her eyes went wide. "Imprisoning me? Until you decide to kill me?"

He grated, "Till death us do part, Josie."

SEVENTEEN

Rune can trace?

Jo wobbled when they appeared on the roof of the building. His teleporting was harder and sharper than hers, as if they'd been shot from a cannon.

Compared to his tracing, hers was like shifting a finely-tuned Caddie into gear. But she couldn't manage it when stuck in these cuffs! Even her ghosting had failed.

He collected his bizarre arrow from beside the crash site. As he surveyed the empty street, sirens wailed toward their location.

He cursed under his breath. "Drawing the attention of humans?" He shook his head at her. "Reckless female." Then he traced them again.

When she opened her eyes, they were in an echoing room with a glass floor. Beneath them was another story with a glass floor, and on and on.

Her lips parted. Each story below was populated with all manner of creatures. Freak-show central.

Some had wings, others four legs. She saw beings with glowing skin, scaly skin, pus-covered skin. She recognized centaurs from comic books and behorned demons from Rune's memories.

Females were interspersed among the males. Most of them sported breasts and wore less clothing.

Everyone seemed inebriated, with goblets in hands, pincers, or tentacles. Peculiar music and loud partying sounded.

"What is this place?" None of her voyeurism had prepared her for scenes like these. When she saw copulation happening everywhere, her heart raced. At least, she hoped that was sex; otherwise creatures were bludgeoning each other to death.

"Ah, you're nervous about what's to come," Rune murmured, mistaking her alarm. "You should be. You're soon to discover something I'm very, very good at."

"Where have you taken me?" And how would she get back to her brother?

Since her resurrection (or her transformation?), she'd often wondered why she'd been given all this strength and speed, all her talents. *I can safeguard him.*

If she could reach him.

Why would Rune target Thaddie anyway? How had her brother gotten mixed up in so much danger? Like sister, like brother? Had he kicked his own ant mound?

She consoled herself with the knowledge that every second Rune was with her gave Thad time to get farther away. Maybe she should stall.

"We're in Tortua, a pleasure den," Rune said. "I maintain a residence here. This is the observatory."

Were any of the freaks below *observing* up her dress?

Reading her mind, he said, "Each floor can view the ones below, but not the ones above."

She craned her head up. A solid dome stretched overhead.

"I've got the coveted top floor. Welcome to your new home."

Wait, Rune meant to keep her in a *pleasure den*? "In other words, you have digs in a whorehouse. If the dark fey fits . . ."

A muscle ticked in his wide jaw.

Oooh, did I jab a tender spot?

"A wiser vampire would be convincing me to spare her life. Not insulting me."

"You won't kill me." How could he? She'd taken six slugs to the face. Unless a wooden stake to the heart could end her?

"Will I not?" he asked.

"You like my bite too much." Not that she'd be giving it to him again. No matter how close she'd come in that basement. She'd been tempted only because she hadn't drunk in twenty-four hours, and she'd used up a lot of energy.

"I could replace it with another vampire's."

His dismissive tone made her nervous. Last night he'd all but told Jo her life depended on keeping him interested.

She'd seen how easily he'd gone from a tender look to a lethal one.

However, there was a surefire way to protect herself from death and Thad from assassination: take out Rune first. "How many people have you killed?" she asked him.

"Can't count that high."

Figured. She'd have to get the better of him. Would he prove as hard to kill as she'd been?

"Come." He turned toward a solid brick wall, pushing a symbol carved into stone. Bricks disappeared to form a doorway. A portal!

A strange memory flashed into her consciousness like a lighthouse's beam—too bright one instant, then gone the next.

But she remembered a place of total chaos, flames, and earthquakes. Though winds had blurred her vision, she'd seen a pale hand raised to the sky. Above, stars had streaked across the night. Behind Jo, there'd been a wall of portals.

No, they were . . . black holes.

They'd been arrayed in tiers one on top of another, black upon black. Like spiders' eyes. Someone had screamed, "It's worldend!"

Was that Rune's memory? Or hers?

Before Jo could delve deeper, he forced her through the portal. It closed behind her with a hiss.

A stone bridge extended before them, lit by torches and flanked with railings. More symbols had been carved into various stones.

He unlocked the cuff around his wrist and reached for hers. He was just going to undo it? For real?

He stashed the restraints in his pocket, then seemed to be awaiting her escape. *Nice knowing you, sucker.* She began to trace back to the Quarter. She'd gotten a good start—when she hit some kind of boundary and bounced right back.

Rune laughed at her. He dug that trinket from his pocket—another point he'd scored against her. With a smirk, he tossed it in the air, caught it in his big palm, then pocketed it again.

"You're such a dick." She couldn't believe she'd been infatuated with him.

"I have wards surrounding this entire residence. I'm the only one who can travel past them. Things inside my lair stay inside, including the sound of your screams—in case you thought to call for help. Even if someone heard you, they couldn't enter, because anything outside remains outside."

Say she got lucky and took Rune out; without help—or the ability to escape—she'd be trapped here.

"Ah, and there went your ridiculous plan to kill me." He dragged her along. "I see you working out all the angles."

Not yet *all* the angles. Could she ghost *inside* the boundaries? If so, maybe she could ghost inside him? He could never shake her. And eventually he'd have to leave this place.

Her heels were loud as they crossed the bridge. She gazed over the railing, seeing only darkness—as dark as a black hole.

She refused to let Rune know how freaked out she was. "Where is Tortua? The South Pacific or something? Didn't they film *Survivor* here? Fire represents life."

"Oh, you are a long, long way from Earth, dove. But you'll like it here—it's perpetual night."

Not on Earth. She'd just have to . . . she'd have to think about that later.

He touched his flattened palm to an elaborate symbol on a pillar, and a second portal opened into a huge bedroom suite.

The inviting space had been decorated in earth tones—probably not called that here—and was a thousand times better than her own "home." Still, she said, "Not bad, I guess. Though the suite looks like it belongs in a blueblood's hunting lodge, not a blackblood's brothel penthouse."

He tilted his head, as if mystified by her. "I hold your life in my hands. My grip on it lessens with each insult."

Then I'll float away. She shook herself.

In the adjoining sitting area, a fire crackled in a large brick hearth. More symbols embellished the stone there. At various places on the walls, similar markings were spaced the way light switches might be.

An enormous bedstand dominated the room. Thick posters supported heavy drapes. The fabric was tied back, revealing tangled sheets. "That's your bed?" She could only imagine what activities had taken place there. Moments ago, he'd cupped her between her thighs in that basement, trying to kiss her, yet he'd most likely enjoyed an orgy here today.

"What of it?"

"I would've thought it'd be bigger," she said. "I doubt you can fit more than five or six nymphs in there."

"Depends on how cozy with them I want to get."

"You don't expect me to sleep there, do you?"

"And if I did?"

She tapped the heel of her palm to her forehead. "I forgot my black light and hazmat suit. But you've gotta have body condoms around here somewhere."

He inched even closer to her. "Condoms? I'm half demon." He leaned down to say, "Even if I needed to wear one, sizing would be an issue. As you well remember."

With a roll of her eyes, she backed away from him. When he got close, she got weak. How could she still desire a manwhore like him? Especially after he'd threatened to kill her?

Because of his blood. Only *his blood.*

He crossed to the wall beside the bedstand, pushing a symbol. One second the bed was unmade, the next it was remade, then freshly turned down.

Don't wig out, Jo. "Handy."

He raised his brows. "Any more commentary?"

"Not at present." She sauntered to the fire to warm herself. Her dress was still wet, and most of her damp skin was uncovered. Plus, thirst always made her chilled.

She turned her attention to a comfortable lounge chair situated in front of the fire. Beside it was a container of feathers and arrow shafts.

He made his arrows there. Alone. "Your sitting area only has one chair?" Was he a loner like her? Not that she cared.

Whatever he saw in her expression made his tighten. "A nymph friend decorated this place for me. The styling choices indicate nothing about myself." He unbuckled the quiver around his leg, setting it against the wall.

"Uh-huh." The styling choices must indicate *a lot* about him.

He unhooked his bow and hung it on a spike above the hearth. "There's a ward over my bow here. Reach for it, and you'll be blown back on your ass. If you'd still like to try, inform me so I can watch."

Dickwad!

"In any case, this is a secondary residence."

"Ruin's whorehouse weekender."

With an irritated look, he pressed another symbol, and a wide doorway opened to reveal a huge library. The shelves had to be three stories high. All those books were like safes full of never-ending treasure, and everyone but her seemed to have the keys.

Another of Rune's symbols opened a second adjoining room with a gigantic swimming pool. Marble columns surrounded it. Torches blazed to life all at the same time, their flames reflecting in the still surface of the water. Steam wafted from a back room.

Cool!

"Copied from an old Roman design." He surveyed it as if seeing the area anew. "Just when I deem mortals completely without flair, a choice century will come along. . . ."

"How many rooms do you have?"

"As many as I wish. It's infinite."

Again, handy. "So this is where you think to keep me."

"Not exactly a hardship, then." He cast her that smug look, the one he wore when manipulating nymphs with his dick, the one that made her want to claw his face to ribbons.

"You've got no idea what my home is like." *Big Sleazy Weeps.* She lifted her nose. "In comparison, I find this . . . quaint."

"Lucky for me I don't give a damn about your lofty standards." He parted his lips, then seemed to change his mind about what he'd been about to say. "Follow me." He turned in a different direction, opening up another area.

When they crossed through the doorway, she stutter-stepped. *Holy shit.* Relics filled the room. Suits of armor, statues, jewels, vases, weapons of all kinds. "Where'd this stuff come from?"

"I've collected these priceless items over my lifetime."

Jo collected things as well. One difference. Everything in here was "priceless." She'd never been to a museum; she wanted to explore this place for days. "Collected? Or stole?"

He leaned his shoulder against a wall. "They're war prizes."

"You some kind of soldier?"

"I suppose you could say that. Do you still think my home *quaint*, vampire?" He cared about her opinion, which surprised her.

She managed a careless shrug. " 'S okay."

He looked like he wanted to throttle her.

"Now that you have me here, what's your plan? My death is on the agenda for some point in the future, right?"

He exhaled. "No. I was angry and wanted to punish you for fouling my shot. A soothsayer like Nïx won't stroll into my sights so easily next time."

His change of tactics put her on edge—

Wait. He'd been aiming at the woman? That Nïx chick?

Not Thad!

Rune closed in on her. "I've realized fighting is the last thing I want to do with you. We'll put what happened earlier behind us. Consider it water under the bridge."

"Oh, really?"

"Don't believe me?" He curled his forefinger under her chin.

"Till death us do part?"

"Killing you was an option I considered and have since permanently discarded."

For some reason, she believed him. At least in that.

He brushed her damp hair over her shoulder, revealing her ear. His eyes grew hooded. Dude *really* dug her ears. "We could sit before the fire and open a bottle of wine. All you have to do is tell me how long you've been in league with Nïx and the other Valkyries."

Valkyries existed? Weird. Why not tell Rune she'd never met this soothsayer before? Nïx had seemed like a friend to Thad—but if so, why had the female been talking about *bait*? Had she been leading him straight into a trap?

What else could be expected of a freak? Jo had encountered few of them, but so far she had been *un*impressed.

Her first impulse was to say, "Don't know Nïx. Put an arrow between her eyes." But then Rune would know Jo had been protecting Thad.

She couldn't predict how the dark fey would use information like that against her. And she didn't trust anyone—under the best of circumstances. No, she'd keep that tidbit close for now.

Which left her with one play: persuade this male to trust *her*, then convince him to let her go. *Will I sleep with him for my freedom?* At the thought of his body over hers, thrusting, she shivered again.

"You must be freezing. You can answer my questions once you're warmed up," he said, considerate as could be. "There's a robe outside the bathing chamber. Etched tiles control the water."

She could handle cocky asshole Ruin. Nice Rune was throwing her. Still, Jo wouldn't mind some time to mull over everything. Though so much had happened tonight, the facts were:

She and Rune had a mutual enemy.

He was presently staring down at her like he wanted to eat her up.

He wasn't trying to murder her brother.

Or her.

Where did this new knowledge leave her? Idiot Jo was kind of crushing on him again. What if she could build a relationship (of some sort) with him (if he quit nymphs cold turkey)?

And then, with Thad possibly coming back into Jo's life . . .

Two connections were within her grasp! Two people to notice if she floated away.

"Unless you'd prefer to remain with me while I dine." His gaze dipped to her body. "I know what I'd like to see on the menu."

EIGHTEEN

At a table in front of the hearth, Rune ate without tasting his food, his mind fixed on the vampire. The naked one bathing in his sauna.

Had he joined her, it would probably have been the most searingly sexual bath he'd ever enjoyed.

Two things stopped him. One: It would probably have been the most searingly sexual bath he'd ever enjoyed. He needed to maintain control. If she bit him at will . . .

Two: He'd decided he would have to secure her to his bed—to make sure she *couldn't* bite him. He intended to draw on his customary coldness when interrogating her, but better safe than sorry.

Contrary to what she thought, Rune didn't entertain bedmates here. It was his sanctuary. His bed hadn't been equipped with restraints, so he'd had to repurpose those cuffs. Task completed, he'd opted for a quick shave and shower in another bathroom.

He scarcely believed he had a female in his home. If another Møriør discovered her, any one of them would annihilate her. She was the ally of an enemy—which meant Josephine was an enemy of the Møriør as well. Plus, she was a security liability.

Killing her was the most logical option. Especially once he'd extracted any information about Nïx.

Yet the demon in him rebelled. Even his rational fey side demanded he first explore why Josephine could drink him. And why she affected him so viscerally.

Everything about her was different. When she'd pointed out his solitary chair, he'd barely stopped himself from explaining that he had allies he'd die for. That they lived communally, and he came here only for respite.

Damn it, information flowed *to* him.

He'd had no impulse to tell the lovely shopkeeper Loa his secrets. Never in all his lifetimes had he divulged one. So why the urge to with Josephine?

He had little appetite, had never been so eager to interrogate a subject. *Get focused, Rune.* He dug in his pocket for his talisman. He rolled it in his hand, contemplating those indecipherable symbols yet again.

He'd received the talisman the day his sire had died, the day Magh had made her decree about Rune's future. He'd pointed out the flaw in her plan to make him an assassin. . . .

"I can't trace." If he could, he would have long escaped.

"You possess demon blood; you can learn from my guards."

Excellent. He would learn to teleport, then use that ability to get free. He hadn't thought Magh the "Canny" would be so stupid—

"I might reunite you with your dam, should you serve me well."

As if struck, he swayed on his feet. "She still . . . lives?" For years, he'd believed her dead, the most likely fate for a slave who'd disappeared in the night. He pictured his dam's lively blue eyes. She'd always had a ready smile for Rune, striving so hard to mask her misery from him. "You or your henchmen killed her."

"As much as I would have enjoyed that, she lives."

"I-I don't believe you." Gods give me the power . . .

"No?" Magh snapped her fingers. One of the guards traced to Rune, handing him a small bag. The homespun material carried traces of his dam's scent—tinged with fear.

He ripped into the bag. Parchment had been folded around his mother's talisman, her sole possession. He opened the note, scanning the familiar handwriting and the language of demons, but some of the script was smudged, illegible:

> *My cherished son, please accept this talisman as a token of my love. It will always remind y* _____.
>
> *I know not the runes, but I believe th* _____. *You must* _____
> *constantly and nev* _____.
>
> *Do not allow the queen to use me to h*_____. *Strength and power flow through our family's line, and the years will bear out the following tru* _____.
>
> *Never forget that. I love you so much and only wis* _____.

Rune swallowed, dragging his gaze from the letter to Magh. "Where is my dam?"

The queen raised her blond brows. "I cannot tell you, else forfeit my leverage."

"The letter is smudged." He held it up accusingly. "I can't read all of it."

"The poor dear wept as she wrote it. I said she lives—I didn't say she was glad of that fact. There are some fates worse than death."

His breath left him. He would do whatever this evil bitch asked of him to free his mother.

And Rune had.

The old queen had been right about his prospects as an assassin, about the value of his seductive nature. His first target had sneaked Rune into her sanctuary, lowering all her protections. A fatal mistake.

He'd been more poisonous than anyone could've dreamed.

With the deed done, Rune had returned to Magh like a trained dog, leaving behind a contorted corpse and a puddle of his own vomit.

But after years of his faithful service, Magh had the last laugh, selling him to a brothel—

A sudden chill overtook him. He glanced around, getting the impression he wasn't alone.

Moments passed. Another chill skittered up his back; then the feeling was gone. Odd. What could have affected him like that?

Josephine returned not long after, distracting him from his thoughts. She wore a white robe and her necklace. Her small feet were bare. A minuscule silver ring circled one of her tiny toes.

His attention roamed upward. None of her makeup had washed off. Those shadows still highlighted her eyes and cheekbones, and her translucent skin remained as pale as alabaster. She must have a glamour in place.

His gaze locked on the helix rings at the top of one ear. Alluring female. "You don't see many immortals with piercings. At least, not freeborn ones." He'd been spared because no one relished drawing his blood.

"Why?"

"Long ago, they were used to mark slaves."

"That so, huh." She sat at the table across from him, meeting his eyes with an unexpected directness—as if she were *challenging* him. Did he detect a hint of superiority?

Strange. He held all the cards. "How was your bath?"

"Water pressure was good. Always a bonus." Steam rose from her wet hair and the fire blazed, yet she rubbed her arms for warmth. Must be thirsty.

He frowned. She'd taken her fill from him just a day ago, and older vampires could go long stretches without feeding. "Did you lose blood over the day? Feeding another, perhaps?" He'd never considered that she might have a mate or a child—because these things had never mattered with his interrogation subjects before.

Now he found himself wondering if she'd rocked a babe to sleep with a warm bottle of her blood. A mother would do anything to get back to her offspring.

Mothers made sacrifices. His own certainly had.

And a child would mean a mate.

"I've never fed someone else." So no child. Why should that relieve him so much?

He pressed a rune carved into the table, and the dishes began to disappear. Another rune materialized a wine service.

She jerked back and stared like a rustic. Did she live magick-free? Primitive.

"You don't get out of the mortal realm much, do you?" He poured a goblet, offering it to her.

"Wine's not really my scene."

"I could sweeten it with my blood." A statement he'd never thought to say.

She tilted her head, as if unfamiliar with the concept.

"I have a vampire ally who lives on blood wine and mead."

"Vampire?"

Why would that mention make her heart speed up? Most of her kind could regulate their heartbeats. Perhaps she was younger than he'd thought.

Then how had she traced with such control? He'd find out all her secrets soon.

"Isn't mead from way back when?" she asked.

Rune had to check a grin. "Blace is a very, very old vampire." The oldest.

"Does he ever visit you here?"

"No. Never." Rune had hidden knowledge of this place from even his allies.

"Oh." She looked disappointed.

What was her interest in another vampire? "Perhaps if you and I can become friends, I'll introduce you to him."

"And what would it take for us to become friends?"

"We'd need to establish some measure of trust between us. Sharing information about ourselves."

"That sounds okay. I'm curious about a lot. Like those symbols everywhere. What are they?"

He could give a little to get a little. "Runes. My mother's people were Runic demons. They had the power to harness and intensify magicks with these symbols. I happen to have fey magicks innate within me."

"So if I carved those symbols, they wouldn't wash my dishes?"

"No. Magick must fuel them." Strong magick. He'd been into his seventies before he could depend on his powers.

"How many runes are there? How'd you learn them?"

"Before she died, my mother taught me as many as she could remember. But there were thousands more." Each consisted of fairly basic shapes layered or connected in various, intricate ways.

He'd memorized every one, had been able to draw them in such meticulous detail that she'd started calling him Rune. He didn't even remember his given name. She'd also taught him reading and languages. By the age of nine, he'd mastered both Fey and Demonish.

"There *were* thousands more? Where'd all the symbols go?"

"Runic demons have gone extinct." Old fury seethed. By the time he'd gotten free of Magh and had gone to search for any Runics, they'd been stamped out. He would never know his people.

A thought arose, like a balm in his mind. *The Møriør are my people.*

Josephine asked, "Couldn't you use runes to neutralize your poison?"

Theoretically, the runes could do anything. "If I knew the correct symbols and combinations."

"Tell me more about them."

Now he knew she was stalling. Most people's eyes glazed over when he started talking about this subject—one he alone loved.

"You have some on your body, don't you?"

"I do." As she'd soon see. "A few are protection symbols, and a couple help with tracing."

"Why would you need help?"

Landing on a moving target like Tenebrous was challenging for any being. Plus . . . "I didn't grow up with that talent." Magh's demons had taught him to teleport—by repeatedly throwing him off a mountain into rapids. In time, he'd figured out how to avoid the fall. "I use some runes for communication." Whenever someone drew Rune's contact symbols, the tattooed band around his right wrist would light up. A blue glow meant the Møriør needed him back at the castle; white meant his nymph spies were alerting him about Nïx's return to Val Hall. "The link can stretch as far as the Elserealms."

"The whatta who?"

"Else, as in uncanny and strange. Those dimensions are exceedingly so. My official home is Perdishian Castle in Tenebrous. It's the capital of the Elserealms and the base of my alliance." Not a secret.

"What does it look like? Is your place there better than this one?"

Better than . . . ? Vexing female! "Perhaps I'll tell you more—when you start talking about yourself. For instance, do you have a mate or family?"

A hint of sadness flashed over her face. "Neither. I'm all by my lonesome."

A lone vampire without even a coven? Maybe that was how Nïx had recruited her. Two could play at that game. If Rune turned Josephine to their side, he could bring Orion a powerful female vampire, an asset.

"Do you have a Mrs. Rune you routinely cheat on?" she asked.

He gave her a thin smile. "I'm all by my lonesome."

"No little Runes running around? Would that take another dark fey?"

There was no possibility of his siring offspring. He hedged. "My kind is very rare in the Elserealms. In Gaia, it's more accepted for different species to breed. Even fey and demons."

"Have you been with a dark fey?"

"I haven't." But he'd once gotten so close. His first brothel master, a sadistic pig, had bought two rare females, promising one to Rune if he satisfied a particularly perverse client over an entire season. *The things I did . . .*

Rune had been moments from kissing the dark fey female—before he'd been yanked away, his bargain ignored. How the master had laughed.

The prick had sold off the pair. When freed, Rune had searched for them in vain.

Yet as much as he'd burned for that kiss, he craved Josephine's *more*. The thought made him uncomfortable, so he said, "I have a lead on a dark fey female in your very city."

The vampire seemed to mull this information. "So you've never been able to do whatever you want in bed?"

"Correct." He longed to twine his tongue with another's as they traded moans of pleasure. He hungered to go down on a female for the first time, to taste her warm honey, straight from the source. He swallowed. He could with this one. "But you learn not to miss what you can't have." A lie.

She gave a bitter laugh. "Bullshit."

"You sound like you speak from experience. What do you miss that you can't have?"

She studied the sash on her robe. A dead end.

For now. "Tell me about Nïx."

Josephine raised her face. "Why are you hunting her?"

"I'm an assassin by trade." He'd been a killer for longer than he'd been a whore. "She's my target because she seeks to bring down me and my allies." She'd bring down the entire Gaia realm and all its connected planes if she continued unchecked.

"Who are your allies?"

"Brothers. Not by blood, but by choice. We've banded together for most of my life."

"But they're not dark fey?"

"They're immortals of all different species." Though they had little in common on the surface, each Møriør sought something in Gaia.

When asked what he desired, Blace had cryptically told Rune, "I want my blood." Typical for a vampire, he supposed.

Allixta intended to find and punish the rebellious witches who'd settled there.

Sian refused to specify, would only say, "In Gaia lies my future."

Before she'd been recruited into the Møriør, Allixta had cursed Sian with a spell that caused unbearable agony. Delirious, the demon had muttered about a treacherous fey girl with one amber eye and one violet.

Maybe Sian yearned for vengeance. He was the only being Rune had ever met who despised the fey as much as he did.

And Orion? Their liege intended to stop an apocalypse. . . .

"Enough about me, Josephine. I don't even know where you hail from."

"Earth," she said. "Texas initially."

That explained her drawl. "You're not afraid of the vampire plague in the mortal realm?" She was probably immune; she'd withstood his poison easily enough.

Yet she looked as if she'd never heard of the sickness that had wiped out females of her kind. "Very little frightens me." She rubbed that necklace.

"Those are bullets."

She dropped her hand. "So?"

Did she keep them because she'd been shot? Rune's fangs sharpened, the demon in him rousing protectively. His fey half was quick to point out that Rune himself had contemplated beheading her—and still hadn't decided Josephine's future. "Who shot you?"

"It doesn't matter. It was a long time ago."

"Those are modern bullets. How long ago could it be?"

She jutted her chin. "It's *past*."

"I wonder if your friend Nïx grew angered when someone fired a gun at you. Perhaps an oracle like her could have warned you what would happen? Or was she busy granting wishes to others?"

Josephine merely stared at him.

"Tell me how you met Nïx." Nothing. "Did your parents die in the last Accession? What was your family name?"

Silence.

"You won't answer any of my questions?" He sighed and rose. "I have other ways of making you talk. On that note, it's time for bed. . . ."

NINETEEN

Jo stood and turned toward the fire, keeping her back to him. *Time for bed?*

After her shower, she'd tested her ghosting, and yes, she could possess him, even in his super lair. If he tried to force himself on her, she had a place she could hide.

Inside him.

He'd been a world away from her previous shells. She'd sensed his power from their first meeting, but inside him, she'd been cocooned by his strength. She'd even perceived his warmth. His heartbeat had lulled her—

Was he removing his boots behind her? He was stripping!

Don't turn around, don't turn around. "What are the other ways you'll make me talk?"

"They involve sexual torture." His voice had grown huskier.

Huh? "Are you going to use whips and chains on me?"

"Only if I think you'd like that." He was so matter-of-fact, as if her participation were a foregone conclusion. "More generally, I'll use orgasm denial."

Just as he'd done when manipulating that nymph. Once the blonde had agreed to do his bidding, he'd rewarded her with orgasms. *Good girls get rewards?*

"Until you give me information about Nïx, I'll edge you for hours, for days even, if that's what it takes."

She frowned at the flames. He said that like it was a bad thing? Before last night, her hookups had always ended with her instructing her partner how to get her off, him failing, and her saying, "Oh, for fuck's sake" and then doing it herself.

Taken all together, her sex life totaled about forty minutes, less than an episode of *Walking Dead.*

Three guys. Seven times. Afterward, she'd always wished she'd watched TV instead. A year or so ago she'd quit altogether.

Edging would mean Rune actually *got* her to edge. For hours.

And every second she was with him meant he wasn't out hunting, wasn't accidentally shooting innocent Valkyrie acquaintances.

Where do I sign? If she neared the brink, she could seduce him to finish her. She might not have tons of experience, but her shells had, and she watched people going at it all the time. If she factored in his thrilling reaction to her bite, Jo figured she could throw him for a loop.

The way she saw it, they were basically about to fight each other, scrapping for the upper hand—except it'd feel good.

She was amped! Her only worry was that Rune wouldn't hold out long enough to make it interesting.

"Ah, your heart beats faster, female. You're right to fear this. Your secrets' lives are about to end."

God, his *voice.* Husky but rumbling. Her breaths shallowed. *Don't look. . . .*

Naturally she did. When had she ever *not* looked?

He stood beside the bed, unbuttoning his shirt. In the courtyard, she'd seen his mind-blowing ass and a side view of his dick. After her hook-up with him, he'd pulled up his pants so fast she'd gotten only a glimpse of the full package. But she'd never seen his chest.

His shirt gaped open, revealing tattooed runes. One circled his navel, another stretching across his collar bone. As her gaze swept over his chest and rigid pecs, her nipples stiffened, straining against the material of her robe.

In the firelight, his skin was tan, except for a few lighter-colored scars over his chest and abs. Those marks—taken together with his tattoos—just made him look like more of a badass.

His jeans were low-slung, revealing the trail of black hair leading down from his navel.

"My heart's beating faster because I'm ready to get busy," she said, removing her necklace and setting it on the table. The only thing she could tell him about Nïx was that she couldn't tell him anything about Nïx. Yet Jo liked all the focus on the Valkyrie and not Thad. She'd keep it that way. "But if you want to keep talking instead of doing?"

Surprise crossed his expression. "And of course I'll deny you my blood."

Oh. Not so good. If anything else were at stake, she'd sing like a canary for his blood.

But more *was* at stake.

She would be winning tonight. And when she did, maybe she could score her freedom as well. If she could just get him to accept a wager. . . .

"Come to bed, Josephine. We're both adults. We both know what's about to happen. I haven't even nicked my skin." When he shrugged from his shirt, his torso flexed in a drool-worthy display, every sinew contracting. His shoulders were broad, his arms long and strong—

Her eyes widened at his right arm. A tattooed sleeve of intertwined runes covered his skin from his shoulder to his wrist.

Red hot, Rune. Red. Hot. His generous biceps bunched when he tossed the shirt away. As his dick hardened, his jeans forced his erection to grow toward the side; it stretched to his hip.

He knew the effect he was having on her, and his lips curved into that slanted half grin/half smirk, the diabolically sexy one that made her pant—the one that said, *I'm about to do filthy things to every inch of you.*

Just to stoke her need, he daubed the tip of his tongue to the corner of his mouth. That tiny movement made her thoughts seize on his mouth—which he'd no doubt intended.

What would he do with that tongue? Those lips? Would he give her a blood kiss?

His eyes darkened to the deepest magenta as he raked his gaze over her body, as if plotting all the places he was about to sample.

She was getting a taste of the smoldering sensuality of his fey half. *Jo like.* She found herself grinning back.

Before she got too caught up in things, she should pitch her wager. "You wanna make a bet?"

"About what, dove?" He started on the bulging fly of his jeans.

"You're going to try to get answers from me. And I'm going to resist you. We should wager who'll win."

"I have thousands of years of experience with this. And no one has ever resisted me—even when I had one hand tied behind my back. Now? There's no chance of it."

"So you've been a sexual torturer for thousands of years?"

"Aside from an assassin, I am also a secrets master. Often I acquire them through my own brand of interrogation. Face it, female, your ass is mine."

"If you're so certain, promise you'll let me go if you lose." Then she could return to find Thad. To start her new job of watching over him.

"What will you give me when I win, other than all your secrets?"

To protect the one she loved, she would withstand this guy. If she failed, then would anything else really matter? "Whatever you want."

The dark fey was obviously liking that prospect. The magenta of his irises began to bleed out over the whites of his eyes. "That's a far-reaching offer. You have no idea what acts I'd commit upon your body. . . ."

His words should've intimidated Josephine; she leaned in closer with interest. "What's to stop you from doing them now?"

"I've never forced a female in my life. I've never needed to. I wouldn't start with you."

She raised her chin. "Do you take the bet or not?"

"Oh, I'll take it."

"How can I be sure you won't back out?"

"We'll vow to the Lore, of course." As every immortal in the realms did.

"Yeah, of course," she hastily said.

Her flashes of ignorance about the most basic things puzzled him. Perhaps she aligned with the Forbearers, an army of male vampires created from mortals. They were a soldiering mass of cluelessness about the Lore. Though she wasn't a turned human, she might've been raised among them.

She flicked a hand at him. "You go first."

"Very well. I vow to the Lore to release you from my imprisonment should you withhold your secrets." His defeat was a ridiculous notion, but he played along.

"Right. I vow to the Lore to let you do whatever you want to me if you get my secrets."

Whatever I want. His cock pulsed with anticipation. What would he begin with? How could he decide? *The starved man presented with a bounty . . .*

"Oh, and one other thing."

"Hmm?" His eyes leisurely devoured her.

"We can't have sex."

He snapped his gaze to hers. "Repeat yourself."

"I can't do it tonight."

Not to be inside her? He was about to shut this down, but curiosity got the better of him. "Why not?"

"I'll only have sex in an exclusive relationship. You're as inclusive as a guy can be. And I don't want you to knock me up."

"A vampire female is only fertile if she's been eating food for some time. Have you been?"

She glanced away. No denial? Hadn't she invited him for coffee? She lived in the mortal world, could have been eating to blend with humans.

He swallowed. Her body might be ready for seed. Inner shake. "In any event, I have a demon seal. I can't ejaculate inside you unless you're my mate. Which is impossible."

He knew his crossbreed species had been forsaken by fate. *But* if a creature like him miraculously had a mate, and if Josephine was miraculously that one female, nothing could be more disastrous than claiming her.

His semen had been awaiting release for seven thousand years, its potency—and poison—strengthening with age, just as the rest of his body had. One of two things would happen if he released it.

She'd withstand his most concentrated poison and become pregnant.

Or his semen would prove so deadly, she'd perish with him still inside her.

But Josephine wasn't his. So this conjecture was moot.

She faced him again. "Define mate."

"Define one of the most universal concepts in the Lore?"

"Define a *demon* mate. Might be different from a vampire's." She had a point.

"It's the sole female, out of any time or any world, a demon male is most compatible with. Destiny would pair her with him, then bond them eternally. But again, I'm only half demon."

"Eternally." Her eyes glimmered, as if she liked the sound of that. "So you figure out a woman is yours because you can come in her?"

"A demon would have some indication before the actual claiming. He would've reacted fiercely to a specific female. He would know there's a good chance of burning away his seal. Still, most demons do try out many, many different females. It's a process known as *attempting*."

"Ah, so you've been out *attempting* nymphs."

"No, I don't believe dark fey get mates. We're anomalies, outside the reach of fate."

That challenging aspect was back in her expression. "Still, I want to be one hundred percent extra careful."

His fists clenched as the demon in him flared. "Extra careful?" Because carrying his offspring would be such a catastrophe? Did she think she was too good for him?

"Is sex all you've got in your playbook?" she asked. "There are lots of other things we can do to each other."

The rich promise of *lots of other things* placated his demon. "Then we're in agreement."

She grinned. "Awesome."

Awesome?

She dashed to the bed, leaping atop it to sprawl on her back. "Let's get to the Q and A."

TWENTY

Jo turned on her side, head propped in her hand as she watched Rune unbuttoning his fly.

She could barely wait to see him naked.

Never taking his spellbinding eyes off her face, he hooked his thumbs at the waist of his jeans and slipped them down, lower.

Lower . . .

His cock sprang free, bobbing for her riveted gaze. The thick shaft jutted from crisp black hair. Smooth skin stretched taut over prominent veins.

Mouthwatering.

His dusky balls looked heavy. She wanted to cup them, weigh them. Tug and watch him groan. His sac tightened before her eyes.

He stepped from his jeans to stand fully nude before her, arrogant as ever.

The sight of his lean, muscled frame and tattooed skin left her dumbstruck. She took her time, gaze roaming from his sexy hair, to his handsome face and penetrating eyes. To his brawny chest. The flexing ridges in his torso called to her claws.

As if Rune liked her eyes on his body, he grew even harder. Blood flowed to his dick so fast, it jerked. The broad crown strained toward her.

Her fangs sharpened for that veined shaft. She tapped one point with her tongue as she imagined grazing him there.

Would the dark fey shudder if she drew a line of blood and lapped it up? She'd never even had a blood kiss, yet her mind had already skipped ahead to a blood blow job.

What fun she would have with this guy tonight. Her lips curled. Best. Date. Ever.

His voice was gravelly when he said, "You like what you see." It wasn't a question.

She nodded happily. Just when she'd realized how wet she'd grown, he inhaled and tensed. Could he tell how he affected her? Of course, he'd scented her.

"You're ready." With a lethal grace, he lay back on the other side of the bed, all seven feet of sculpted fey/demon physique. A long, tall drink of blood.

He used a claw to prick his finger, and a bead of black arose.

Her eyes locked on that drop. The scent filled the air, making her light-headed.

He curled that pricked finger, summoning her. "Come and get it, dove." Then he drew a line directly over that maddening pulse point in his neck!

Her fangs were *aching*.

"Look at your little fangs sharpen. You crave the forbidden, don't you?"

Gaze fixed on that line, she went to her knees, climbing over to join him. She couldn't believe he was giving her his blood this easily. She bent to lick—

He grabbed her arms with his unnatural speed and tossed her to her back, securing her wrists in metal.

"What the hell?" The cuffs from before? He'd attached them to a chain leading from the wall. She fought to get free, but they were still unbreakable. "This wasn't part of the deal, Ruin!"

"This is my show, vampire. You follow *my* lead. And do not call me Ruin again."

"Asshole!"

His dark laugh sent shivers over her. "Do you want to rethink our wager?"

"It'll make it that much better when I win!"

"Vampire, I'm going to have you begging for me." He leaned forward as if to check on the cuffs, putting that line of blood in front of her face.

"Oooh! You dick!"

Blood had dried on his thumb, the scent remaining. He rubbed it on her face, along her cheekbones and jawline. Her lids slid shut, her head spinning.

"My vampire loves her baneblood, thinks it sweet."

God, I do. I do. Her eyes flashed open when his other hand glided to her chest. Through the thick fabric of her robe, he kneaded one of her tits.

They felt swollen, aching as much as her fangs.

She moistened her lips, and he groaned. "Fuck, you make me hard when you do that." His accent was heavier than she'd ever heard it.

"Will you kiss me?"

"I've wanted to. Have imagined it. But you'd steal blood from my tongue, wouldn't you?"

She couldn't deny it when she was licking one sharp fang.

He sounded as if he'd stifled a groan. "Then a kiss will be your reward for confiding in me. Once you've told me all, I'll take your lips and give you blood. But not before." He shook his head hard, reaching for the tie on her robe. "I'm keen to see the rest of your body."

She wanted to feel his gaze too, was panting in anticipation. Slowly, he bared her.

At the sight of her tits, black forked out over his eyes. He unsteadily sank back on his heels. "Your nipples are pierced? Were you a pleasure slave?" Had that been a hopeful note to his tone?

"No, I was never a slave."

He leaned forward, his head descending. He put his mouth right above one peak, so she could feel his hot breaths.

Her nipples had never been so hard. "Oh, God . . ." She didn't know where to look—was greedy to see every detail about him. His sensual lips. His rapt eyes. Were his hands balled into fists? His cock was *pulsing*.

"You had this done yourself?"

She nodded.

"You wicked little girl." His tongue flicked one nipple.

Sensation shot through her. "Ahh!"

He wetted it. Blew on it. She arched up to the sizzling stimulation.

"Did a lover want you pierced?" He widened his knees. His straining shaft swayed with the movement.

"N-no. I like it."

He gazed at her face, as if to gauge her truthfulness. He held her eyes as he bent down . . . as he took the peak between his gorgeous lips . . . as he sucked. God, that smoldering sensuality was in full force.

Over her moan, she heard his teeth click against the piercing, which seemed to delight him. He sucked harder, tugging at her nipple to the point of discomfort—as she'd always wanted it.

Though he hadn't touched her below the waist, she wondered if she could come this way. She was soaked, her clit throbbing. Her core tightened, lusting for something to fill it.

He kneaded both of her tits, his black claws digging in. Something about his possessive grip on her body turned her on even more. She panted, perilously close to coming. So much for edging!

Against her nipple, he murmured, "Sweet as a meadowberry." Leaving that one wet, he kissed his way to her other breast. "You're already close." He couldn't sound smugger. "I haven't even touched your pussy, but you're drenched." His lips were just above her other nipple.

She arched that side of her body up. "Rune . . ."

"Patience, vampire. We've days of this ahead of us."

Days? She'd pass out. Die. Combust.

He touched the tip of his tongue to the peak just as his fingers tweaked the little barbell.

"Ah, yes!" Her pussy quivered in readiness, her own claws digging into her palms. So close to coming . . .

As he suckled with hungry pulls, her eyes slid closed, and sounds bombarded her. Her desperate moans. The rattling cuffs.

The wet suction of his mouth . . .

Heightened emotions brought on ghosting. But she didn't fear it. She was tethered by the cuffs, by every throb and every pang that told her she was more than air.

She was embodied. Carnal. How could she ever float away when it would mean missing this?

Once he'd left both nipples damp and swollen, he kissed down her torso to her pierced navel. With another groan, he nuzzled the tassel there.

Hips rocking, she widened her knees.

He hissed in a ragged breath. "I scent your sweetness. Need to *see* it." In a blur, he clawed through the robe's arms and yanked the entire cloth from her.

When he'd left her nude and gasping, his gaze descended from her face to her breasts to her navel to her pussy. He narrowed his eyes at the tiny ring at the top of her clit, as if he wasn't seeing correctly. "Gods almighty."

She swallowed. Before, she would've killed to have him between her legs; now she grew nervous.

He looked like he was about to *consume* her.

She drew her knees up protectively.

"Ah-ah." He'd shoved her legs open before she could blink. "Never close yourself to me." Like an animal, he glided between them.

Licking his lips, he gently parted her folds. His nostrils flared and his cock jerked. He wrapped his big fist around it to give an absent stroke. "I am going to eat my wicked girl alive."

TWENTY-ONE

The vampire's glistening sex was offered like a prize before him. At his words, she rolled her hips, tantalizing him with her spread lips, with her intoxicating scent.

Sounding out of his head, he growled, "You pierced your pussy for me." He leaned down to tease the ring with his tongue.

She went wild, her thighs flexing around his ears. "Yes, Rune!" They met gazes over her mons. Her eyes were bright, glimmering black. Between breaths, she said, "You. You are exciting. This is . . . so freaking *fun*."

Fun? She wouldn't think so for much longer.

Though he could have played with that ring for decades, the scent of her arousal drew him to her opening.

Honey. Warm from the source.

His first time to enjoy this act would be indulging in the most beautiful pussy he'd ever imagined. Mouth covering her, he thrust his tongue for his first taste.

"Ahhh!" She twisted in her bonds.

His eyes rolled back in his head. He dug his claws into her ass, then panicked, retracting them.

No, no, my vampire can take it. She even seemed to like it. He flexed his claws again and gripped her hips. She moaned and undulated to his mouth.

"Fuck, you get so wet. You needed this, didn't you?" How was he going to keep from plunging into this tight slickness? The pressure in his cock made him gnash his teeth. The crown swelled, the slit so sensitive. His balls ached as if they'd been booted. Was this what it felt like with seed?

Agony! *Want more.*

He curled his tongue for another helping, groaning against her entrance. He would never get enough of this. Her little lips flared in offer. He sucked one, then the other.

She was watching him, eyes hooded. "You haven't done this before, right?"

He shouldn't call attention to his inexperience with this.

"Well, what do you think?"

Power dynamics, he reminded himself. But he wanted to roar about his discovery, to share it. "You're fucking addictive," he rasped with another lick. And another. Another. *Can't get enough!*

"Oh! Good. *Ohhh.*"

I'm eating her, and it's bliss. He pinned her to the mattress as he began to feast in earnest.

Her head thrashed, her long hair streaming over the bed. She was about to come, and he didn't care. Nothing could tear him away.

"Oh God, oh God!" She yanked against the cuffs, writhing under his kiss. "You're doing it!"

He gazed up her body. Her pierced tits quivered, her mouth open from her cries.

Between licks, he said, *"There you go, Josie."* He sounded crazed. *"Give your come to me."* His vision blurred until she appeared to flicker before him.

"Rune, I'm . . . COMING!"

She screamed with pleasure; he tasted her orgasm; his mind turned over.

He buried his face between her legs. Snarling. Sucking. Feasting. Fucking her with his tongue. Groaning as he consumed her.

Her pussy was a revelation. Her body was everything.

The throbbing in his length commanded him to move his hips—to rub his shaft, to sink it, to penetrate her wet core with cock instead of tongue. He fucked the sheets, rutting the bed in a frenzy. Anything for the agonizing pressure to end. Friction burned the crown, the slit. His heavy balls drew up.

About to come already? Control it, hold off!

She was peaking again, and he wanted more of her luscious honey. "AGAIN!" he ordered, clawing her ass.

She obeyed with a wanton cry, bucking against his probing tongue to give it to him.

Sensation coursed up and down his spine. His shaft jerked violently between the mattress and his torso. Pleasure lashed him, so much pleasure . . . so much—

He gave a brutal groan against her slippery, plump pussy.

RELEASE.

He threw back his head. His yell was a fucking war bellow—as wave after wave seized his body, flinging him to some place he'd never been before.

He was out of control. Control was a jest. He surrendered. Shattered.

His back bowed, his cock pulsating as if to shoot seed. Heart-stopping tremors . . .

On and on and on.

Gradually that exquisite pressure relented, and his yell ebbed in his chest. As the world spun, he lay with his head on her pale, trembling thigh, heaving his breaths. Only the two of them existed; he was certain.

He licked his lips, her taste proving what he'd experienced was real. An hour passed, a day, an age. He didn't care; he needed to rest. *Not* because he was sated—solely because his release had seemed to alter him.

"Rune?"

Her drawling voice roused him. What the hells had he done? So much was at stake, and he hadn't even asked a single question!

With effort, he sat up. Making it to his knees, he swiped his forearm over his mouth. He'd seen her naked and lost his godsdamned mind—as if he hadn't been doing this his entire life. As if he didn't pride himself on his prowess.

He'd come from rutting the sheets. How the old queen would laugh. He gritted his fangs. *Get control of the situation. Begin anew.*

He surveyed Josephine's body for the next round. Where was his clinical detachment? For the first time in his life, he didn't know what sexual thing he wanted to do next. Bed sport had always been about limitations—*can't do that, can't touch that, can't put my mouth there.*

Now the options were dizzying. His repertoire hadn't prepared him for this. "Good. We got that out of the way." His voice sounded off. Strained. From his war bellow.

Still panting, she said, "I was *so close* to telling you everything. No, really. Swear." She flashed him that bedazzling smile. "Next time I'm sure I will. Should we get to it?"

Rune was going to make her eat her words. "You've just made me that much more determined, vampire."

TWENTY-TWO

Maybe Jo shouldn't have taunted the dark fey. Over what had to be hours, or even days, he'd teased her mercilessly.

Again and again, he would take her right to the edge, patiently toying with her. Whenever she reached the very brink, he backed off. At times, he would nick himself, spicing the air just to make her insane.

Her body from the waist down was one tender ache. The cuffs had chafed her wrists. Her eyes were wet with pink tears, her mind reeling.

But . . .

She was a woman of flesh—a yearning, empty, horny woman. And she *loved* it.

Releasing his suck on a nipple, he leaned up over her breasts, his expression ominous. He'd questioned her as he tormented her, to no avail. "You must be so thirsty." He sliced the pad of his forefinger.

The scent hit her. Her thirst scalded her. "Just a taste, Rune. . . ." Her claws dug into her palms till her own blood spilled. With a cry, she punctured her bottom lip with a fang.

"Tell me anything about Nïx."

She shook her head. "Can't."

He ran his bleeding finger across her chest, painting her. His blood was searing, a brand over her skin. He traced it over one swollen nipple, and she could only moan.

He eased down her body, making himself comfortable between her thighs once more.

She whimpered, anticipating what was to come—namely, not her.

"Look at your lush little slit." He'd discovered what his dirty talk did to her. "My cock would fill you to the brim, vampire, have you screaming for mercy." He tickled her opening with his tongue, French-kissing it. "For now, do you need my fingers fucking you, dove?"

"Yes, fucking me!"

He slipped in one, and her needy core clenched it, her body trying to capture it.

"Your pussy's nice and tight." His voice was so deep, like the thrust of a finger. "Good call not to fuck yet."

Yet.

He curled that finger inside her. "Here's something you'll enjoy." He stroked one . . . specific . . . spot.

Bursts of light appeared before her eyes. *"Ohmygodyesmore!"* He'd done it—he'd made her see stars.

"That's it, baby." Over and over, he rubbed that spot. "Getting so wet for me. Doesn't it feel good?"

"Uh-huh—AHHH!"

He leaned down to tongue her clit while rubbing inside.

Some woman was spluttering nonsensical words and sounds. *Me?*

In a lower tone, he said, "Need more, Josie?"

When he called her *Josie* her toes curled. She nodded. *All I am is need.* She was need in the shape of Jo.

He worked another finger inside her. "So hot and soft and hungry." When he plunged both fingers, her head thrashed, arms catching against the cuffs.

"Hear how wet you are? Wouldn't you do anything to come on my hand? Just tell me how you met Nïx." He sucked her tender clit between his lips, tugging at it.

She gasped, shaking her head.

Suck. "Why did she target my brethren?" *Tug.*

"Brethren?"

"What's your involvement with the Valkyries?"

Jo nodded.

He made a sound of frustration. "You're the strangest creature I've ever met. You should despise me. I feel how swollen your little clit is—it throbs against my tongue. Your pussy's begging for my cock. How can you not want this ache to end?"

"Never end. Never . . ."

"No? Then you're not hurting for it enough." He began working a third finger into her.

The fullness made her eyes roll back in her head. She imagined his dick was penetrating her. So close . . . so close . . . She wriggled her hips on his long fingers, fucking herself with them.

He groaned. "Damn it, Josephine, do you want to hurt this way? Do you like this?"

She raised her head, telling him honestly, "You. I *like*." A tear streamed down her cheek. "I like you so much."

Never had Rune tortured himself by torturing another.

His shaft felt as if it'd explode. His heart hadn't stopped pounding, his lungs heaving. He now knew what all his victims had gone through.

And never had he broken skin—unless he'd meant to. Yet the vampire's wrists were bleeding. "Gods damn it, woman!" Injuring her was *not* part of the plan. He slid his fingers free, then rose from the bed.

She might want this never to end, but unlike his body, hers was suffering from more than thwarted desire. Pink tears had spilled from her eyes. Her skin was pale from thirst, her eyes black and glassy with it. Her fangs were sharp as daggers.

He couldn't keep hurting her. Which meant she'd won. He bit out a Demonish curse and punched a hole in the stone wall. She'd defeated him.

"Rune?" Her finely boned face looked exhausted.

Flexing his fingers, he collected the key to her cuffs, then returned to the bed to unlock her. He knew just how she'd want to celebrate her release. Her predatory gaze had zeroed in on his neck.

He freed her, and she rose up on her knees. She shoved him back on the mattress, and he let her. Where would she bite him first? She'd likely drain him dry. His cock surged at the idea, even as his mind rebelled.

She won.

He told himself he could take her to the brink again. But he had no taste for it any longer.

Torturing her tortured me.

She straddled him, seating herself right atop his aching rod. Her sex was drenched, tormenting him with what he couldn't have. Would she fall upon him?

She seemed to be resisting that urge. Why wouldn't she move on his cock? She was edging herself! *I don't understand her!*

She reached forward to cup his face with shaking hands. He had no idea what she was thinking. She telegraphed nothing—

She leaned down and pressed her lips to his cheek.

A gust of breath left him. Why would she do this?

Then she tenderly kissed his chin. The tip of his nose. His forehead. She nuzzled the sensitive point of one ear.

"Are you . . . thanking me?"

She drew back. "Yes."

"For hurting you?"

She shook her head, the silky curls of her hair cascading over her shoulders. "For making me feel alive."

His gaze dipped to her mouth. He had to kiss her, couldn't wait any longer. He clutched her nape. "I've wanted to take your mouth from the moment I first scented you."

A lie. He'd wanted it all his life.

To kiss without killing?

She licked her carnal lips in invitation. "Take it, Rune."

He tugged her head down, pulling her closer. Their gazes locked. When only an inch separated their lips, he swallowed. The moment was laden. "So long I've waited . . ." He pulled her in.

Contact.

Soft, giving lips trembled against his. He stilled, basking in this luxury, his senses drinking her in.

In time, he slipped his tongue into the welcoming heat of her mouth. He knew she was immune to him, but habit made him tense.

As if to reassure him, her tongue met his. When she gave a gentle lap, he felt it in every single inch of his body. His shaft pulsed so hard, it lifted her.

She moaned with pleasure. Only pleasure.

The most erotic sound his twitching ears had ever heard.

His grip on her nape tightened, his hand beginning to shake as he deepened the contact. He claimed her mouth possessively, his tongue twining hers—until they shared the breaths from their lungs. Until her heartbeat drummed in his ear alongside the sound of his.

This kiss was *right*. Her lips were *right*.

He'd wanted this so badly. And it was so much fucking better than he'd dreamed. He groaned for more.

She lovingly cradled his face again, and something inside his chest twisted. Her lips . . . her lips were teaching him to need. To feel again.

This woman. This vampire. With her slow, sweet kiss.

He wanted to teach her as well. To demonstrate why he was a man she should desire. That he had strength enough for both of them. She would listen to this kiss—just as she did to his blood.

He licked one of her fangs. The instant his blood hit her tongue, her body stiffened.

They both went motionless. *Heartbeat . . . heartbeat . . . heartbeat . . .*

"Ummm." She cried out, lapping at him. He set back into the kiss, giving to her as she was giving to him.

Yet she still hadn't moved over him. He gripped her hips and pulled her along the top of his shaft.

That was all it took.

She screamed against his mouth. Her orgasm made her suck on his tongue and rock atop him, her slickened pussy slipping from the base to the crown.

Ecstasy.

He shuddered, on the verge of coming instantaneously. The reasons why he couldn't pin her down and rut, spending so deep inside her, grew dim.

She pulled back to rise up over him, undulating her hips as her eyes slid closed. Blood spilled from the corner of her lips. *Mindless.*

Voice thick, he said, "You'd drink me till eternity, if I let you. Become a little glutton for it."

"I would," she moaned, piling her hair on her head. "Pierce you day and night."

"You'd drink me alone, forever."

She licked her lips as her hands dipped to caress her body. "You alone."

"Already you can't live without my kiss."

"I can't . . . *can't* . . ." Blood trickled from her chin, hitting her breast. His lifeblood had never looked blacker than against her alabaster skin.

Like paper inscribed with ink, her flesh was marked by him. Marked with his scent. She was his *possession.*

Obsession.

Yet he knew nothing about her. He reached forward, caging her delicate throat with his fingers. "Tell me *anything*, woman. Anything I don't know about you."

Dazed, she murmured, "Your blood isn't tainted. I can taste heaven."

His breath left his lungs. His fingers went limp. His arms fell back. "Move on me, then," he ordered her. "Make me come!"

As she snapped her hips, that urge to shove himself inside her grew overwhelming, his body fevered for release.

Right on the edge, he stared up at this female. Hair wild, eyes onyx with need, lips black from his blood. Pierced sex, navel, nipples. Plump breasts quivering.

He'd never forget the sight of her like this. Not even if he lived for another seven thousand years. He'd never seen anything so stunning.

She could make me wish I got a mate.

But she was still weakened, hadn't drunk enough. His undeniable urge to come battled an inexplicable need to care for her. He sliced his neck and pulled her down to him. "Feed." Arms coiled around her, he awaited her fangs.

"I don't want to take too much."

"Drink!" he commanded her. "Feed from my body till yours is sated."

He growled as she sank her fangs in so slowly, penetrating his flesh like a leisurely lay.

Lids heavy, he stared at the ceiling, struggling to process his actions, what he was feeling. As her bite made him come, he nearly bellowed once more. Instead he clasped her tightly to him and rocked her as she fed.

TWENTY-THREE

With her head upon Rune's chest, and his heart beating against her ear, Jo tried to stay awake to replay everything.

All the pleasure he'd delivered when questioning her, and then in the hours after she'd fed.

All the things she'd learned—about life, him, herself.

Before they'd even gotten started he'd told her vampires had to eat to be fertile. She'd never thought she could have children of her own. Now, there was the possibility.

She couldn't get the last fourteen years back with Thad, but maybe she could have a kid who reminded her of him as a baby. Maybe, one day, he would be an adoring uncle.

Possibility. The future began to spread out so brightly before her. With that thought in her mind, she slipped into an exhausted sleep.

Dreams arose. More memories of Rune's? Vague impressions filtered through her awareness. . . .

—Queen Magh viewing him in his court dress, her pride over the "sexual weapon" she'd molded.

—His sense of foreboding when he spied desire in her eyes, and then her fury at him for causing it.

—His sleepless nights leading up to his first mission. He'd traveled with a Sylvan delegation to the Wiccae nation of Akelarre, masquerading as the son of a fey ambassador. His presence was to be a token of goodwill from one healing kingdom to another.

But his target was not what he'd expected. Even to save his mother from a fate worse than death, Rune wasn't certain he could go through with this.

Because Magh had no interest in assassinating the warlock who'd cursed her husband. She wanted the warlock alive to bear the sorrow of his beloved daughter's death.

A girl turning sixteen years old—Rune's age.

"You've been invited to her birthday celebrations. Seduce her, cur," Magh ordered him. "Make her love you, as you have all the others. Then strike. She'll die with a heart full of love, a mind full of dreams, and a body riddled with your poison. . . ."

Compliments through dinner, murmured flirtations during cards. It wasn't long before the young witch was infatuated with him. She was fair of face, but young for her age.

Had he ever been so naïve?

She whispered in his ear, "I want you for my birthday present." Then she gave him directions to a hidden alcove beside her bedchamber. "I'll raise the protection wards for you."

He forced himself to smile. She was guarded like a treasure by magicks and warlock sentries. Nothing could possibly get to her.

Nothing but me.

He followed her instructions, finding the alcove. There, he paced. If he saved his mother by carrying out Magh's killings, would his dam be able to forgive him? If he confessed, "I took the life of an innocent girl to free you," would the guilt be too much for his mother?

A door glided open. Eyes alight, the witch peeked out. She'd changed from her dress to her nightclothes and let down her hair. "It's clear." She'd foiled her own protections, unwinding those wards as she'd unwound her braids.

She took his hand, guiding death into her bedchamber.

Her room was a palace all its own, filled with charms and priceless jewels. At least her sixteen years of life had been plenteous.

She crossed to her bed, patting the cover beside her.

How could he go through with this? "Perhaps we're moving too quickly. You're young yet." *If he didn't obey Magh, he couldn't return to Sylvan. Where would he live? Here? Maybe if he told the witch the truth, she would be moved to help him.*

And abandon my dam?

"Nonsense, fey. I'm old enough. As of this night especially." *In a wistful voice, she said,* "Only one thing could make my birthday more magickal."

I can't do this. My gods, I can't. "We'll meet another time, dove. I know the way to your room and will come each night."

Her eyes watered. "I want you now."

"I'll be here for weeks yet."

"But no other night will be my birthday." *Tears spilled down her cheeks.*

In lowered voices, the witch and Rune continued quarreling.

Finally she said, "I'll scream for the guards if you go."

His jaw slackened. Are all nobles so underhanded?

"I'll do it!" *She drew a deep breath.*

He leapt for her, putting his finger over her lips. He could still tup her without killing her. He had with all his other conquests. But those females had been more mature; they'd known the risks and how to avoid them. This girl didn't.

When he heard the sentries changing shifts outside, he glanced over his shoulder. He should trace away. But then she'd know what he was. And where could he go?

He turned back. "I need you to listen to me—"

Her mouth was against his. She'd lunged forward, pressing her opened lips to his. She'd stolen his kiss.

He flung her away and traced to a wine service, hastily pouring a goblet. Maybe the tales of his poison had been exaggerated. How did they know? He returned to her in an instant. "Drink!"

Eyes wide with terror, she choked on the liquid. The poison was already in her system. Her limbs contorted, muscles knotting.

The pain in her expression . . .

He watched her body ceding its life, the sound of her panicked heartbeat fading to nothing. The young witch perished in seconds.

The tales hadn't been exaggerated. Rune was deadlier than anyone had ever suspected.

He turned to the side and vomited over and over until nothing remained in his stomach. He wiped his mouth, comprehension dawning: he'd stepped upon a path and could never go back. . . .

Jo woke, opening her eyes, confused she wasn't in a magickal bed-chamber filled with girlish charms and death.

Rune was petting her hair, his breaths deep and even.

She stifled shudders from that lifelike memory, fearing it'd only gotten worse for him. When he'd been even younger than Thad was now, Magh had forged him into a lethal lover with a kiss of death. She'd used Rune's mother against him, the mother who'd been everything to him, just as Thad was everything to Jo.

What would Jo have done to save her brother? *Anything.*

Absolutely anything.

Did she want to relive more of these memories? Would they come each time she took Rune's blood?

Her preferences didn't matter. Though she fought against sleep, she drifted off, lulled by the steady drumbeat of his heart.

Another dream began to play out. She was in the Sylvan court. She could hear water fountains, could smell the rose arrangements and candle wax. Magh sat upon her throne, gazing at Rune, now a grown man.

She'd summoned him because she'd come to a conclusion: his utility had reached its end. . . .

"You've done your job so admirably, I have few enemies left. The remaining ones know of you, are on their guard against a silver-tongued fey who disappears into shadows."

"And spying? Interrogation?"

"The same problem. Who will you target?"

"Then I've kept my end of our bargain," Rune told her, excitement building inside him. "You vowed to reunite me with my mother."

"So I did, cur," she agreed.

Too easy. He'd spent enough time in fey company to pick up some of their ever-rational ways, so he knew his hope was illogical. He should expect trickery from Magh. Ultimately, she would make him suffer.

If Rune's mother was in a slave camp, Magh would dispatch him there, enslaving him as well, but he didn't care. He pictured his mother's affectionate blue eyes, and the smile she always had waiting for him.

Together he and his dam would escape. They would start their lives over. All the killing, all the disgust, all the hatred over these years could finally come to an end.

Magh snapped her fingers for a guard. "Take us to the cur's mother."

A reunion is truly happening? At long last? Rune's heart thundered as they traced to a realm wrapped in night and buffeted by winds. He squinted against the gusts, seeing nothing but a towering mound of dirt.

"There she is." Magh pointed to the mound.

"Wh-what are you saying?"

Her demon guards traced in front of Magh. "She's buried there, with hundreds of others. Has been for centuries."

Shock engulfed him.

"She was a favorite of my husband's, enjoying his protection, but your position was precarious." Magh's voice sounded distant. "Your mother knew I had you in my sights, would soon strike. She begged me to spare your life. I vowed that I would, but only if she agreed to quietly abandon you for a life as a pleasure slave in a faraway brothel. Anything to save you! Alas, the poor dear hadn't been frozen into her immortality yet—which she must have known." Magh sighed. "Ah, the sacrifices we mothers make. Don't worry, she wasn't long in that hellish place. After a bit of rough bedsport, she was . . . broken." Magh examined the end of one of her flaxen braids. "Her life was short, her death brutal, and now her bones are naught but dust."

Buried.

Brutal.

Dust.

His lungs constricted. His legs buckled. As he knelt in front of the mass grave, Magh's guards collared him and bound his wrists.

"On to the next stage of your life," she said in a mirthful tone. "I have a new occupation for you, cur."

"Gods give me the power," he bit out. The collar prevented him from tracing, the bindings from fighting. "I will destroy you and all your spawn."

"Oh, I think your next employment will keep you far too busy for that. . . ."

TWENTY-FOUR

Josephine's breaths were light against Rune's chest. He sifted his fingers through her hair, trying out this "afterplay." He'd never stuck around after he'd used a female sexually. Certainly not after an interrogation.

As he stroked her silken locks, he smelled meadowberries anew, calling to mind recollections from his boyhood. He remembered the times he had briefly escaped to the high meadows, to a glen filled with berries. Their taste had been even sweeter than their irresistible scent.

With sugar on his lips and breezes rustling the leaves, he'd lain among them in bliss, never wanting to return to the sweltering fens.

The taste of Josephine had been sweeter than anything he could've imagined. . . .

Though he'd lost his wager against her, he was surprisingly relaxed. She hadn't won per se; he'd been defeated by his own loss of control. But how could he blame himself?

Her bite gave her an unfair advantage.

When her fangs had entered his flesh so slowly and her tongue had flicked in readiness, he'd nigh lost his mind. Even now he shuddered.

After she'd fed, he'd been dazed, wanting only to explore her. For hours as they'd pleasured each other, he'd listened for every hitch in her breath. He'd awaited the telltale flush across her breasts that signaled her approaching orgasm. He'd watched for her irises to flicker.

In the past, these reactions had been benchmarks to gauge a subject's willingness to talk.

Tonight each of her responses had been a *discovery*—about a woman who aggravated him, invigorated him, enthralled him.

He'd nuzzled her ears until her little toes had curled. He'd tongued that tiny dip in her bottom lip. He'd taken her mouth—at his leisure, whenever the impulse struck him—so many times his own lips were bruised. He ran a finger over them now.

For eons, his last kiss had been a lethal one.

No longer. There'd been no barrier between him and Josephine, between their bodies, their desires.

Was the insatiable Rune sated? He was still erect for more, yet he could swear he was almost drowsy. Perhaps not sated, but satisfied.

Again and again, he'd wondered if she could be his mate. If he actually got one. But even if she was his, nothing would change. He had no interest in settling down with one woman. The Møriør still required his talents—which included extracting information from targets—whether through fair or foul means.

And he wasn't going to simply *retire* his burning need to stamp out the royal line of Sylvan.

Though Magh was long dead, she lived on through her vile spawn, like her first son, King Saetthan. There were only fourteen left. Most lived on Gaia, in hiding from Rune.

With each Accession, hidden things came to light.

The Møriør would help him hunt those fey, just as Rune would help in his allies' endeavors. No, he wouldn't surrender his dreams when he was so close. Which was why Josephine would never lie so trustingly with him again; he had plans to use her against Nïx. His will would be done in the end.

Best to savor this now.

Josephine shifted against him. Like many vampires, she was a deep sleeper. She hadn't even awakened when he'd inked a temporary tracking rune on her back.

Her eyes moved behind her lids. Would she dream his memories? What would she think about his past? He wasn't ashamed he'd been violated and used.

Just that he'd eventually submitted to it. . . .

Hours passed as she slumbered on. He occupied himself tracing the contours of her breathtaking face and musing which memories she might see if she had the ability.

When she woke, she blinked open thick lashes to reveal those bright hazel eyes. She drifted upright. "Will you really let me leave? I have to get to—I need to get home."

He bit back his irritation. Her first thoughts were of escape. If he'd pleasured any other female so thoroughly, he wouldn't have been able to get rid of her.

Not so Josephine. "I made you a vow."

"Lemme get dressed." She hopped from the bed, giving him a mind-scrambling view of her taut ass, and hurried to the bath.

He reached for his jeans, regretting he hadn't said, "After another round." He'd just strapped on his bow and quiver when she returned, fastening her necklace.

She'd stolen one of his shirts to wear over her dress, tying the ends and rolling the sleeves up. Her hair was pulled back in a haphazard ponytail. Even like this, she couldn't look more fetching.

"Are you ready?" she asked.

He took her hand. "Of course."

She stared at their clasped hands for several moments.

"Josephine?"

"Uh, yeah, can you trace me back to the Quarter?"

It'd be full dark there, roughly midnight. "I will." An instant later, they were standing on a side street off Bourbon.

She regarded the area, then turned back to him. "So. We're here."

"So we are. Run along, little dove, back to your roost."

She hesitated to release his hand, gazing up at him. The flickering light from a gas lamp reflected in her eyes. "This is it, then? You go from thinking about killing me to freeing me?"

"I believed you were a security risk. I no longer do."

"Got it." She opened her mouth to say something, closed it, then tried again: "I know you're the hit-it-and-quit-it king, but for what it's worth, I would've liked to see you again."

Oh, you will. And shortly. He could follow that tracking rune anywhere. He was merely using her to locate Nïx.

Though Rune would have the vampire back soon, he was still reluctant to let her go. They might be on opposite sides of an immortal war, but he wasn't finished with this female. He'd use his silver tongue to persuade her back into his bed—even after he killed her ally. He forced himself to let go of her hand. "Perhaps we'll cross paths."

He thought he spied a hint of sadness in her eyes. "Sure. Cross paths. No big deal." She started down the street.

Once she'd turned the corner, he drew another rune combination on his forearm, a concealment spell to cloak his scent and render him invisible.

He traced to the rooftops to pursue her, traveling from one building to the next. At first she strode through the neighborhood. Then she paused, seeming to catch a scent. She took off in a sprint, scanning each street she passed.

No doubt she was frantic to find Nïx and divulge everything she'd learned about Rune. He felt an unexpected sting over that, but reminded himself all was fair in love and war.

Wait—wasn't that the Valkyrie's scent? Yes, there Nïx was, silently trailing Josephine, with that bat on her shoulder.

Eyes locked on his enemy, he fingered the flights of his arrows, selecting one-and-done.

Rune nocked it and drew his bowstring, fingers to his chin. Had there ever been an easier shot?

Yet his fey curiosity stayed him. Perhaps he should eavesdrop on their conversation, to uncover how much Nïx knew of the Møriør's plans. Secrets there for the taking. He could always kill the Valkyrie directly after.

Follow Orion's orders to the letter and make the shot? Or listen in?

Old habits . . . He returned the arrow to his quiver, then dropped to the ground to spy.

TWENTY-FIVE

After leaving Rune, Jo had picked up Thad's scent, but it was always just out of her reach.

Was he in a departing car? A trolley heading away from the Quarter? No, the opposite direction!

She sprinted toward the Mississippi, following his trail to a riverside industrial lot. Stacks of rail containers bordered a worn-out patch of cement. She traced past the perimeter fence into the middle and scanned the shadows. Where was he?

She'd lost the thread altogether. "Damn it!" Somehow she would find him.

If possible, she was even more determined to reach Thad, to make sure he was safe. Rune's memory of being separated from his beloved "dam" had devastated Jo. And then to learn of her death, to feel his grief . . . she'd woken in a panic to find her own beloved brother.

Alongside her worry for Thad, she hurt for Rune, the involuntary killer who'd only wanted to save his mother.

What won't we do for the people we love?

She hoped Rune had gotten revenge on that vicious queen for his mother's murder—if not for more. Magh's mention of Rune's "new occupation" had given Jo chills. . . .

"Oh, Shady Lady."

Jo spun around to find that black-haired woman standing behind her. Nïx. Jo had never heard her approach.

So this was Rune's target. "What do you want?" Jo peered past her. "Where is Thad?"

"I have our handsome lad tucked away." Nïx was carrying that bat again. Tonight she had two boots on. Her eerie golden eyes glowed even more brightly than before.

Her T-shirt had writing on it, but Jo couldn't decipher the words. "Tucked away where?" If need be, she could take this . . . *Valkyrie.*

A breeze flowed off the water, ruffling Nïx's wild black hair. "He's safe. Well, safe-*ish.* Perhaps, Josephine, if you cooperate, I will allow you to see him."

"Allow?" This bitch had no idea. Jo didn't cooperate; she squeezed till things broke. She Hulk-smashed. If Nïx didn't take her to Thad, the Valkyrie would learn a lesson she'd never forget. "How do you know my name?"

"I'm a very important oracle, a leader of the Vertas army, and a soon-to-be goddess. Just have one teeny-weeny task to complete." She gave a laugh. "I've been watching you for some time. Oh, the things I know."

"You've spied on me?"

"Did you ever see that movie *Broken Arrow*? Naturally you have—it's a cinema classic. Anyhoodles, I would *never* let my nukes out of my sight. Except for when I would."

She was a nut-job. "Why would Thad be with you? Does he know what you are?"

"He does. And I know what *he* is."

Jo's mouth went dry. "What do you think he is?" *Is Thad like me?* No answer. "All you need to know is that he's *good.*" Charity work, community service, generosity.

Nïx grinned. "If you say so."

"What does that mean?"

"I have plans for Thaddeus this Accession. We all have parts to play."

Plans? *Plans?* The Valkyrie was freaking dead. "No one makes plans for him—no one. Get me?" She closed in on Nïx. "You are going to take me to him. *Now.*"

"Not possible."

Jo stared down the smaller female. "You say you know me? Uh-uh. Otherwise you'd know I'm about to break all your bones, one by one, until you tell me where he is."

Nïx remained amused. "Break all my bones? One by one?" Lightning flashed nearby. "What a fascinating idea."

What the hells? From his vantage atop a stack of rail containers, Rune listened in disbelief.

How wrong he'd been. Josephine hadn't been protecting Nïx; she'd been protecting the male. The vampire had mistaken Rune's aim!

No, she wasn't in league with Nïx, but she might be in love with *Thad.* What kind of ridiculous name was that?

Rune thought back. The male had been tall. Females would find him attractive. More than attractive.

If Josephine was in love with another, then everything she'd done in Rune's bed had been a ploy to get back to this other male.

Rune ground his fangs. She had offered to let him do *anything* if she lost her bet, because she'd been desperate to return to another. From what Rune understood, a female could actually get *stronger* if she gave her heart into someone else's keeping.

Josephine had known she wasn't going to lose that wager.

That little bitch! For the first time since Magh had singled him out,

Rune had pleasured without artifice. Without using. Yet tonight *he* had been . . . used.

I like you so much, the vampire had cried—with a tear streaking her face. Bullshit!

She and the Valkyrie began circling each other. "Are you sure you want to challenge one like me?" Nïx asked. "You're such a tender young creature. Just a quarter of a century old."

Quarterwhatthefuck??? Josephine was only twenty-five?

He'd taken her to bed. He'd *devoured* her and given her a font of forbidden blood. Talk about taboos! *Gods, I sicken myself.*

"Oh, I'm positive," Josephine told the Valkyrie.

"Are we about to mix it up? No, no, that would indicate both sides landing blows. You won't."

Josephine raised her brows. "Just remember: you could've avoided this."

"Very well." Nïx turned to her bat. "Bertil, spectate!" The creature took to the air.

Josephine possessed formidable strength, but she was too young to go up against an ancient Valkyrie. Nïx would wipe the street with her.

Rune should let her, to punish Josephine for her trickery. But he had a kill to make. He readied his bow.

"You'd do anything to get to Thad, wouldn't you?" the Valkyrie said in a taunting voice. "But you don't understand. He's not yours; he's *mine*." Another bolt of lightning flashed nearby.

Josephine's body shook—with rage. They were about to godsdamned catfight over the male! "That was the exact wrong thing to say, bitch." She lunged to tackle the Valkyrie.

"I know!" Nïx pivoted, neatly dodging her. "You've always thought of him as yours alone, belonging solely to you."

Josephine traced for Nïx, but the Valkyrie anticipated her move and evaded.

"I *will* catch you. And then I will *break* you."

"Josephine, you rare and wondrous thing. Such untapped potential.

You're death and death all rolled into one. There's only a handful of your kind."

Mad ramblings? Or partial truth? If Josephine was rare with potential, she might have more value to the Møriør than Rune had suspected.

Josephine drew up short. "Tell me what you know!"

"You come from a long, long, long, long, long, long, long, long way away. You remember flames replacing seas. A hand holding up the night. Broken stars and spiders' eyes."

These utterings made Josephine go pale, swaying on her feet.

Time to end this. The air crackled with electricity as he tautened his bowstring and loosed his arrow. *One-and-done . . .*

The end of a long-lived immortal.

Lightning bolts shot down from the sky. White spears intersected, forming a cage to shield Nïx.

His arrow disintegrated to ash.

TWENTY-SIX

Jo whirled around, stunned. A huge cage of lightning had descended, trapping her with the Valkyrie.

First thought: *I'm screwed.*

Second thought: *Screw that, I'm Jo.*

Nïx didn't seem to notice all the blinding bolts. "You've known unutterable beauty." Her eyes went from gold to brilliant silver, matching the lightning. "On your way here, you saw things no one in the universe ever has."

"What are you talking about?" Jo's head suddenly felt like it was splitting. Clouds thickened around them. Winds whipped across the lot, rocking the rail containers and tossing the river. Spray hissed against the lightning cage.

That bat screeched as it swooped and played among the bolts.

Jo ignored all the weirdness, focusing on the Valkyrie who stood between her and Thad. "You'll give me answers, Nïx!" She traced behind the woman, drawing her fist back on the way. Just as Jo solidified to land a blow, Nïx twirled around. Her own fist shot out, connecting with Jo's chest.

Bone snapped; Jo's body soared upward, the heat from the crisscrossed bolts scalding her. Her control wavered. She landed fully embodied, crashing into the cement. Pavement sanded her face.

A man's bellow sounded in the distance. *Rune?*

"Stay down, child," Nïx said. "This isn't my first cage fight. Won't be my last."

"Fuck that!" Jo traced through the air to tackle Nïx. The Valkyrie dodged her again.

"No one's taught you to fight like an immortal." Her tone was sing-song, even more enraging.

Jo hurtled forward, ducking under Nïx's swing—

Just a feint. The Valkyrie's knee shot up to catch Jo in the face. Her cheekbone cracked; she flew across the cement again.

Nïx chuckled. "It's all about prediction."

Jo spat blood, attacking, but Nïx was too fast. She punted Jo like a kickball.

Zooming. Speed. *Pain.* Jo crashed down on the other edge of the cage, landing on her side. Her ribs were toast.

In an instant, Nïx stood over her. "Stay down, little girl."

Little girl? "Ahh!" Jo lurched to her feet, facing off once more.

"You don't know half of your talents. You fear one of your greatest. The ground should be your best friend."

She vaulted toward Nïx, tackling her!

The Valkyrie turned them in midair to pin her to the ground.

Jo tried to ghost. Failed. Pain robbed her of even more control. She struggled to get free, but Nïx was too fast, too strong.

More lightning bolts jagged down around them. One struck behind Nïx. Without looking, the Valkyrie snared it.

The light fried Jo's eyes, but she could make out Nïx molding the bolt—into a blade. "Why would you ever become tangible in a fight?" the Valkyrie asked, pressing that crackling heat against her throat.

Jo couldn't wrestle for the blazing weapon, could only endure it. For once, she wasn't the predator in the night. She was prey.

"Why embody?" Nïx shoved the blade harder, searing skin away. "Answer me."

She's going to take my head. Bet that would kill me. "Only w-way to strike."

"Your information is erroneous. I'll give you a tip about your powers. Your mind is your greatest weapon. Use it to strike; use it to defend. As the woman once did."

"Wh-what woman?" Another flash of memory arose, the lighthouse's beam. . . .

"It's worldend!" someone screamed. The sky was falling. Failing. *Wounded stars plummeted to their deaths, as bright as sparks from a flint.*

Jo clung to the edge of a vortex, her claws digging into the ground. All around her, more black holes hissed open, a wall of them, black upon black upon black.

Like spiders' eyes.

No idea where those sucking chasms would lead—taking one was their only chance at survival.

Some relentless force was crushing their dimension. They'd heard rumors of a being who could crumble realms using naught but his will.

But a pale woman with dark-smudged eyes fought back, trying to shore up the world—her delicate hand was raised to emit power. "I can't falter!"

Pain erupted, wrenching Jo back to the present. Nïx had broken her arm! She screamed, *"Why?"*

"Ah, I have your attention once more." Nïx smiled. "Let's not forget that breaking bones was your idea. I'm merely paying homage."

Jo felt trapped in her solid body, yet out of her mind. She imagined she heard Rune yelling again. "Who is the . . . woman? From my dream. Where . . . ?"

"She played her part, just as you will," Nïx said. "They believe they know my role. They think I hasten the apocalypse. They think *to Nïx* is *to destroy*. They think *Nïx* means *nothing*."

Jo bit out, "Wh-who?"

"The Møriør. The Bringers of Doom. They're bogeymen, ones you never even knew to be terrified of. Nightmares made flesh. Imagine having one's bones pulverized. It'd probably hurt something like this—"

SNAP. Jo screamed when Nïx broke her other arm. *"STOP!"*

"Their wasteland realm approaches," the Valkyrie continued, oblivious to Jo's pain. "Inside their castle . . . monsters and devils. A dragon who

could burn the world. A poisonous bane who slips into your secret fantasies. A malevolent demon risen from hell. They're bent on enslaving us all."
She laughed. "Though it sounds terribly fun and exciting, the Undoing is
anything but. He'll soon have us all in the palm of his hand."

Nïx loomed over her with that crackling dagger-bolt, her face twisted
but beautiful. "He says worlds are like glass spheres. When he handles
them, he leaves his mark. Sometimes only the faintest smudge." Her
expression grew vicious, her voice rising to a shriek: "Other times, he
obliterates—*them—back—to—sand*!"

Lightning speared down. Cement exploded; the river boiled. Grit
blasted Jo's eyes, and steam scorched her face.

Nïx tossed away her dagger and leaned down to murmur at Jo's ear,
"Each has such fabled abilities. Together they attain synchronicity. On a
battlefield, if interconnected, they will win. But if we can't defeat them, we
can appease them."

"D-don't understand."

The Valkyrie whispered, "If you want to see Thaddeus alive, you'll
learn about Orion."

"Don't even know . . . who that is."

"And yet he'll impact your life in so many ways." *SNAP*.

Jo's left femur. "*AHHHHHH!* S-stop! Why?"

"Sometimes you have to be cruel to be kind."

"You're . . . crazy!"

"There, there." Blank-eyed, Nïx petted her face, her razor-sharp claws
slicing Jo's cheeks. "Shhh. I want us to be friends."

Jo couldn't fight back with broken limbs. "I-I'll do it." *I'll say anything*.

Nïx pressed her forefinger over her own lips. With her other hand, the
Valkyrie grasped Jo's neck and squeezed.

Black spots swarmed her vision as she stared into this monster's eyes.
Consciousness faded.

Delirious. About to die.

Who would save Thad from the Valkyrie?

TWENTY-SEVEN

Can't reach her. No arrows left . . .

When all attempts to shoot through the cage failed, Rune had attacked the bolts bodily, snatching at lines of them until his hands were charred.

The light was searing his corneas. He closed his eyes, willing them to regenerate quickly. Unable to see, he could only fight, burn, and *hear*.

The crack of Josephine's bones. Her strangled breaths.

He roared with fury, striking out at the lightning with even more force. Nïx would likely spot him. She could begin to clock his future, lessening his chances of a successful assassination.

Rune didn't give a fuck. To reach Josephine, he grappled to breach the cage—

The lightning began to dissipate.

He swiped his sleeve over his eyes, blinking repeatedly to regain his sight. In the distance, Nïx had vanished, and Josephine lay motionless on the ground.

He traced to her. The damage was even worse than he'd thought. He dropped to his knees beside her battered body.

Shattered bones, cracked skull. Skin blistered and slashed.

He'd suffered enough internal injuries to recognize them in this small female. Her organs were bleeding inside her. With a curse, he lifted her. Her head lolled unnaturally. Nïx had broken her neck.

He yelled into the night, "I'll fucking kill you, Valkyrie!" He traced Josephine to Tortua, to his bed. He sliced away her clothes, wincing at what he revealed.

If she was truly so young—and hadn't made the transition to full immortality . . .

The vampire could die. *As brutally as my mother did.*

He cut his wrist for blood, dripping it between her pale lips. She didn't wake and wouldn't swallow. He needed a healer. How to find one? Immortals had scarce use for them! All they had to do was rest and wait for regeneration to happen.

Rune's ears twitched. His heart raced as her heartbeat slowed. She might perish before he could return with help. *Think, Rune!*

In theory, he possessed enough magicks to heal her, but he would need a runic combination to access them, a spell of symbols. Could he remember the precise order and form of the runes?

He'd utilized healing spells to regenerate quickly after a violent brothel patron, but that had been thousands of years ago.

Racking his brain, he gathered black blood from his wrist. He pressed his forefinger to her chest and willed his mind to remember. . . .

Jo woke, blinking at her surroundings, her body in agony.

She was at Rune's? He'd been at the riverfront! He must have saved her from the Valkyrie.

Jo raised her hand to her forehead, wincing. Dizziness made his bed feel like it undulated in waves. She dared a glance down. Bandages covered her. Strange markings peeked out from the edges.

She tried to make sense of that, but her head felt like it was stuffed with cotton, yet echoing at the same time. The harder she stared at the bandages, the more her vision blurred. Soon she saw two of everything.

Two of Rune appeared beside the bed. Both of his faces looked exhausted. "You're awake." He sat next to her and rolled up his sleeve. "You should drink," he said, but his manner was cold.

Why? He now knew she wasn't in league with Nïx. "How did you find me?"

"I never *lost* you. I released you solely to follow you back to the Valkyrie."

"I was bait?"

"As if you wouldn't have done the same," he said, tone even colder. "Seems you're quite good at using others."

"What are you talking about?"

"Forget it. You need to feed again." He offered his wrist.

Pain ramped up her nausea. "I can't. Not yet."

He shrugged. "You're on your way to making a full recovery, regenerating all on your own." He hesitated, then said, "You should've told me you didn't know Nïx."

She couldn't read his expression. "Would it have mattered?"

"It would have, yes. What did she mean when she called you rare?"

"I have no idea," Jo murmured. "Did you bandage me?"

"I did. And I finally got you to drink over the last two days."

She'd fed, and didn't even remember? *Wait* . . . "Two days?" She needed to get back to Thad—he was still in that woman's power! "I've been gone that long?" She sat up, and the room spun. All the pain in her body grew sharper. In response, her mind went foggier. She collapsed back.

"You had a cracked skull, among other things. It's too soon for you to rise."

"Oh." Recovering from bullets to the face had been easy compared to this.

"I'm going to have a hell of a time assassinating an oracle now that she'll be clocking my every move. And she made it sound like she'd already been watching yours."

"I guess." Jo's cloudy brain couldn't recall the things Nïx said, only the ass-kicking she'd delivered.

He reached for Jo's hand, smoothing the edge of a linen bandage. Without looking up, he said, "The male you two were fighting over. Thaddeus. You thought I was aiming at him that night."

She nodded, then grimaced at the deep pop in her neck. Waves of dizziness washed over her. The urge to throw up grew.

"You attacked me with all your might to protect him. You must really care for him."

Confusion. "Of course I do."

Rune shot to his feet, starting to pace. "Who is he? What is he?"

She tried to follow his movements, but the effort was grueling. *What is Thad?* She didn't know. Was he like Jo?

Thad was good. "He's the best man I know." Her voice sounded more and more distant.

"In our wager, you were able to resist me because you wanted to get back to him."

"Uh-huh."

"Won't tell me his species? Then what is he to you?"

Everything. "I'd die for him." Her words were slurring.

Black forked out over Rune's eyes. "You love him?"

"Whaa?" Silly question. "More than anything."

Rune sank down on the side of the bed again. Just as abruptly, he rose. He dipped his hand into his pocket, rolling something there over and over. The trinket? "You love him so much you drank from me? Then you gave me your body for a night? How would he feel to know you can't get enough of my forbidden blood?"

What did that have to do with anything? "You wouldn't understand."

As she slipped back into sleep, he muttered, "I understand the demon in me demands his due. I'm off to service a harem of nymphs."

TWENTY-EIGHT

Rune's head pounded, his ears ringing.

Josephine had used him, sighing his name and coming on his tongue. She'd given him his first real kiss. But her reactions had been feigned so she could return to the one she loved.

Loved. She'd given her heart away. Lore females didn't do that lightly. *And I'd actually been worried about her getting attached to me?*

The night she'd fouled his shot, she'd been dressed like a man-eater—because she'd known she was going to see Thad. The body Rune had lost himself in belonged to someone else.

He pinched his temples. He'd planned to go to the tree nymphs' covey, but couldn't quite bring himself to leave. His headache worsened, and an unfamiliar, churning aggression filled him. Damn it, that night with her had meant something to him.

Shared breaths, discovery, barriers broken. It'd been different; it'd been *more.* How much had been real for her?

He did the using. Artifice was *his* specialty. He gritted his fangs, pacing the room. He craved angry sex, a good hate fuck. He wanted to hurt Josephine. *Needed* to.

He could return to New Orleans and take down her male. From his ever-present quiver, Rune pulled a gray arrow. The eraser, they called it. A shot to the chest with this one, and there'd be too many pieces to find.

The demon in him whispered, *Do it. Then piss on his grave marker.*

The fey in him said, *She's too young to know what love is. She's too young for you! Just* think *about this and calm yourself.*

She might have a man, but Rune would keep her from him. He couldn't allow a security risk like her to be freed—

One of the symbols on his arm began to glow and tingle. An alert. Someone had tripped his perimeter wards. *A trespasser in my sanctuary.*

He pictured Josephine—small and helpless in his bed. The demon in him commanded *protect.* Fangs bared, he unslung his bow, then traced to the observatory. His scowl deepened. He had a *guest.*

Sian was drinking from a flask, gazing down at an orgy, his customary war ax sheathed at his side.

By way of greeting, Rune said, "How did you find this place? And trace past my ward?" He shouldered his bow once more.

Sian cleared his throat. "You concealed your knowledge of this location, but when I read your mind, I uncovered enough." The demon's striking face was stamped with fatigue, his intense green eyes bloodshot.

How long did he have before his appearance started changing? With his twin's death, Sian had become the King of Pandemonia and all Hells—which meant he would transform from one of the most physically faultless males in the worlds into his own most monstrous state.

Sian offered his flask. "Brew?" The favored libation of demons.

Rune found the taste harsh, but as a lad, he'd drunk it just to have more in common with demons. The habit had stuck. From his pocket, he retrieved his own flask.

He raised it and took a generous swig. "What are you doing here?" Would Sian scent Josephine on him? How would Rune explain that he smelled of only *one* female? "You could have contacted me." His wrist tattoo was dark. "Now is not a good time."

"You must have a thousand nymphs in need."

Rune corrected him: "A thousand and one." *Soon.* He'd gone two nights without release, holding vigil for a female who didn't want him. Two nights abstaining! *That* was why he was conflicted. Rune wasn't the only one. "You look like hell, demon."

"Soon to be literally," Sian said in a bitter tone. "I'm now the king of it and must fit the part."

Rune had nothing but sympathy for Sian. He loathed change, had been altered so many times during his life, he refused to be ever again. "How long do you have?"

Sian didn't respond to that, his focus on a racy scene below—a demoness with three males inside her. "Gods, I will miss the attentions of desirable females. They flock to me now. Anon, they will gaze upon me with horror."

There was only one cure for a demon like him, and it was so implausible, Rune had little hope for his friend. "Will you resemble Goürlav?" Sian's twin had been a giant with green skin and slitted yellow eyes, considered repulsive by most.

Curt shake of his head. "Already I sense different changes. I'll be my own brand of monster." He drank again. "I asked around about my brother, couldn't understand why he would enter a contest for a kingdom. He already had the demonarchy of Pandemonia."

The source world of all demons. "Then why'd he do it?"

"Also up for grabs was a queen, a sorceress who'd volunteered to be won." Sian met Rune's gaze. "Don't you see? He craved a willing wife and could see no other way to get one." Sian took a long swig from his flask, then stared down at it. "The spectators of that contest considered him a monster, when all he wanted was a companion. Soon, I'll be the one who's hideous and yearning. How amused *she* would be about this."

"The fey girl? With different colored eyes."

Sian glanced up. "We have so few mysteries among all of us."

"Was she your mate?"

"I never attempted her, so I can't know for certain," he answered. "But I had a strong sense she was mine."

"You once said she was treacherous."

"As duplicitous as she was lovely." Sian rubbed his head, a gesture he often did—a telling one. A full-blood hell demon like him should sport sleek black horns, but his had been shorn when he was too young to regenerate them. Even after so long, he felt their absence. Like phantom limbs.

A predatory and defensive feature, horns were also sexual organs, sensitive to the touch. Amputation would be a nightmare.

"I would give anything for vengeance." Sian turned up his flask, draining it, then swiped his sleeve over his mouth. "Let's think not on the past. I've come to call you to battle."

Even better than a covey visit! "Against?"

"The Ice Demonarchy. They've been making sacrifices to old deities, attempting to wake them."

Idiots. They had no idea what they were doing. The Møriør ran into this sometimes, were old enough to have personally encountered most of those gods before they'd slept. The ice demons played with powers more evil than the Møriør could dream of being.

Was Nïx steering that faction as part of her Vertas army? If so, she was steering them straight into an apocalypse. Yet she would blame the Møriør and Orion?

Few knew a fundamental truth about the Møriør: The Bringers of Doom didn't *cause* the apocalypse; they *heralded* it.

Sian pocketed his empty flask and stood. "I traveled to that realm ages ago. I know our meeting place."

"Then let's be off." Rune grabbed one of his brawny shoulders, and the King of Hells transported them to the frozen reaches of the ice demons, landing atop a snow-covered shelf.

Chill winds gusted. A waxing moon illuminated lines of warriors below them, stretching all the way to the horizon.

Darach, Blace, and Allixta were already on the ledge, along with the witch's familiar. Curses' whiskers were frozen white.

Darach appeared on the verge of turning, his eyes as blue as the glaciers all around them.

Blace looked as impassive as ever. One would never know he prepared to enter the fray.

Rune glanced from Blace to Darach. Had either coveted a female to distraction? Wondered if she might be his mate?

Had either been used by someone he'd desired?

"Oh, it's the baneblood," Allixta said as she fought to keep her hat on against the winds. "The assassin who can't take out a single Val . . ." She trailed off when Rune rested an arrow against his lips, eyes narrowed with threat.

Silence, witch, or die this night. He might be crazed enough to do it.

Though her palms glowed with defensive magicks, she turned away from his challenge. Smart girl.

Blace told them, "We don't know who's listening in these rocky crags. Speak silently." They often communicated telepathically in the presence of others. —*The Valkyrie has eluded you, Rune?*—

—*For only so long, vampire. I have this well in hand.*—

Blace raised a brow. —*Then why are you in such turmoil?*—

Did the vampire recognize that so well in others because he rarely felt it?

—*If I am, it'll be short lived.*— Rune would celebrate this victory with an entire covey of nymphs.

Blace drew his sword, then turned to Sian. —*You don't have any hesitation about killing your own kind?*— Was the vampire getting soft in his old age?

Sian readied his war ax. —*The* Møriør *are my own kind.*—

Exactly Rune's thoughts! Sian knew where his loyalty lay. Why had Rune allowed Josephine to live after she'd taken his blood?

Because she makes me weak. He'd risked his standing among the Møriør for a female who didn't even want him.

His alliance meant everything. Rune focused his gaze at the battalions of demon warriors below. Every one of those males was bent on defeating Rune's brethren. On stealing victory from their grasp.

Stealing the triumph I've enjoyed since joining the Møriør.

Allixta asked, —*This army was given a chance to surrender?*—

—*We* always *give them that chance.*— Sian twirled his ax. —*Let's get this over with.*—

Rune nodded. —*Good warring, Møriør.*— As he awaited Blace, Darach, and Sian's charge, Rune's thoughts turned to a memory from long ago.

He'd been target practicing in Perdishian's training yard, growing more and more frustrated. In the distance, Kolossós, one of the first to join Orion, had been having some fit or another, so the ground—and Rune's target—had quaked.

Orion had appeared beside Rune. "How fares this, archer?"

"I don't understand why I can't take up a sword and leave this bow to another." He'd pointed an arrow at Blace, sparring with Sian. "The vampire is teaching me."

If Rune mastered swordplay, then he could fight his half brother Saetthan on equal footing. Saetthan carried the sword of their ancestors, a weapon passed down through generations. The ancient metal had been forged in the fires of a world being born: Titania, the second of the three great fey realms.

Saetthan was rightly proud of that weapon. But then, he'd always enjoyed lording over Rune anything he'd inherited as the legitimate Sylvan heir.

Orion had said, "Could you match Blace's talents? Become our swordsman?"

Rune showed promise. But he could never be better than Blace.

Just then Uthyr had soared overhead, unleashing a stream of fire. The gigantic dragon had flown into the flames, warming and cleaning his scales. Yet another fantastically powerful Møriør.

Orion had gazed up with his fathomless eyes, musing, "Why not take up fire breathing?"

Rune had scowled. Already he'd felt as if he didn't belong here. Blace was the oldest vampire, filled with the wisdom of ages. Sian was the prince of hells, son to the first demon, and a second generation Møriør after his sire had died.

Rune? A killer from the shadows and a whore.

"Just as the Møriør are limbs of one entity, that bow must become a part of you." Strolling on, Orion had said, "Remove the leathers from your hands."

His archery guards? Rune had called, "My fingertips will be shredded."

Without turning back, Orion had spoken into his mind. —*Did you think to become the Archer without pain?*—

Rune roused from his memory when Sian gave his fearsome roar.

Battle on.

Sian and Blace began tearing through that army's ranks with little resistance. Rune loosed strategic arrows to cover the two, though they had no need of help. From the icy forest beyond, Darach howled, fresh on the trail of something.

Within a quarter of an hour, victory was nigh.

—*Shoot the bonedeath, Rune!*— Blace commanded. —*West flank.*—

Rune plucked a white arrow from his quiver.

Allixta warily said, —*You've configured those magicks to make Møriør immune?*— She was understandably nervous.

—*You'll soon find out.*— Rune drew his bow to the limit, aiming for a boulder in the rocky field below. He adjusted for winds, gauging the direction with the sensitive tips of his ears.

Silent, he let fly his arrow.

It sliced through the air. When it implanted in stone, the icy rock exploded.

Waves of heat and pressure expanded from the target, scorching snow, striking the closest demons, then sweeping out farther for miles.

All around Sian and Blace, demons fell to their knees with yells of anguish as their bodies broke and broke. Soon their bones were dust, and they could only writhe on the ground. None would regenerate; each would become an immortal burden on what was left of his people.

The battle was over. The bonedeath always ensured a decisive—and talked about—victory.

Watching his enemies helplessly squirm made Rune even more unsettled! He understood why this needed to be done; the show of force would cow enemies and prevent future conflicts. Besides, if the Møriør didn't prevail, all these demons would be dead anyway.

But he didn't relish this.

Nïx had described the Møriør as pure evil, an alliance of monsters and devils. That malicious Valkyrie had long allied with the fey; would she have deemed the outwardly beautiful Magh a monster?

Sian and Blace traced from the devastation and rejoined them with grave faces. No one would celebrate this as a victory.

Rune strapped on his bow. —*I wonder why Orion didn't merely destroy this dimension in the palm of his hand.*—

Dear gods, had Rune spoken that to the others?

Apparently. Orion materialized that moment, his uncanny gaze boring into Rune. Tonight, the Undoing resembled a demon, a gruesome one like Sian's twin Goürlav had been. Standing over twelve feet tall, Orion had thick-plated skin, two rows of horns, and dripping fangs. But his chilling black eyes were the same. —*This demonarchy has strategic value and is filled with resources. Do you harbor other doubts, archer?*—

Feigning nonchalance, Rune shrugged. —*None, my liege. If I've discharged my duty here, I'll take my leave.*—

—*By all means,*— Orion said, his demonic expression giving away nothing.

Rune was tempted to return to Josephine, but he couldn't predict his behavior. His hunt for Nïx wouldn't resume until night fell in New Orleans. Only one thing left to do.

He traced to the Dryads, his favorite nymph covey. They lived in a hollowed-out tree as large as an apartment building. Each nymph had her own quarters, her "nest." They were spread throughout the interior of the tree's limbs. The main gathering area was a bar at the base of the trunk.

When he appeared inside, nymphs cheered his arrival. They were all topless, their voluptuous bodies painted with leaf designs. Amber jewels adorned them.

The other males present scowled, knowing Rune had just skipped them in line.

"Well, hello, doves." He cast the nymphs his wickedest grin. They crowded around him, fawning, hoping to be chosen.

This was what he'd needed! He'd already fucked most of them, which meant they craved a repeat.

Josephine, however, had woken from a night in his bed with one question on her lips: *Will you really let me leave?*

Here, he was the best choice, the ultimate for any female to enjoy. Here, he had one worry: deciding which nymphs to honor with his dick.

Second best? Not among these beauties.

TWENTY-NINE

R une?" Jo called when she woke in his bed alone. She tested her body, moving her arms and legs.

She was totally healed! Time to return to New Orleans.

Yet Rune didn't answer. She rose, gazing down at her many bandages. He'd cared for her. So where was he?

She checked the other rooms he'd shown her. No sign of him. She dimly remembered speaking to him when she'd been in such pain, but not much of what they'd said.

Until he returned, she was trapped in his home again. Which meant Thad remained unprotected, under the control of an evil bitch. Jo shivered to recall Nïx snapping her bones like dried twigs.

The Valkyrie wanted her to spy on some guy named Orion and report back. Nïx had said he would impact her life in so many ways. That might be true, but Jo had no idea who he was.

Struggling to make sense of that fight, she headed to the bathing chamber. As she unwrapped layers of bandages, more details filtered into her consciousness. Rune had used her as bait for Nïx! But he'd also saved her in the end. Why else would the Valkyrie have stopped mid-murder?

He'd yelled as Nïx tortured her—as if he were desperate to save Jo. As if he gave a damn about her.

Naked, she gazed down at her body. Black runes covered her. He'd painstakingly crafted shapes from his own blood.

That delicious wine.

She trailed her fingertips over each one, loving his marks on her flesh. She would've healed on her own in a few days, but he hadn't known that. She recalled his panic, and the dread rumbling in his voice.

The dark fey was starting to feel more for her!

After their night together, Jo's own feelings might have deepened into something more than infatuation. Her dreams of his past had affected her as well. Seeing him so vulnerable and young, yet so cocky, had touched her. The love he'd felt for his mother had softened her.

She'd been swamped with disappointment when he'd traced her to the Quarter and told her to run home to her roost.

Huh. That had merely been part of his ruse.

In the spacious shower area, she pressed some tiles, and warm water cascaded from the ceiling. She was reluctant to erase his symbols, but she needed to clear the cobwebs from her head.

She stepped under the water, staring at the drain. The blood washing from her skin colored the water like ink, and quickened her appetite. When Rune returned, would he give her a top-off? She nearly moaned at the prospect.

Could she trust him enough to reveal Nïx's deal? Maybe he and Jo could work together on their mutual Valkyrie problem.

After her shower, Jo padded in a robe to his closet to steal an undershirt. His clothes were rough-and-tumble, many ripped and frayed. She loved his devil-may-care look.

Lady-killer with a big swinging dick? Oh yeah.

But she didn't need to be mooning over a player like him. Nothing mattered more than saving Thad from Nïx. As she dressed, Jo replayed the madwoman's every word. Some things stuck out more than others.

The ground should be your best friend. . . . Why would you ever become tangible in a fight? . . . Your mind is your greatest weapon. Use it to strike; use it to defend. . . .

Had Nïx given Jo pointers to help with her spy mission? Jo was leery about believing the Valkyrie, yet she got the sense Nïx had been telling the truth. Great. Now all Jo had to do was figure out how to use her mind to strike.

The Valkyrie had also mentioned a woman. Had Nïx been talking about the one in Jo's waking nightmare, the one who'd emitted power to shore up the sky?

Though Jo wasn't a trusting person (understatement), maybe she should reveal to Rune everything she'd learned and remembered. Damn it, where was he?

Another memory hit her. Just before she'd passed out, he'd told her he was off to . . . service a nymph harem!

Her eyes went wide. "Manwhore!" He was in bed with another female at this very moment. Or *females*, plural. Apparently, Rune *wasn't* starting to feel more for her.

That gigantic dickwad.

What was it with him and nymphs? She clenched her fists, and the lights flickered. The furniture vibrated.

She gasped. That hadn't happened since all those years ago at the morgue. She'd all but forgotten it.

Had she just moved the furniture with her mind? One way to find out. She returned to his museum, filled with his precious relics. His *priceless* ones. What better place to test an unpredictable power!

She eyed a small vase across the room. She inhaled, exhaled, then pictured lifting it. . . .

The vase wobbled!

Holy shit, she *was* telekinetic! More clearly she saw that vision of the crumbling world and the dark-eyed woman—she'd been using her hand to control her telekinesis.

Jo aimed her palm at the vase and tried to raise it. The thing shattered.

Uh-oh. Hope he didn't like that one. She turned to another antique, a delicate-looking box atop a marble pedestal.

Pressing down telekinetically would have to be easier than lifting. She concentrated on flattening the box and waved her palm down. The box—and the pedestal—were crushed.

Awesome!

But she wasn't managing a focused beam like that woman's. Jo needed more practice. Rune's collection was making a great shooting gallery.

She turned to a medium-size bust of some man who'd probably written books Jo couldn't read. *Asshole.*

BOOM! She laughed as chunks of marble landed all across the room. Okay, not focused, but Hulk-smash was more Jo's style anyway.

Then came the real test. Would she be able to wield her telekinesis while ghosting?

She dematerialized. Floating like a speck of nothing, she gazed from one treasure to the next. Which one to practice on? He'd said these were war prizes, but she'd bet some were gifts from women he'd screwed.

When Jo pictured him in bed with beautiful nymphs—gazing down at them with those seductive eyes—a wave of power blasted from her mind.

The sound of destruction rang in her ears. *Crashing, ripping, shattering.* Once the dust settled, she blinked in disbelief. She'd trashed everything in the room.

Hulk. Smash.

He was overly proud of his home, would be furious when he saw the damage. Lady Shady gazed around with a discerning eye.

I'll smash it all *to bits.* Payback for hurting her heart.

She turned to the next room to *practice* some more. She'd been a killer before. With these new talents, she would be an undefeatable one.

She frowned. Nïx had made it sound as if Thaddie was like Jo. If so, how could he cope with changes like these?

With the Valkyrie's help?

Jo had been forced to let MizB raise Thad; she'd be damned if Nïx took over from here on out.

Change of plans, Nïx. Jo would definitely be getting access to Thad, but not in the way the Valkyrie had envisioned. Jo wasn't going to spy on anyone; instead she'd do what she did best.

Before Rune got another chance at Nïx . . .

I'm going to kill her.

THIRTY

Rune's face was buried between two of the finest nymph breasts in Loredom, his hands full of them, and he was kissing his way toward a taut nipple.

Just what he'd needed.

His soon-to-be-shed trews were the only thing preventing him from shoving inside his partner, Dalliance.

The word had been derived from her, the epitome of amorous toying. She had been for millennia. She had long black hair, wide gray eyes, and a body men had actually killed to possess.

She arched her back in readiness, her fingers threading into his hair. His lips closed around a nipple, but his teeth didn't click against a piercing. No warm metal teased his tongue.

Often imitated, never duplicated.

Concentrate on what you're doing! He knew what she liked, could satisfy her in his sleep. The two of them went way back, had shared clients and patrons, fucking for the entertainment of others at exclusive gigs.

Every now and then, they'd hook up for old times' sake. He'd selected her today, instead of a bevy all for himself.

The difference between him and Dalli? She'd chosen her line of work at the outset.

The night Magh had sold Rune to a brothel, he'd just seen his mother's grave and been devastated to learn of her fate.

Then he'd learned of his.

"You've been a whore for so long, I thought we should make it official," Magh said. "Here, you will please your customers, cur. Or perish. At the end of each night, a guard will raise a sword over your neck. If you were a good whore, you'll retain your life. The first complaint you receive will be your last. You had better hurry. Dawn nears, and no one in your long line appears . . . pleased."

The creature at the start of the line had been hideous, yet he'd known he would somehow have to pleasure her, to bury his disgust and ignore the blistering wrath he'd felt over his mother's death.

Please or perish. In the intervening years, many of his customers hadn't been "pleased" with anything less than his body beaten and bloody.

Concentrate. Soon Dalli would notice his distraction. He turned his thoughts to the vampire to stay hard.

His mind raced from one image of her to another. Her little fangs. Her incomparable curves that seemed made for him alone. Her ethereal face when she was about to come. Her flashing hazel eyes when she smiled.

He'd made her smile. She'd smiled in bed with him. Had *thanked* him.

No! The vampire loved another. All that had been an act. Everything about their night together had been false.

Dalli cleared her throat and sat up. "I called your name twice. But you're not even here, are you?" He didn't deny it. "I can always tell when you check out—your eyes glaze over." She knew more about his early centuries than anyone still living. She alone knew he feared becoming so deadened he'd never feel alive again.

"What's the problem, Dalli? My cock's hard enough."

"Please. I've seen you get it up for a pus demon."

He drew back and sat on the edge of her bed, head in his hands. "Lot on my mind." He stood and began to pace, bare feet silent on the plush carpet of her nest.

She pulled her robe back on. "Will you please tell me what's wrong?"

"It doesn't matter." Maybe on some level he'd suspected he wouldn't be in the moment. Maybe he'd chosen Dalli because he needed a friend more than a fuck.

"Clearly it does matter." Rays of sunlight stole inside from the carved-out window, catching her gray eyes. "Will you not confide in me?"

He shook his head. How could he possibly explain a creature like Josephine?

"I don't ask where you go when you're not here," Dalli said. "I don't ask what you're doing with your life, or what plans you have for the future." She knew he was a secrets master in a shadowy alliance, but he'd given her no other details.

"Which is why we're still friends."

As if he hadn't spoken, she continued, "I've never asked those questions, because I could see for myself you weren't *utterly* miserable with your life."

He paused his pacing. "Why would I be?"

Dalli rose, heading to her wine service to pour them goblets. "Someone your age with no mate? No offspring? It wears on a soul."

"Speaking from experience?" She was almost his age, the oldest nymph he'd ever met.

"We're talking about you today. And how you are now completely, utterly miserable."

He scowled. "I just want to get laid. It's why I'm here."

"Uh-huh. This has got to be over a female."

"Why do you say that?"

She handed him a drink, then crossed to the settee with her own. "Give me some credit." Taking a seat, she motioned for him to join her. "I've been in the desire game for a long, long while."

He stabbed his fingers through his hair. "There is a girl. She's got me tied up in knots."

"I think you better bring the bottle over."

Good thinking. He grabbed it and joined her, setting it on an amber side table. He sank down beside Dalli. "I've only known her for four days." Out of the millions he'd lived. "In my lifespan, that's a blink of an eye." In Dalli's too.

"Do you think this girl could be the one?"

Maybe? No. *No!* "I will never have a mate. I've expected no destined female for myself."

"Because of your poison? I know how much you despise it."

I hate it so godsdamned much. Yet for a while, his hatred had faded—because Josephine bloomed whenever she fed from him. She'd craved him. But he didn't want to be dependent on a vampire just because she could tolerate his hated blood!

He didn't want to want someone who loved another.

Even if Josephine chose Rune instead, what kind of future would they have? He would never be exclusive with her, couldn't imagine spending the next several millennia in bed with one female.

Especially when his value to the Møriør depended on him sleeping with others.

He emptied his goblet and set it aside. *Forget the vampire.* "Let's just do this." He rubbed the heel of his palm over his cock until he was hard enough. "Does it matter to you if I'm engaged or not? I'll make you purr. I always do."

"Are you sure?"

I want inside Josephine. Inside the silken heat he'd pleasured with his tongue. *I want to see her reaction when I enter her for the first time.* "Hundred percent."

Dalli pursed her lips. "You might as well start talking. Tell me her name. I want to know all about her."

He exhaled with resignation. "Very well. Her name is Josephine." He poured another healthy serving for them both.

"What is it about her?" Dalli asked, excitement in her demeanor. "Why is she different from all the others?"

How to put into words what he was feeling? "She's a walking contradiction. She's powerful, but young. She seems world-weary at times, but again, she's so bloody young. She's insanely secretive—and yet she's outspoken to the point of being blunt." He recalled her telling him, "You. I *like*. I like you so much." How could she have been so believable in the throes?

"When you say young . . . ?"

He hesitated, then admitted, "Quarter of a century."

Dalli coughed on her wine.

"I know. And, damn it all, Dalli, she's a vampire."

"How can that be? Female vampires are so rare."

"I don't know a lot"—*anything*—"about her. But she's definitely a vampire."

Dalli's excitement faded. "Rune, I'm so sorry. No wonder you're miserable." She put her hand over his. "Maybe your Josephine could drink bagged blood or something like that. Not feeding from her partner would be a sacrifice, but I'm sure she'd want to try for you."

Over the rim of his goblet, he said, "She drinks my black blood. Couldn't crave it more." His tone was smug.

"What? How is that possible?"

"She says it's because she's 'wicked strong and all.'"

Dalli's eyes grew merry. "I like her already. Is she transitioned?"

"She was injured recently. I slathered her with runes, but I suspect she would've regenerated on her own." He still couldn't believe he'd remembered those rune combinations after so long. *But then, I'd needed them enough in that brothel.*

"Are there no physical boundaries between you two? Can you be with her fully?"

"So far, so good." Though he hadn't been inside her yet. If she *was* his mate . . .

"This must mean she's yours. You've found *her*, Rune! Do you understand how blessed this makes you?"

That word had *never* been used to describe a being like Rune.

Dalli studied his face. "Are you . . . engaged when you're with her?"

"Engaged? When I come with her, I yell so hard my throat hurts. I say things before I think them. Speak in bloody Demonish!" His head fell back against the settee, and he stared at the leafy ceiling. "I lose control totally. The first time I got a taste of her sex, my eyes rolled back in my head." Those plump lips . . . that maddening clit ring . . .

Lost in memory, he said, "She gets so wet. When she comes on my tongue, it's a luscious reward for me. And gods almighty, when she pierces my skin with her sharp little fangs, my heart thunders, and my balls tighten and ache as never before. My cock feels like it's going to explode. . . ."

Dalli cleared her throat.

He blinked, amazed that he'd been stroking himself. She grinned. He scowled and yanked his hand away. "This is what I'm talking about—no control!"

"You can't have it both ways, Rune. You can't fear losing control *and* becoming deadened."

Dalli was right.

"I think you're falling for her."

"As in love? My kind doesn't love; we're not capable of it. Much less me, with my past."

He'd lived with the threat of that sword over his neck for ages before a fair master had come along, freeing him and offering a percentage. Numb to violation and blind to an alternative, Rune had said, "Why not?" He'd considered himself nothing more than a coin whore.

His thoughts had never strayed toward the future. His feelings had been stunted, as cold as ash.

Were they still? Josephine had gotten him excited and frantic and agitated. Frenzy had overcome control. Was that sparking cinder inside him catching flame?

With her, he'd been flung into some place he'd never been before.

I want to return there.

Dalli said, "In the past you had to distance yourself to survive. But no longer."

To survive his patrons—and Magh. When she'd learned he was volunteering to be used, she'd been enraged. Evil to the core, she'd recaptured him, imprisoning him in her dungeon. She'd desired him and hated herself for it. Then the real torture had begun—

"Stop right now," Dalli said, reclaiming his attention. "Stop reliving days gone by. You can begin again with Josephine. Someone so young will help you see the worlds anew."

"I don't *want* to begin again." Magh had reshaped him so many times that the mold should have broken. He'd gone from slave laborer, to killer, to involuntary whore, to voluntary whore, to whipping boy. All because of a vicious woman. He was *done* changing.

Yet hadn't he considered himself altered after his first orgasm with Josephine in his bed? "All of this is moot anyway." The cinder inside him had caught flame for the wrong female. "She wants . . . someone else." Rune downed his goblet, then stood to pace again. "Some asshole who wears cowboy boots." Was Josephine's male searching for her? Wondering why she hadn't returned to his bed for yet another moonset?

"What manner of species is he?"

"I don't know." Rune had been focused on his target, had only paid passing attention to Nïx's companion, *Thaddeus*. Unable to recall the male's scent, Rune pictured his appearance. "He's big. Tall with broad shoulders." The prick's face was much handsomer than Rune's own. Which meant it was boring. He grated, "Attractive, I suppose."

"You sound jealous."

"I'm not jealous; I'm pissed. She tricked me. We had a night together, and it was . . . different. I didn't even swive her." *Shared breaths, broken boundaries. All an act.* "She played me just as I played patrons, making them believe I loved each one alone."

"What did she do?"

"I thought she was half-infatuated with me. All along, she plotted to get back to him, the one she truly wants."

"Then win her from the other. You and I both know you're an unparalleled lay. Unleash your arsenal upon her—your full arsenal—and she'll be yours."

Rune stopped pacing. "You're right. If I hold nothing back, I could have her eating out of the palm of my hand." Yes, he would make her love him instead of the other. And once she did, Rune would hurt her as he'd been hurt.

Not that he was hurt. He was simply *irritated*.

"That's the spirit!"

He frowned. "Say I did win her, I think she's the jealous type. She'd expect monogamy, and I can't do that."

Dalli gave him a rueful grin. "It's not so bad. Most beings want a devoted partner they can call their own."

"Nymphs don't."

"Maybe we desire freedom just a bit more." Her gaze grew distant.

Daydreaming of someone in particular? "Dalli?"

She raised her face. "By the way, I suggest you shower before you go. The scent of nymph arousal wouldn't be a good opener if she is indeed the jealous type."

"She needs to get used to it, because I *will* be bedding others."

"Rune, trust me on this."

"Very well. Just this once." He stripped off his trews, then headed for her bathing chamber.

As he strode past her, cock swaying, Dalli sighed. "I'm going to miss that."

"Trust me, dove. It's not going anywhere. Rune the Insatiable does not do monogamy."

THIRTY-ONE

That little vampire bitch!"

When Jo strolled back into Rune's demolished museum, she heard him muttering, "Should've fucked Dalli *sideways.*" Whatever that meant.

He twisted around on Jo. "What the hells is this?"

She shrugged with a smile. "Dunno."

"I don't understand you! You knew how much I valued these things." The ends of his hair were wet from a recent shower. How many had he been with this time? "You knew this collection was priceless."

"Yep." How could she still find him so attractive? With his black leather pants and white tunic, he looked as gorgeous as ever. The bow slung over his shoulder and the quiver on his leg just amped his hotness level. Outside—gorgeous. Inside—*not.*

His expression turned menacing. "Do you think I won't punish you?"

Try it. You won't like what happens. She didn't necessarily want to show him her powers—no reason to since she would never see him again—but she would if worse came to worst. She started toward the bedroom, making her way to the fire. "I'm ready to be let out now."

He followed. "You destroyed everything because you couldn't get out? You aren't a prisoner! The wards are for protection as much as anything."

"If I'm not a prisoner, then let me go." She sat on the arm of his favorite chair.

"Without repercussions . . . ?" He eye-fucked her T-shirt clad body, as if he'd just realized she was naked beneath. *He really is insatiable.*

"I could've trashed your library too." She'd left it untouched; though she couldn't read, she revered books. Maybe all the more because she'd never delved into their mysteries.

"The only reason I'm not tanning your ass right now is because you're going to pay me back sexually." He closed in on her, towering over her. "And, Josephine, you can't imagine the tab you just ran up."

A laugh burst from her lips. "You're so not serious."

He drew his head back in confusion. "*I* am the one who's been wronged here! Me! In thanks for tracing you to safety and treating your wounds, you wrecked my home. I saved your life!"

She stood to show him she wasn't intimidated. "Please. I would've rallied."

"You're young. There was chance you hadn't been frozen into your immortality yet."

"Frozen means . . . ?" At his frown, she said, "We might call it something different where I'm from."

"When a Lorean is at his strongest and stops growing older. When he can regenerate from lost limbs and such. The transition to full immortality."

"Oh, yeah. When did you *freeze*?"

"What? I was twenty-nine."

"Then you think twenty-five would be a good age for me to?" If so, how had Jo regenerated her face and brain at eleven years old? Another question to add to her list.

"It's within an average range for a female. Males freeze later. How could you not know these things? You align with the Forbearers, don't you? And of course, you're further sheltered by your age."

Forbearers? "What do you suppose a Forbearer to be? We might call ourselves something different."

"An order of vampires who were once mortal, still living as humans do. They refuse to drink from the flesh, like vampire monks, and they're uninformed about the Lore. If you were raised among them, it would explain a lot."

"Gotcha." With so much in common with them, maybe she should try to find them.

"No denial?" Voice gone rough, he said, "Is my flesh the first you've taken?" His black brows were drawn, his magenta eyes flickering.

She found her body responding to that look. *He was just inside someone else, Jo!* But she refused to reveal how jealous she'd been. "I'm ready to be let out."

"To go where? So quick to leave me behind?" His tone was surly.

The nerve! He'd been out screwing nymphs—was freshly showered from his adventures. "I have my own life. I have things I need to do."

"Namely, your male."

"What are you talking about?"

He pulled a flask from his pants pocket and drew deep. "The man I saw with Nïx is yours."

"I can promise you he's not."

Rune's menacing expression eased, before returning full force. "Then why would you say you loved him? Ah, it's unrequited? That's got to hurt. I'd wondered why you'd dressed like a man-eater the other night. You sought to impress him!"

She considered telling him about her brother, but again, she had no reason to. The less Rune knew about her, the better. "I'm done talking about this."

"I'm not going to let you leave until I've bedded you."

God, he confused her! "Didn't get your fill of nymph?"

"I haven't swived anyone since I first saw you! Four days!"

She glared. "So you went out just to take a shower?"

"I did go to a nymph covey. I was with an old friend, and we started to fool around." As if the words were pulled from him, he said, "But I didn't go through with it."

"Should I believe that?" *I* want *to believe that.*

Shrug. "Don't care if you do."

He was telling the truth! Their night together *had* meant something to him. He'd been true(ish) to her. Because he was already falling for her!

Speaking of falling . . . What if *she* was his fated mate? What if destiny really did pair people up? Rune had told her a mate was the one female in all times and places a demon was most compatible with.

Compatible? Oh yeah. He'd reacted to her much more intensely than he had with those nymphs. Plus, Jo was the only one immune to his poison.

Seriously. Dude couldn't kiss another female without offing her. *Ding ding ding.*

He believed dark feys didn't get a mate, but she mentally waved that away because men often believed stupid shit.

She bit her bottom lip as she thought about his museum. She'd probably found the other half of her unbreakable bond, and she'd kind of destroyed all his things. Maybe she should tell him about her telekinesis?

He interrupted her thoughts: "You're way, way, *way* too young for me. And you've got this weird jealous bent. You annihilated my belongings—like a godsdamned hellhound pup escaped from a kennel. But I still believe I want to bed you." He gazed to her side as he gruffly said, "More than once."

"Is this your idea of asking for a relationship? Is that why you were faithful?"

"Faithful?" He looked aghast. "Slow down, vampire. I don't want to give you the impression I would be monogamous, because it will *never* happen. If we spent time together, we'd have to work on your jealousy."

She wanted to strangle him! "You're one to talk about jealousy—you're eaten up with it! Over my 'male.'"

"Bullshit. I'm *pissed*, because I don't appreciate being used. Everything we did in bed . . . the things you said. All lies."

"Like what?"

"You said you'd drink me, only me, for eternity. You said you couldn't live without my kiss. Pretty words to get back to your male."

Rune could deny it all he wanted, but he was jealous. Which meant he *did* give a damn.

Maybe after so long, he couldn't see himself as anything other than a bachelor, and was struggling against his feelings. After all, he'd left here, intending to have sex, and he hadn't been able to follow through. If he went in the future, wouldn't the same thing happen? It'd be even worse if he fell for her!

Her thoughts drifted to that wedding she'd ghost-crashed. Once Rune loved Jo the way the romantic groom loved his bride, he'd never be able to stray.

Now if only she could learn to trust the way that bride had.

In any case, Jo's path was clear. Make Rune fall in love with her—perhaps through bonding activities such as Valkyrie assassinations.

"Why would you care if I was with a nymph or not?" Rune asked. "You're in love with another. You're already taken."

Josephine rolled her eyes again. "I'm not."

He couldn't believe he was quarreling with her like this. Nightfall approached in New Orleans. He needed to be on the ground, stalking his target. "But you want to be taken by that male." Rune's fists clenched. *Kill Nix; kill this vampire's would-be lover. All in a night's work.* "You set out to seduce him. Admit it."

She headed toward the fire, but he caught a glimpse of her disbelieving expression as she turned away.

Wait . . . What if the male was connected to her in another way, maybe by blood? She wasn't old enough to have a son that age. Perhaps a brother.

Rune joined her by the hearth. Curling his forefinger under her chin, he lifted her face for his scrutiny. Not much resemblance to Thad overall. But if she removed her glamour, especially around the eyes . . .

Their eyes' unique color was the same.

The ringing in Rune's ears started to subside. Perhaps he'd cared about this more than he'd admitted to himself. "He's your brother."

She shrugged. He was beginning to realize her shrug meant *Yes, Rune*. Suddenly, the destruction of his things felt like a mere irritation.

She hadn't been using him. There'd been no artifice. "Why didn't you tell me?"

"Because I didn't want you to use this as leverage."

"We're not enemies, Josephine." *She doesn't have a male*. Rune was going to kiss her tonight till her lips got sore.

"He's my little brother. There's no such thing as being too protective."

This development brought its own set of challenges. "Thaddeus allies with Nïx?"

Her expression hardened. "Not for long."

"You might be protective of him, but I'm not seeing the reverse. Did he know Nïx was going to attack you?"

She shook her head. "He doesn't even know I'm alive."

"I don't understand."

"We were separated when he was just a little kid."

"How old is he?" As a younger brother, Thad couldn't be over twenty-four—because she'd lived for *only a quarter of a century*. The back of Rune's neck flushed.

"Thad's seventeen."

Big fucker for his age. But the boy wouldn't be frozen into immortality yet. Which meant Josephine had a glaring vulnerability: she cared for a being who could easily be killed. "How were you separated?" When immortals had offspring, they tended to keep a family united. *Unlike my own sire*. "Did your parents die?"

She crossed her arms over her chest, pulling taut the material of his T-shirt across her pierced nipples. "Rune, I like you. And I loved what we did in bed."

He snapped his gaze from her chest to her face. He'd known that night had been different!

"But why would I reveal more to you? Give me a reason." Her eyes were almost . . . beseeching.

"Because you can trust me."

She exhaled with clear disappointment. "Which is exactly what an untrustworthy person would say."

Rune let it go. "I'll get your secrets soon enough." He planned to introduce her to blood mead at the earliest opportunity. Before she could ask more, he said, "Nïx's allies are staunch. Your brother might choose to remain with her."

"Oh, that will never happen."

"Why are you so confident?"

Her eyes flickered, her irises black as night. "Because I'm going to kill her."

THIRTY-TWO

I admire your optimism, but she trounced you." Rune hit that flask again. "She amused herself with you."

"Our next matchup will be different," Jo assured him. "I'm ready for it."

"You are a very, very young vampire who should never pick a fight with a primordial."

"Relative to you, the big bang is young. And what's a primordial?"

"Don't know that either, Forbearer? It's the firstborn of a particular species, or at least the oldest one living."

"Are you the primordial dark fey?"

A shadow flashed across his face. "I may never know."

"Whatever she is—I've got this."

"Say you could somehow prevail over her, why would I give up my kill?"

"Is it personal?" Jo asked.

"It's *important*. She's been playing with forces she's too young and confused to understand, forces that can throw the entire universe into chaos. She flirts with an apocalypse. I happen to be one among a group that opposes her."

"What did Nïx mean when she talked of the Møriør?"

"That's the name of my alliance. I'm a Møriør."

"But you're not a nightmare made flesh." Not a Bringer of Doom. Jo figured Rune would need to keep it in his pants for more than a hot minute to be a *doom bringer*.

"And you're not a bomb," he said. "Can we agree that Nïx alleged ridiculous things?"

The Valkyrie had said she'd kept her eye on Jo and Thad: her nuclear weapons. "Do you share a castle with monsters?"

He ran his hand over his chin. "That part is true. But not material."

"The hell?" Her potential guy lived with monsters? Girlfriend/roommate issues would take on a whole new level.

"We're speaking about Nïx."

"Fine." Jo would address his monsters in the future. "What does she intend with me?" *With Thad?*

"Depends on what you are. Nïx said you were rare. You're half vampire, so what's your other half? The first time we met, you cut me off as soon as I asked you what you are—as if I'd reached the limits of my usefulness. But you do *know*?" Whatever he saw in her expression made his lips part. "How could you not know? If you were raised by one parent, were you told nothing about the other? You said you were all by your lonesome. The generation before you is gone?"

Jo couldn't bring herself to share her story yet. If he'd given her just *one* good reason to trust him . . .

"I'll have your secrets soon enough, Josephine."

The second time he'd said that. Why was he so confident?

"Since you can stomach my poison, you could be one of the mystical species," he said, "like the Sorceri or Wiccae. It's possible you could be fey. Most fey have magicks in them."

She recalled her dream of Rune's first kill. "Maybe you're enemies with the Wiccae or Sorceri. You're half fey, but you still might not be a fey fan." She wondered if he would admit to hating them.

"I despise the fey, but I wouldn't make you my enemy just because you possessed fey blood. As for the Wiccae, I've sworn allegiance to a witch. She's one of the Møriør. I don't care about the Sorceri either way." He took another swig from his flask, his mind on this mystery. "Vampire hybrids are uncommon, but would any of those combinations be enough to attract the attention of a primordial Valkyrie?" He met her gaze. "When I kill Nïx, this information might go to the grave."

Never to know? "As long as Thad is safe, I don't care."

"Then let me deal with her. As I told you, I'm an assassin by trade and have been for thousands of years."

"I need to make sure you don't accidentally off my brother. I *will* be watching over him. Either we go together, or I go alone."

He leaned his shoulder against the hearth mantel, examining his black claws. His silver rings shone in the firelight. "Then I'll keep you trapped in here."

"Asshole! So I'm back to being a prisoner? And you wonder why I don't trust you with more information about myself?"

"You need to clean up this mess. And more . . ." He traced away for a split second, returning with a weighty book. He dropped it on his fireside chair. "You can read this and learn about the Lore."

Lemme get right on that. "What's in the book?"

"Everything you ever wanted to know about immortals."

She pursed her lips. *Of course it is.* The treasure trove she needed most. "No dice, Rune. Nothing matters more to me than keeping my brother safe."

He smirked. "I'll do my best not to make him a collateral casualty."

So arrogant! Rune seemed to take those vows to the Lore seriously. Why not try one? He loved it when she drank from him, so . . . "If we aren't partners in killing Nïx, if I don't go everywhere you go when involved in that mission, then I vow to the Lore I won't drink blood."

"You did not just say that." He actually reeled a little. "You will be bound by that vow, compelled by it, even if you later decide differently. You gave few qualifiers—and no time limit."

"What's the big deal?"

"Say I returned here in five seconds with the Valkyrie's head and your brother safely in tow. All your problems would be solved. Yet because you didn't accompany me, you wouldn't be able to drink blood—ever. The vow would prevent you from ingesting it. You'd be incapable of it!"

He had to be overreacting. No way a few words were so powerful.

"So I either have to partner with you or allow you to starve." He pointed his finger at her. "Guess which way I'm leaning, vampire!" He was madder than he'd been about his stuff. "You shouldn't throw those words around, much less so broadly! It was an immature move. Which is *completely* understandable given your age."

"Look, I've never made a vow like that before I did with you, okay?"

"Yet you refuse to read the *Book of Lore* and educate yourself?"

Ugh! She wanted nothing more! "I'm having a hard time believing words could make me starve."

He pulled that trinket from his pocket. "Vow to the Lore you'll never take this talisman from me without my permission."

"So it's gone from trinket to talisman?" She stepped closer. "Tell me what that is."

"Perhaps I will in time. If you make the vow."

"Fine. I vow to the Lore I'll never take that from you without your permission."

He held it out to her.

When she reached for it, her hand veered to the right as if repelled by some invisible force. Brows drawn, she attempted again. Same result. She raised her chin. "Then my vow is bulletproof. Good. That means we'll work together to kill Nïx."

"I *have* done this by myself a time or two, vampire."

"You've failed with her twice already. I botched your attempt from the roof—"

"Because I *chose* not to kill you." He squared his shoulders, clearly un-used to criticism about his skill. "In a nanosecond, I could have shot you and strung another arrow for the Valkyrie."

"You couldn't hit her when she attacked me. I assume you were try-ing?" When he'd been yelling for Jo.

He ground his fangs.

She had him! "Then that settles it. We're partners in crime for this mission."

"I'll make sure it's a *very* short mission." He strode closer to her. "We begin now."

"I need to get clothes from my place first." She gestured at her bare feet.

"There's more I want to say about your actions—my wrath is in no way appeased—but I'm curious about your home, since you found mine *quaint*."

"After that, will we go to Nïx's?" Jo tried to picture a mad Valkyrie's crib. "Does she live in a different dimension?"

"She resides not far from New Orleans on a property called Val Hall. But there's no need to go there. I have spies watching it every minute of the day. They'll alert me if she returns there."

"How?"

"This rune will glow." He pointed to a band inked around his right wrist. "In any case, we hope she doesn't. The wraiths guarding Val Hall make it the safest place for her."

"Wraiths?"

"Spectral she-beings. They fly around the mansion, keeping intruders out."

"How do you kill them?"

"You don't; they're already dead." He took her arm. "It'd be best just to show you. But say nothing about what we intend. The nymphs concealed around Val Hall would overhear it."

Concealed? "So?"

"So they're there to help me for two reasons. One: I fucked them. Two: They believe I only want to sleep with Nïx. They can't hear us arguing about how best to assassinate her." He traced Jo to an overgrown stretch of misty bayou countryside.

Moss dangled from oaks. Fog draped the area. Lightning rods jutted all over the property, corralling repeated bolts.

"We're in Valkyrie territory now. They give off lightning with emotion. Feed from it too."

"Do they all control it like Nïx, making cages and blades?"

He shook his head. "As the primordial of her species, she must have learned to wield it."

"This place looks like a mad scientist's laboratory."

"You haven't seen the worst yet."

As she and Rune approached a clearing, a sprawling, creepy mansion came into view. Against a background of lightning, ghostly females in ragged red garments flew through the air, circling the structure. "The wraiths?"

"Also known as the Ancient Scourge," Rune said. "They're as strong as Titanian steel, and even older than I am. You can't tunnel under them, can't fly over, can't trace past. Overpowering them is impossible."

She raised her face to scent the air. Thad was here! Behind their guard? She'd just tensed to do *something* when Rune clamped her forearm and traced her back to Tortua.

"Why'd you leave?" She flung her arm away. "Thad is inside! I can challenge Nïx. She might come out to fight me!"

"She's not in Val Hall."

"We can wait there until she shows up."

"The other Valkyries wouldn't tolerate it. I could keep you safe, but I couldn't do anything for your brother until we handled the guard dogs. If you anger Val Hall's inhabitants, they might take it out on him."

Jo made a sound of frustration. Resigning herself to a wait, she said, "I can't believe Thad's in there." At least she hadn't scented his fear. He and Nïx *had* seemed chummy. "If Nïx isn't there, who's watching him?"

"Her Valkyrie sisters. They're likely coddling him, convincing him to join their alliance."

In other words, they were brainwashing her brother. "There has to be a way around those wraiths." If tracing past them wouldn't work, ghosting and walking right through them probably wasn't an option.

"For now, our best bet is to hunt Nïx. You have to be patient."

"Patient? Not my strong suit. You got a plan B?"

He gazed away and murmured, "Always."

Why did that one word send a chill down her spine?

THIRTY-THREE

Josephine took Rune's hand to trace him to her home, what promised to be some grand manor or stately castle. As she began to teleport, she and Rune seemed to fade before traveling. Whereas Sian's tracing was quick and seamless, the vampire's left him swaying.

Rune frowned at his new surroundings, a small dingy room with red carpet worn down to the foundation and paint curling away from the cinder block walls. A garish floral cover topped the bed, and the air conditioner rattled. "Where did you take us?"

"To my digs."

"*This* is where you live? It's a rat trap! You had the nerve to call my place quaint?" In one corner of the room, next to stacks of comic books were stacks of cash. "If you've got money, why not get a nicer place?" This one was pitiful and demoralizing. The only positive he could discern? It was spotlessly clean.

"I like to fly under the radar. I don't mind it here."

A picnic table stretched the length of one wall, covered with random things: a phone, a tiara, plastic beads, a metal stick with a camera on the end.

"Immortals with power simply don't live like this."

"I can't get an ID, okay?"

"I could get you one in an hour." He bit the inside of his cheek. She'd never need an ID because he could never set her free in the world. She still potentially had his memories. "So this is where the fair Josephine sleeps. Since you've taken my blood that first night, have you had dreams of me? Experienced any scenes from my past?"

"Oh, yeah, constantly. I love watching you screw two hundred nymphs at one time and kick puppies."

"I have *never* kicked a puppy."

Rolling her eyes at him, she crossed to a garment rack filled with dark clothes, all in various stages of disrepair. She selected black jeans and a sleeveless T-shirt with some band logo, then tossed them on the bed.

"Why did you dress as a man-eater the other night?" Definitely not to seduce Thaddeus. "You wore that skimpy red dress to impress *me*."

"Don't flatter yourself." No denial.

A cracked full-length mirror hung on the bathroom door. Had she inspected her reflection there before setting out to find him? "Perhaps that's why you made your earlier vow—your power play—because you yearn to be near me. And now we're trapped together for as long as the mission continues." He should still be pissed over that play; yet he found the corners of his lips curling.

And for some reason, his cock was semihard.

"Believe whatever you like, Rune, but I told you why I made that vow." To protect her brother.

If Nïx found the two siblings valuable, then the Møriør should as well. Though Rune might have difficulty assassinating the oracle, he could hurt her by recruiting the weapons Nïx wanted: Josephine and Thaddeus.

It wouldn't matter that Josephine knew his and his allies' secrets if she became an ally herself.

He crossed to the picnic table, reading the inscription: *Orleans Parish Parks*. He inspected a sequin-covered phone, then moved on to the next item. "What is all this stuff?" He twirled a plastic tiara on his forefinger.

She snatched it from him. "Mementos from my experiences." She set down the tiara, arranging it just so.

"So you took my talisman to remember me by?"

Shrug. The one that meant *Yes, Rune.*

"How *do* you steal so easily? And why not anything of significant value?"

"Like your relics? All you're doing is inviting B&E."

At his blank look, she said, "Breaking and entering? People coming into your territory to boost your stuff?"

He'd noticed a brace on her motel room door. She might be a hybrid, but she was just as territorial as other vampires he'd known.

She walked to a set of drawers, opening one filled with underwear, selecting two pieces of black lace. "So what's up with your talisman anyway? I've seen you roll it in your pocket."

"I'll start talking about my past as soon as you tell me anything about yours." He sat on the bed, his good mood unaffected. How could he feel this way after what he'd lost? For millennia, his collection had been his one nondeadly pursuit. Perhaps it'd masked his lack in other areas.

No generations to discover before him; no generation to come from him; no hope of a mate.

Now as he gazed at the vampire about to undress, he had difficulty recalling which piece had been his favorite. Which one his newest. At least she'd spared his precious library. Still, he said, "I should destroy everything here for turnabout."

She smiled over her shoulder. "See where that lands you."

He leaned back on the bed, hands behind his head, inhaling the meadowberry scent of her pillow. "So you believed I was out diddling nymphs, and you smashed my belongings? You must've been in a fit of jealousy." Possessiveness had always rankled the hells out of him. Strangely, hers made his cock grow harder.

He'd still break her of it though. "This is why we need to work on your jealousy issues. . . ." He trailed off when she removed the shirt she'd borrowed from him, leaving her naked in front of the cracked mirror.

He rubbed his now-aching cock. When he could drag his gaze off her ass, he met her eyes in the mirror. Black forked out over his. "If we're going to be partners on this mission, we'll partner in other ways."

"How's that?" As she wriggled into a tiny thong, light glinted off the metal of her nipple piercings.

He needed to suck those nipples so hard she'd feel him the next day. "Prepare for blood and bed play." Once his task was complete, they wouldn't leave his room for weeks.

"You're bringing up sex again? I'm not looking for a meaningless hookup. Be warned: I'm going all-in with the next guy I sleep with. Relationship, trust, commitment, love. The works."

So young. So immature. "What do you know about any of these things?"

She fastened a lacy bra over tits that should *never* be covered. "I've seen love, and I want it for myself." The combat-boot-wearing blood-drinker wanted romance?

Fascinating woman. Still, he made a scoffing sound.

Her eyes flickered as she explained, "When two people form an unbreakable bond, it's like a reactor, feeding them power and heat and a sense of belonging. It makes them *strong.* They're the true superheroes."

She was so passionate about this, he could almost find himself believing. Then he remembered *reality.* "Dark fey don't love. We aren't capable of it."

She glared at him as she reached for her jeans. "Don't pull that Spock shit with me. Everyone's capable of it."

"Spock?"

"*Star Trek?* TV show? He's all logic and pointed ears."

"So Spock is a fey? They are known for both." Rune was somewhat versed in this world's popular culture since his sources—mainly the nymphs—were. But he wasn't a hundred percent certain about Spock.

Josephine rolled her eyes. "Anyway, I'd never sleep with you unless we were exclusive."

"In your strange imaginings, how long am I not to take another?" That he was considering even a *day* of monogamy . . .

"If you have sex with me, you'll be telling me you want a commitment, a bond between only us. That you will never want another female as long as you live."

He tilted his head as she tugged jeans over her ravishing ass. Then her words sank in. "Given your parameters, sex is decidedly off the table," he said, even knowing he'd bed her soon. He'd seduce her into thinking his way.

Seduction was what he did. "Your views on this are naïve. Not surprisingly."

She pulled on her T-shirt. "Your loss."

He was fine with his life right now. Or, at least, not *utterly miserable*, as Dalli had said. Any other male would kill to have Rune's existence, traveling worlds, warring, and swiving new females each night.

Now this vampire wanted to change Rune once more? "You've known me for four days—and you were passed out for two of them. Yet you think you know me well enough to have a relationship?"

She shrugged. *Yes, Rune.* "I know I won't sleep with a guy without a commitment first."

"Naïve," he repeated. "I'll talk you out of this. Like I said, we're going to work on your jealousy issues."

"I vow to the Lore I will never have sex with you unless we're—"

He traced in an instant, putting his palm over her mouth. *Exclusive?* "Don't say that word. You do not mean it."

She squirmed from his grip. "You sound terrified!"

"Have you not learned your lesson? These vows are not to be played with."

"Okay, okay. You know how I feel on the matter." She fetched her combat boots and socks. "And you know how stubborn I can be."

"Demons need sex multiple times a day," he informed her, stating a fact well known by Loreans. Did he believe she was a Forbearer? Not particularly. But he believed she knew as little as they did. "I'm going on days without." Not since the four nymphs.

When he recalled that rendezvous, he felt not even a twitch below the belt. But imagining Josephine up against that courtyard wall as he pistoned between her thighs got his shaft so stiff, it pained him. "Don't you even want to *try* to land me through sex?"

She stomped into her boots. "Pass."

No matter. Her resistance now would make her eventual surrender all the more rewarding. He turned to the set of drawers, opening one. Inside was a backpack and a scrapbook with the edges of pictures sticking out. She'd drawn abstract designs on the cover.

She sidled in front of him, closing the drawer with her hip. "I'm ready."

"Now I know where to look when I return." So many secrets for a master to uncover.

"Better make sure your return doesn't have *anything* to do with the mission to kill Nïx, or I'll never get to drink again."

What if he went to a nymph covey and Nïx showed up? If he killed the Valkyrie there, that assassination would trigger Josephine's vow! How could he leave the vampire at all? Again, the pressure to kill Nïx weighed on him. "Come, then. We need to start hunting. Besides, I'm keen to leave this pitiful place."

"Go to hell, Ruin."

His shoulders tensed. "I told you not to call me that." The vampire did *not* want to challenge him, not when he was still hard from watching her change and his demon half suffered from lack of sex. Not when their futures were becoming more entangled with every hour. Pressure increased from all sides. "So shut the fuck up."

Her eyes went wide. "*You* shut the fuck up, *Ruin.*"

Gods, she was sexy when pissed. "I wasn't jesting about tanning your ass, little girl." Picturing that got his demon in a lather.

She gave a haughty laugh. "Try it, old man."

Her *defiance* . . . it called up his every primal need to pin her down and make her submit. To cover her and rut till the pressure within him relented. "You wouldn't be able to sit for days."

"I dare you, Ruin." She shoved at his chest with a flash of her fangs.

Like flipping some kind of switch.

The demon in him reacted outside of Rune's control. He lunged at her, one hand gripping the back of her head, the other palming her ass as they flew into the wall. Cinder blocks cracked. He trailed his lips down her neck. "You defy me?" *She wouldn't if I marked her. She'd be too busy coming, surrendering.* "When I'm so much stronger than you?" *She'd respect the male who mastered her.*

"Wall's still standing. Is that all you got, limp dick?"

He shoved between her legs. "I've got your fucking limp—AHHH!"

She'd sunk her sharp little fangs into his neck.

He threw back his head. Fighting not to come at once, he growled, "You can't get enough of me!"

She nodded, lapping and sucking.

"Ah, gods, that's it, baby. Drink me. I want you to swallow me down." Using his grip on her ass to hold her in place, he rocked his swollen shaft between her thighs. *I need on her, in her.*

She couldn't seem to get close enough to him either. Her claws dug into his back, her legs locking around his waist.

This tiny creature wants me as prey. The thought made his balls ache. "Suck me. Drain me!"

"Ummm." She met him, grinding her sex against him faster.

"Ah, I scent you! Your tight little pussy gets so wet. Sweet and slick. Can't stop thinking about your taste." He tried to hold back, to draw out their pleasure. But he could hear her swallowing as she consumed him, could imagine his hot lifeblood filling her lush body, coursing all over her. "Ah, *fuck*," he groaned. "Too good! You going to come for me?"

She whimpered against his neck, sucking wantonly, grinding, grinding. . . .

"Harder!" His shaft throbbed, his ballsac tightening. "You told me you'd fuck me with your fangs—*do it*."

She dug her claws in deep, and she bit down *hard*.

His mind turned over. His cock jerked in his pants. He shoved and shoved, words bursting from his lips. Pleasure racked him, whipped him, made his knees go weak. His bellow was like an explosion from his lungs.

She released her bite to throw back her head. Still writhing on him, she screamed, her pale throat working.

He rasped at her ear, "That's it. You like the way I make you come. . . ."

When she finished with a shiver, she met his gaze. Her irises were black, her lips so plump as she licked them for more of his taste.

They caught their breath, still languidly moving against each other. The moment was thick with . . . something. He felt as if he might say words he'd regret. Or she might.

But he couldn't seem to let her go—

A knock sounded, and she hissed at the door.

He reluctantly set her down, then adjusted his sensitive cock. Curious how she would interact with others—he'd only seen her with Nïx—he said, "By all means."

She traced to open the door. A human male stood outside.

"You *want* me to flay you," she told him. "To contribute to my man quilt. Come back Sunday. That's my sewing day."

The man's face was pale, and he reeked of urine. He offered up a piece of paper. "A woman named Nïx left a message earlier."

THIRTY-FOUR

Jo snatched the note from the motel owner's hands, then slammed the door in his face.

"Come on, then," Rune said. "What did the Valkyrie write?"

Good question. Jo handed over the note. "Too angry to read it."

He unfolded the paper and read aloud: "'Catch me if you can. I'm on a boat to China for some high tea. The highest.'" He met Jo's gaze. "She wants us to chase her."

"You think she's really going there?" Would *they* be going there? Jo had never been out of the South, had only gone as far west as Texas and as far east as Florida. But after a fresh intake of Rune's blood—and a heart-stopping orgasm—she felt ready for anything.

"I believe so. She's too crazy to fear her enemies, and she likes games. She's worse than Loki." Whoever. "If she's leaving us messages, we can be fairly certain she's clocking our moves."

"Then won't she foresee our every attempt?"

"Probably." He crumpled the note. "Gods damn it!"

"Now what do we do?"

"We hunt her there." He cast Jo a resentful look. "This doesn't mean I simply get to quit."

"Maybe she'll make a mistake."

"I don't suppose you've visited China during the scant years of your life?"

"Nope."

He threaded his fingers through his hair. "I can't trace us there either."

"How do you know? Have you tried?"

As if speaking to a child, he said, "Because Loreans can only trace to places we've previously been or places we can see."

"I knew that. Wait . . . You're so old, but you've never been to China?"

"I lived in the Elserealms most of my life. I *visit* Gaia. I've only been to Australia and America."

"How are we going to travel? I don't have a passport." She couldn't take a plane. Couldn't even copy a page out of Nïx's book and take a boat. Not that she could read Nïx's book.

"We go via demon, finding one who's been there. For a price, he'll teleport us." Rune crossed to her stash of cash. "For our journey." He pocketed bills, leaving large gold coins in exchange.

"How do we find a demon?"

"They like to hang out at nymph coveys."

"Naturally, the solution to our problem involves nymphs in some manner." Rune was a one-trick pony. He reached for nymphs the way a gambling addict reached for dice. "What is the big deal with them?" At his disbelieving expression, she said, "We might value them differently where I come from."

"The nymphs are hidden everywhere. If you have a secret conversation, don't have it beside a tree, a rock, or a puddle, because a nymph could very well be within it."

"The ones watching Val Hall for you are *inside* the oaks there?" It sounded as if they ghosted!

He nodded. "They're Dryads, tree nymphs."

"There are different kinds?"

"Yes, based on the elements. Since immortals first kept records, the Nymphae have remained neutral during Lorewide wars, fighting only to defend themselves. Their coveys are battle-free zones and draw every species of immortal, which means you can observe your enemies without worrying about death. Or you can find a demon who can trace you to another country."

"You couldn't sound more admiring."

As if she hadn't spoken, he continued, "Due to their neutrality, they live exceptionally long lives and grow very knowledgeable—that also means there are legions of them. Some say the coveys are the glue holding the Lore together."

"Well, they certainly seem to stick to you."

He gave her a thin smile. "We can swing by the Nephele covey."

"Nephele?"

"Cloud nymphs. Their visitors are more interdimensional. But first we have to pinpoint a more precise location for Nïx, namely the highest place to get tea in China. Fire up your computer and Google it." He frowned. "I can't believe I just said that sentence."

"Google?"

"I learned of it from—"

"Lemme guess. The nymphs?"

"A few of their *patrons* told me Google is like the Oracle of the Elserealms. If you ask the exact right question, you'll be provided a suitable answer."

Jo studied the frayed hem of her shirt. "I don't have a computer. I pretty much shun technology." She was deeply embarrassed by her illiteracy, and didn't want Rune to find out about it before he'd fallen head over heels for her and all.

Again and again, Jo had imagined what would've happened if she'd taken MizB up on her offer of adoption, living with a freaking librarian, a wrangler of books.

Jo would be able to read. She wouldn't have been shot in the face. Wouldn't have been reborn.

Yet now she was beginning to think her transformation had been inevitable. Was it inevitable for Thad? The evidence mounted.

And if he was like Jo, how would MizB handle her precious son drinking blood?

Rune said, "If you don't have a computer, then we'll go to a library."

Jo visited them often—alone. With Rune there, it would be the hardest place to disguise an inability to read. "Or we could head to an internet café near the local college." Still dicey.

"Lead on."

Outside the café, Jo watched Rune extricating himself from a throng of female admirers. Women had lined up to show him how to Google.

Jo had continually thought, *I just got off with this guy.* And yet he'd flashed each one his panty-melting grin.

With one girl's help, they'd learned about Mount Hua, a towering mountain in China. Rune believed Nïx's note referred to the tea house on Mount Hua's soaring summit.

To reach it, one had to inch along a rickety patchwork of boards nailed to the sheer face of the mountain. The ascent was considered the world's deadliest hike. Treacherous sections of the trail had names like Thousand-Foot Precipice, Sparrow Hawk Flipping Over, and Black Dragon Ridge.

Mortals fell to their deaths all the time. Jo was amped to travel to such an exotic and exciting place; Rune had seemed far less enthusiastic.

Now all they had to do was find a demon to get them to China.

Finally, Rune emerged. "Let's get somewhere secluded so I can trace us."

If she'd been alone, she would've disappeared in front of anybody. With a shrug, she strolled alongside him. "The guy who worked in the internet café knew tons about computers, but you chose a random coed to help us?" Jo would bet Rune didn't play well with anyone who had a dick. She couldn't picture him having a lot of guy buddies.

"The female mortal had sexual interest in me, and so was particularly motivated to help with my queries."

"Do you always boil everything down to sex?"

He blinked at her. "When I want something from someone? Yes."

Could she really expect anything different? Rune the Insatiable had used seduction as a weapon for ages. Still did.

Jo frowned up at him. *Does he have ulterior motives for seducing* me?

THIRTY-FIVE

"The Nephele are close," Rune said. He'd traced Jo to a meadow beneath a star-strewn sky.

With no city lights, the stars appeared so much brighter. After that memory flash during the fight with Nïx, would Jo ever look at them the same way? She was growing convinced the answers to her past resided in the stars.

"Ahead is the covey." Rune pointed to a dense patch of fog. "They enjoy mating earthbound creatures, so much so they brought their clouds to the ground."

As a fog bank.

He took her elbow, and they started toward it. *Here I go. Into the Lore.* She could handle this.

She squinted through the mist, murmuring, "Why do you think Nïx went to Mount Hua?"

"You didn't read the history?"

She gazed away. "Got distracted."

"Pilgrims used to seek immortality among the peaks of that region. Maybe there's a grain of truth to the tales, and something is drawing her in. Maybe she wants to test herself on a deadly climb. It's best not to contemplate the motives of the mad, or you'll wind up mad yourself."

Music and laughter carried through the fog. Like a stray drumbeat, groans rang out.

"Do you truly think she's insane?"

"The human who brought us that note reeked of fear. She must've demonstrated her power to him, outing herself, and for no discernible reason? That alone proves her insanity."

"It's that bad for us to demonstrate power in front of humans?" Like crushing a guy's balls one-handed while chewing gum? In front of all the folks in the neighborhood? Enough to get a supervillain name?

"You're jesting, right? It's the one law in the Lore all factions respect. The gods could rain down punishment for any infraction. At the very least, outing oneself to humans is thought to bring horrible luck."

Hunting always seemed to get her in trouble. So why couldn't she stop?

"Have you been attracting attention?" he asked. "Besides shoving me through a building?"

She shrugged. "Sometimes I punish humans a little. When I move to a place, I feel like it's my territory—and like the people within it are mine too. If pimps and drug dealers and gang bangers mess with what's mine, I hunt them. Hurt them. Disappear them."

He looked unsurprised. "Vampires are notoriously territorial."

We are? No wonder she'd been compelled to hunt! "I'm kind of a protector of prostitutes."

He stiffened beside her. "Is that meant to be funny?"

She blinked at him. "No. I really am." She'd need to plan a maintenance visit soon. "So why do the gods get mad when we out ourselves?"

"This is the mortals' world. Though Loreans like to believe it's theirs as well, it *isn't*. They trespassed when they colonized here. Deities look the other way as long as Loreans don't change the course of human history."

"Why do beings come here then?" The fog grew increasingly thick, the grass wetter.

Rune placed his warm palm on the small of her back to guide her. Not as good as when they'd held hands, but a promising start. "Gaia is all but a heaven plane," he said. "Life is very easy here compared to the home dimensions of many species. Immortals gather in certain Lore-rich cities—such as New Orleans. Established communities benefit them further."

That explained why Jo had seen so many more freaks there. "How many dimensions are there?"

"Some say the number is infinite. Many remain unexplored."

Infinite. Whoa. How cool would it be to explore new worlds? Maybe with the guy at her side.

"We near the covey." He pulled up his collar to conceal his bite mark.

"You embarrassed by that?"

He turned to her, his voice going deeper. "Just the opposite. I have a beautiful vampire who can't keep her fangs out of me."

That's fair.

"But I don't want to reveal what you are. Of all the species nymphs fraternize with, vampires are among the least welcome, have been known to drink a nymph dry. You have clear eyes, and you lack a vampire's scent, so you shouldn't have any problem passing for another species. I also don't want to reveal your immunity to my baneblood, not until I figure out the other half of your hybrid."

"Got it. I'll try not to shotgun-drink a nymph while I'm here."

Giggling females traipsed through the mist nearby, wearing wispy dresses that looked like they'd been fashioned from the fog itself. Silvery fringe jewelry dangled from their ears, with more pieces in their hair.

Jo wore jeans, combat boots, and a ratty *Red Flag* T-shirt.

The nymphs joined a group of burly demons with curved, shell-colored horns. Those horns were seriously badass. Jo tilted her head. What would they feel like?

She sensed Rune's gaze on her. She was used to spying at her leisure. Now he was watching her watch others.

Farther along the meadow, they came upon another group. She blinked. Couldn't be seeing right.

Centaurs were mounting ecstatic nymphs. "How is that even possible?" Centaurs had been in Tortua, but seeing them *midmount*, or whatever, made her squeeze her legs together—the way guys did when racked.

Rune glanced away. "An immortal body is capable of unbelievable things."

"I guess you see nymphomaniac orgy scenes like this all the time." He *starred* in scenes like this.

"You haven't? Loreans aren't shy. And nymphs can be witnessed fucking everywhere in the Lore. Especially in a pocket realm like this."

"Pocket what?"

He exhaled. "I can't remember when I last met someone so unacquainted with the Lore. A pocket realm is a dimension that shares the same characteristics of Gaia. Same sun, moon, stars, weather, et cetera." He cocked his head. "You've obviously been sheltered, and you're only twenty-five. That makes me wonder how many lovers you've had."

She jutted her chin. "Three."

He laughed. "Three? Yet more evidence you were raised among monks." He again muttered, "Three," as if that were the punch line of a joke. "How long has it been?"

"A while." What would he think if she told him she'd only had sex a handful of times? "How many have you been with?"

"Can't count that high."

"That's the same answer you gave me when I asked how many you've killed."

All his previous good humor disappeared. Casting her a strange look, he said, "You'd be amazed how closely tied those two numbers are."

No. No, she wouldn't. Jo knew some of the specifics. She considered confessing to the dreams, but reminded herself that four days ago he'd reached for his knife—because he'd *suspected* she might be a *cosaș*.

Probably not best for their burgeoning relationship if he again decided to kill her.

They approached a clearing in the mist, spread over a section of the meadow. The fog floated above, resembling a giant awning. In the center, a fountain flowed with wine. Nymphs congregated there, like super-models at a vino convention.

"Rune!" one squealed.

The rest cried his name and clapped excitedly. When they jumped up and down, their cloud dresses slipped, boobs flying.

They acted like a rock star had entered the premises.

Nymphs surrounded him, jockeying for position, crowding Jo out of the way. With worshipful expressions, they petted his arms and chest. Each promised him secrets. They definitely had his number.

And I thought I could get Rune to fall for me? Stupid Jo. Why on earth—or anywhere else—would a male give up this kind of lifestyle?

"Doves, I'm here to find a demon," he told them, and they quieted. "One who can trace me to every continent in Gaia."

"I know of one," said a nymph with an arrangement of thick blond braids piled atop her head. "What would that information be worth?"

Was the chick angling for Rune to screw her? *Would* he?

"It'd be worth a small favor," he said smoothly. "I can find a demon on my own, but I'm asking you ladies in order to save time. Which also means I can't linger here as I normally would."

Jo could just imagine him *lingering.* How would a one-man orgy work? Would it be a nymph free-for-all? Maybe they lined up the way they had in the courtyard. Her fangs sharpened with aggression.

As much as she liked Rune, she would never share a man. So unless he could keep it zipped, she'd have to move on. Which might be a problem if they were linked by destiny and all.

She reminded herself that nothing mattered more than freeing her brother. Soon Thaddeus would be in Jo's life again. If he was like her, she'd teach him everything she knew about ghosting and telekinesis. They'd learn the rest together. Hope made her giddy. Her future was so freaking bright.

Why should she care if all these women were pawing Rune? Yes, Jo had a crush on him, but crushes could end.

The braid-y nymph said, "I'll tell you, but only if you vow to the Lore you'll attend our next Bacchanal."

"Easy enough," he said grandly. "I vow to the Lore I'll be in attendance—unless an emergency crops up." Tacking on that qualifier.

"You'll wear traditional attire?" another asked excitedly.

"How could I attend a Bacchanal in anything but?" he said, slanting them all that grin.

One nymph *swooned*.

Filled with importance, the braid-y nymph said, "I know a storm demon named Deshazior. He used to be a pirate, but now he's a transporter. He's been all over Gaia."

A pirate? Interesting!

"Where will he be, dove?"

"He and his crew like to hang out at a place called Lafitte's. It's in New Orleans."

Rune looked puzzled, so Jo said, "I know where it is."

Nymphs turned to her and frowned, as if they'd just become aware of her presence.

Braid-y nymph asked, "Who's she, Rune?" No jealousy in her tone, just mild interest.

"Oh, me?" Jo buffed her black claws. "I'm just the chick who made him nut in his pants. *Twice*."

THIRTY-SIX

Move ... move ... move. Outta my way," Josephine ordered pedestrians as she and Rune strode through the Quarter. The sign for Lafitte's was just ahead.

Mortals scattered. Sensing on some level she was a predator?

"Move ... move ... move your ass." No polite *excuse me* from the vampire. As males made way for her, they stared, agog at her otherworldly looks and figure.

"I could lead," Rune offered, increasingly irritated by their reactions.

"Got this. Clearly."

He wouldn't have thought he'd be this attracted to a brash female—especially not one who'd delighted in telling a covey he'd twice come with his pants on. Alone with her again, he'd grated, "Have your fun?" She'd shrugged. *Yes, Rune....*

When the crowd thinned, she asked him, "Did you sleep with all those—what did you call them?—Nepheles?"

"Nephelae. I'm almost certain I slept with them all. I like to spread the love around. If I don't, they feel slighted." Important to avoid.

Hell hath no fury like a sexually neglected nymph.

Apparently he'd burned through every Dryad at Dalli's covey except

one, the comely Meliai, and she was fuming about the oversight. Before
he'd left Dalli's earlier, the nymph had stopped by, hoping to join in.
When he'd blown her off, she'd told him she possessed a key that could
get him around the wraiths—and she'd trade it only for sex.

His wrist rune still showed no alert from the nymphs at Val Hall. Until
Nïx was in residence, the wraiths were a secondary concern. . . .

Josephine had stopped in her tracks, forcing him to turn around.
"What?"

"Slighted? Spread the love? I go through cycles with you. Sometimes I
think you're the greatest thing since bagged blood. Other times, like right
now, I can't figure what I ever saw in you." She passed him, heading toward one of the doors of the crowded bar.

He stared after her. She couldn't lie; she'd truly meant that.

Just as information flowed *to* him, females flowed *to* him. All he had
to do was be himself around them, and situations worked themselves out.
Now was he to monitor everything he said?

No, no, once he started bedding the vampire, her attitude would im-
prove. He caught up with her.

As they entered, he scanned the premises for enemies. The fey
kingdom of Sylvan was a pocket realm of Gaia. Sooner or later Rune
would run into either Sylvan bounty hunters or even King Saetthan
himself.

He pictured his half brother's face, one so like Rune's own. Though
Saetthan had inherited Magh's blond hair and blue eyes, he'd gotten his tall
build and features from their sire.

Saetthan was Rune's most coveted target—of the fourteen left from
Magh's line—and considered himself a protector for the others. . . .

Rune spied no fey within, but in the shadowy back of the bar, a gar-
rulous gang of five demons sat at a table. Each had a different shape to his
horns, indicating his species.

"I believe that's our contact." Rune nodded toward the biggest one.
The male had a colossal chest and the large forward-pointing horns of a
storm demon. When standing, he'd be over seven feet tall.

Josephine breathed, "I'm going to meet a real-live demon." Her steps quickened.

Rune followed. "You've *been* with a real-live demon. I'm half demonic, remember?"

"Yeah, but you don't have wicked cool horns like that dude."

I should. Rune had wished for them his entire life, just as he'd wished for red demon blood.

His gaze roamed over the vampire. What if his blood *were* red? As much as she loved baneblood, how could she crave another kind more? What if baneblood *specifically* attracted her? Later, he would demand to know which kind she preferred.

At the table, Rune addressed the storm demon, "You're Deshazior?"

"Aye, that'd be me," he said with an undeniable piratic accent. His huge paw of a hand curled around a tankard of brew.

"We heard you can assist us with travel."

Deshazior ignored him, turning in his chair to face Josephine. "Are ye lookin' for a ride, me beauty?" A thorough perusal of her body accompanied his words.

Rune did not appreciate this. Deshazior had to assume she was with Rune. At best, the demon's open interest was disrespectful. At worst, it could be taken as a sign of hostility against Rune.

"Yes, we are," she said.

The demon stood, far too close to her, then held out a paw. "I'm Deshazior. You can call me Desh."

She shook his hand, his swallowing hers. "Josephine," she said, craning her head up, seeming enthralled by the male. "You can call me Jo."

Jo?

"Ah, me lovely Jo, let's mosey outside and talk." He finally released her hand. "I need to know where and when I can take ye."

Really, demon, double entendre? As if this pirate had game!

Neither paid attention to Rune as they turned toward the exit. Nearing the doorway, Josephine said, "Oh, duck! You don't want to hit your horns."

Deshazior slanted her a heated look. "And she's considerate to boot?"

Sheltered or not, she must know a mere reference to a demon's horns could be construed as an invitation!

On the street, Deshazior gestured toward Rune. "I figure him for a fey. But what might ye be?"

"I'm a vampire." She would tell the demon that, yet she refused to reveal basic information to Rune.

"Never had much use for vampires," Deshazior said, "till I met a l'il bit named Jo, me first female one." He waved from her toes to her head, asking, "Are ye all this eye-catchin'?"

She beamed, her smile dazzling. "Are demons all so charming?"

Deshazior leaned in even closer. "I've been hard on yer species in the past; teach me the error of me ways."

She leaned in as well, eyeing him. "Do it again, bilge rat, and I'll bite you smartly, then keelhaul your hide."

Deshazior put his paw over his heart and breathed, "Blow. Me. Down."

She chuckled. *Chuckled!* "I speak *Pirates of the Caribbean.*"

Rune was all but forgotten.

"Where would such a winsome vampire need to be goin'? 'Cause I'll trace ye across the worlds."

Rune interjected: "We need to go to China. To Mount Hua."

Deshazior told Josephine, "Ye're in luck. Been all over that country. I can put ye straight at the base."

"All over?" she asked. "No one ever asks you about your horns?" Mentioning them again!

"See me T-shirt?" It was emblazoned with the words *Big Easy Casting.*

She tilted her head. "I see it."

"Folks think I'm wearin' prosthetics for a movie."

"Oh, cool. They're really big," she said, which turned the demon on, those horns growing. Her eyes went wide. "That's wild! Can I touch them?"

Rune's jaw slackened.

Deshazior couldn't dip his head fast enough. "Woman, make me dreams come true!"

"That's enough," Rune cut in. "We're running out of time." They were in no way running out of time.

"Rain check?" Josephine asked.

Voice gone low, Deshazior said, "Oh, decidedly, luv."

Jo was digging Desh!

Not like she did Rune, but she felt a curiously strong pull toward the affable demon.

Desh was handsome in a supernatural linebacker-y way, and his accent was kind of sexy. His horns were even more badass up close.

When he grinned down at her, she gazed up at him with a puzzled smile. For someone who pretty much hated everybody, she had a good feeling about this guy. She could almost imagine she was making a friend.

Her first!

So many things were beginning to change in her life. The future spread out so brightly. . . .

Yet while she'd taken an instant liking to Desh, Rune and the demon seemed to hate each other on sight.

"Name your bloody price," Rune demanded.

Was the dark fey jealous? Or was this another instance of Rune not playing well with anyone who had a dick? She suspected the latter.

"The lady's ride is gratis." Desh didn't back down an inch. "Ye'll be payin' me a gold doubloon—or she goes alone."

Jo muffled a laugh.

With narrowed eyes, Rune took a coin from his pocket, flipping it to the demon.

Desh caught the piece, seeming to weigh it. "It's good gold." He sank a fang into the edge. "It's *old* gold. Where ye from, stranger?"

Rune's lips drew back. "A place where demons mind their own business."

Jo glared at him.

"Ye look like a fey, but ye're barin' the fangs of a demon. Should've known by yer eyes." Desh frowned at her. "Ye understand he's a scurvy baneblood, luv? Walkin' poison and poxy bad luck to boot. If ye're thirsty, the blood of a storm demon"—he pounded his broad chest—"is stout and hearty. I'm a thousand years old, so I'd be aged like fine wine."

Rune bit out, "What the fuck is this, demon? We're here to transact."

Desh turned to him. "I see no mark upon her neck." *Mark?* "If ye reckon she's yer mate, I'll respect that. Otherwise, she's fair game. The fairest."

Rune didn't believe dark fey got mates, much less that Jo was his. So how would he answer that challenge?

"She's not my mate." Rune squared his shoulders. "But she's in *my* bed." Then he added, "Currently."

Her flare of excitement fizzled. Currently. One of his qualifiers—to indicate she wouldn't *always* be in his bed.

Dickwad! Jo told Desh, "We're not exclusive at all. Earlier today, we were discussing how *un*exclusive we are. He insists on it. We haven't even slept together."

Rune grated, "Yet."

Jo ignored him. "Ever."

"Good to know. I'll be givin' ye me number."

"Awesome! Or stop by my digs. I live not far from here at the Big Easy Sleeps." She pointed over her shoulder.

"No shite? The Big Sleazy." He laughed.

"Exactly!"

Rune stepped closer to her, telling Desh, "We need to leave for our destination. You're either taking us, or you're wasting our time."

"I accepted the gold, baneblood; I accepted the gig."

Rune nodded at Jo and said, "Head somewhere sheltered."

"Already thought of that. I know of a place." The demon held out his big hand to her. "C'mere, me beauty." Turning to Rune, he snapped, "Yer arm." He clutched Rune's forearm, then traced them. His teleporting was hard and fast like Rune's.

When Jo blinked open her eyes, they stood in the shade of a rock over-hang. Past the shadows was an expanse of blue sky. Puffy white clouds elbowed the sun. The day was crisp, a one-eighty from the humid night in the Quarter. The scent of pine tickled her nose.

I'm in freaking China! "This is amazing!" She could see the bases of two mountains, but not the peaks. The stone was light in color, the surface dusted with tufts of green. She wanted to see more! She traced to a nearby field, peering up at the white-capped tops.

She reeled on her feet, mind boggled. *So beautiful. So big.* Her first real mountains.

Desh traced to her side. "Gods almighty." His stunned gaze flickered over her face. "Ye're a day-walkin' vampire."

"That a big deal?" She glanced past Desh. Rune was just as astounded.

"Huge," Desh said in a choked-up voice. "Ye should've burned to ash."

So sun did burn vampires. "The light's never bothered me." If she'd ever made friends, she would've liked to go to the beach with them. Lie out. Sip blood from a glass with a little umbrella. "Must be because I'm wicked strong and all."

"I've seen a lot of things in me days, but never something like this. Never." Desh stared at her—the same way she'd stared at the snow-capped mountains. "Ye truly drink blood?"

"One hundred percent of my diet."

Suddenly Desh's body hit the ground, plowing through solid rock. Rune had lunged for the demon, now had his knife against Desh's throat.

"What is wrong with you?" she screamed. "Don't you dare hurt him! I vow to the Lore I'll make you regret it!"

"Another vow?" Rune snapped. "He knows too much! If I don't do this, you'll be hunted. It'll never end."

She'd be damned before Rune decapitated the nice demon in front of her!

"I'll not say aught about the girl!" Desh's eyes met hers. He looked like he worried more about her than himself. "Get away from this poxy bastard, l'il bit. One way or another."

She teed up her telekinesis, but Rune had that blade pressed to Desh's vulnerable throat. She didn't have enough control to focus a precise beam, could end up blowing them both to bits.

But one talent of hers was honed to perfection.

"Make me regret it, then, Josephine." Rune's tone was like steel. "But I can't risk it." He tightened his grip on the blade handle.

Which meant it was time to reveal all her secrets.

THIRTY-SEVEN

Josephine the vampire stood beneath a blue sky. In godsdamned sun-light. In front of this random demon.

Too many thoughts to process:

She's a day-walking vampire, a hybrid. But of what?

Such an asset for the Møriør.

Not even Blace can go out in the sun.

Protect the asset.

Protect. What's. Mine.

Rune snatched Deshazior's hair, yanking the demon's head back.

Suddenly a chill swept over him. He glanced up. Josephine was gone—

His blade hand flung away from the demon, outside his control. His other hand balled into a fist—and slammed into his own jaw! Then again! "What the fuck, demon?"

Freed, Deshazior traced across the clearing. "Not me, baneblood."

Rune fought with all his strength, finally able to overcome the force.

Another chill ran through him. Then Josephine *stepped out of his body.*

She was a faint outline, the skin around her eyes so dark. Her hair billowed as she floated.

She'd been *inside* him. She'd possessed him! The shadowed eyes, the immunity to sun . . .

Josephine was half *phantom*.

He turned to Deshazior, saw the demon's recognition of the same. *Can't allow him to live.*

"Didn't get enough, Rune?" Her voice was as ghostly as her appearance. She sank into the ground.

He pivoted, jerking his head around. Where the hells was she?

A spectral hand breached the surface, clamping his ankle, dragging him down.

He fought, but his own body was dematerializing! Every kick passed through the ground. There was no defense against this. If she wanted, she could haul him to the core of this world, where he'd be crushed to death.

Or worse, what if he *didn't* die?

He bellowed with frustration when he'd sunk to his waist and his arms uselessly passed through rock. "Josephine!" To his horror, she crawled up his body until they were face to face, her ghostly hands clinging to his chest.

She was faint, her visage almost colorless, except for her irises. In her phantom form, they glowed, brilliant blue and amber.

"We've talked about your hurting Desh. It's not happening, understand?"

"Release me!"

"If I do, you'll go solid. Sure you want me to?" They began to rise, like heated air. Once clear of the ground, she let him go.

As he materialized, she levitated, face frightfully beautiful. "You"—she pointed at Deshazior—"vow to the Lore you'll never say anything about me. You"—she pointed at Rune—"vow you won't hurt Desh."

The demon readily said, "I vow to the Lore that I'll say naught about ye to anyone."

Rune's gaze was locked on Deshazior. "You and I both know what she is. And we both know that vow's not good enough." He traced to his knife, telling Josephine, "Will you trust me for once? The demon has to go." When he lunged for his foe, she gave a panicked cry.

Rune's body went flying, crashing into the rock face. Stone cracked; ribs cracked. The entire mountain vibrated.

He fell to the ground. Telekinesis too? Struggling for air, he grimaced from the pain in his side. "Enough, woman!"

Her otherworldly face was filled with menace. "Get it through your skull: you're not going to murder him, okay? I'll keep doing this until you make the vow!"

When she raised her hand at him, Rune bit out the words: "I vow to the Lore not to harm this demon. Today." As soon as night fell . . .

She rolled her vivid eyes at that. "Another qualifier."

"Accept that vow; it wasn't easily given." He forced himself to his feet, his ribs screaming. "We three will live. Today." Though his bow was nigh indestructible, he checked it for damage. Unharmed. He exhaled in relief, then cringed with pain.

Deshazior cautiously approached her. "I'm good with the vow, Jo." His awed gaze flicked over her pale face. "Ye never know what will pop up during an Accession, eh?"

She embodied, sinking to her feet. "You really know what I am? Because I don't."

"Ye're part"—the demon's voice dropped to a murmur—"phantom. Ye're a shapeshifter betwixt life and death."

"Phantom." Her irises wavered again. *"Phantom."* She said the word like she was trying it on. "Yeah. I like that."

Nïx had said, *Death and death all rolled into one.*

"Ye saved me, l'il bit, and I'll not forget it."

She grinned. "Told you I was wicked strong."

Rune regarded her with disbelief. *She has no idea.* He'd already had no intention of letting her go; now there was even more motive to keep her close.

Which had nothing to do with the fact that—in the heat of the moment—he'd thought of her as his.

THIRTY-EIGHT

Y e think she'll be hunted?" Desh said to Rune. "I'd like to see who could catch her."

Damn straight, Jo thought.

With malice in his gaze, Rune ran his fingers down the bowstring over his chest. If she had to guess, he was planning an assassination at his earliest opportunity.

She'd have to extract more vows or something. "Maybe you better go, Desh." She was even more respectful of Rune's strength. He'd somehow fought her possession! No one had ever come close before.

The demon glanced past her at Rune. "This is where an old salt makes his exit." He took one of Jo's hands into both of his own. "Ye ever need anything, ye know where to find me. Fair winds, me beauty." He kissed her hand.

Awww. He was like a big, hot, horned teddy bear.

"Till we meet again." Desh disappeared.

Meet again? Try this weekend at Lafitte's.

"What the hells, Josephine?" Rune snapped when they were alone. "You attack me? I'm on your side, remember?"

"*Currently*, you might be. But as soon as this mission ends, we'll go our separate ways. You made that clear." And it'd really hurt. She'd suspected he would nail and bail her, but to know . . .

"Don't speak for me." He lumbered over to a boulder to sit. "I was protecting you, and this is how you repay me? You couldn't reveal things about yourself to Deshazior fast enough, but you left me in the dark! How could you not tell me about these powers?"

She was stoked she hadn't telekinetically Hulk-smashed him! *An A+ for Jo!* "I kept my abilities close to the vest because I figured I might need to use them against you. Obviously, I did."

"Where is your family? Which parent was the phantom? Where did you come from?"

"Why should I tell you anything about myself? We've traded some orgasms. We both want to off the same Valkyrie. As you were so quick to point out—there's no bond between us. We're only together currently, which means *temporarily.*"

"Bond? Let me explain something. You're going to need allies. And quickly."

"Why are you making such a big deal about this? Wiccae or Sorceri must have similar powers. Can't your witch ally move things with her mind?"

"Yes, but she can't harvest power through another's blood. She can't trace. She can't possess an enemy and sink him into the ground."

"Oh."

"Oh?" He was getting angrier by the moment. "No wonder Nïx called you special! No wonder she's so interested in you and your brother. I should've killed Deshazior."

"He won't talk. He made that vow."

"And what if a *cosaş* drinks him? If this gets out . . ." Rune caught her gaze. "Vampires will want to study you—at best. Others would breed you for day-walking progeny. If the Horde ever crowns a new king, you can be assured he'll try to capture you."

Then she would ghost that king beneath a mountain. "Do you know other phantoms?"

"They're rare. I might have met a handful in all my years. But a vampire/phantom hybrid? I didn't believe they existed. Are there any other powers I need to know about?"

I can dream your memories. "Nope. That about sums it up."

"As if those aren't enough. We need to be on the move as soon as possible, but know this: you *will* tell me your history today." He tugged up his shirt to assess his side. His torso was mottled dark purple.

Oops.

"Internal bleeding. Great work. I'll have to heal this before we face Nïx." Lips thinned, he removed his bow. "The demon's right about one thing. You must be a product of the Accession."

"Keep hearing that term." Nïx had said they'd all have parts to play.

"Let me guess—you might call it something different?" He pulled off his shirt, his muscles flexing.

Despite everything that had happened, she was primed for him, ogling his broad chest.

"An Accession is a mystical force occurring roughly every five hundred years. It brings immortals into contact for good or for ill. Loreans can find mates and make alliances, but mostly death comes to reduce the immortal population. The Lore is already a violent place; it's about to get much more so."

"Accessions sound disturbing."

"They're also times of historical wonders and discoveries. For instance, a vampire/phantom hybrid might surface." His brows drew together, the wheels definitely turning. "Not just one. Your brother is in play as well."

Jo raised her hand again. "Leave him out of this, Rune! You don't even get to think about Thad."

"*You* should've thought about him. If Loreans know what you are and you reunite with him, he also becomes a target."

Shit, he was right. "You left me no choice but to show my powers. Besides, Nïx already knows about us. We're as safe—or as screwed—as she decides."

"That's a precarious position to be in, Josephine. Rumor holds she's steering the entire Accession, bringing about a great war, instead of a drawn-out one. I've told you she flirts with an apocalypse."

"Now you see why I want to fight her. I can drag her down to the center of the earth and make her go solid."

"You've given me a hint of how horrific that fate would be." He pricked his wrist with a claw. Dipping a finger to the welling blood, he used it to draw on the injured side of his torso. The heady scent swept her up as a fascinating symbol took shape.

He'd drawn that on her! She wanted to know what each rune meant. To re-create them. "Will that speed up your healing process?"

He nodded. "Necessary because my *partner* has delayed us." In a surly tone, he said, "I reacquainted myself with curative combinations—when I treated *your* broken body. Without a single word of thanks from you."

He was making her feel like a bitch. To be fair, he'd only wanted to kill Desh to protect her. And he had saved her from Nïx. Because of Rune, they were on the Valkyrie's trail.

Yet Jo had kind of broken all his stuff. Guilt weighed on her. "Thank you for helping me."

He wasn't listening, his attention on her face. "You don't wear a glamour."

"Not quite sure what that is."

"Some creatures use spells to enhance their appearance. I thought the shadows around your eyes and the pale skin were part of your look."

"They *are*."

"Good," he said. "Good." Seeming to drag his gaze away, he checked his side. Beneath that symbol, his bruises were fading. "No wonder your tracing felt so peculiar. You made us intangible first."

"Yep. I can make things I touch turn to air, if I want them to."

"The ramifications . . ." He was clearly working out all the angles. "Is it easy to possess others?"

"As easy as breathing. I sometimes call it ghosting. I *ghost* into a *shell*."

"How many *shells* have you *ghosted* into?" He drew his shirt back on, then slung his bow over his chest.

"Tons. I hang out in them."

"So I was just another shell today."

She shrugged. She needed to steal a memento from him. Unfortunately the talisman was out. "Shouldn't we get a start?"

"This conversation is in no way over. We'll revisit it later."

"Just like we'll discuss how you're *not* going to hurt Desh once the day ends."

Rune pointed his finger at her, opening his mouth as if he was about to lay into her, but then he just scowled.

In the distance, she heard excited voices. A tour group? Their enthusiasm was contagious. "Come on, Rune." Jo waved at one of the mountains. "Time to climb!"

His irises flickered as he gazed up and up and up. "Can't wait. . . ."

THIRTY-NINE

Rune's harried thoughts weren't enough to keep his mind off the yawning drop beneath his feet.

He and Josephine had navigated carved steps to reach the Plankway in the Sky—a wooden path thousands of feet in the air, affixed to the side of the sheer mountain, one of the steepest on this world.

Strangely, the lift that would've saved them hours of ascent was out of order.

Senseless thrill-seeking humans were about, so he and Josephine couldn't trace to the top. Besides, he couldn't see where to land, and he'd never been there before.

He sidled along the narrow path, cobbled-together from scrap boards. The plankway had no railing, just a length of chain stretched across the rock face for a handhold. He gripped it with clammy palms. The sun beat down on them, and sweat dripped from his forehead, burning his eyes.

Rune had few true fears; acrophobia, the fear of heights, was one of them.

Ahead, Josephine bounded along, utterly fearless.

Utterly *surprising*.

Rune's determination to bed her had only deepened. Her show of strength fueled his desire, but sex would also bind her to him—and therefore to the Møriør.

His mission had expanded: kill Nïx and recruit Josephine. And once Rune did, would the brother follow his sister to their side?

The Møriør could have *two* hybrids of unimaginable power.

He lost sight of her around a sharp bend. Not far behind him, adrenaline-pumped mortals laughed and yelled to each other.

He transferred his sweating grip from one chain to another. He was seven feet tall; these boards weren't intended to hold someone of his size.

When Josephine skipped back to him, the planks vibrated just from her scant weight. The rusted bolts attaching wood to stone squeaked.

Perspiration dotted her forehead and misted her thin T-shirt. Tendrils of her shining hair were damp. Sun struck her face, and he marveled anew that she was a day-walker. In the light, she seemed as delicate as gossamer, her pale skin slightly pinkened. She was exhilarated, her eyes appearing even brighter against those seductive shadows.

He was glad she wore no glamour. Her looks were forever unique to her. He could stare at her spectral face for hours.

"Up ahead, the view is sick! You can see miles down." She'd discovered his discomfort and delighted in giving him grief. "There're no more planks. It's just little foot holes carved into the rock. Hmm. Your feet are really big. I wonder if they'll even fit."

Josephine could float or ghost or whatever she called it. She could all but fly.

When she casually leaned a shoulder against the rock and crossed her arms over her chest, he wanted to snag her close.

"Why are you afraid? If you fall, you can trace right back here."

"I'm not afraid. I'm . . . cautious. I've told you I didn't grow up with the ability to teleport. My *cautiousness* developed during my childhood."

"But you can trace now."

He knew that. Yet phobias weren't rational. "This is not my natural element." He'd been born and raised to labor in the fens, assassinate Magh's enemies, and fuck her political targets. He was never supposed to climb mountains.

"Your natural element seems to be on top of nymphs. Starting to realize how limiting that is?" She gave him an exaggerated frown.

Despite his unease, he yearned to kiss her quiet. "I want to be on top of you."

She shimmied around him, holding on to the chain with the crook of a finger. "All you have to do is whisper promises in my ear."

She made no secret she wanted more from Rune—talking about love and commitments—but he suspected this was merely the infatuation of a *very* young female. "I'll have you eventually. I know you crave sex with me."

"I crave a lot of things I don't get. Them's the breaks."

"It's not possible for me to be exclusive."

"Possible?" She snorted. "Because you're such a lady-killer? Because your big swinging dick says, 'Baby, I gotta be free'?"

"Maybe it's not that I would desire other women. As a secrets master, I use sex to get information. That's my job—but you'd expect me to quit it right at the Accession?" What in the gods' names would it take for someone to accept him as is?

She nodded with understanding. "One day you'll find a nice female who'll put up with your 'job'. Listen to my words, Rune: I am not that woman. If you stepped out on me, I'd kick your ass to the curb."

"You think I couldn't seduce you to see things my way?"

"Never. Your best bet is to forget all this"—she gestured at her body—"and find that dark fey you had a lead on."

He frowned at the reminder. During the two days he'd held vigil over Josephine, he could've returned to Loa's, enjoying the shopkeeper *and* getting that lead. In the past, he would've hounded Loa.

Now, he had difficulty picturing himself with any female other than Josephine. "Perhaps I could be persuaded to try an open relationship with you—a long-term commitment that allows us to stray, but always to return to the bed we share."

"That's your idea of a commitment? Maybe we call it something different where I come from." The little wench winked at him. "In any case, why would I settle for less than I need when I'm only twenty-five?"

"Because you aren't fixed in your ways."

"Says who? I want promises that my guy'll be in one bed: mine."

"No doubt a vow to the Lore? You're power-mad for those vows. What if we committed, and you realized your feelings for me were just an infatuation? A schoolgirl crush? We've known each other for such a short time."

Instead of reassuring him she felt more, Josephine said, "I bet I could get Desh to make me a pledge."

Rune's eyes narrowed. "By the way, a male demon's horns are considered sexual organs. Your asking to touch them was as good as offering a hand job. You probably didn't know that, since you're mentally the equivalent of a human. I'll give you the benefit of the doubt."

"You're right. I didn't know that." She tapped a black claw to her chin. "But I will the *next* time I ask him."

Rune clenched his jaw. She *could* proposition Deshazior—doing anything she pleased with the demon—and Rune couldn't say a word about it.

Whatever she read in his expression made hers light up. "My old man's jealous of Desh! I'll bring you around."

"Or maybe I'm furious that a fledgling storm demon disrespected me. He was only a twinkle in his sire's eyes when I was six thousand years old!"

In a singsong tone, she said, "Jea-*hel*-lous." She floated higher to nip the tip of his sensitive ear!

He didn't know if that made him want to fuck her, spank her, or hug her. "Perhaps I'll run into some *Orea* up here, nymphs who live on high mountaintops. Then we'll see who's jealous."

She alighted on the plank again. "And what would you do with them? Bone them? When you're so scared?"

"I'm not scared. I'm just not overjoyed."

"My man is old and jealous and scared too." The sun hit her dazzling smile.

Gods, she was stunning. "I'd simply rather be somewhere else. Now, shut up, child."

"So it wouldn't bother you if I did this?" She jumped up and down, bouncing the plank. "Will the Orea come and save their favorite stud?"

"You'll pay for this when we get to solid ground."

"What if I did this?" She inched closer to him. Closer. She didn't stop when she reached him, just proceeded—into his body.

"Josephine, *no*." Chills skittered up his spine. Yet at the same time, having her inside him was curiously . . . erotic.

They began to dematerialize. "What are you doing?" Dread overwhelmed him when his fingers passed through the chain.

She stepped off the fucking ledge; they hovered in the air.

He peered straight down at the drop. His lungs seized, his heart about to explode. *Trace away!* Would she move with him? Or would he throw her off? What if she lost control and fell? Mind in chaos, he yelled, "Enough!"

She floated him back to the plank, then disentangled herself. Once she'd solidified beside him, his phobia kicked in with a vengeance, applying to her as well. "Stay on this godsdamned plank." He shoved her between him and the mountain—leaving room only for his toes to remain on the board.

"What'd you do that for? You're hanging off the edge now."

He bit out, "I don't *know*. You need to be kept close. But not bloody inside me." In this position, he could see straight down her shirt to her pale cleavage. Just to distract him, a bead of perspiration trickled past her necklace, down between those alabaster mounds. When he focused on that view, he found this situation wasn't as troubling. In fact, he was hard. He wanted to lick the sweat from every inch of her skin.

She walked her fingers up his chest, twining her hands behind his neck. "My dark fey's protecting me again?"

He dragged his gaze to her face. "It wouldn't be the first time. I did try to safeguard you below."

"You were so fast against Desh! And you're a lot stronger than I thought. Which is saying something since I saw you drop a building when I spied on you."

He'd never scented her when she'd watched him—because she'd been *air*. "My strength comes with age. In the Lore, *old man* means *strong man*."

"I feel your strength when I'm inside you. Possessing you gives me a high."

"You've done it to me more than once?" It struck him. "In Tortua."

She nodded. "I wanted to make sure I had an out if you tried to gank me or something. So I found an *in*."

"Why would you ever materialize? You're invincible as long as you're intangible. Why not go twenty-four hours a day?"

"I like having a body."

He would like having her body as well. "Have you possessed others when they have sex?"

She grinned. "Oh, yeah."

He clutched her closer. "Do you make them do things?"

"I'm a voyeur only. I try not to make shells move. Messes with their minds."

"You don't say." His jaw was sore from his own hits. "I had no idea why I was punching myself in the face. And then to step off the ledge?"

"I usually can't sense anything inside a shell, but I tasted your fear and felt your heart thundering. Sorry I scared you." Just as her delicate fingertips had climbed up, they began to trail back down.

"What're you doing, Josephine?" He barely recognized his voice. Gods, she made him feel reckless. And exhilarated.

Young.

"It's like I've got *you* cuffed. You can't escape my clutches." Her hand dipped to the waist of his trews, then inside. She gasped to find his cock erect and aching for her attention.

"Why would I ever want to escape?" he asked, hissing in a breath when she thumbed the crown in a mind-numbing circle.

She moaned, her nipples hardening against her shirt. He needed to touch her too! Battling his fear, he released the chain and rewarded his palms with plump flesh.

FORTY

I would kill to take you," Rune murmured, nuzzling her ear. "I'd fuck you right here."

He cupped Jo's tits, getting so caught up he seemed to have forgotten all about the drop below. "You really would?" She shivered when he swept his thumbs across her nipples.

"Say the word. Though I wonder if I could last long enough to get you ready." His brows drew together. "That's another sentence I never thought I'd say."

"Get me ready?" Next to his bowstring, his shirt opened into a V, revealing damp skin and that rune on his chest. She wanted to trace it with her tongue.

"You're so tight, Josie. I'm going to do everything I can to keep you from hurting."

She grasped his dick at the base. Couldn't fit her fist around it. "I take your point. But you don't have to worry about how tight I am"—she leaned in to kiss that rune—"because I won't sleep with you unless we're monogamous." She darted her tongue to his skin. He tasted delicious, the salt of his clean sweat making her moan.

She wanted to keep kissing down his torso, to the rune around his navel. Then head lower to the hot, swollen part of him that pulsed in her palm. When she stroked him, he rocked to her grip.

"You're a wicked little tease." He tweaked her nipple, drawing a whimper from her. His other hand dipped down her front.

"Tease? You haven't seen anything. What if I used telekinesis to stroke you?" She moved her hand on him. "You could be standing across the room, and no one would see I was jerking you off. You'd never know when to expect it."

His eyes lit with excitement. "I want this!"

Then stick around. "Soon. It's still kind of new to me. I just learned how to do it at your place."

"Is that why you destroyed everything?" He started unbuttoning her jeans.

"Partly. Plus I *was* jealous."

He unzipped her, then grazed his fingertips above her thong. "I knew it."

"Is it so bad to want this"—she squeezed his dick—"all to myself?"

His nostrils flared.

"And then you could have me exclusively too."

"I want . . ." he trailed off. "Damn it! Mortals approach."

The mountain was teeming with them. With a last stroke that made him shudder, she drew her hand from his pants.

He cursed under his breath, then zipped her back up.

"Rain check?"

"The second time you've asked for that today," Rune said. "Will mine or *Desh's* be honored first?" Totally jealous!

He could deny it all he wanted to. Hell, he was even trying to deny *her* feelings. Schoolgirl crush? Bullshit.

She gazed up at his penetrating eyes—glowing magenta in the sunlight—and things grew clear. The facts: He'd pleasured her more than anyone ever had, and his expression promised more soon. He was the strongest male she'd ever met, the smartest, the most accomplished. Taking his blood made her feel connected as never before.

She knew from his memories that when Rune loved, he loved deeply. Why *wouldn't* she want him for her own?

He and Josephine sat on a bench, watching the sun begin to set, and even Rune could admit the sight was a spectacle. Maybe she *was* making him see the worlds anew.

Earlier, they'd reached the summit and explored, then cased the teahouse. He'd detected no sign of Nïx, no lingering Valkyrie scent. They'd beaten her here.

Most of the humans were dispersing—leaving a few couples and the occasional night climbers with headlamps on—so he and Josephine had found seats to soak up the last of the sun.

Both of them were lost in thought, but the silence was companionable.

Josephine was likely imagining her reunion with her brother. He feared she was building up their meeting so much that disappointment was sure to follow.

A troubling notion.

He ought to be plotting their next move, but his musings were fixed on the day-walker beside him.

He ran his hand over his chin, replaying their interaction. He really had expected her to deny his crush accusations, perhaps convincing him of her feelings.

What *would* happen if her infatuation waned? Wouldn't that be ironic? Rune wanting a tart more than she wanted him.

He still couldn't believe she'd possessed him. More unbelievable—he wouldn't mind if she did it again, as long as she didn't float him off a mountain. . . .

When a young vendor strolled by with a cart of wares for sale—food, gloves, even jackets—she asked Rune, "Will you buy something?"

She didn't look cold and wouldn't be interested in the food. "Ah, you want a souvenir, then. To go with your others," he said, clearly delighting her. "What shall we get for the table in your motel room?"

Her entire visage seemed to glimmer. "It doesn't matter what—so long as it's from here."

He stood and surveyed the cart. Candy bars, Red Bull, peanuts. The only thing with distinctly Chinese lettering was some kind of drink in a ceramic jug.

Rune pointed to it, raising his brows at the vendor. The mortal male mimed drinking, then stumbled in a circle. Josephine laughed.

Ah, alcohol. Rune took one. The vendor was happy to accept U.S. currency.

Returning to her side, Rune asked, "Do you want to try this?"

"You drink it, you poor thing. After the stressful day you had?"

He grinned. "Have your fun." He uncorked the jug, eyes watering at the smell. "Good gods, this will be strong." He tried a taste.

"What's it like?"

Unusual. "It doesn't burn going down, and yet I can tell the alcohol content is high." Perfect. When she fed later, she'd grow intoxicated. He took a healthy swallow, drinking for two.

He'd already planned to loosen her inhibitions to get information from her, but now he had even more reason. Though today had answered a lot of questions, it'd raised so many more.

Why had she been separated from a brother she loved? And why hadn't she known her own species? Where were her parents?

Why hadn't she been taught to read?

Earlier, when he'd suggested they stay near the summit, she'd said, "Where will we sleep? Maybe in one of the hermit caves we passed? You probably didn't see them, with your eyes squeezed shut and all."

Smart ass. "We'll get a guest room on the mountain."

"How do you know they have them?"

"There was a notice in English on the bulletin board." She'd stood beside him, appearing to read it.

"Oh, yeah." She'd shifted her gaze away. "I remember reading that."

With that statement, Rune had realized two things.

Unlike natural-born vampires, Josephine was physically able to lie.

And she probably couldn't read.

In Tortua, he'd tossed the *Book of Lore* at her. Thinking back, he could see how frustrated she'd been. And the fact that she hadn't harmed a single page in his library was telling; he believed she *wanted* to learn.

Teaching her English wouldn't be hard, but it would take time and commitment. For once in his life, he didn't know where the future lay with a particular female. He took another long draw from the jug.

The final light of the day hit the peaks, rays streaking the stone. When was the last time he'd watched a sunset?

As night fell over the mountain, the temperature quickly dropped. He wrapped his arm around Josephine, pulling her close. An unfamiliar wave of . . . *something* washed over him.

Relaxation? Satisfaction?

She drew back to gaze up at him with those luminous eyes.

Death and death rolled into one? Then why did she look so *alive*?

"What?"

After a hesitation, she leaned her head against him and sighed.

"Right now, I bet you think I'm the greatest thing since bagged blood."

"Right now, you're not so bad, sport."

For a male who'd never hoped to have a fated female, he was settling in with Josephine at an alarming rate.

Only known her for a blink of an eye. . . .

Then why was he picturing his emotions as an expanding flame?

FORTY-ONE

Jo and Rune sat next to each other in a mountainside restaurant. Outside, the temperature kept dropping and the wind picked up, making the structure quiver, but their spot in the corner was warm and cozy. Paper lanterns cast a muted glow. Soft strains of exotic music sounded.

Even to a blood-drinker, the food scents were appealing. She needed to steal something from this place to remind her of her first dinner date.

Rune had arranged for them to get a room in a guesthouse and a meal. Dinner and a bed. She wondered how often he'd done that with a female.

Just three nights a year meant twenty-one thousand times.

Let that one alone, Jo. She wouldn't overthink this, not when she'd shared such an incredible day with him. He'd bought her a souvenir—her first *real* one—and then he'd held her on a bench, like that couple in New Orleans.

This was really happening!

After sunset, they'd taken a few minutes to return to Tortua and her motel for warmer clothes. She'd placed that emptied jug on her table beside the groom's cufflinks.

With her new memento, she would remember the day she'd spent exploring a mountain in China with her dream guy.

"What are you thinking about?" he asked now.

"This entire day."

"What was your favorite part?"

"Teasing you on the plankway was fun. And I loved watching the sunset with you." When he'd put his arm around her, Jo had concluded that the more he got to know her, the more he liked her. So she'd decided to open up to him tonight.

Of course he'd been holding back—because *she* was. Once he realized she was awesome, he'd fall into line.

The restaurant host, an elderly man with a shaved head and a bounce in his step, brought them menus, indicating they should read one side.

One side, Chinese. The other, *English*. Shit. She'd have to get food to look human!

"Shall I order for you?" Rune asked.

Relieved, she handed her menu back. "Sounds good."

He ordered something that sounded like *bee-yang*, along with some *bie-jo*.

"What'd you get?" she asked when the host bustled away.

"A noodle dish and more of that drink from earlier. Now that I think of it, I should have asked you. Certain foods might spice my blood and skin. You probably have preferences."

She didn't know. In the interest of opening up more, she admitted, "I've never bitten anyone but you. Well, except for my own wrist." Vampire masturbation.

He inhaled sharply. "If I saw you do that, I might spontaneously come." Then the rest of her admission hit him. "*I* was your first?" His tone couldn't have been smugger.

"Yep, your blood converted me. I can't go back to bagged."

He grinned. "It's that good. I'd wondered if you like mine *because* it's black."

"Maybe red blood would taste different coming from the flesh. Like the difference between fresh and packaged food." Even so, it could never compare to Rune's. "I've got time to figure it all out."

His grin faded. "You expect to drink indiscriminately? Only Horde vampires do that. They take so many memories their eyes grow red and their minds rot." He'd been relaxed, but now irritation simmered.

"You're jealous to think of me biting another, huh? It *is* kind of like sex—with the licking, and the lips, and the penetration. Just think, other guys would react the way you did. I'd get blood; they'd get a nut. Just as nature intended."

He didn't say anything, but his fists clenched.

Exciting! "Well, it's not like I have to worry about any of this right away. I'm drinking only from you." She cast him a nonchalant smile. *"Currently."*

The host returned, interrupting the tension at the table. He set down a decorative jug, similar to the one from earlier, and two small glasses. When he poured the clear liquid, the strength of the alcohol stung Jo's nose.

Rune sipped it, nodding his approval. As the host walked away, Rune shot the glass, used his fey speed to down hers as well, then poured another round.

"Do you always drink so much?"

"I'm drinking for two."

"Ohhh. I would get tipsy from your blood?"

"Let's find out." He turned to face her, his big frame concealing her from view. He used a claw to pierce his forefinger. "Look at your gaze lock on my blood. You think you could give it up for another's so easily?"

She grasped his hand. "I never said I didn't love yours."

In the lantern light, his irises darkened to the deepest plum as he rasped, "Suck."

She pulled his finger to her mouth, closed her lips over it, and drew. His blood did taste different tonight.

He stifled a groan, using the heel of his other palm to adjust his erection. "Look at me when you feed."

She gazed up, and he murmured, "That's it. Fuck, I could come right here."

Her claws dug into his skin. She knew the feeling!

"You love my taste."

Growing light-headed, she eased her suck, but he said, "Ah-ah, a little longer."

She took a few more swallows, then released him, licking her lips.

He palmed himself again. "How was your dinner?"

"Delicious as ever, but with a kick."

As if she'd proven some point, he said, "That's what I thought." His good mood was restored. "And how are you feeling?"

She couldn't stop grinning. "Wonderful."

"I suspected it would hit you quickly. The alcohol will get into your system much faster than it does mine."

"Is that stuff the strongest you've ever drunk?"

"In the realm of Pandemonia, the demons make a brew called lava liquor that will put you to your knees."

He was so world(s)ly. Was it any wonder he fascinated her? She put her elbows on the table, resting her chin in both hands as she stared at him. "How many realms have you been to? Wait—lemme guess—you can't count that high."

"Exactly." A hint of a smile curved his sexy lips.

She sighed. "Remind me to figure out how high you can count. What's your favorite world?"

He held her gaze. "Right now, Earth is ranking *very* high." Flirtatious Rune was irresistible.

"Would you have come here if not on a mission?"

"I visit on occasion. But Tenebrous—the home of the Møriør—has been very far from Gaia and its planes. Tracing that distance can be demanding, even for immortals our age. The realm is moving closer as we speak, but still takes days to get there."

"Realms can move?"

"Ours can."

"Tell me about the Møriør. How many are there?"

He seemed pleased by her interest. "Including myself, ten. But we'll eventually be a dozen. Møriør means *twelve*. Or *soul's doom*. Most of us have been together for thousands of years."

"How did you get involved with them?"

"I was in a dungeon. Orion, our leader, freed me. He's descended from gods, *very* powerful."

She laid her hand on Rune's forearm. "Why were you imprisoned?"

"Long story short—"

"Lemme stop you right there. If it concerns you, I will never want the short story."

He gave her a considering glance, but she could tell he'd liked that. "Very well. My father was the king of the fey kingdom of Sylvan. My mother was a slave he used. When I was born, he spared my life—against custom—but didn't give me a life worth living. He died when I was fifteen. His widow, Queen Magh, forced me to become an assassin by holding my mother's life over me. I later learned she was already dead."

"I'm sorry, Rune." He'd just confirmed those dreams of hers were indeed his memories. What else would she see? "Then what happened?"

"I was too good at my job. In time, there was no one to kill, no one to interrogate. So Magh sold me as a . . . slave. I suppose she expected me to lose my mind or wallow in misery. But I became cold, and I endured. She forced me back to Sylvan just to torture me. Orion found me in her dungeon and freed me. Because of him, I was able to exact my vengeance on Magh."

"Then he has my thanks. I'm glad I never planned to spy on him."

"What are you talking about?"

"Nïx wants me to get information on him, won't let me see Thad until I do."

Rune raised his brows. "So your solution is to assassinate her? Seems like a blunt-tool approach, doesn't it?"

"Yep. It eliminates the obstacle. My motto? Squeeze until something breaks."

"I'm discovering you like to keep things simple."

She nodded. "Even though I'm not spying, I want to know more. Had you met Orion before he freed you?"

"No, never. Yet he somehow knew I would become the greatest archer in all the worlds."

Rune said this matter-of-factly, as she did when she informed folks she was wicked strong. *It's not bragging if it's true.* "You told me your bow was a priceless gift. Was it from Orion?"

"Yes, the Darklight bow." He plucked at the string. "You do listen to me on occasion."

"Every now and then. Why's it called Darklight?"

"It was crafted from Yggdrasil, one of the world trees. The wood was harvested beneath a full hunter's moon, but cured with the fire of a sun dragon. Even my strength won't break it. Which means I can shoot very, very far, and very, very fast. With the right arrow, I could pierce a mountain with ease. In the Elserealms, I'm known as Rune Darklight. It's my surname, as much for the bow as for my species, I suppose."

Josephine Darklight. Sigh. She would love to take his name, to finally become someone other than Josephine *Doe*. He'd asked her for her family name only once, but he'd promised to get all her secrets. Soon, she'd entrust them to him.

"Maybe I'll take you shooting one day," he offered, his tone casual.

One day equaled *future.* "I'd like that." She glanced down at his ever-present quiver. "Why are your arrows different colors?"

"They each have a specific purpose. I use blood runes to bespell them."

"I want to learn those symbols."

He frowned. "Why?"

"Because they're badass. And they're how you got your name."

"Learning them is easier said than done. Perhaps I'll teach you a couple."

A couple? She'd already memorized all the ones he'd drawn on her and the one he'd used today. "Let's see your arrows."

He drew out one with a white shaft and feathers. His runes shone in the dim light.

She noted the symbols.

"This is a bonedeath arrow," he said. "Shot into the ground, it will pulverize the bones of anyone within screaming distance." His expression was impassive; he didn't sound proud or ashamed.

Yet he considered her ghosting him into the earth horrifying? "That arrow doesn't hurt you or your allies?"

"I make us immune. I'll add runes to spare you as well."

"So that's what Nïx was talking about." *When she'd been breaking my limbs.* "Have you ever shot one of those?"

"Today I used it against troops of ice demons before I went to Dalli's. She's my friend I told you about." He returned the arrow.

"Dalli's a friend with benefits?" No denial. He'd gotten with that female less than a day ago. Jo's claws sharpened. It seemed like weeks had passed. "So you had time to get busy with a nymph *and* go into battle?"

He shrugged, his demeanor all *no big deal*, then moved to the black arrow. "We call this"—he tapped the feathered end—"one-and-done. When I shoot a target in the neck, the arrow severs his head cleanly, which makes things tidier when I need proof of a kill." His fingers skimmed a gray arrow. "This one is the *eraser*. It will explode an immortal's body into small chunks."

That'd probably be a trip to see. "And the red arrows?"

"I've dipped the arrowheads in my poison. Most Loreans won't survive even that dose."

"Who was the last person you assassinated?"

"A descendant of that queen. Before I killed Magh, I swore I'd stamp out her entire line." Just talking about that female made his eyes glint with hatred. "Each Møriør wants something in the Gaia realms. I work toward retribution."

"Do the others have vendettas?"

"Some, but there's more." He seemed to be deciding how much to tell her.

"Like what? Do you plot worlds domination?" she asked, trying to lighten his mood once more.

Deadly serious, he said, "Yes."

Whoa. "Are you going to set up some kind of dictatorship?"

"How would that be different from what you do in your neighborhood? You police it and protect your people from threats. Imagine if your actions alone kept your entire neighborhood—no, your *nation*—from absolute destruction." He shot his glass, then picked up hers. "I want you to meet Orion. He'd best explain it to you."

Rune wanted to introduce her to his people? "You'd arrange a meeting?"

"In time. As I've said, you need allies. You could have none finer."

"Do any of the other ones have a mate?"

He coughed on his drink. "Why would you ask that?" He cleared his throat, emptied the jug, then signaled for another.

"Because I'm totally yours."

He looked rattled. "I'm not even a demon. I'm a dark fey—and they don't get mates."

"Says who?"

"I've never met a dark fey who had one."

Funny how he didn't say *Jo* could never be a possibility. "But you don't know a lot of them, right?"

"I thought we agreed you had a crush."

She crossed her arms over her chest. "Nope. Wouldn't have agreed with that."

"Then explain how you can be so sure."

"The first time blood touched my tongue, I knew I was a blood-drinker forever. I didn't need to date Blood for a few months and then move in with Blood and meet Blood's family to be sure."

"Yes, but that's instinct."

"Exactly. Don't you trust yours?"

Instead of answering her, he asked, "Do you think the reverse is true? That I'm yours?"

"I thought they went together."

"Often, but not always." He leaned in closer, peering into her eyes. "Am—I—yours?"

She leaned in as well. "I'd—lay—odds."

He drank again. "When a Lorean male finds his mate from a different species, the female is usually resistant. I've seen more than one acquaintance go to hellish lengths to secure a future with a mate who is *other*. I'd expect you to fight every step of the way. Not ask for a commitment on day four!"

"What a breath of fresh air I am. Look, I know what I want, and I've been waiting for this. So just spitball with me. What would happen if I was your mate and we had sex?"

"My body would recognize yours. I'd begin to produce seed for you," he said, his voice getting huskier.

"You like imagining that?"

His eyes darkened even more. "The idea of filling you with my cum? Fuck yes, it's erotic as hell." He scrubbed a hand over his mouth. "Yet the reality would prove to be anything but—if this were even possible. Everything in me is poisonous. Why should I expect my semen to be different?"

"But I'm immune to everything in you." She turned his question back on him: "Why should we expect your semen to be different?"

"Would you take that risk? If there's an infinitesimal chance you're mine, there's a chance you could die in agony."

"I'm immune to you; you're delectable to me. Seems we're *compatible*, huh?"

He was either surprised or frustrated by her blasé attitude, or both. "There's more. After giving you seed you might not survive, the demon in me would need to mark your neck with a bite, forever signaling to other males you're taken."

So that was what Desh had mentioned. "It'd be like getting a tattoo? You have tattoos—I want one!"

"No, no, it's not like that." Definitely frustrated. "It would be invisible to all but demons."

She pouted. "I wouldn't be able to see my own tatt?"

"Will you let me get to my point? I would sink my fangs—also lethal—deep into your flesh. Could you withstand so much poison in your body? What if the effect is cumulative?"

"You'd screw me, come in me, *and* bite my neck? You just described my dream date." She shivered. "So what will I do?"

He shot another glass. "Females climax from a demon's bite."

"Sign. Me. Up."

He was getting agitated. When he poured more of his drink, some sloshed over the rim. "Why would I go seven *thousand* years without a mate? What's your explanation? I'll tell you mine: because it was never going to happen anyway. You can't change my thinking on this. I've had eons to accept my fate."

"It's because I wasn't born yet, sport." She poked his chest with her forefinger. "I just arrived on the scene twenty-five years ago. Plus, it's an Accession. You said Loreans find mates around those times. So while seven thousand years sounds bad, in truth I've only missed the first thirteen Accessions of your life."

He swallowed.

Boo-yah. "Hadn't thought about it that way, huh?"

"You truly believe you're mine?"

"Yep."

He stared her down. "I guarantee you're not."

She nodded with understanding. "Because I'm Desh's? I guess I could have my dream date with him."

Rune ground his teeth until a muscle ticked in his wide jaw.

The host returned with a tray of food then, serving two large bowls. Each had a big noodle folded into it with vegetables on top. It smelled appetizing, and poor Rune was going to need his strength tonight.

"Go on and eat. I'll still be your mate in twenty minutes."

FORTY-TWO

I'm gonna go out on a limb here," Josephine began grandly as they strolled along a terrace, "and make a blanket statement. I like alcohol." She swerved, so Rune put his arm around her.

He might've given her a jot too much. She'd had two more draws from his finger. "I think I've created a monster." At least she was prepped for questioning.

"That blood mead you mentioned? Completely down with trying it. Hey, been thinking about phantoms . . ."

She'd asked him myriad things about her species, but he'd had little information to give her.

In all seriousness, she said, "If a phantom has an orgasm, is it a phantasm?"

He grinned. "I'm certain of it."

She craned her head up, coming to a stop. "Look at the stars. I love stargazing."

"Have you ever flown on a plane?" Over dinner, she'd admitted she'd never been out of the American South.

"Uh-uh."

"Then at this altitude, you're closer to the stars than you've ever been."

Her red lips curled. But then her brows drew together. "Wasn't there another time . . . ?"

"Another time?"

"Aren't they tempting? Maybe I'll float up to them." She reached up as if she could touch them. "They're mine. I saw them first."

"What do you mean?"

"'S nothing." Josephine faced him again. "Where are you taking me?"

Arm draped over her shoulders, he led her down a stone path. "I told you. It's a surprise." He lifted his face to the wind but scented no Loreans on this mountain. He heard no Orea. Time for questions. "I'm curious about something. How could you not know what you are? Did you never know your parents?"

"I don't know."

Even drunk, she was going to stonewall him? "You either knew them or you didn't."

She kicked a pebble on the path, tripping, but he steadied her. "I don't have any memories from before I was eight or so. It's just a blank slate."

He stopped, turning her to face him. "How could that be? What's your first memory?"

Her gaze grew distant. "There was a shroud of crystal covering me, and a warm bundle in my cloak. I jerked upright, banging my head against the crystal, shattering it. Then the bundle moved! I was holding a baby."

Dear gods. "Go on."

"I assumed he was mine, because I didn't know how old I was. In the end, Thaddie was my kid anyway."

No wonder she was so protective of him.

"I didn't know where I was. Who I was. *What* I was. But I knew the baby would need to eat. My God, he could scream. So I set off. Walked till my feet bled, till we were found."

She and Thaddeus had been foundlings. Rune pinched the bridge of his nose. "Who discovered you, humans or Loreans?" he asked, though he knew the answer.

"Humans. They said I'd been speaking gibberish. They blamed my memory loss on a head injury."

That explained why she knew so little about the Lore. "Then what happened?"

"They gave us names, posted bulletins to find our parents, then put us into social services. We were the 'Doe children'. We crapped out on our first foster placement."

"Why?"

"Guy stuck his hand down my pants."

Rune's fists clenched, claws digging into his palms with the need to kill. "You will tell me how to find him."

She waved that away. "Got him back. Burned down his house with his own Zippo."

In time, Rune would track down that male and do far, far worse. Somewhere in this world, a human had no idea he'd just been marked for torture and death by an immortal assassin. But even Rune's dark plans didn't appease the wrath in him. He inhaled for control.

"I took Thaddie, and we started living on the streets. I raised him from an infant. He was my number one."

"You were a girl! What did you know about taking care of a baby?"

"I knew jack shit, had to figure out everything quickly. I learned to speak English in record time."

She and Thaddeus would have been utterly vulnerable, yet she'd somehow kept them both alive. Adding to the difficulty, she'd been a hybrid in a world of humans. "How did you hide your powers? Your need for blood?"

"I got my powers and began to drink on the same day. Not until I was eleven."

"Why then?"

"I kinda burned down this gang lord's house—sensing a theme?—so he kinda shot me in the face. Six slugs to the head. *Ow*, you know?"

Rune's gaze dropped to her necklace. He hoped she hadn't already offed that fuck. *Adding him to my kill list.*

"I woke up in the morgue, in a body bag. I thought I was a ghost."

At eleven years old. Though she was only twenty-five, she'd experienced more shock and uncertainty than some immortals who'd lived for centuries.

"That same day, I slit the asshole's throat."

Already dead. Pity. "Go on."

"When his blood sprayed, it hit my mouth."

"You didn't bite him?"

"I was squeamish about putting my lips on him, much less my tongue and fangs." She peered up at him to say solemnly, "I'm a very picky eater, Rune."

"Noted. Why were you separated from Thad?"

"After I 'died' from gunshot wounds, this librarian took him in. MizB. When I went to steal him back, he didn't recognize me 'cause I was all vamped up—my looks change with proper nutrition, I guess. MizB and her husband were good for him, and I thought I was some kind of evil resurrected demon or something. I thought Thad should be with his own kind," she said evenly, but she was alternating between intangible and embodied, betraying her feelings. "I should've been in a grave; what right did I have to him?" She lifted her necklace. "That's why I wear this. It's a reminder of the day I became something that should never be around an innocent boy." She frowned. "Or it *was* a reminder."

Not to know about the Lore . . . or her own species? How had she developed such a strong sense of herself? Where did her confidence come from? As before, these answers only begged more questions.

"I tore myself away, letting Thaddie live his life. Somehow I kept my distance, never seeing him again." She fixed her gaze on Rune's. "Not until the night I thought you were trying to kill him."

FORTY-THREE

Jo had left out certain parts of her story, like her fear of floating away, but she was proud of herself for revealing so much. *Baby steps.* Alcohol had made it easier to confide stuff and had her feeling . . . spectacular. Specter-tacular! So what would Rune think about her history?

Though his expression gave away nothing, his grip had tightened on her. "What will you do now that you know Thad is a Lorean, the same as you?"

"I'm not sure he is. I don't think he drinks blood." A few months ago, he'd been in a hot-dog-eating contest for charity. "And he's not pale like me, was never sickly like me."

"But if he's your full blood brother . . ."

"He is. I sense that strongly. Sometimes I have the vaguest memories of a woman with shadowy eyes. I think she might be . . . our mother. But why would I have powers while he has none?"

"Perhaps your shooting was a catalyst, speeding up your transition."

"You talked about females freezing into immortality in their twenties. How'd I regenerate so young?"

"I don't know," he admitted. "I can't think of another species where the young regenerate. That must be a hybrid power."

"So I couldn't have been transformed from a human or anything?"

He shook his head. "Transformed into a vampire? Perhaps, though females aren't known to survive the transition. Into a phantom? Again, it's unlikely. Into both? Impossible."

"Then Thad *is* like me," Jo breathed, ghosting again.

"Nïx's unusual interest in him only serves as more evidence."

"I stayed away from him for so long." Grief rose up inside her. All those lost years . . . "I can't explain how hard it's been."

He laid his warm palms on her shoulders. "Did you have no one to lean on? You took three males into your bed—did you have a relationship with any of them? Love one of them?" Earlier, he'd laughed when she'd told him her number. Now his eyes flickered as he awaited her answer. "Well, have you been in love?"

Jo shook her head. "I didn't fit in with humans, and I'd never even talked to a Lorean before you."

Josephine had been completely alone.

Those two nymphs in New Orleans had told Rune she would roam the streets, appearing sad. He hadn't been able to understand it then. . . .

She was gauging his reaction. He sensed she'd stop talking if he looked like he pitied her, so he kept his expression neutral. "The woman you remember—do you think she was a phantom?"

Josephine nodded.

How had that female been separated from her two offspring? Had she been in a war? An invasion? "Aside from the Valkyrie, is there anything to prevent you from reuniting with Thad?" *From both of you joining our cause?* Thaddeus would become as much a target in the Lore as Josephine; the Møriør could keep him protected until he'd transitioned.

"He has that human adoptive mother. Even a grandmother. He's really close to them. MizB didn't accept me when I was eleven—I doubt she will now when I have so much blood on my hands. In any case, I want what's best for Thaddie. I'd keep away if I thought that would help."

It won't. "You can take it as it comes, once we remove the Valkyrie from the equation."

"I know you think I'm telling you all this 'cause I'm drunk, but that's not why." She eyed him. "When we were watching the sunset, I made a decision to be more open with you."

She'd been thinking about me? "Why now?"

A light snow began to fall. She raised her pale face to the flakes.

He gently pinched her chin to get her attention. "Why now?"

"Because the more you know about me, the more you like me."

He couldn't deny that. "Are you so determined for me to like you?"

She shrugged. *Yes, Rune.* "You should like your mate."

He dropped his hand. "This again?" He was about to fall back on his known-each-other-for-only-four-days argument—

Wait. No, it was worse than that. She was infatuated with him—simply because he was the first Lorean she'd ever spoken to!

She'd never known another being with powers. Fate could have substituted any immortal male for Rune the night they'd met. Josephine would've drunk the other's blood, then grown attached.

Damn it! Hadn't she responded to Deshazior with like enthusiasm? If that demon had come upon her first, she would fancy herself in love with him!

"Why's the breeze warm?" She glanced over her shoulder. "What's around the next corner?"

"Go see," he bit out, following her into a narrow canyon. How to turn infatuation into something more lasting? So he could secure her for the Møriør.

When the canyon opened up, she rushed toward a small pool. "Hot springs? This is amazing, Rune." He'd read about this place today.

Steam rose from the water. Tall boulders circled the pool, buffering the wind. Snow accumulated on the stone, but flakes melted a couple of feet above the water. Strings of paper lanterns stretched from one side to the other, making the haze appear to glow.

She wasted no time undressing: boots, jeans, shirt. In her lacy thong and bra, she descended the natural rock steps into the water.

That body would be the death of him.

She ducked under and emerged, smoothing her wet hair back, revealing her perfect ears. "Come in!"

He recalled Dalli's words: "Win her." He wanted an iron bond with Josephine.

Then the forge had best be hot.

FORTY-FOUR

Jo didn't know what had gotten into Rune, but as he strode toward the edge of the springs, with his eyes so dark and threatening, her laughter died. As if in response to a threat, her body tensed, her mind becoming more alert.

He started to undress, his movements growing quicker and quicker, until parts of him blurred.

She blinked, and he was in the water with her naked. She swallowed hard as he stalked closer. Steam dampened his smooth skin and his black hair. As his torso flexed, his tattoos glided over chiseled muscle. Soon the water would erase that blood rune on his side.

Standing before her, he used a claw to slice away her bra and then her thong, tossing the scraps away. "Nothing comes between us." He grazed his knuckles over a nipple, his silver rings clinking against her piercing. "Tell me why you've seized on me, Josephine." He coiled his arms around her, drawing her close, trapping his straining dick between them. It was hotter even than the water. "Why do you want more from me?"

Breathless, she said, "Because you're mine."

"Why. *Me*?" He grasped her nape. "I'll tell you—because I'm the first

Lore male you've ever known. If you'd met another before me, your attentions would be fixated on him."

Dickwad! As if she didn't know her own mind? *And* he was harshing her buzz.

"You're too bloody young and inexperienced to—"

She cupped his sac and tugged.

"Josie?"

"You're making me sound like an idiot. Which doesn't mesh with me being extraordinary in every way, now does it?" Yank.

Groan. He eased his legs farther apart for her and rocked his hips.

"If you underestimate me, Rune, I will always have you like this: by the balls. Get me?"

His gaze locked on hers. "Two can play at that." He cupped her pussy with a firm grip.

She sucked in a breath.

He rubbed the heel of his palm against her clit as he murmured, "Do you want to play nice with me?"

Jo did, she really did. She let go of his balls—and grasped his shaft.

Each time he kneaded her, she stroked. "That's it, Josie." His free hand caught hers, and he linked their fingers.

They stared at each other, both fondling beneath the surface of the water, both breathing heavy. Their clasped hands squeezed rhythmically.

Then he leaned down to take her mouth, his tongue seeking and twining with hers. She moaned into the kiss, making him groan again.

Still cupping her, he slipped his middle finger into her pussy. She dimly realized her feet were no longer touching the bottom of the pool; he held her in the palm of his hand. She gave a cry, stroking him fast.

He took her mouth over and over, slanting his lips. He kissed her like he wanted to scald her. *Brand* her.

Her breasts slipped against his rigid chest, her nipples raking along his skin. When she thumbed the head of his cock, another of his fingers found its way inside her.

By the time he broke away from the kiss, she'd gone boneless, happily resting in his hand.

In a husky voice, he told her, "I'm going to take you."

First thought: *Where?* "Ohhh, *take* me take me." Maybe she was still a *little* drunk. "But today, on the mountain, I was thinking. . . ."

"About what?"

"I'll need my hands for this."

Curiosity lit his eyes, and one of his sexy ears twitched. He freed her and set her down.

She ran her palms up his tattooed torso, rubbing his flat—and clearly sensitive—nipples, then laced her hands behind his neck. She tugged him down so she could reach his ear. Nipping his lobe, she whispered, "I wanna suck your cock, Rune. Can't stop thinking about it."

He shuddered. "A *very* feasible alternative." He traced from her to the steps, sitting on a higher one, which put most of his dick above the surface.

She rose in the waist-deep water taking her time to join him, loving the view.

Molten gaze eating her alive, he started to masturbate his big cock for her. "You want to take this between your lips," he rasped, his tongue daubing his own. "You need to suck on it." That smoldering sensuality . . .

She nodded, spellbound. Each stroke of his big fist made need tighten in her belly. *Up. Down. Up . . . Down . . .*

Once she reached him, she leaned in to kiss his throat, but not to bite. She eased lower to lick drops from his chest.

He cupped her tits, weighing and massaging them.

When she grazed her teeth over one of his nipples, all the muscles in his mighty body tensed. "I'm not to be teased tonight." He gave her breasts a squeeze to show her he meant business.

"Uh-huh." Ignoring him, she moved to the other one, twirling her tongue as she gave it a sizzling suck.

A gust of breath left him.

When she nipped it, his hips bucked.

"You're sensitive." Continuing down, she nuzzled the damp hair at his navel. As she'd fantasized today, her lips followed his tattoo, her tongue flicking.

"Enough! Don't you see what you've done to me?" He tilted his hips, jutting his cock upright. "Put me out of my misery."

She grasped his dick, about to kiss it.

"Ah-ah. Meet my eyes. I want to see your true reaction."

She raised her face. "Reaction?"

"Some females crave this; some don't. Never gave a fuck before. Now . . ."

Gaze holding his, she slowly licked the tip.

He groaned and tightened his hold on her tits.

She swirled her tongue around the head, then licked the slit. When she probed that dip with the tip of her tongue, his legs quaked around her.

"Wicked little girl."

His taste! She could do this forever. As she flicked kisses all over the plump crown, she tried to keep her eyes on his, but bliss made her lids heavy.

"You love it, don't you?" He rocked his hips up so she could reach his balls.

When she nuzzled them, his head fell back. Then she tongued that rippled flesh. He growled when she sucked on one, then the other. But his shaft called her back. "Hard as stone." Beneath his taut skin, veins pulsed. She hungered for his magnificent cock *and* the blood stiffening it.

He lowered his head again to watch her. "You said you're never duplicated. I'm not so easily replaced either, am I?" His lips curved into that arrogant grin.

She wanted to wipe it off his face. *You asked for it, dark fey.*

She grazed a fang along his shaft, drawing blood.

Rune inhaled a shocked breath, lusting for more of this blood play, craving her darkest kiss. Could he coax his *picky eater* to bite him there . . . ? The idea made him even harder.

Both of them watched black blood welling.

She lapped at it with delight, panting for more.

"Do it, then! Sink your fangs into my cock." He cupped her lovely face, commanding her with his eyes. "You'll pierce me as you were pierced."

With a nod, she opened her mouth to take him. He felt her breaths against the bulbous head as she stretched her lips around it, enclosing it.

"Yes!" Her mouth was a sultry paradise. "Now bite. *Do it.*"

Below the crown, her fangs slowly sank into flesh, pricking it.

He bellowed to the sky, "*AH!* My gods!" He palmed her head, trapping her to him.

Her wanton moan vibrated his length. With her first draw, his back bowed uncontrollably, as if a physical force was arching him to her. He almost came instantly, hovering right at the edge.

But he needed to see her, to witness this female's taking. He lowered his chin. "*Fuck,*" he breathed as she sucked.

The most erotic thing he'd ever seen.

In an awed tone, he said, "You're feeding from my cock." How could a male care about power dynamics when a female this beautiful seared him with forbidden pleasure?

This was a fantasy come to life, one he'd never known he had. He threaded his fingers through her hair, reveling in her bite. Just when he thought this sight couldn't get hotter, one of her hands dipped below the water, between her thighs.

Disbelief. "Are you fingering your pussy?"

She didn't have to answer; her mesmerizing eyes grew even more hooded.

Fingering herself. While she suckled his raging dick for blood. "Gods almighty." His balls drew up, but he struggled to hold out.

With her other hand she fisted the base of his shaft, claws digging in.

Were her instincts telling her to secure her prey? Vampires were posses-sive. Did she consider his cock hers?

"Take more!" His swelling veins felt *too* full of blood. He had more than enough for both of them. "I want you greedy for it."

Her moans grew louder, keening. She released her fangs, still sucking from his pierced skin as she eased her head down. When her carnal lips slipped along his shaft, his hands guided her lower, his hips rocking.

She took him deep—then sucked until her cheeks hollowed.

"Uhn!" He could *feel* her drawing from his veins. Pressure pooled at the base of his spine, his release imminent, but he needed to last till she was sated, slaked in more than one way. His voice went guttural. "That's it. Suck it like it belongs to you."

She swallowed more of him, and he wished he had semen to give her too. "If I could spend, I'd make you drink every drop of my cum."

She whimpered. Beneath the water, her hand sped up.

"You'd like that? I'd fill you with blood and seed. Make you accept everything from me." Pressure kept building. His muscles flexed in readi-ness. His balls ached; his rod throbbed. Unfamiliar impulses struck him.

He needed to bite *her*. Sink his demon fangs into her pale phantom flesh.

Possess *her*. Be inside *her* body.

Own her.

When she jerked against her hand, and his length muffled her scream, he yelled, *"I can't hold out!"*

She was orgasming with his dick in her mouth. She *was* greedy—as she came, she took more and more of him, till her throat closed around the entire crown.

"Oh, FUCK!" The pressure was anguish. He was helpless against it. Nothing mattered past releasing it.

Heat exploded inside him, radiating out from his cock. *"AHHHH!"*

Ecstasy lashed his body, piercing him like her fangs. His shaft pulsed against her tongue over and over as he came.

Head spinning, he floated, feeling as weightless as when she'd possessed him. . . .

With a tender kiss, she released him. Her face was flushed, her eyes lustrous. "Dessert was heavenly."

"Come here, beautiful." He reached for her, drawing her into his lap, squeezing her too tightly. He rested his forehead against hers, catching his breath. He barely recognized his voice as he said, "Is it time for your breakfast yet?"

FORTY-FIVE

Later that night, Jo dreamed.

She'd fallen asleep in a guesthouse bed, her limbs tangled with Rune's; yet now she found herself in a dank cell, beaten and bloodied after a session with Magh and her torturers.

This had happened to Rune, was another of his memories. . . .

He stared at the ceiling of his cell. Anything that bitch wanted of him, she'd gotten, changing and reshaping him so many times he thought he would break.

Now she was breaking his body over and over in this putrid hell.

She'd just finished with him. "You will surrender your pride, cur." She hung up the whip she favored. "I won't rest until you beg for my mercy." Each time he refused, she set her demon guards upon him.

Tonight they'd broken his right leg; the jagged end of his femur jutted through his skin. Two ribs breached his flesh as well. His hands were bound behind his back, so he couldn't use runes to heal himself. "Shouldn't a lowly whore be beneath a queen's notice?" he bit out, spitting black blood in her direction. "But I now know why you visit me each night. You believe if you could only make me grovel, you could shake your desire for me. Then you'd stop fantasizing about me when you're fucking others."

Rage flashed in her eyes. "Tomorrow night will not go so well for you, cur. I'm going to bring out the pincers. . . ."

For hours after she and the guards had gone, Rune stared at the ceiling in agony, muttering his usual prayer: "Gods give me the power to destroy that bitch, and the entire royal house—"

"And what if we did?" a grating voice interrupted.

Rune jerked his head around to find a stranger in the shadows. The male's face was indistinct, but his eyes were dark, like bottomless pits.

"We?" Rune attempted to sit up against the wall, choking back his pain. "Are you one . . . among the gods?"

The towering male crossed to stand outside the cell, far closer than most did. "I'm one among the number five. In time, I'll be one among the number twelve. I'm known as Orion."

"Why are you talking to me? You must not know who I am."

This Orion merely stared, his expression unreadable.

"I'm Rune. I've been a whore for centuries." He nodded down at his body. "Presently, I'm Magh's favorite whipping boy."

"I've come to this place for you," Orion said. "Now answer the question, archer."

Archer? "If you gave me the power to destroy her and all her line?"

"Would your resolve never falter?"

This being had no idea! Gritting his fangs, Rune fought to stand. Though one of his legs was shattered, he managed to rise on the other. "Never."

Orion stepped back to inspect the cell door.

"The bars and cell are mystically reinforced," Rune said between ragged breaths. "No being can break—"

The door flew open.

Rune's jaw slackened. "How did you do that?"

"The universe is inundated with weaknesses, archer." Orion entered the cell. With another wave of his hand, he freed Rune's manacles.

No time for shock. Rune pierced a finger for blood, then began to draw healing symbols on his leg.

As Orion gazed on with interest, Rune told him, "I had to relearn these when patrons got too rough." The magicks mended skin and knitted bones. Experience had taught him how to manipulate the bones to facilitate the healing.

His broken arm was next. Orion waited patiently until Rune's body was restored, then said, "Why don't you make your farewells to Sylvan, archer?"

"I'm not an archer," Rune said. "If you freed me because you believe that, I appreciate the mistake, but I won't pay for it."

"You will *be an archer."*

If you say so. *Rune had never picked up a bow in all his life. Still, there was something so mesmerizing about the male. As if Orion saw secrets Rune could never know without him.*

Orion said, "Upon your taste of triumph, return to me, and you'll know still more. Lifetimes of it."

After lifetimes of failures?

Rune didn't have time to argue. No one had ever escaped this dungeon; Magh would never expect him. She might not have blocked off the secret tunnel leading to her chambers. If he could defeat her personal guard, she'd be helpless.

Like a crazed animal, he traced to the tunnel. It was unsealed? Such hubris!

With each foot closer to his target, Rune grew more enraged. Tonight she would die. Her long immortal life would end.

Yet even in the midst of his fury, he kept thinking of the mysterious male in the dungeon. Rune could tell Orion hadn't wanted to fuck him—or break him. So what was his interest? Why save someone like me?

Lifetimes of triumph? Rune craved that so badly, he shook.

First, vengeance. He set upon Magh's guards. Moving so fast he was a blur, he used his fangs to tear out their throats before they could yell.

Inside the queen's chamber, he gazed down at her slumbering form with revulsion. His sweat mixed with demon blood and dripped from his forehead, splatting her face.

She woke, eyes widening as she drew a breath to scream.

He snatched her by the throat, throttling her. "The monster you made has returned to its creator." He traced her to his dam's grave, then released her.

She rubbed her neck. "H-how did you get free? Did you offer sexual favors to a traitor?"

"Guard your tongue, Magh. Or I'll take it from you."

Her gaze darted to the burial mound. "What do you want from me?"

"Payment."

Expression calculating, she stepped closer to him. "I can give you a castle filled with gold."

"Think it will be that easy? How much are you offering for my mother's life? For the centuries you forced me to whore?" Every dawn, to be under that sword . . .

"And you obviously loved it!" she hissed. "Offered freedom, you still preferred to mate creatures for coin."

"Loved? As you love to torture me? You're maddened with desire for your whipping boy, and it guts you!"

The truth was there on her face.

"If you harm me, my offspring will avenge me," she told him. "Saetthan will take your head with his ancestors' sword. The last thing you'll know is Titanian steel."

"No. Because I'm going to hunt down your spawn and all of theirs. Saetthan will fall like the others."

"That's your plan? My heirs are guarded far better than I was. Most live in other dimensions. How will you find them?"

"One—at—a—time."

She swallowed. "Will you murder me first? Burying me here?"

"Pollute my mother's grave site with your foul body? Never."

Confusion. "Then what?"

"I thought about taking a like retribution. Selling you into whoredom, and watching customers brutalize a former queen. They'd pay extra for you to wear your crown," he said, relishing her look of horror. He'd always envisioned centuries of revenge on her. Yet that would take time and involve risk.

A stray thought arose: Orion awaits, promising triumph. *"Instead, I'm going to give you what you've always needed and secretly wanted."*

"And what is that?"

"My kiss."

True terror shone in her eyes. He yanked her closer. She tried to turn away, but he was far too strong.

His kiss was cold as ash. As deadly as flame. . . .

Jo woke in shock, gasping a breath. Rune had endured that torture? Surviving it?

For ages, Magh had claimed his last kiss. The lips that brought Jo pleasure brought others doom.

Good. She was glad he'd gotten his revenge on that bitch! Jo's satisfaction faded when she recalled what she'd learned.

Earlier, Rune had confessed Magh had sold him, only to buy him back for torture. But he hadn't only been a slave; that queen had forced him into sexual slavery.

Jo remembered him asking her in bed, "Were you a pleasure slave?" There'd been a hopeful note to his tone. When she'd told him she was a protector of prostitutes, he'd tensed.

She put her hands over her face. She'd called his home a *whorehouse weekender.*

Cheeks burning, she sat up and stared at him sleeping. Pre-dawn light filtered in through a window, lovingly painting her dark fey. His face was relaxed, calling to her. His head was turned, his hair fallen back to reveal the side of his shaved scalp and his ear. It twitched. *Even in sleep, he's listening for enemies.*

Her heart ached at the thought. Had he never known peace? She hoped Orion had given him the triumphs he'd promised.

She would have to confess these memories to Rune soon. But he and Jo had come so far, even over the last day. How would he react knowing she'd discovered his innermost secrets?

She exhaled a long breath. Wanting only to comfort him, she gazed over his body. He was hard beneath the cover.

He needed; she wanted to give. She might not be able to deliver peace, but she could deliver pleasure.

Mission accomplished, Jo thought when she heard Rune whistling from the nearby washroom.

They'd just shared a brief, lukewarm shower after "breakfast." As she waited for him to finish shaving, she dragged clothes from her bag.

She'd only intended to give him a blowjob, was kissing the tip when he'd awakened. "I was just dreaming of this very thing," he'd said in a sleep-roughened voice. "Does my beautiful girl want her breakfast?"

He'd maneuvered her body until she straddled his mouth at the same time. Between kisses, he'd commanded her to feed.

After she'd come till her vision was blurry and he'd released so hard his heels had planted into the mattress, she'd tried to crawl off him, but he'd smacked her ass. In a surly tone, he'd growled, "Want my breakfast too," then he'd lazily licked and nuzzled until her toes had curled. . . .

Despite her recent cataclysmic orgasms, lust kicked in yet again. How was she going to hold out from having sex with him?

When he'd worked his fingers inside her, telling her how badly he wanted his cock to replace them, she'd wanted it too.

After her dreams, she didn't know if he would ever commit to her, mate or not, considering what he'd suffered in the past. But she did know she could never share him.

She'd just finished dressing when he returned with a towel around his waist and a wide grin. Could he be any finer? "Somebody's in a good mood."

"A stunning hybrid woke me with head and rode my mouth. I'm in a *great* mood." He dropped his towel, reaching for his clothes. "I'm going to have to insist on breakfast in bed every day."

As he pulled his leather pants up his long muscular legs, she followed the movements of his shaft until he tucked it away. "Roger that."

"Did you wake hungry or horny?" He drew a fitted gray shirt over his head.

"Actually neither. I just wanted to make you feel good."

He frowned, as if this didn't compute. He sat on the bed and beckoned her with a crooked finger. "You're going to have to explain this to me." He dragged her onto his lap. "Will I have to get you drunk first?"

She laid her palms on his face and tenderly kissed his lips. When she pulled back, his brows were drawn.

"Little female, you say a lot with your kiss. But I don't understand the language—"

A boom of thunder sounded, shaking the guesthouse.

They shared a look.

"Nïx?" Jo bolted to her feet.

He ran out of the room like a bullet. She was right behind him. The sun was creeping up over the horizon, rays striking clouds and sparkling off the new snow.

With his hunter's eye, he surveyed the area and pointed to the highest terrace. "It came from the top." He took a split second to grab Jo's hand before he traced there, ever careful to have her on the mission.

The clouds might conceal them from humans. Didn't matter at that moment. They both wanted Nïx dead so badly, they risked exposure.

None of the stragglers on the terrace had noticed Jo and Rune appearing, were too busy rubbing their eyes after what must've been a hellacious lightning strike.

Jo pivoted in place, didn't spy the Valkyrie. "Do you scent her?"

He shook his head. "What is she up to?"

"Did she return to Val Hall?"

He checked his wrist. Dark.

A monk padded out of the teahouse, heading straight toward them. With a welcoming smile, he handed them a note. He spoke in Chinese, but Jo made out "Nïx" a couple of times.

Thanking the man, Rune accepted the parchment, and the monk bowed and walked away.

"Another clue?" Rune ripped open the envelope. "The Valkyrie plays with us. She's digging her own grave." He skimmed the note.

"And?" Jo asked.

"And now we go to Rio."

FORTY-SIX

Rio had been a total bust. So had the next eight locations the Valkyrie had lured them to.

Now Jo and Rune waited on the Bridge of Spires in Venice, with no sign of Nïx.

It was after three in the morning, and the bridge was empty. Jo had spotted a stray drunk driver—gondola version—but passersby were sparse.

Rune paced, bow at the ready, scanning the night with those intent archer's eyes. The breeze ruffled his hair and his loose white shirt, and moonlight sheened off his leather pants.

Every day he seemed to grow more gorgeous. Where was the upper limit?

The bite mark on his neck from earlier was healing, and soon he'd insist on feeding her. They'd discovered twice a day was optimal for her. When they went too long, *he* would get antsy.

"She's not coming," Rune said. They'd been here an hour before three, the time given in the Valkyrie's last clue.

Considering how easily Nïx had evaded them, she must be using her soothsayer powers to predict their movements.

Though Jo worried for her brother, Rune assured her he would be safe—even more so with the unpredictable Nïx constantly away, out leaving bread crumbs for them.

Rune had decided to give this pursuit one more night before requesting help from the Møriør. Unfortunately, the moving realm of Tenebrous was still days away. And he hadn't wanted to call them in to assist with *his* responsibility. But for Jo, he would.

Which meant she'd have Thad back soon. What would he think of Rune? For the first time, Jo had to consider how different parties in her life might get along.

Rune did not play well with other men, so he might come across as arrogant to the easygoing Thad. Her brother might strike Rune as woefully immature.

By Thad's age, the dark fey had been a seasoned killer. Yet never had he tracked a target as elusive as Nïx. . . .

Over the last twelve days as he and Jo had followed the Valkyrie's clues across remarkable worlds, Jo had encountered one wonder after the next. She'd witnessed a "million-hoof" stampede in the centaur dimension. She gawked at mind-blowing exhibits in Brooklyn's Morbid Anatomy Museum. She'd dodged ginormous feet in the land of giants and ascertained that they went "true toga" (hot poker for her eyes!).

Yesterday, Nïx's clue had led Jo and Rune to the Fremont Troll under a Seattle bridge. Humans thought the cement sculpture had been created as art, but it actually marked a portal to the troll realm.

If I never go back to Trollton, it'll be too soon.

She'd enjoyed watching Rune in action in the various lands they visited. He was always collected; nothing freaked him out. So many beings they'd met looked up to him, except for the giants, of course. But they'd respected him.

Rune spoke tons of languages, and if he drew that Darklight bow, creatures quaked. He was more well-known on other dimensions than on the mortal plane, and he seemed to like it that way.

Oftentimes, Jo and Rune had been forced to delay their travel, waiting for a demon transporter or for a Trollton muck-nado to pass.

In those lulls, they'd continued exploring their combustible chemistry, yet he'd still given no indication they would be exclusive. She maintained she would never accept anything less.

How much longer can I deny him sex? Especially when she'd begun losing her heart to him.

Last night, he'd murmured in her ear, "Refuse me, then, but we both know it's inevitable. It has been since the first moment I saw you. From the first moment I scented you. . . ."

Jo gazed down at the moonlit currents streaming under the bridge. She and Rune were stuck at an impasse.

Why can't he commit to me? Despite their sexual tension, they'd settled into a companionable ebb and flow. If one of them got discouraged, the other brought the fun. If one didn't feel like talking, the other would pick up the slack.

They were becoming so attuned, they often finished each other's sentences. The last time it'd happened, he'd given her a puzzled look. "Sometimes, it seems like you know me better than the allies I've fought beside for millennia—allies who can read my mind and speak telepathically to me."

She'd smiled pleasantly, telling him with her expression: *It's because I'm your mate, sport. . . .*

After Mount Hua, they'd awaited Nïx in Rio, laying up in a beachfront hotel. With Jo's head on his chest, they'd listened to the waves roll in. She'd told him, "I want to know more about the symbols you draw."

"Most people's eyes glaze over if I talk runes. Do you recall any of the ones you've seen?"

She'd leaned up. "I can draw all of them."

Smirk. "Sure you can."

Glare. "Watch me."

He'd been shocked when she'd drawn one—much less thirty. "You did remember them all!"

"Like it's difficult?"

He'd translated them for her. Most were simple. "That one indicates *purity of purpose*. The second means *victory*—or rather, *domination*. That one means *nightmare*. The combinations are just as important as the rendering."

Whenever they had time, he'd taught her more. As he sketched, he would grow relaxed, often giving her additional details about his mother. "She could have hated me, the son of a despised foe—not to mention that I was considered an abomination—but she adored me."

As he'd spoken, Jo had experienced a flash of a memory: the sight of his mother smiling down at her son with utter love on her pretty face—and the fullness in Rune's heart for his beloved "dam." Jo had realized she might not remember all of her memory-dreams until something triggered her recollection.

He'd told Jo that his talisman had been a last gift from his mother, was his most cherished possession.

Then Jo had stolen it. Twice. "Rune, I'm sorry."

"I got it back." He'd brushed his knuckles along her jawline. "And more."

Wondering if he'd confide in her, Jo had asked, "How did your mom die?"

He'd dropped his hand before it clenched into a fist. "Magh sent her to a brothel. Though my mother hadn't transitioned into full immortality, she went so that Magh would spare my life. My dam was too young to survive the . . . demands."

And then Magh had sold *him* to the same place. If his mother had died there, what had Rune *lived* through?

He never mentioned a word about that time in his life, but Jo had been getting glimpses from his blood—torture scenes that turned her stomach; no longer did she question his need to wipe out the Sylvan royal house.

His blood had also delivered glimpses of his allies. Jo had stopped delving into the past—reminders of Magh enraged him—and started asking about the Møriør.

He spoke about Orion in respectful tones, but he admitted he wished he knew his liege better. Rune's manner grew more casual when he talked of his compatriots, like Darach Lyka—a real-live werewolf!

"His Lykae form is petrifying to most," Rune had told her. "Darach is the primordial alpha, the largest and fiercest of their entire species, but he has little control over himself."

Sian, a demon and now the King of Hells, was notoriously good-looking. "The expression 'handsome as the devil' was coined because of him."

Rune had frowned when explaining his ally Kolossós. "I find him indescribable. Let's put it this way: There are twelve seats at our table. For some Møriør, they're merely places of honor. . . ."

Now Rune exhaled, recalling her attention to their surroundings. Yet again, he checked the band on his wrist. "Nïx isn't there. And she's not here."

During their travels, they'd also searched for a lock of Valkyrie hair. Rune had told her the wraiths guarded Val Hall in exchange for it. When they'd braided the locks to a certain length, they could bend all Valkyries to their will. Rumor held the braid was nearly complete.

Death controlling life. Jo wished the wraiths all the best with that. "How much longer do we wait?" she asked him.

In a wry tone, he said, "Do you have something more pressing to do?" His eyes flickered as he said, "I know where I'd like to be instead."

Her body responded as if he'd touched it. He continued to make comments about her supposed infatuation, but she *felt* like they were destined. How to convince him?

If he'd just commit to her, she'd sleep with him, and then his seal would break, proving what she'd known all along. He couldn't deny evidence like that! Nothing could be more convincing—not her arguments, not her holding out.

What if she gave it up? Would the undeniable proof jump-start their future together?

Or break her heart?

FORTY-SEVEN

Though Rune and Josephine had been releasing pressure a few times a day, just being around her ratcheted up his need. He was having difficulty concentrating. Right now, he should be on guard against threats along the Venetian canal, not staring at her.

But in the moonlight, her creamy skin looked even paler, her eyes darker. Her hair shone, appearing almost black. At that moment, she tucked a curl behind her bewitching ear, as if to tease him.

She turned back to the water, but not before he saw her irises waver with desire. He wasn't the only one in need.

"Let's give it fifteen more minutes." She leaned forward to rest her forearms on the bridge railing, drawing his attention to her black mini-skirt.

Erection straining against his pants, he fantasized about taking her just like that. He'd smooth that skirt up her hips, tug her thong aside, then work his cock inside her right here. If she was his, he would come in her, claiming her.

He forced his gaze away from her to study their surroundings, marking vantages and blind spots. He knew Nïx was playing with them, foreseeing their movements, yet these weeks hadn't been wasted. Rune had used the time to recruit Josephine.

He could now admit he was securing her loyalty for himself far more than for the Møriør.

How long will she bloody hold out from me? While his will seemed to weaken, Josephine grew more powerful in all aspects. Even she'd noticed it, attributing her increased speed and strength to his blood.

His regular donations left him with no negative effects. Just the opposite. He felt energized. But if they went too long between feedings, he'd get heated, as if he had too much blood, his body overfull with it.

All parts of his body. His throbbing shaft woke him each morning. He would cut himself, waking her with the scent of his blood, then eagerly steer her to his cock.

He'd told her she couldn't go less than twice a day. When she'd asked if that included "snacks," he'd thrown her over his shoulder and whacked her on the ass, informing her that nothing about him was snack-sized. She'd laughed and laughed. . . .

As much as she'd been drinking, had she dreamed his memories? At times, when he revealed something about himself, she wouldn't seem surprised at all.

He was apprehensive about her seeing his past in that brothel. Would she run screaming? Or pity him? He didn't think he could handle her pity.

As if he could handle her running away from him? Already he was addicted to her laugh, her candor, her blazing sexuality. She was more tempting than meadowberries to a halfstarved slave. . . .

I'm going to have to tell her soon.

"She's not coming," Josephine muttered. "This is getting old."

"I thought you were enjoying yourself with me."

"You, I like. This—not so much. She could at least make these no-shows more interesting."

"Each time I figure we're walking into an ambush." And why, he wondered for the thousandth time, hadn't Nïx contacted his enemies, passing along Rune's predicted location? King Saetthan, for one, had a colossal bounty on his head and was a fey ally of Nïx's—

"Rune, look! In the water."

A model boat floated down the canal. He turned to Josephine. "All yours."

She started to go intangible.

"No, Josie. Use your telekinesis." He'd been encouraging her to practice.

She nodded, aiming her hand at the boat. Her brows drew together as she lifted it, directing it closer. Off by a ways, she levitated to snag it in the air. But at least she hadn't destroyed it outright. She ripped free a note affixed to the mast.

She no longer acted as if she could read, just handed over the missive.

In one week, she'd learned much of the runic language; she would pick up reading English so quickly. He tore open the envelope, finding a crisp invitation card. Once all this was over, when he had her settled in Tortua, he'd teach her. For now, he read aloud:

YOU ARE CORDIALLY INVITED TO ATTEND
THE 2915TH ANNUAL TITANIA COURT BALL
10:00 ON THE EVE OF THE PINK MOON

"What's Titania?" she asked.

"A fey kingdom." The pink moon was this month's full moon. He gazed up at the sky. The ball would be tonight. With the time difference, they had roughly eight hours till it started.

Josephine canted her head. "Okay, so what's this ball thingy?"

He crumpled the invitation. "A trap."

Rune stood by the fire in Tortua, gazing at the flames. He'd dressed in his formal attire for the *ball thingy*, was only awaiting Josephine.

He wanted to leave her safely behind, but her vow compelled him to keep her close. So he'd debated not going. Titania was a staunch ally of Sylvan, and he wagered Nïx would never show.

In fact, he believed the soothsayer had planned these twelve days to lead up to this ball—as a favor to King Saetthan.

Yet Rune's duty to the Møriør demanded he attend, which meant Josephine would too. She was eager for it, though he'd explained everything they'd be up against.

Namely Saetthan's bounty hunters. Rune expected at least a hundred of them.

Despite their similar ages, Saetthan would never fight Rune one on one. As a full fey, Saetthan was faster; Rune's demon half made him stronger. It'd be a good fight if Saetthan had enough mettle to face him.

The king refused, even though he'd deemed it his sacred duty to protect his kinsmen. They all considered Rune a monster, a bogeyman who preyed on their innocent family members.

Bogeyman? Yes.

Innocence? He'd yet to find it in Magh's line. . . .

After he and Josephine had left Venice, he'd taken her shopping for a gown. He'd told her money was no object, that they could go anywhere in the universe.

Just to be contrary, she'd taken them to secondhand stores off bloody *Canal Street* in New Orleans.

He'd paced while she tried on garments, never allowing him a glimpse of what she might wear.

Outside one dressing room, he'd murmured, "Fey nobility wear obscenely expensive materials. Females favor pale colors and gauzy fabrics. Perhaps you should as well."

"Uh-huh," she'd said, clearly ignoring his suggestions.

Rune didn't want her to stand out any more than necessary, else she'd feel distressed. "Though we're likely stepping into an ambush, we should at least *try* to enjoy ourselves."

He already had plans for Josephine tonight—seducing her fully—so he'd made preparations. Barring an attack, the setup was ideal. Females went crazy for balls. He and Josephine would drink a little, dance a little, and she'd be his.

Barring *his death*, he was going to be inside her.

Yet his plans wouldn't work if she was miserable. She was a woman. A *young* woman. Weren't they overly sensitive about things like standing out?

"Gauzy, huh?" she'd said from that dressing room. "Like fairy-airy?" Then she'd peeked out past the curtain and whispered, "You know I'm probably not fey nobility, right?"

"Smartass."

"But I'm gonna need something from you. To put my whole ensemble together."

Ensemble. He'd inwardly cringed. Not just *one* inappropriate garment or accessory. "And what would that be?" He'd expected her to ask for jewels.

She'd cryptically answered, "Your blood in a glass. . . ."

Now she called from his room, "I'm coming out. Warning: I look wicked hot."

"Come on, then," he said, tone resigned. "Don't keep me in suspense any longer."

She stepped out. His feet shuffled to keep him from keeling over.

"You . . . you're . . ." *Vampiress. Phantom.* Somehow she'd complemented both sides.

She wore an unadorned strapless gown of jet-black satin that accentuated her seductive vampire curves. Her generous breasts were pushed up above the tight bodice.

The material was so smooth it reflected light, playing up her translucent skin and high, graceful cheekbones. The shadows framing her luminous eyes were darker, highlighting their unique hazel color.

She'd piled her silken hair atop her head, baring her be-ringed ears and her delicate neck.

Around her throat . . .

He swallowed. She'd used his blood to draw a choker, with her own tiny inlaid runes.

"Do you like the design? I had to cut out a stencil with my claw. Don't try that at home. It's got the runes for luck and victory."

She's painted with my ink. Possession. *My halfling female wears blood runes of her own.*

No force in the worlds could stop Rune from taking her tonight.

FORTY-EIGHT

Y ou look okay, I guess," Jo told Rune, though she'd barely recovered from her first glimpse of him in formal fey-wear: fitted fawn pants, black boots, and a tailored coat of some unusual cream-colored material that molded over his muscles.

He was long, lean, and elegant, but with that hard-core layer underneath the polish.

When she could drag her eyes off his obvious wood, she noticed other details. His hair was tied back, revealing the shaved sides of his head and his fey ears. Black was forking out all over his eyes as he stared at her. "You . . . just . . ."

"Rune, I did warn you. Get yourself together, man."

His gaze met hers. His lips curled into his slanted grin, and she sighed.

"Ah, Josephine, you're one to talk. I knew I was wearing you down."

"Whatever, old-timer." She wished she could deny that more convincingly, but he *was*.

"This is the first time I've seen you without your bullet necklace."

"I don't need to wear it anymore." It'd served its purpose.

"Just so." He donned his bow and strapped on his quiver, both of which turned invisible. "If we survive tonight's ball, I'll take you some-where you've never been. A favorite place of mine. We'll drink wine, and you can stargaze to your heart's content."

Stargaze? With another person? "I'd love that! Even more incentive to survive."

He offered his elbow. "Come."

She took it, and an instant later they arrived in a moonlit garden. "Where are we?"

"Titania. I can't have everyone seeing my mode of travel, so I traced off-site. The palace is just ahead." He pointed out a castle not far in the distance.

The structure looked like something from a fairy tale, aglow in the night, with towering spires and snapping flags. One entire wing was made of glass, its facets sparkling like diamonds. Strains of orchestral music reached them, and exotic flowers scented the warm air.

Arm in arm, they started forward. Closer to the castle the walk grew more crowded with formally attired Loreans of all species. *Back into the Lore I go. . . .*

He escorted her up a set of stairs to the torchlit entrance. Liveried demons manned the doors. Their polished horns shone in the firelight as they bowed to arriving guests.

Rune handed one his invitation, then ushered her to a landing over-looking the event.

She gasped at the sight. The ballroom was as large as an auditorium and made completely of glass. Huge chandeliers dangled from a soaring dome. The center of the transparent ceiling framed the moon above. The walls had been frosted to resemble leafy woodlands, glaciers, flames, and oceans.

Below, a gleaming glass dance floor was already packed with immortals. In the background, musicians played.

She was here at a ball—without the comforting security of a shell. Yes, this was real life, and yes, she was truly living, but she felt naked. The tall, graceful females below all wore gowns in soft colors—a sea of blue pastel, dotted with pinks and seafoam green. "I stand out like blood in water."

"All the more with that choker." He'd gazed at her neck so often, she could swear *he* was the vampire. "Are you uncomfortable?"

"If I were a guy and I had to choose one girl here, I'd pick me hands down. But you yammered on about the fey style so much, maybe you like that better." She tapped her chin. "Rune, maybe you *are* an idiot."

"If you couldn't tell by my speechless reaction earlier, you nearly put me to my knees. You're easily the sexiest female here. And you're with me alone."

"I'm more used to being inside a shell for gigs like this."

"You're welcome inside me." Over the last two weeks, he'd concealed her in his body a couple of times.

"And if I get too excited and embody?" She still had trouble controlling her ghost-mode.

"Then you'll have to remain by my side, where I can show you off." He led her to a grand staircase.

"Are these things always so popular?"

He nodded. "Especially during an Accession."

Had these Loreans attended to find their mates? Or their foes? "So ballpark this for me. How many here have you slept with?"

"I don't think you want to know that. But I'll tell you I *want* to sleep with only one here."

Awww. He was good.

As they descended the steps, he said, "You're attracting even more admirers than I am."

She'd noticed guys whipping their heads around to check her out, females too. "Good thing you never get jealous."

He raised his brows. "Shall we dance?"

"I thought we were here to fight." She nibbled her bottom lip. "And I can't dance."

"I'll lead. Just go with it, love."

She froze. "You called me 'love.'"

"Nonsense. I called you 'dove.'"

She squared her shoulders. "Bullshit. You said 'love.'"

"I've told you dark fey aren't capable of that, but imagine whatever you like, *dove*."

"If we were in my motel room, I'd tell you to fuck off until you slammed me into a wall."

"I recall that night often." He ran a hand over his mouth. "In lieu of that, we could ballroom dance."

"Same diff, I guess."

He took her in his arms and swept her onto the floor. At first Jo was awkward, but as soon as she let him lead, a miracle happened. "Look at me! I'm a wicked good dancer. You're passable too."

His lips curled. "You're wicked good at everything." Then he grew serious. "Do you know how proud I am of your runes?" His gaze was so solemn.

How could she resist him when he was like this? When the entire experience was like a dream?

I'm falling headlong. . . .

So many things reminded Jo of that grand wedding she'd crashed. She felt like a bride in her elegant gown. The music wasn't too dissimilar. The dancing seemed about the same.

She peered up at Rune. *He's my guy. My groom.* When his eyes held hers, she didn't bother hiding what she was feeling.

Adoration.

The message must've been received, because he gave her a nod, then swallowed, as if with nervousness. *Yeah, this is the real deal, Rune.* And she suspected he was falling right beside her.

As he twirled her around the floor, she gave herself up to the night. Trusting him, she leaned her head back and simply *felt*.

Giddiness. Dizziness. Joy. She almost ghosted from pleasure. She was living a fairy tale; she never wanted it to end—

"I'm about to get blitzed." His torso muscles tightened under her palm.

Jo raised her head. "Like trashed?"

He murmured, "No, *rushed*." He scanned the crowd. "Fifty swordsmen are about to descend on me."

FORTY-NINE

The imminent attack puzzled Rune.

If Saetthan had dispatched these bounty hunters, then why not hire twice the number?

Rune concluded they were all fey, but probably not ex-military. Carrying short swords, they displayed neither the martial showiness of Sylvan soldiers nor the distinctive longswords of the Titanians. They wielded no Draiksulian bows.

Perhaps these males might give him a challenge. Perhaps that was why there weren't more.

"Josephine, I want you to stand over there by the wall and become intangible." He wished he could send her away completely.

She laughed. "Forget it. I'm fighting too."

"If you give me room, I'll return to you within minutes." Nearby guests made outraged sounds as hunters elbowed their way toward the dance floor. The orchestra went quiet, one instrument at a time. A hush fell over the ballroom. The wiser attendees dispersed.

One sword-bearing male stepped onto the floor, then another, and another. Each was focused on Rune.

His only trepidation was due to the female at his side. "If you're vulnerable, my thoughts will be divided." He unstrapped his bow.

"I can use telekinesis while I ghost."

"Can you focus it enough to pick out my foes alone? I mean this. Trust me, Josie. Let me show you what I do."

She hesitated. "If you get killed, I will kick your ass so hard."

Though Jo dutifully moved to the wall and ghosted, her nerves made her outline flicker, so she remained visible in flashes.

She was a wallflower who wanted to be out on that ballroom floor—so she could fight.

Everyone had fled the area, except for a few idiot spectators peeking out from doorways and balconies, scandalized by the promise of a clash.

Bounty hunters advanced on Rune, surrounding him. How could she not fight for him? They kept coming, their circle tightening.

One gave a battle yell. Heart in her throat, she watched them charge.

Utterly calm, Rune strung *five* red arrows—poisoned ones. He turned his bow horizontal and let them fly. The arrows fanned out in the air, drilling through the first line of men, then the second—then the third.

Fifteen men down! They moaned on the ground, dying from Rune's agonizing poison.

He nocked five more arrows, repeating the shot. At least a dozen dropped.

Like a blur, he swept through the fallen, collecting arrows from the last wave of bodies. As he refilled his quiver, he kept one arrow in hand to stab necks, wasting even more swordsmen.

He was faster than blood splatter, dodging jugular sprays. Compared to Rune, his attackers seemed to be moving in slo-mo. They plodded and slipped on the bloody glass.

She'd seen him in action, but never like this. Never against so many opponents.

With his quiver full, he vaulted to a balcony. Three couples were hiding there. Though Rune gave them only a passing glance, the males gazed at him with terror. The females sighed over him, about to swoon with desire. One reached for a meager touch of his leg.

Rune's next round of arrows flew in a curving trajectory. He'd arced them to make impossible strikes, then leapt down for another arrow harvest. Not a drop of blood marked him.

Her worry faded. On occasion, he'd spoken of his fey and demon halves, one more methodical, one more aggressive. The methodical fey was at the fore as Rune coldly and efficiently destroyed the threat. Only a few were left standing.

He was magnificent. And he *knew* it. In the middle of a kill, he turned to take in her breathless, awed reaction.

The cocky dark fey *winked* at her.

She'd never wanted him more.

Once he finished taking out this trash, she'd kiss those smirking lips and nip the bottom one till he groaned. When they were alone, she'd strip, revealing the lingerie she'd bought today.

And if she let him have her tonight? He'd told her he would take pains to get her ready. She imagined him petting her with those amazing fingers until she was wet and aching, then he'd work his big shaft inside her. When he entered her to the hilt, would his kiss steal her cry?

As she fantasized about his ripped body thrusting and moving over her, she started to pant. Her heartbeat quickened. *That's my guy.* She needed him desperately.

Tonight. Tonight she was going to surrender—

Steel kissed her throat.

FIFTY

A soft gasp.

Rune whipped his head around. He'd defeated all the swordsmen who'd engaged him, but one had sneaked in to target Josephine.

Gods damn it! Why had she embodied?

The male yanked her back to him, a knife against her fragile neck.

This was why Møriør had no mates—because Orion allowed no vulnerabilities. Rune couldn't have a more glaring one than his need for Josephine.

When the blade nicked her tender skin, he all but lost his mind. He bared his demon fangs, yearning to maul that male, to savage him with poisonous claws.

Blood slipped down her throat. *Black* blood.

From drinking his. A thought arose that he couldn't even acknowledge.

Despite the danger, she wasn't afraid. Her irises darkened and the shadows around her eyes deepened—a predator signaling her threat.

In his panic for her, Rune had forgotten that she was no mere female. She was a force. She was death and death rolled into one, and she looked like she could barely wait to strike.

Rune told the man, "Release her. Or die a nightmare death. I'll warn you once."

Movement on a balcony. He whipped his head up.

Saetthan.

Rune's half brother strolled out, clad in formal attire with their father's sword drawn. A pair of royal guards flanked him. "What a mess you've made, baneblood." He regarded all the bodies with an amused expression that resembled Rune's own.

"I thought you were behind this," Rune said. "Ill-planned and ineffectual is your signature."

Like a dragon twitching its tail, Saetthan twirled that sword.

Rune expected more guards to file out on the balcony, yet none came, leaving only the two. He never got opportunities to strike his half sibling this unprotected. "Next time I hope you'll send me a real challenge," he called. "Are funds tight in Sylvan?"

"I didn't need an army to take you down. I only needed to distract you—while I collected your mate. My spies told me you'd found yours, but I scarcely believed an abomination like you got a fated female."

Rune's hand dipped to his quiver. He'd wanted a fair fight; Saetthan had targeted his woman. All bets were off.

His fingertips brushed the flights of one-and-done. He'd string it among four poison arrows. Those would hit lower; the guards would dive and take them leaving Saetthan to contend with Rune's most precisely lethal arrow.

"Ah-ah, Rune," Saetthan chided, all confidence. "If you aim for me, your pretty pet will lose her head."

Rune gave a laugh. "If you believe that, then your spies didn't tell you quite *enough* about her."

Saetthan shuttered a look of puzzlement. "You'll forfeit either your life or hers this night, to pay for taking my mother's."

Keeping Saetthan in his sights, Rune said, "Josie?"

"I got this. Do what you gotta do." She began to dematerialize, to the swordsman's shock. Descending through the floor, she forced the intangible male down as well. She made it slow, eerie.

"What trickery is this?" Saetthan demanded. "Your mate's as much an abomination as you are!"

While Saetthan gaped, Rune nocked his arrows, unleashing them with all his might.

Each guard caught two.

Reacting with uncanny speed, Saetthan swung his sword up to deflect the one-and-done.

The arrowhead connected with the blade.

Light erupted. A boom like a thunderclap.

The sword . . . *exploded*!

Charred metal bit into Saetthan's skin. Shards hissed and cooled as they plummeted, clanging against the glass floor. The blast hit the glass dome above; ominous fractures forked out.

My gods. Rune had destroyed the sword—the uniting symbol of that entire accursed family. He quickly fired another volley into the smoke.

By the time the air cleared, Saetthan had disappeared.

Rune turned to Josephine. She'd dragged the swordsman to his waist, and he'd comprehended his fate; there was no fighting her. The hunter was terrified, his short yells chilling.

The two sank below the glass floor, visible for a few moments as a dwindling flicker. Gasps sounded among the attendees still present on the outskirts of the ballroom.

Josephine surfaced. Alone.

Her secret was out. She must have the strength of an alliance to depend on.

She gazed around at the appalled spectators. "Anybody else want to go to their grave tonight? I'll bury you so deep, they'll never find your body down there. You might die. Odds are . . . you *won't*."

Oh, yes, he could get used to having her around.

She turned to him with a sunny smile. "Best. Date. Ever."

His lips curled. And it was in no way finished.

Rune might have missed his opportunity to kill Saetthan, but that sword had been annihilated. Josephine was unharmed. All was well.

As soon as the thought occurred, another crack sounded from above as fractures spread out like webbing.

"Quickly," he told her. "Let's see if we get a clue." They hastened to a swordsman who hadn't yet succumbed to poison. Wide-eyed, the male twisted in pain, his limbs contorted. Rune bent down to him. "Any message from Nïx? She's surely the one who gave you my whereabouts."

Silence.

"Talk, or the phantom will take you to hell."

His eyes somehow got wider. "We each carried . . . a note for you. Pocket!"

Rune retrieved it.

Congratulations on reaching the bonus level! Now's your turn to try and get past my wraiths. Thaddeus and I will be in attendance at Val Hall tomorrow night, awaiting the pleasure of your (failed) arrival (attempts).

XOXO, Nïx the Ever-Knowing

Rune rewarded the male with a quick decapitation.

"What does it say?" Josephine asked.

"Nïx invites us to Val Hall. Tomorrow we'll face her—in her den." Considering the damage his arrow had done to that sword, how would the wraiths fare against a volley of them?

When Josephine nodded, his attention dipped to the nick on her throat, and his heart thundered anew. Her dried blood matched the color of her choker.

My blood courses through her veins. Only mine.

Fractures continued to fork out above. *Need to trace her away—*

She took his hands. With a grin, she made them intangible. She gazed up at him with that same adoring look she'd given him on the dance floor. Females had cast him that look for ages.

For the first time, he wanted to *earn* it.

The ceiling splintered, then shattered in a deafening burst. He and Josephine smiled at each other as shards fell like rain, passing harmlessly through them.

FIFTY-ONE

I'm in freaking Australia, wearing a ball gown!

Rune had picked up a pack of supplies in Tortua, then traced her here: to the base of Ayers Rock in the middle of the outback.

He stood behind her, his hands covering her shoulders, his rings warming against her skin. "What do you think? Do you find it *quaint*?"

She elbowed him. "This place is unreal!" The rock was the same color as a terra-cotta pot. Yet as the sun set, purple tinged it.

The shade of Rune's eyes when he was relaxed.

Over her shoulder, she asked, "You've been here before?" The full moon they'd enjoyed in Titania was just rising here.

"On occasion. The portal to the Quondam realm is nearby. Among mortals, this monolith is central to Aboriginal lore. It's known as the ancestors' rock. The Aborigines revere their ancestors." He traced her to the plateau.

"Oh my God!" She spun in place. "I never thought I'd see stuff like this. For two weeks it's been sick." From this height, she surveyed the alien landscape. They could have been on Mars.

She craned her head up. Had she ever seen so many stars? They glimmered like beacons.

"You approve?"

She lowered her gaze to take in just as riveting a sight: Rune grinning. He knew he'd blown her mind.

From his pack, he drew a thick blanket and spread it on the ground. He waved her to sit, then tossed her a jeweled flask.

"What's in this?"

"Blood mead. You'll like it."

She settled herself happily, her satin rustling. "Is it black?" Heat emanated from the surface of the rock, making her even more comfortable.

His grin deepened. "It's baneblood, as my vampire craves."

"Aren't you full of surprises?"

"I'm told stargazing is thirsty work." He dropped down beside her with his own flask of demon brew.

She took a sip of the mead, and her eyes went wide. "It's really good. Got a kick to it."

"When blood bites back, huh?"

"No wonder your friend Blace loves this stuff." So stars, and a blanket, and booze? Definite seduction vibe.

Rune knew this final step would mean they were exclusive; she couldn't have made her feelings clearer. And still, he'd brought her to this dream place with sex in mind.

He was ready. In her excitement, she briefly dematerialized.

And once his seal was broken, he could never doubt their fated connection again. *Which is why you're about to give in, Jo.*

"Did I tell you how beautiful you look tonight?" He reached forward to tuck a stray curl behind her ear. "Your ensemble was a huge fuck-you to fey snobbery. Jet satin trumps pale gauze any day."

"This old thing?" she teased. Compliments as well? *I'm a sure thing, sport.* "Speaking of fey snobbery—who was the blond guy? He kind of looked like you." He'd referred to her as Rune's mate, and Rune hadn't denied it!

"King Saetthan, my half brother."

"Why is he so bent on killing you?"

"Probably because I'm so bent on killing him. He's now the head of the royal line I plan to wipe out. If you're with me, situations like tonight will keep happening. The bounty on me is steep. You'd be hunted just for associating with me."

Rune was giving her a chance to cry off—before they went eternal. "I'll already be hunted just for what I am, right? Makes for another level of excitement." She sipped her flask. "What about that invitation? How will we get inside Val Hall?"

"If my arrow can destroy a sword made of Titanian metal, why not wraiths?"

"That was seriously badass." She play-punched his shoulder. "Big ba-da boom."

"Indeed. At Val Hall, we'll use my most powerful arrow. If that doesn't work, you could try your telekinesis."

"Maybe I can nudge their hula hoop of evil off its axis. Before they get back into position, we'll trace for the door. You'll take care of Nïx, and I'll snag Thad." She sounded optimistic, but she had to wonder: why would Nïx have alerted Jo to her telekinetic potential?

Either Nïx was a shitty psychic and a really stupid Valkyrie—or she was playing with them yet again.

"If all else fails, you can try to ghost us inside," Rune said. "We have options."

"Nïx seemed so cocky in that invitation."

"Perhaps she's slipping. She is mad after all."

"Still, do you want to tell me about your plan B?" Maybe he'd already requested his allies' help, and they were on the way to gather like the Super Friends. Hmm. What was the villainous equivalent of the Hall of Justice?

Rune brushed his knuckles over her cheek. "It probably won't come to that. For now, let's celebrate tonight's victory and drink to our upcoming battle."

Reassured, she raised her flask. "Good warring." She bit her tongue as soon as the words left her lips. In her dreams, she'd heard Rune say that to his allies, even to foes he respected.

All relaxation left him, and he stood. "How long?"

She scrambled to her feet. "Since the night I met you."

"What have you seen?"

"In the beginning I saw Magh summoning you and your first kill. You were really young."

Muscles gone tense, he grated, "I stole, I killed, and I fucked for that bitch. I did anything she wanted of me, and I still couldn't save my mother." He narrowed his eyes. "Have you seen what happened after Magh sold me? I wasn't merely a slave, as I told you." He loomed over Jo, a challenge in his tone. "She peddled me to a brothel, Josephine."

Did he think this admission would send her packing?

" 'Please or perish,' Magh told me. Each morning, a guard would raise his sword over my neck to take my head if I'd failed to please a single patron over the night." Rune let that sink in. "No commentary? No blunt remarks?"

She needed to touch him, but didn't want him to think she pitied him. "I wish that hadn't happened to you, but I'm glad you did what it took to survive. To get vengeance. I saw that too, Rune. I only wish Magh was alive so I could hunt her and drag her into the earth over and over again."

He drew on his flask. "Why didn't you tell me about the dreams?"

"At first because I was worried you'd try to kill me again. Then I didn't want anything to get in the way of . . . us."

"What else did you see?" As if his head was suddenly splitting, he pinched his temples.

"Your first meeting with Orion. And I saw a battle—it seemed from long ago—where you were all fighting together."

"Have you seen me sleeping with others?"

She shook her head, admitting, "But I saw you tortured in that brothel."

His gaze slid away. "Once I was freed, I chose to be there."

She eased closer to him. "You couldn't imagine life getting better, because for so long it hadn't. Orion has my loyalty just for showing you a new future."

"But the past can never be undone, and mine is sordid. I'm tainted in more ways than one." He drank deeply. "I bet you've never been with a whore before."

Unable to stop herself, she laid one hand on his strong face. "That's not you anymore." *I'm falling for you. I want to be with you always.* "You're a different male."

"Different." He gave a humorless laugh. "How many times can a male be *different* in one lifetime, Josephine? I'd like to get to a place where I never have to change again." He peered at her, as if saying more than just the surface words.

She'd realized he was ready for her; now he'd just confirmed it. "I'm sorry I didn't tell you. I kept waiting for the right time."

He exhaled. "You didn't do anything wrong. Just the opposite; you saw my past and didn't leave. And you didn't pity me." As if just registering these facts, he grasped her nape. "Gods, that means a lot to me."

"You won't get rid of me that easily, Rune Darklight. And how could I ever pity a male like you, my archer?" She could tell he liked that.

"I'm relieved you know. I would've confessed all this to you eventually."

Before they made love? Before they went forward? "I'll tell you when it happens again."

He nodded, then wrapped an arm around her shoulders. "This is supposed to be a celebration." He pulled her down on the blanket with him. "Gaze, woman."

Little by little, his tension dwindled, and their usual companionable ease settled over them. In silence, they watched as full night fell and the moon climbed higher—though she could have sworn Rune was looking at her more often than the sky.

All the times in the past when she'd turned her questioning gaze to the stars, she'd been alone.

No longer.

He drew her closer. The sky above was vast and unknowable, rounded over them like a shield. She sighed, "The world is so big. . . ."

FIFTY-TWO

Rune turned on his side, taking in Josephine's sweet profile.

His gaze flickered over her lips, nose, cheekbones, and eyelashes. Stars reflected in her eyes as she stared up in awe, and he felt a tugging in his chest. *This world's actually so very small, love.*

He could show her thousands of worlds. They'd need lifetimes to see them all.

He drank more brew. He'd been with her for the merest blink of an eye, yet now he was going to travel? Live a life of leisure? He had wars to wage, and secrets to uncover.

Maybe *after* the Accession . . .

His brows drew together as he watched her. She wasn't just gazing at the stars—she seemed to be awaiting something. Almost as if she were *listening.*

"I want to know why stargazing is your favorite thing," he said.

"Whenever I stare at them, I feel like I might be on the verge of re-membering my past."

"Do you think your parents are still alive?"

She shook her head. "I don't believe my mother is. I have these vague impressions of fire and chaos. Like there was a natural disaster or some-thing. I've never had an impression of my father."

"Your mother could've traced away from a natural disaster, no?" Unless she'd never been away from her home.

"I don't even know if those scenes are dreams or my imagination or part of my memories." She sipped her flask. "I've wanted to know my parents so badly and for so long I could be making stuff up."

For so long? *Says the twenty-five-year-old.*

At least Rune could name his parents. "Is that why you want a bond so much? The absence of a family?" Surely recovering Thad for her would help fill that need—and alleviate some of the pressure she'd been putting on Rune.

"No, it's more than that. When I hang out in shells, I get to experience other lives. One time I ghosted into a bride on her wedding night. Her groom ended up being a dream man who gazed at her like she was everything. He promised her he'd die for her—and I believed him." She turned on her side as well, facing Rune. "This man was looking *me* in the eyes and telling me these things. I know, not really me, but I was still staggered. Other people take being cherished for granted. But if you've never had it and then you get a hit, you need it."

Dream man. Everything. Promises. Cherishing.

Damn, no pressure there, Josephine. She'd taken a wedding—an event engineered to be ideal—and she'd built a template for her love life.

Not for the first time, Rune recognized he wasn't the man to give Josephine her dreams. He tried to make light. "The combat-boot-wearing blood-drinker wants romance."

"If I had that bond, things in my life would get . . . fixed."

"Like what?"

"I have a fear as strong as your phobia about heights." She nibbled her bottom lip. "I'm afraid I'll just float away. Especially if I sleep-ghost."

"Sleep-ghost? Like sleepwalking?"

She nodded. "I float through the bed into the ground. When I come to, I'm basically in a grave. Why shouldn't I fear going the other way? And those stars seem to call to me."

"You never did that during the past two weeks."

"It only happens when I'm filled with . . . loss. Or yearning. If I had a bond with someone, it would—I don't know—maybe anchor me here."

She fears floating away; I fear extinguishing my emotions forever.

Every time he went cold with a target, he wondered if he was like Darach—one fateful transition away from permanence. Or like Uthyr, the dragon shifter, who'd abandoned his human form and became a dragon forever.

Josephine wanted Rune to be her anchor? To hold her hand and keep her tethered to him? That, at least, seemed achievable. In return, she could make sure his heart never fell to ash again.

Maybe we could be each other's anchors.

He reached for her, smoothing his thumb over her full bottom lip, that little dip. Her eyes grew even more luminous. As he stared into them, he said, "I could keep you with me."

Her face lit up; his fell.

He'd used zero qualifiers. Was she mesmerizing him again? Exasperated, he said, "I want you, Josephine. I'll wait no longer." He was about to go into all the reasons her refusal was ridiculous—

"Okay."

Huh? "I want you completely."

Her lips curled.

"As in sex. I want sex." He was fumbling. What in the hells was wrong with him?

Her smile deepened.

He could disabuse Josephine of her hopes right now. Or he could let her believe they would be exclusive, when he had every intention of bedding others.

Every intention of remaining the same.

She'd told him she had expectations, and they were sky-high. Tomorrow he would manage them for her. *She* would change. If they were to have any kind of future together, it would be on his terms—or not at all. "Are you sure you want to risk my poison?"

"Already told you I don't think there's a risk. But if we're even talking about this, then you must think there's some chance I'm your mate."

"I'm not going to lie. I do think there's a chance. I've got protection." He rolled up his sleeve to reveal a runic combination he'd inked in preparation.

"I've never seen those symbols."

"It's an ancient contraception spell to keep me from spilling seed." He was about to get what he wanted. He'd won. He had seduced the impressionable Josephine with a ball and drinks and compliments.

If she knew how much he'd manipulated her—a millennia-old master versus an inexperienced young woman.

"But how will you know if I'm your mate?"

Rune already did. In that ballroom, when he'd seen her black blood . . . even amid his panic, a bewildering thought had arisen: *She's me, and I'm her.* "Does it really matter? Tonight won't change how we go forward. We're still going to be together."

Together in bed. In the Møriør. In war.

FIFTY-THREE

I loved this on you," Rune murmured against Jo's choker.

She was sitting in his lap as he nuzzled her neck. Beneath her ass, he was rock-hard.

"Loved seeing you wear my baneblood." His warm breaths made her shiver. When he claimed her as his mate tonight, he would bite her neck. "Your own blood is black now. I saw when that swordsman nicked you."

Get out! "Can I kill with my bite or my claws?" More powers!

"Your blood might be deadly. But I doubt anything else would be."

"Oh."

"You sound disappointed." He pressed his forehead to hers. "For all my life, I've hated my poison."

"Until you met me." She leaned in for a kiss.

His lips were firm when he grazed them over hers. Just that light contact made her heart race. She parted her lips, welcoming his clever tongue.

He leaned her back against his arm so he could take her more thoroughly. For a male who hadn't kissed often—or at least not for extended amounts of time—he was an amazing kisser.

She threaded her fingers into his thick hair, loosening it from his queue, pressing herself against his body. She was already wet for him. He'd made a big deal out of readying her for sex—she was *raring*.

When she wriggled over his dick—*hint, hint*—he groaned into the kiss, adjusting her on his lap. As their tongues twined, she tugged on his neck, arching into his grip. Why wasn't he feeling her up? Why did they still have clothes on? She wanted his dick warming her palm. She wanted his mouth on her tits, his tongue playing with a piercing.

Against Jo's lips, he muttered, "Damn it." He drew his head back.

Catching her breath, she said, "What's wrong?"

"Maybe we should get back."

"To Tortua? I wanted it to be here at this epic location."

"Perhaps we should wait for another night or so." Her dark fey was getting cold feet.

Jo had outlined her parameters for sex. Yet he'd still been about to do it. To commit. The bond with him was so close she could taste it.

His Adam's apple bobbed; he was nervous. Because it meant that much! She'd known he was falling for her. Hadn't he called her *love* earlier?

"And if I said we're staying?"

He set her away, then traced to his feet. "We've only known each other for so little time."

"We're role-playing, right? You're playing me, giving excuses why we should wait. I'll play Rune. 'But, *baby*,'" she crooned, "'we only live once, and we have a battle tomorrow.'"

He cocked a brow. "Smartass."

"Seriously, what's up with the one-eighty?"

He shrugged. "Changed my mind."

Awww. He was skittish about such a drastic change. After countless centuries of sameness . . .

It was up to her to drag him to the finish line. She replayed his reaction in her motel room, when she'd goaded him and flashed her fangs at him. For her "defiance," he'd shoved her against the wall, kissing her like his life depended on it.

"Changed your mind?" She nodded with understanding. "Problems with little Rune, old man? Do you know the Viagra symbol?"

Eyes narrowing, he gestured at his bulging shaft. "Obviously that is *not* my problem."

It's working. "I bet Desh doesn't need Viagra. Hey, on the way back, can you drop me at Lafitte's?"

Rune's muscles tensed, his fangs becoming more prominent. "You're wearing my godsdamned blood on your skin, and you're talking about fucking another demon?"

"You want me to be all dressed up and nowhere to go?" She pinched the hem of her dress, sliding it up her legs.

"Stop what you're doing." His sexy ears twitched at the sound of satin skimming her hose.

"Look at these." She exposed her black garters, adjusting them. "I won't wear them for just anyone. But you don't appreciate them?"

His fists clenched. "I told you to stop this." As if he had no control of his body, he dropped to his knees in front of her, just to pet a hose-clad leg. "You're defying me once more?"

She collected her dress hem again, drawing it even higher. "I was so busy choosing my hose and garters, I forgot panties."

"You wouldn't defy me if I'd marked you. You'd come to heel."

Intense male! She brought one knee up. "Don't you want to see where you should be?"

He inhaled deeply, his pupils blown. "You're playing with forces you don't understand. The demon in me . . . needs . . . to make you surrender."

She spread herself to him. "How's *this* for defiance?" She'd never felt more exposed. But dark urges gripped her. She wanted to be vulnerable, to put herself in his control.

One second he was on his knees staring; the next he'd traced atop her, pinning her down on the blanket. . . .

Like flipping a switch.

Rune had barely withstood the mouthwatering scent of her sex. But to see it, to see the little shadow of her opening? His cock throbbed to claim it. His demon half was in a lather for it.

Her defiance maddened him. Provoked every primal need in him. *She'll respect the male who masters her.*

He *felt* demonic. Savage. Out of control.

Claim. . . . Her dress was an obstacle. He wanted her naked but for those garters. He fisted her bodice, ripping it away. She gasped as he tore the dress from her body.

He couldn't kiss her bared tits fast enough. He wrapped his lips around a nipple, suckling hard. His teeth clicked against her piercing. *Perfection.*

Never releasing his suck, he tore off his own clothes, his tongue flicking when his rigid cock met cool air.

He dimly remembered the need to prepare her. His hand shot between her thighs, cupping her possessively. *Mine.* He slipped a finger in, groaning against her breast.

Her pussy was hot, giving. He thrust his finger, fucking her with it.

"More!" She rocked her hips.

Another finger. He spread them wide inside her, opening her up for him.

"I'm ready, Rune!"

"Ready when I say you are." He lightly bit her nipple.

She cried out, her claws raking his heated skin, spurs to a beast.

Her honey drenched his fingers, wetting his palm. Still he worked her pussy. He wedged a third finger inside.

She bucked to his hand. "About to come!"

He stilled his fingers. "No."

"No? Then fuck me!"

Can't wait any longer! He slid his fingers free. He sucked them with a snarl as she watched with those sultry eyes.

"Need you, Rune! *Now.*" She raised her arms and spread her thighs to welcome him.

He'd waited seven thousand years for this! On his knees, he leaned over her, aiming his cock. He tilted his hips, and her lush wetness kissed the tip. *Claim!*

He yelled and thrust. The crown slipped along the plump folds of her pussy. *"AHH!"* He nearly came. *"Get so wet!"* He didn't recognize the sight of his own member. Never so engorged.

He sweated, his muscles straining. His aching balls tightened. It took everything in him not to fall upon her in a frenzy. He gnashed his teeth as he fought his instincts. *Have to get control!*

The head rubbed her swollen clit, and she cried, "Rune, do it!" Her little fangs sharpened.

For my flesh. The demon in him roared with satisfaction. *She drinks me alone. After tonight, she fucks me alone.*

His own fangs readied for her neck. *About to know my mark.*

For the first time in his existence, he could perceive semen climbing up his shaft. *It's for her. It's all hers. Give it to her . . . put it where it belongs.*

Her head thrashed, her hair coming loose, silken strands haloing her head. He went awash in her scent.

The crown tucked against her entrance. No turning back.

Her thighs fell wide in surrender, her heart racing. Its beat spurred him as much as her claws.

Her eyes were as frantic as he felt. "Put it *in*." She needed; he provided.

Emotions? He was *raw*. Scalded. With a bellow, he shoved home.

Pleasure seared him. Her body gloved him. *"Ah, gods, YES!"* A demon covering his mate.

Her back bowed, her pierced tits slipping across his sweating chest. She screamed, "Rune!" Her core clenched his rod, her wet flesh quivering around it.

He snatched her nape, forcing her to meet his gaze. "You're mine now! Belong to *me. . . ."* A groan replaced his words. Unbearable pressure kept building in his shaft.

It was agony! *Want more.*

He needed to rut like a demon. He needed to *fuck*.

To *bite*. His fangs throbbed as badly as his cock. *Mark her forever.*

He withdrew to thrust, sensation climbing his spine. Too much sensation.

He froze halfway. *Coming in two thrusts . . . ?* "Josie, I'm spending! Can't stop!"

As if she'd been trained for him, her head turned to the side, baring her neck for him to mark.

Another war bellow to the night, to this entire godsdamned world. Then, one word: *"MINE!"* He sank his fangs into her skin and plunged his cock as deep as he could reach.

"Rune, I'm . . . Oh, God! You're making me COME!" She screamed, helplessly rocking on his length. He perceived her orgasming—her sheath milked him with greedy tugs.

Fire erupted inside him. He snarled against her skin when his demon seal burned away, and semen shot from his slit for the first time.

Ecstasy. Pinpoints of light flashed behind his lids as he ejaculated. His mind turned over, instinct ruling. *Put your seed where it belongs.*

His shaft pulsated to empty his cum, jet after mind-numbing jet. *So hot, so hot.*

Still buried deep, he fucked to ease a pressure that had been building for ages. . . .

FIFTY-FOUR

Jo was boneless by the time Rune was spent.

He released his bite with a shudder and collapsed over her. Heart thundering against Jo's chest, he continued to lazily thrust, as if he couldn't get enough of her.

Her eyes slid closed, but she was smiling to herself. Sex should always be like that! She got her man, and he did the job *right*.

The rune on his arm, however, hadn't. She'd felt him coming inside her—hot, hard spurts. But she wasn't worried.

"Wait." His voice was hoarse. He leaned up on straightened arms, a look of confusion on his face. "I thought I was dreaming it . . ." With a hiss, he pulled out. "Dear gods, the rune didn't work! I came inside you."

"Yeah." She patted his ass. "I felt that in real time, sport."

His gaze fell on his arm.

Ohhh. She'd clawed his skin, disrupting the rune. "Oops?"

"How can you be so calm about this?"

" 'Cause Jo just got laid properly? Okay, okay. I'm calm because I feel amazing. I *knew* I was your mate. I got marked"—she traced the bite on her neck—"and apparently drenched with seed." She wriggled her hips with a thoughtful expression.

He flinched. "I need to get you somewhere, get you clean!"

She stretched her arms over her head. "Forget that. I'm basking." She replayed the moment when he'd looked into her eyes and told her she was his. Nothing had ever made her feel more connected, not even drinking from him.

Fate considered them bound. Destiny said they were joined. No union was stronger than that. She couldn't stop smiling. Yes, everything was looking so bright.

"You don't feel pain? You don't feel any effects from this?" He tenderly brushed his fingertips over her marked neck. "Please, tell me. I don't want you to hurt. Josie, you can't . . . I can't hurt you."

She was going to be sore tomorrow—no matter how much he'd readied her—and she regretted *nothing*. "You wanna know what hurts me? Not yelling, 'I told you so!' at the top of my lungs."

Some of his panic seemed to lessen.

"Now you can't argue with me anymore," she informed him. "First step of our matehood? Accepting I'll always be right. Also, I need to know when we can do this again. It's very important we do this again as soon as possible."

"Matehood." He sat back on his haunches, stunned. Must be sinking in that he'd just reached a life milestone—after a gazillion eons.

"Oh, yeah." With a teasing grin, she said, "And just think, if I had been eating, you might've knocked me up."

Breath left his lungs. "I never allowed myself to imagine. . . ." His face fell. "My offspring would be poisonous."

"Maybe, maybe not. Worst case scenario for *our* offspring: having to score a wicked awesome mate like you did."

"You would want"—he cleared his throat to gruffly ask—"you'd have young with me?"

Even *more* people in her life! She pictured a baby with magenta eyes and a crooked grin who reminded her of Thad. The baby she'd never thought to have two weeks ago. "Hell yeah, why not?"

Black forked out over his eyes, and his dick surged.

Her gaze widened. "You like that idea?"

"The idea of impregnating my mate? My gods, it makes me hard for you. Once the Accession passes, you could eat." He swallowed. "We could see."

"Sounds like a plan."

He returned to the cradle of her thighs, those dark fey eyes blazing with emotion. He was looking at her—really looking—and his expression promised things she'd only dreamed of.

His eyes held hers as he rolled his hips, feeding his length back inside her.

Connection. "This is even better than I fantasized." She sighed, undulating to receive him. "A girl can't feel more anchored than this."

He eased down, giving each of her nipples a ruthless suck, making her moan. Then he pulled out to the tip and slammed his big cock home. "Ah! So *tight.*" Another shove. He watched her tits bounce with obvious delight. Another thrust. "I just came, and already . . ." He went to his knees, pulling her up to straddle his lap. His powerful arms coiled around her, squeezing her body against his. Against her ear, he said, "How did I live so long without this?"

"It feels different?"

He pulled back, his eyes heavy-lidded with lust, but gleaming with excitement. "So different . . . can't decide if I'm going to come until my testicles scream—or lose my mind. I can *feel* semen climbing." He frowned. "It's *too* good. I've as little control as when I was new to this."

"Maybe we're both new to this." She'd certainly never made love before.

He nodded slowly. Lips inches from hers, he said, "I've had a taste of this, and there's no going back. You're mine." Just uttering those words heightened his aggression: "I want to hear you say it. Now." He wrapped her hair around his fist, tugging to show he wasn't fucking around. "Tell me what you are." His demon intensity made her crazed.

She dug her claws into his shoulders. *"Yours."* She wanted to bite *him.*

He thrust upward, growling, "You're going to bear my young."

"*Yes.*"

"Your blood's black. It's like mine. I'll always be inside you."

At the thought, Jo rocked on him and arched her back, feeling the cool air on her nipples.

He hissed in a breath between clenched teeth. "Don't move."

"What's wrong?"

His big hands clamped her waist, holding her still. "*Too* good. I look at those pierced nipples of yours, and I'm about to come." He drew back his cock with a shudder. "I look at your lips—the same. Your sexy ears. Dear gods, your eyes. Your fangs . . . when they sharpen I know I'm about to feel them somewhere on my body." He pulled her hair to force her to his neck. "I've fantasized about giving you seed—while you take my blood."

The idea turned her on so much, she grew wetter in a rush, clenching his dick inside her.

He felt her, repeating her question, "You like that idea?" His pulse point was beating furiously, calling her. Like a devil in her ear, he murmured, "Take what's yours, Josie."

With a cry, her head shot forward, and she pierced him. When his firm flesh closed around her aching fangs, she almost came.

A deep groan rumbled. "Ah! That's it, baby. Take from me. I'm going to last till you're fed."

She scented more blood. It spilled down her back—because he was sinking his claws into his palms. Pain tempering pleasure. Anything to hold out for her.

"My mate," he rasped. "My beautiful female."

As she consumed him, their heartbeats . . . changed. The wild drumming in her ears matched beats, synchronizing.

As if they shared a heart.

"Do you hear that?" he murmured in bewilderment. "*Feel* that?"

She whimpered against his skin. Joined. Connected. Nothing had ever aroused her so much—her body, her mind, her heart. The tightening in her core escalated past the point of no return, gathering to explode.

He bucked upward. "Come with me," he commanded.

She hovered . . . right on the verge . . .

"You're never going to be alone again, because I will never let you go. Understand me, Josie—this is *forever.*"

At that, she went over the brink. Her climax ripped through her. Fiery and relentless. She released her bite to scream, *"Rune!"*

She clung to him as he pounded upward inside her, unmercifully. She clung to him as their sweating bodies writhed together.

Demonish words left his lips, a sign of his mindlessness. With a brutal groan, he wrenched her hips down as his surged up. A yell burst from his chest, and his seed shot into her, filling her with heat.

As she trembled against him, her dark fey mate threw his head back and roared her name to the night.

FIFTY-FIVE

For the first time in his unending life, Rune the Insatiable had been sated. He'd come with his stunning mate so many times, his tender balls had pled for a reprieve.

Lying in their bed in Tortua, he stroked her hair as she slept. He was getting to like this after-play business.

Toward the end of the night, he'd been able to hold his seed longer, but he'd still had as little control as when he'd been a lad. Yet then, *everything* had seemed new to him. Dalli was right—he did feel as if he were starting over with his mate.

He pressed a kiss into Josephine's hair, inhaling her scent. *Mine.*

She'd seen his past and accepted it. She'd accepted *him*. Before she'd drifted off, she'd told him, "Something in me changed when our heartbeats synchronized. I don't know *what*, but I know I'm different."

He understood. He felt as if he'd discovered the answer to a mystery he'd been teased with his entire life. A secret like no other.

Though his body was sated, his mind wasn't. Would she wish to wed? Probably, if she'd been raised human. He would do it for her—if she could compromise as well.

Despite how powerful tonight had been, he couldn't let that affect how he went about his life. He'd tried to postpone this with her, but she'd pushed. He suspected she might even have mesmerized him at one point.

The Møriør were still his priority, and war loomed. As the eyes and ears of his alliance, he couldn't shirk his duties at the cusp of an Accession.

And without the Møriør, his quest for vengeance could fail. He'd been so close to taking Saetthan out, but the prick had escaped him. Destroying that royal sword had only whetted Rune's appetite for retribution.

He would stay the course, refusing to change his existence yet again. It was someone else's bloody turn. Tomorrow he would inform Josephine what he had to offer, knowing it was far less than she expected.

Using his silver tongue, he'd seduce her into his way of thinking, and she would adjust. She was addicted to their sex, enamored with the idea of not being alone.

She'd never give him up.

"Rune," she drowsily murmured.

"Hmm?"

"You love me." She drifted off again.

His eyes flashed open in the dark. That hadn't been a question.

To go from cold ash to inferno in two weeks? Couldn't be possible. But then, he'd also believed he could never have a mate. Or progeny.

A generation to come after him. Offspring with Josephine. She'd be fiercely protective of them.

Them. Already he'd jumped from a single potential child to plural.

Lorean parents were the true immortals. They lived forever in memories. If he had children, he would tell them about his own mother, whose sacrifice had allowed Rune—and his entire line—to live.

He would avenge her, help win the coming war, and then a life with his mate and their young could be more than a dream. If his stubborn female could see things his way.

FIFTY-SIX

Jo watched Rune as he prepped his arrows for their upcoming battle. Black, gray, red, and white.

With no weapons to prep, she'd been ready for a while, had dressed in frayed jeans, a funk-band T-shirt, and boots. Her version of war wear.

Night would soon fall on New Orleans, and he had on his game-day face, looking deep in thought.

Ever since Jo had awakened, he'd seemed like he needed to talk to her about something. But they'd gotten distracted by dozens of bouts of sex. Wild, immortal sex.

They'd showered together, breaking the tiles. Handy magicks had already repaired them!

Her guy was *strong*. To keep up with him, she'd fed throughout the day to speed up her healing—of rug-burned knees, sore muscles, and more love bites.

She suspected he wanted to talk about their future, solidifying things. *Broken seal* equaled *commitment*. Fate said so.

Did dark fey marry? Would he get her a ring? Shit, they were probably poor after she'd destroyed his expensive stuff and all. She'd have to go out and roll tourists—or Fort Knox. Since he'd be quitting his gig as *secrets master*, she could be the main breadstealer of the Darklight family.

Today between kisses, he'd told her they would find a new place to live. Somewhere for them to start fresh. A place where Thad could—at the very least—visit. In other words, no orgy observatory.

"You'd really do that?" she'd asked.

"You're my mate—which means he's my brother by fate."

Now she sighed as he strapped his quiver to his leg. Her long, lean, dark fey assassin.

He glanced over at her, caught her grinning stupidly at him. Yet he didn't return her smile.

"I'll be back in a minute," Rune told her. "I need to take care of something."

She frowned. "Okay."

With a last glance at his mark on Josephine's neck, he traced to the observatory.

Over the day, he'd had time to think about his plan to retrieve Thaddeus, and doubts were creeping in. Last night, Rune had been high from victory, but now he wondered if he could remove the wraiths.

Should his arrows—and Josephine's telekinesis—fail, would he have to resort to Meliai, the nymph from Dalli's covey? She'd promised him a key. He suspected it was a lock of Valkyrie hair.

When he'd rebuffed her, she'd made her own vow: "I'll never give you my possession until you bed me, and bed me well."

Sleeping with another female for this mission had always been a possibility.

Sleeping with another female for the Møriør was a certainty.

Now that he produced seed, he'd have to use that contraception spell routinely. Not that he would ever take release with another female, but he feared even his pre-cum could kill.

He rolled up his left sleeve and gazed at his unmarked forearm. Though Josephine would be hurt, she needed to get used to this reality of their lives.

This is bigger than just me, than what I want. I'm the eyes and ears. Hadn't Rune sworn his resolve would never falter?

Of all the beings in the worlds, Orion had chosen him—for some reason considering him a worthy ally.

I've striven every day since then to be one.

Rune began to ink the runes for that spell once more.

FIFTY-SEVEN

When he joined her ten minutes later, Rune was still as serious as before.

"Everything all right?" she asked with a forced smile. "Was I too rough with you today?"

He raised his glowing wrist. "Nïx has gone to ground." Ah, he was now in ultra-game-face mode. "Are you ready?"

"You bet. Let's put the *breaking* back in B&E."

With a nod, he looped an arm around her shoulders and traced to Val Hall.

Into chaos.

Jo clapped her hands over her ears against the deafening sounds. Constant thunder boomed so loud she could feel the percussion in her belly. With piercing shrieks, the wraiths swirled like a furious red tornado. Their skeletal faces looked enraged, their jaws hanging low around their screams.

Nïx had invited Jo and Rune; the Valkyries' guards were prepared for an attack.

Eyes watchful, Rune yelled to Jo, "Is he here?"

She barely heard him. She had to yell back, "Here!" She'd already caught Thad's scent coming from the manor.

Rune waved at her. *Ladies first*, he mouthed. *Let's see what you've got.*

She nodded, starting to ghost. "Get ready to trace inside!" As she fixed her gaze on her target, her body levitated, her feet floating above the ground.

All she had to do was nudge the wraiths away for a split second. She raised her hands. Power leapt from her mind to her palms like Tesla coils.

The force kept building until it was *too* strong, about to blow up in her face. She needed an emergency brake! Her eyes darted. She was losing it, couldn't contain that power any longer!

With a scream, she hurled it at the wraiths.

Contact!

Their circle shifted. She and Rune traced at once—

The next thing she saw was a cloudless sky above a silent field. They'd caught her and thrown her?

Across the field, Rune shot to his feet, shook his head hard, then traced to her. "Are you all right?"

She took his offered hand, standing. "How'd they touch me? I was ghosting."

Rune inspected his bow. "They're dead warriors. You're half spirit."

"Well, I crapped out. It's up to you," she said, puzzled by how disappointed he appeared. Surely he hadn't been laying odds on her success. "Batter up, Rune."

Back at Val Hall, the wraiths' shrieks were even louder. The red funnel bulged outward, like an inflamed wound.

Rune nocked *seven* arrows, all black. One-and-done. He drew the string to his strong chin, and his archer's gaze grew lethally focused. This male was her mate. He'd overcome so much—to become a hero.

My God, he's magnificent.

He exhaled. Body frozen like a statue, he released the string.

The arrows were a detonation. *IMPACT.* Shockwaves fanned out. Smoke billowed.

She was about to trace for the manor, but he grabbed her arm, shaking his head.

The shockwaves faded, revealing an inner ring of wraiths. The scattered beings in the outer ring congealed again, their low moans joining the other shrieks. Had those freaks arranged for cannon fodder?

She thought Rune muttered, *"Failure."*

The wraiths were immovable. Thad remained trapped. She rocked on her feet when she caught her brother's scent again. He smelled of . . . fear.

Rune clasped her shoulder. "Josephine, your heart's racing."

"Thad's *afraid*." She was desperate to reach him, to protect him. "I'm ready to hear about your plan B now."

Without another word, Rune teleported her to a location amid a rustling stand of woods. The air was cooler here, the winds even more blustery. It took her a few moments to register what towered before her.

The largest tree she'd ever seen.

Boisterous laughter and music sounded from within the hollowed trunk. Floors were carved into the wood, lit with lanterns. Rooms occupied the gigantic limbs. Between enormous roots was an arched entryway. "Where are we?"

He released her and slung his bow over his chest. "The Dryads' covey."

"As in tree nymphs? Naturally the solution to our problem involves the nymphs." Jo wrapped her arms around herself, wondering why he was being so standoffish. "Not even surprised anymore."

"There's one here named Meliai. She's supposed to know of a way inside Val Hall. I suspect she owns a lock of Valkyrie hair."

"The key! Let's go talk to her."

He gazed to Jo's right as he said, "She won't talk for free."

"Okay. Then we'll pay her. I've got cash and can get more like nobody's business." Fort Knox, anyone?

Finally he met her eyes. "This one has no interest in money."

FIFTY-EIGHT

Josephine asked slowly, "Then what is she interested in?"

In their time together, Rune had never seen her afraid for herself. Fear for Thad had made her breaths shallow, her lovely face gone even paler.

Rune had failed his mate the day after he'd claimed her. *I got used to winning.* But the game wasn't over yet. She wanted her brother back. Rune could turn his failure into triumph. Storm Nïx's lair in the process? All the better.

With one measly lay. "Meliai won't talk unless I fuck her. And well."

Josephine's vivid eyes dimmed. "You've gotta be kidding me."

"It's a status thing," he said. "I've been with everyone who lives here, everyone but Meliai."

"How many?"

He exhaled. "I don't think you want to know."

"Because of my jealousy issues, you mean?" She started toward the tree. "*I* can get that bitch to talk."

He grabbed her arm. "Ah-ah. You do *not* threaten a nymph. If you commit violence on a covey's grounds, you'll be shunned by every single one of their species."

"So?"

"They are everywhere, and they are necessary. They can make life very easy, or nightmarishly difficult."

"When you offered me your 'open relationship'—to stray but then meet up after—you were talking about nights like this?"

"It was going to happen eventually, Josephine. I told you I broker in information, and I use sex to get it. This is part of my job. I can't retire from it right at the Accession." He curled his finger under her chin. "Better to get this out of the way, so you know what to expect." *So you don't get your hopes up.*

"You would choose your job over your mate?"

He dropped his hand. "I am choosing to *remain myself*. My mate should try to understand why that matters to me!"

"This is your plan B? The one you had in place *before* you screwed me last night?"

"Yes, I've known I might need to transact with Meliai," he said, his ire at the ready.

Josephine's was just as much so. "I made it clear if you had sex with me, it was as good as saying we were exclusive. Maybe you should've thought about that before you did the deed!"

"Did I ever agree to those terms?"

She blinked repeatedly, as if she'd been slapped. "Wow. I *am* as naïve as you accused. You schooled me, didn't you?"

"I tried to back out, for just this reason. You manipulated me into it."

"Maybe I did—the *first* round. But not the next twenty!" A gust of wind blew her hair over her pale face. She tossed it back. "What are you going to do about your poison? Your demon seal's gone."

He shoved up the sleeve of his shirt.

Her eyes widened at the contraceptive rune. "You really were planning on this."

"I prepared for any eventuality."

"Meliai better not claw your skin like I did *last night*."

"Nymphs don't have claws."

In a disgusted tone, Josephine said, "And you would know."

"The sooner I get done here, the sooner we can free Thad." Rune hadn't been able to save his own mother, but he could save his new brother. "Do you want him back or not?"

She looked stricken. "Of course I do."

"I intend to protect both of you, and right now, we're wasting time—more of it than you think. Each minute here equals several in the mortal world."

Her lips parted wordlessly. Then she rallied to say, "I don't want Thad to be in that house of horrors a second longer than he needs to be, but there's got to be another way."

"Do you think I *want* to do this tonight? Do you think I wouldn't rather be back in our bed, anticipating the night with you?"

"*Our bed?* You say that like it's sacred or something. You've taken me to this place because you intend to be in *her* bed."

"Any other time, I would keep these parts of my life separate, out of respect for you." He started toward the lantern-lit entrance. Over his shoulder, he said, "However, this counts as part of our mission to kill Nix—which means you're to stay with me." To himself, he grated, "Yet another example of my mate getting her way."

Less than two hours ago, Rune had been inside her. Less than one hour ago, Jo had been thinking about wedding rings.

She'd yearned for a relationship with him so badly that she'd ignored the countless warnings—while he'd had other intentions all along.

But if he was too stupid to realize how amazing things could be between them, why would she want to be with an idiot? Maybe she should accept his offer of help, closing off her feelings for him.

I'll use him to get Thad back, then my brother and I will leave New Orleans together, leave Rune in the dust. She could get another lover, but she couldn't get another Thaddie.

Barely maintaining tangibility, she caught up with Rune.

He must've thought she'd signed on with this plan, because he took her hand in his, gripping it possessively. "We'll get past this. With age, you'll see things more realistically."

She gaped down at their hands. How many times had she dreamed of walking like this with a guy, the other half of their whole, two souls linked in an unbreakable bond?

They *were* bound by fate, supposedly in an eternal union. She'd thought her dream had come true with Rune.

Now she felt like she was going to the gallows, dread making her queasy. The noisy laughter and blaring music coming from the tree seemed to mock her feelings.

No, no, Rune could talk about this open relationship all he wanted, but he'd been crazy jealous when he'd thought she had a mate. He'd been jealous of Desh.

Over the day, Rune had gazed down into her eyes as he'd rocked inside her, and she'd *felt* his love. They hadn't just had sex; they'd made love.

When it came down to it tonight, he would balk. Surely he would. He had the last time with that other nymph!

They neared the huge arched entryway. *Any minute now, he'll pull the plug on this.*

But he kept going, squiring her inside a loud barroom packed with partying immortals. Dozens of demons were here. Some of the other guys looked human, just bigger and more animalistic. Lykae?

She could pick out the gorgeous Dryads. They wore nothing but gauzy skirts, their bare chests painted with leaf images.

Rune had slept with all of them.

Except one.

When he entered, cheers broke out. As in the other covey, these creatures acted as if a rock star had come to visit.

He smiled at different females, greeting them.

Any minute now . . . Meliai might not even be here. Or she could be screwing someone else. With more time, Rune would see reason.

"She's here." He jerked his chin toward a redheaded nymph at the bar.

Jo's stomach dropped. Meliai was . . . off-the-charts. Flawless body. Waist-length red hair and porcelain skin. Pink cheeks glowing with health. Doe-brown eyes. They sparkled when she caught sight of Rune.

She was the most beautiful female Jo had ever seen. Even the tall, graceful fey at the ball couldn't compare.

Rune had asked, "Do you think I *want* to do this?"

After looking at the half-dressed Meliai, she could honestly say, "Yes, Rune the Insatiable. Yes, I do."

If he screwed the redhead, Jo was done forever. She was about to lose him, just when she'd found him. Her claws decided to dig into his hand.

"I'll return with what we need as quickly as possible." He tugged his hand away.

To her shame, she clung before letting go. "Wait! You expect me to just sit here?" With all the other women he'd previously enjoyed?

As Meliai sauntered over, he told Jo, "You must stay—because of the terms of *your* vow."

Jo swiped at her forehead, her queasiness worsening. She might have to chance never drinking blood again.

Meliai smiled at Rune in welcome, seeming unconcerned he'd brought another woman with him. "How wonderful of you to visit."

The nymph, with all her experience, was probably a much better lay than Jo. Would Rune arrive at the same conclusion? Nausea churned. *Too hot in here.* Jo was about to throw up blood, needed air.

Would Rune make Meliai scream?

Of course he would. He was supposed to fuck her "well."

He wasted no time with the nymph, lowering his voice to say, "You can get me past the wraiths?"

Meliai looked him up and down as if he were a piece of meat. "I have the means." Her throaty voice dripped with innuendo as she said, "And I just so happen to need something of yours very badly."

FIFTY-NINE

Josephine's face was paper-white, her outline flickering.

Why couldn't she understand how little swiving another would mean to him? He was a taken male; he was Josephine's. Meliai was a grudging chore to be done with—

Josephine darted for the exit.

Fury welled inside him. He'd told her over and over this would happen. But she'd chosen to believe whatever she wanted to.

"I'll return shortly," he said to the nymph. "Be available."

Meliai raised her brows. "I'll only wait so long."

He made his way past admirers, nodding absently at them as he followed the only female he wanted.

Outside in the windy night, she leaned against the trunk, facing away from him.

"What is wrong with you?" he snapped. "You got jealous before and destroyed all my things. Once more, you're jealous, throwing a tantrum to get your way." Giving no concern for what *he* wanted. "I won't be manipulated again!"

She turned to him with her eyes glinting.

He bit out a curse. "Why this hang-up, Josephine? You got past how many I was with before you. Why does the timing of this matter so much?"

"The timing?" Her voice was strained. "Explain to me how this would work. After screwing someone else, you'd shower, then hop in bed with me? Would we laugh about funny things that happened at work? Would you call if you got tied up with a client?"

"It wouldn't occur every night, and probably not often after the Accession." Then a thought struck him. What would happen once the Møriør seized control of the Gaia realm? Rune's means were particularly fruitful when rooting out dissension; his duties might ramp up even more.

The mere idea exhausted him.

"Not every night? Will you listen to yourself? You are talking about *being inside* other females. About taking their bodies with your own."

"This is my job! You saw me with the four nymphs that first night. Did I look overwhelmed with passion? Or did I look bored?" *Like I'd rather be making arrows in my chair by the fire?* Would he never be free from this chore? "You remarked on my lack of reaction."

Josephine's tears spilled over—they were blood tears, *his* blood—and it was killing him. She was too young to be losing nourishment, and she couldn't have fed enough during the many times he'd taken her today.

He wrapped his palm around her nape. "If you tell me Thaddeus will be fine for just a while longer, we'll go home for tonight. Say it, Josephine."

Her gaze darted. "We can figure out something else. If we work together. So I need you to stop thinking like this!"

His hand tightened on her neck. "Like this? This is *me*! You've told me you feel more than infatuation for me. Then aren't you supposed to accept me as is? Why do you have to try to change me? What is so bloody wrong with how I am right now?"

"You're trying to change me too! You're making me give up something I feel like I'll die without."

Jo and Rune had traveled worlds together and had encountered creatures of all species. They'd seen wonders.

He'd never looked at anyone or anything with this much bafflement. "You've gotten what you wanted. I'm yours, and you're mine. I plan to spend the rest of my life with you. Have children with you. You're not alone anymore, Josephine. You have me. And you'll have your brother—if I do what's necessary."

He was making promises to her, just like that groom. Except Jo's actual groom was about to spend his wedding night with a nymph.

And Rune could act like he was nobly doing this for Thad, but he was also doing it for the Møriør, for his mission. He still needed to kill Nïx.

His eyes widened as he lit on an idea. "You can ghost inside me. We'll both be present, and you'll see how little I'm affected."

"I've been kidding myself." This male was never going to be faithful. He wasn't going to balk tonight. She shoved his hand off her nape. "I told you I wanted monogamy. Not a threesome."

"Monogamy?" He gave a bitter laugh. "There's obviously no reasoning with you, because you're too young to see the bigger picture. You like to keep things simple? Sometimes life isn't simple."

"It won't bother you when your mate takes advantage of our open relationship? You got jealous of Desh, and I wasn't even screwing him. Yet."

Black forked out across Rune's eyes. "I'm not a hypocrite, but there would be no *reason* for you to bed others. No *need*. That wouldn't be like for like. You'd probably think random sex means something. I'm old enough—and experienced enough—to know it means less than nothing."

"Experienced? You're letting your past color the way you see this!"

"Of course I am! That's exactly how I know it's meaningless! Why can't you get that through your head?"

Her tears kept spilling. She wasn't normally a crier, but she was about to lose the second person she'd ever wanted to keep. Should she have fought more for Thad when she'd had the chance? Desperate, she told Rune, "If you sleep with other people, I vow to the Lore I will too."

"Gods damn it, do you never learn? You're acting like a child! Fine. Fuck other males. You won't coerce me with yet another vow!"

"When I return home from my dates, will you ask if my lays satisfied me? You'll probably be put out when I'm full of another's blood and can't take any of yours."

He drew his head back, as if this was insane talk. "Again, there's no *need* for you to drink from another! Why would you even consider that? Your eyes can grow red if you drink indiscriminately."

"Then I'd better stick with a few trusted sources."

"And how will that work? You have black blood. I don't think your bite will be poisonous, but would you risk it? You either drink me—or you drink others. You can't have it both ways."

"Your blood will run its course in a day or two. If your job calls you away too many nights, I'll have to share suppers with someone else." A lie. Once he slept with Meliai, she would never take from him again.

What if she dreamed of him with the nymph? Jo would lose her everloving shit.

He gritted his teeth. "For future reference, mate, this is *not* how to deal with me. Emotional manipulation and tears? Ultimatums and childlike behavior? You are pushing every wrong button. All you've done is compound my anger and reinforce my intentions." He looked at her like she was pathetic. "I don't even recognize you."

She *felt* pathetic. But she had all these unfamiliar emotions, and no experience with them. No outlet. Her body flickered from solid to air.

"Why are you losing control like this?"

"Control? *Control?*" She flew at him, solidifying to beat on his chest. "You asshole! You're breaking my heart, and you can't even see you're ending us!"

He snatched her wrists, capturing her hands against him. "Ending?" His voice turned tender, but it was menacing at the same time. "Oh, Josephine, there is no *ending*. We're bonded mates now, so you're stuck with me. *Eternally.* That's why I'm confident you'll get past this."

She wrenched her hands free. "You're wrong!"

"Do you really think you can exist without the pleasure I give you? Or the companionship? You were alone for the last fourteen years. How'd that work out for you?"

She beat on him some more. "Do *you* really think I'll let you give me a steady stream of new nightmares? I'd rather starve than relive all your late nights 'at work.'"

He bit out, "I *want* you to dream my memories of this, to experience what it's like feeling utterly *nothing*—"

"Rune?" Meliai walked outside, her gauzy skirt whipping in the winds.

Jo turned away so the nymph wouldn't see her tears. She reminded herself that Rune—Ruin—was about to be in the rearview mirror. But that only made her cry more.

"How much longer?" Meliai asked. Impatient for her stud? "It's now or never."

"On my way." He turned to Jo, pulling her close to kiss her, but she averted her face.

He murmured, "From my vantage, I've got to weigh whether you'll be more angry I swived a nymph—or that I let your brother suffer. You're about to learn a lesson I grasped very early: one measly fuck can equal something you want badly."

Maybe that was true. Maybe she wasn't being rational. But it was difficult to stay rational—when she felt like she was being throat punched. She murmured back, "How is this different from your past? You'll be having sex in exchange for something. You're going to be a whore again, only this time there'll be no excuse for it."

He ground his teeth so hard that muscle ticked in his wide jaw.

"Obviously I was wrong when I said you weren't that man anymore," she continued. "But then, I *am* naïve."

At her ear, he grated, "If it makes you feel better, I can honestly say I'll be thinking of you."

He straightened, then started toward Meliai. They strolled off together, leaving Jo behind.

Knife in gut. Knife in gut. Knife in gut.

That's when a realization hit her like a Valkyrie's fist: *I'm completely in love with that prick.*

Tears ran freely down her face. Of all the times for her to recognize this . . .

She knew she was in love—because nothing else could hurt this much. Nothing ever had, except for when she'd left Thad behind.

Rune glanced back at her one last time before turning a corner.

She could get another lover, but she couldn't get another Rune.

SIXTY

Dalli stopped Rune and Meliai in the corridor. "What in the gods' names are you doing?"

He flicked his hand at Meliai. "Her, apparently."

Dalli told the other nymph, "Wait in your room. I need to speak to him."

Meliai asked him, "Any requests for lingerie?"

"Whatever's quickest."

"Eager. I like it." Meliai traipsed away.

When they were alone, Dalli said, "Have I heard correctly—you brought Josephine here?"

He nodded. "She's truly my mate, Dalli."

"Then what could possess you to do this?"

"Meliai has information I need to free Josephine's brother from a dangerous situation. I've been tasked with getting him back." Success would go a long way toward soothing his mate's feelings. She'd see that Rune's means were often an efficient solution to a problem. She would better understand *him*.

"You expect her to wait outside while you gather your information?" Dalli was incredulous.

"I brought Josephine with me because she vowed to the Lore she wouldn't drink again—ever—unless she was with me on this mission. So unless you can force Meliai to cooperate with me, I don't have much of a choice." He knew Dalli couldn't. Despite her age, her authority was limited. The Nymphae power hierarchies weren't like those in other factions.

"If I could force her to tell you, I would."

"Then my path is clear. You know I won't enjoy this. Mentally, I won't even be there. I damn sure won't come." He'd have to fantasize about Josephine to stay hard.

"Rune, *I* know you won't be there—your eyes are already glazing over—but others can't understand that. There's got to be another way."

"Should I leave Josephine's brother in danger? Now my brother as well? You've never encountered a creature who loves her sibling more. And besides, she needs to accept this is what I do. Damn it, I'm too old to change!"

Even if she's my destined female. The one he'd never hoped to have.

"You're about to harm your relationship irreparably."

"And what do you think the death of her brother would do?" He lowered his voice even more. "While I'm standing here talking to you, a seventeen-year-old boy is in Val Hall, trapped behind the wraiths. I can't get to him without Meliai's information on the Scourge."

"You're going up against the Valkyries?"

"I'll do whatever it takes to protect my new family." His mission for the Møriør seemed far removed.

Dalli exhaled. "Meliai used to repair Val Hall's oaks from lightning damage. She could know of a way in."

"Good. Will you go talk to Josephine and smooth things over? Make her understand this will have no more effect on me than tying my shoe."

"I'll do what I can."

"She isn't feeling . . . She isn't doing well." Those blood tears tracking down her face had wrecked him. "Just watch out for her." He headed to Meliai's chambers. Her door was open, and the nymph was lighting candles.

How bloody romantic. The cloying smoke mingled with the overblown perfumes in her room. "Give me your vow you have what I seek." He shut the door behind him. Amid this haze, he lost Josephine's reassuring scent.

"My vow, is it?" Meliai grinned coyly. "Would it be so awful to sleep with me? If I'm lying, you'll still get the lay of your lifetime."

At his unbending expression, she said, "Very well. I vow to the Lore I possess something you could use to get past the wraiths." She shrugged out of her robe, leaving her in only a transparent teddy.

Josephine, with every inch of her body covered in bandages, was sexier to him.

"I should warn you, I've been satisfied dozens of times today." Meliai reclined on her bed. "You're going to have to work for it. It'll take hours and hours and hours." She reached for a goblet of wine on her bedstand. "Do strip off all your clothes."

He ground his fangs, longing to strangle this bitch—not pleasure her. Pride stinging, he removed his bow and quiver. How triumphant did he feel right now? He kicked off his boots and yanked his shirt over his head.

"Very nice." She watched him avidly, like his brothel patrons of old.

He felt as much disgust for her as he had for his first customer, a hideous serpent shifter with keyhole pupils, slits for nostrils, and a scaling bald head.

Please or perish. Though the demon in him had bayed for Magh's throat between its fangs, the fey in him had reasoned that fucking the serpent female was a mindless biological function. Servicing her body with his meant nothing. *She* meant nothing.

A freeing calm had descended over him. He'd become untouchable: *I'm not even here.*

Though the serpent's forked tongue had flicked across his throat, Rune's slanted grin never wavered. "Ah, dove, the things I plan to do to you. . . ."

He'd gotten through that; he could do this. *Turn your mind from this room, this situation.* That familiar coldness washed over him.

He'd told Josephine he'd be thinking of her. He should have told her the whole truth: *I'll be holding on to you.* He'd cling to what he felt for her.

Because right now his heart was cold ash.

If he did this, would he extinguish what Josephine felt *for him*? She'd seen his memories and had accepted his past—until tonight. *"You're going to be a whore again, only this time there'll be no excuse for it."*

Magh's words: *"You've been a whore for so long, I thought we should make it official."*

With a smug look over the rim of her goblet, Meliai said, "I can't wait to see your cock. It's supposed to be legendary."

"It's the only part that matters, right, dove?" As Rune removed his pants, one thought stood out: *I never* stopped *being a whore.*

SIXTY-ONE

Rune is ruin.

Jo paced outside the tree entryway, her hands balled into fists. She needed to go somewhere and scream. What was so weird—if she left, Rune would come find her. *After.* He'd told her he would never let her go, and she believed him.

Last night, before they'd made love under beckoning stars, he'd brushed his fingers over her cheekbones and assured her he had a plan B.

He'd known screwing the nymph was a possibility.

A flash of a dream hit her, a snippet from his memories. He'd been sitting back in his chair in Orion's stronghold. "If one of my tarts is stupid enough to want more," he'd told his allies, "then she deserves all the heartache in the worlds."

Huh. This stupid tart got what she deserves.

A beautiful blonde loitered by the entrance, watching her intently. Could that be Dalli, Rune's "friend with benefits"? Add some more humiliation to the pile. Jo was about to tell her to go fuck herself with an oak splinter when she scented a demon.

Deshazior??

He'd just traced inside the barroom! Standing taller than everyone else, he seemed to scent her as well, lifting his face, then turning toward her outside.

Jo had a friend! "Desh!"

He grinned and traced to her. "Hello, little luv!" He wrapped his brawny arms around her and squeezed.

"You don't know how happy I am to see you!"

"Why these tears?" He cleared his throat and backed up a step. "These black, poisonous tears?"

Oh. Blood had dried on her face. She must look like hell washed over.

"Bet this has somethin' to do with yer baneblood. Where's the poxy scum?"

"With another woman." And Jo was sitting outside, waiting like a tied-up pet, more pitiful than she'd ever been.

"He's up there in a love nest?"

"Is that what they call them? Hi-fucking-larious." Tonight, Rune had gone out on a limb. She laughed bitterly.

Desh's gaze landed on her neck, her *mark*. "The baneblood claimed you as his mate, and he's still with another?"

"He's here to get information."

Desh scratched his head with confusion. "I'm not followin'."

Jo found herself telling him parts of the story—her fight with Nïx, her brother's captivity, the failed attempts to overpower the wraiths—ending with: "And now I'm supposed to cool my heels while he bones Red."

"All this to get into Val Hall? If ye wanted in, I wish ye'd come to me."

Jo's breath caught. "Do you know a way?"

"Gettin' in's the easy part. Gettin' out'll be the kicker."

She grabbed his big hands, squeezing to urge him on.

"If ye fought Nïx, go surrender to her. They'll take ye inside in a heart-beat. Ye'll likely be dispatched to Val Hall's dungeon, but at least ye'd be closer to yer brother."

Thad was in a dungeon? "How do you know all this stuff?"

"I know a few Valkyries." He scratched his chin. "And ages ago, Nïx mentioned somethin' I was never able to figger. She says to me, 'Demon, when ye see the girl with black tears, tell her to surrender.' Drove me mad with curiosity, but she'd say naught else about it, seemed to have forgotten the entire conversation."

Tell her to surrender. Yet another invitation from Nïx.

Jo had thought she'd known Rune. She had been wrong. She'd thought she needed him to save her brother.

Wrong again, girl.

His mind filled with Josephine, Rune touched Meliai by rote. He was as out of his body as he'd been with the serpent.

If the nymph noticed, he didn't care.

Normally he would've been inside her by now. He could replay the last twenty-four hours with his mate to get it up, but his mind resisted that trick.

To stay hard with another, he was going to have to make a conscious effort. A conundrum. Because he couldn't stray in the first place if he was mindful of what was happening.

His thoughts were turned inward, puzzling over his fight with Josephine. Why in the hells had she been *that* upset? She hadn't cried when Nïx had been snapping her bones, but tonight tears had flowed.

Was Josephine so used to getting her way she'd cried out of resentment? She'd vowed she'd sleep with others, was all but making plans to drink from them. Yet another ridiculous vow. He'd never known anyone who abused them more.

In the future, while he was struggling not to become deadened in some distant covey, she'd be making besotted males come from her bite.

When Rune had claimed her, he'd thought, *She drinks me alone. After tonight, she fucks me alone.*

Not quite, baneblood. No one could pleasure her more than he did—but what about his taste? What if . . . what if she preferred another's blood? She'd never bitten anyone else.

She's me, and I'm her. What if she never wanted to darken her blood again?

He would recognize her little bite anywhere—in a way, it was like his claiming mark. If he encountered one of her lovers and saw it . . .

He ground his fangs. She didn't *have* to feed from others. What was the point? They would keep that separate from any arrangements between them. He'd make it a condition.

Maybe *he* would use a vow to the Lore!

He would convince her blood-drinking was for them alone, their special act. As she'd described: *with the licking, and the lips, and the penetration.* Damn it, that should be private! Just last night, their heartbeats had synchronized; she'd commented on the bond, how she was different.

Why would she *ever* share that—

He stilled. Josephine viewed sex the way he viewed her feeding. As private and special. As something that bonded them and altered them. She'd left her claiming bite on him, just as he'd done with her.

It didn't matter that he gave little meaning to sex with others. *She* did.

He hissed in a breath. Unfortunately, he'd come to this gut-wrenching conclusion when he was naked in bed with another female, after deserting his mate—while she'd looked as if she were dying inside. *Fuck!*

He yanked Meliai's hands off him and sat up.

"What's wrong?" she asked, her voice sounding far away.

He shook his head hard, bringing himself back to this room. When Josephine had told him that they'd think of another way to get her brother back, Rune had been confused; wouldn't she do anything for Thad?

She didn't care *less* about her brother; she cared *more* about Rune. Just the fact that she hadn't sent him off with a smile and a wave told him how much.

Her heart had opened up to another!

His spike of excitement faded. Tonight, she'd cried, *You're breaking my heart.*

She hadn't been throwing a fit like a scorned lover; she damn sure hadn't been trying to manipulate him.

Josephine had reacted like a female *grieving a lover she'd lost*.

She would be finished with Rune after this! Panic seized him by the throat. He swung his legs over the edge of the bed, tracing to his clothes.

He could still fix things with her. She'd be outside waiting—because he was supposed to return with the means to free Thaddeus.

"Rune, answer me!" Meliai cried. "What's wrong?"

He yanked on his pants. "I'm done," he said, and he meant it. Rune had just retired from his millennia-old job as secrets master. He had time to figure out something with the Møriør, but how was he going to save Thaddeus?

Meliai scrambled to her knees. "You can't be serious!"

By spurning her, he risked angering coveys the worlds over. There was no worse insult to her kind.

"What do you need to get back into this? I'll do it." She cupped her breasts, tweaking her nipples. "Imagine your filthiest fantasy, and it's yours."

His fantasies all involved the beautiful, brash, courageous mate he didn't deserve. The one waiting outside for him to finish bedding another.

"*Anything*, Rune."

He stomped into his boots, then pulled on his shirt. "No." That word, from his lips, about this subject . . . "*No.*" Gods, that tasted delicious.

"Why? At least give me a reason!"

"I've changed." A thought struck him. He would *never* have to do this again—dragging on his clothes, wishing for a shower and the peace of his chair by the fire.

He was free.

Meliai sputtered, "Short of sex with me, there is no way you can get past the wraiths."

"I'll figure something out."

"Are you going to fuck your way in there? You'd do it, wouldn't you? Screw creatures as repulsive as the Scourge?"

How was he going to face Josephine? By promising her he'd get her brother back, Rune had set himself up to fail her in one way or another.

I don't want to fail her. He strapped on his quiver, slinging his bow over his shoulder. Just as she'd said, there had to be an alternative, something he wasn't seeing. . . .

He traced his fingers over his bowstring. Tonight, he'd forever sheathed one weapon.

I have another.

He unslung his bow and nocked a bonedeath arrow. He stared down Meliai, his voice deadly as he said, "Give me that key, or I'll release my arrow, pulverizing the bones of anyone within screaming distance."

Meliai gasped. "You risk a war with the Nymphae? You'll never enter our sacred places again!"

"So be it. Now talk. What do you have?"

Her gaze betrayed her, darting to her wall, to a raised knot in the wood. A concealed hollow?

"Something to show me?" He waved his bow. "Retrieve it."

With a fearful look, she crossed to the wall. "My sisters and I will make you pay dearly for this." She pressed a hidden latch, and a compartment opened. Among her cache of amber jewels was a glass case.

When he realized what she possessed, sweat beaded his upper lip. No, not a lock of Valkyrie hair. In the case was a fire-red feather.

A *phoenix* feather. He could sense its mystical power from here.

To an archer, it was priceless; to Rune, a game changer. He could use it to fashion the flights of an arrow, amplifying his magicks exponentially.

With that feather, he could create the most destructive arrow ever to fly.

SIXTY-TWO

Standing at the gates of hell.

Wraith shrieks pained Jo's ears, thunder booming in her stomach once more.

Desh bent down to her ear to yell, "Sure ye have this, little luv?"

Remembering her last meeting with Nïx, Jo stifled the urge to rub her arms and nodded.

"Gotta warn ye, smells like they've got an army in there."

Since Jo had been here earlier (who knew how long ago, with the weird time flow?) dozens of cars had been parked near the manor, as if a party was happening inside. The scents coming from Val Hall were different from before. The sounds too.

Desh glowered at the entrance. "Scurvy wenches didn't invite me."

"I've got it," Jo yelled.

"I'll be at Lafitte's, in case they don't accept yer white flag."

"Thank you, Desh. Fair winds."

He met her gaze. "Good luck." Then he disappeared.

Jo marched toward the spine-chilling Ancient Scourge. What wouldn't she do for Thad?

As she neared Val Hall, the new sounds and scents bombarded her.

She couldn't place so many threads: fur, smoke, a cool slice of ice. So many hisses, growls, and mutters.

Hadn't she once recognized these creatures as fellow Loreans? Why couldn't she remember? Out of habit, she gazed up at the stars, seeking an answer, but clouds hung low, concealing them. Just as a cloud stood between her and her memories!

Her entire life was a mass of frustration. Her inability to remember her early childhood basically meant she didn't have one. Same with her parents. Her inability to retrieve her brother tore at her.

My ex, my former guy, is inside someone else right now. I love him, and he's inside another woman.

Before coming here, Jo had flagged down Dalli and left a message for Rune. Because she was done with him.

Done.

So damned frustrating. She couldn't fix Rune, or her memories—but she could reach Thad.

All she had to do was scream, *I surrender.* But that galled Jo.

As if in another lifetime, she'd watched girls retreat from Wally's house with their fight stolen. She'd seen it happen to the women around her motel.

Rune expected Jo to surrender her dreams, to stop fighting for what she wanted? That made her more furious than the actual infidelity!

He expected Jo to just lie down? Like he did?

Like I once did. I surrendered Thad as a baby.

She needed to scream two little words. But Jo didn't surrender; she Hulk-smashed. She squeezed until things broke.

She'd forgotten that over the last two weeks.

Just outside the wraiths' reach, she turned intangible, then launched a fist into the tempest. When she drew back her arm, gashes covered it.

"We're alike, then?" Jo was death and death rolled into one, a shapeshifter between the living and the dead; it made sense that the Scourge could harm her if she was in ghost form.

The whirling wraiths slowed. One swooped down, hovering inches from Jo's face. They met gazes; the wraith's eyes were black pits. Yet then a flash of another image crossed the creature's face. She saw a beautiful woman for an instant, as fleeting as the lighthouse's beam. "Let me in," Jo murmured. "Or suffer."

The thing canted her head.

What are you seeing, wraith? Jo's tears had dried into hard tracks on her face. *Are you seeing Josephine Doe, a half-dead girl with absolutely nothing to lose?*

A girl with a lot of unresolved anger and abandonment issues? Jo whispered to her, "If I can bleed . . . so can you."

The thing was sucked into the tempest once more. Still in ghost form, Jo backed up, bringing power into her hands.

The wraiths screamed louder, sensing her growing threat.

I surrender?

Never. Fucking. Again.

The ground quaked from her building fury. What did she need Rune for? Jo would kick the ant mound, making the Valkyries—and anyone else—spill out. Once she'd dragged enough of them into their new graves, she would demand Thad's freedom.

Jo popped a crick in her neck and smiled. *No, Rune, some things* are *simple.*

Dalli was waiting for Rune at the edge of the barroom, her expression grave.

Outside of Meliai's perfumed room, he'd tried to catch Josephine's scent. And failed. "Where the fuck is she?"

Whatever Dalli saw in his bearing made her nervous. "I tried to stop her, but she left."

His lungs constricted. "She left me."

Dalli frowned. "That's what I just said."

"No, Josephine *left* me. She ended this." She'd warned him she would kick his ass to the curb.

"She gave me a message for you."

He straightened. "Talk."

"She wasn't quite . . . alone." Dalli fidgeted with the sash of her skirt. "She said she'd be thinking of you the entire time."

Having these words thrown back in his face made him realize how ridiculous they sounded. How hurtful. *Hateful.*

"Who took her away from me?" He'd accused Josephine of having jealousy issues? Rune was about to rip this place to the ground.

This godsdamned world.

"What male?" Who was about to die?

"Fair's fair, Rune. You were just with another."

He bared his fangs at her. *"What. Male?"* With the different time flows, she could already be beneath another.

"A demon named Deshazior."

Rune's claws stabbed into his palms, spilling his poison. Would Josephine go with that demon to his home or to her motel?

"I heard them talk about Valkyries," Dalli said.

Josephine couldn't have gone to Val Hall on her own. He'd *rather* she be in a motel room with Desh.

"About her surrendering—"

"The baneblood broke our deal!" Meliai cried, storming into the barroom. The crowd began to quiet. "Instead of bartering, he robbed me of a treasured possession! He threatened me and the entire covey!"

"Is that true?" Dalli asked.

Nod. He unslung his bow and nocked an arrow, readying for a return to Val Hall.

Dalli raised her face to him. "You are yet again the coveys' most wanted man—but for an entirely different reason." Just before he traced, she mouthed, *I am so proud of you.*

SIXTY-THREE

As more and more power gathered inside Jo, low creatures in the surrounding swamps fled with whimpers.

They should flee. Nïx had compared Jo to a nuclear weapon.

Ah-ah, Valkyrie, try supernova. No longer did Jo wish for a power emergency brake; she let her telekinesis mount.

The force was as strong as steel, yet light as air. Just like her, it was hot and cold, alive and dead.

Black clouds gathered above that eerie red funnel, mushrooming. Lightning bombarded the property, striking the copper rods.

With a wave of her hand, she raised one rod and launched it at the wraiths. They shrieked even more piercingly, but repelled her javelin. With both hands, she telekinetically lifted *all* the rods, letting them hover menacingly. The wraiths tightened their ring, bracing for impact.

"How's this for a white flag?" She hurled half of them at the wraiths. The red tempest jolted and recoiled with each hit, but managed to reform.

Hmm. All this pretty lightning . . . She brought the remaining rods to the very edge of the Scourge, positioning them just so—

BOOM! The first lightning bolt struck a rod; the metal channeled sizzling electricity straight to the wraiths.

Jo grinned. Fires had always been free fun, but this was so much better.

Rune didn't know what shocked him more: the sight of his mate attacking Val Hall, or the presence of Blace, Sian, Darach, and Allixta with Curses. He'd spotted them watching from a distance.

Josephine had arranged copper rods in the air, using the Valkyries' own lightning against them. She looked so small and delicate to be wielding such power. Those black tear tracks were like war paint against her ghostly white skin, highlighting her uncanny eyes. Her outline shimmered between bolts.

And I thought I would need to save her?

He wanted to trace to her side, but knew she'd unleash her fury on him. Though he deserved it, he needed to be in one piece once the Valkyries attacked.

Any second now, they'd spill out.

Seeming bored with the lightning, Josephine let fly all the rods, a volley of spears. The Scourge shrieked as one.

Then her attention fell on the closest oak tree. Immense, old. Probably filled to the brim with eavesdropping nymphs.

Josephine waved her hand, and the tree shot into the sky, roots exploding from the earth, like a rocket dusting off.

Nymphs within screamed, which she seemed to enjoy. When the tree plummeted, she batted it into the wraiths.

It connected in an explosion of groaning wood. She teed up another oak, then another, batting them one at a time, a barrage of cracking trunks and limbs.

Rune traced to the other Møriør. Never taking his eyes off her, he asked them, "What are you doing here?"

"We're watching your mate," Sian said. "Well done. She's horrifyingly lovely."

Rune slung his bow over his chest and returned his arrow. "How did you know Josephine's mine?"

"Orion told us days ago she would be revealed this night at Val Hall," Blace said. "He suggested you might need our assistance."

Rune needed all the help he could get. On his own, he was fucking up the most important thing that had ever happened to him. It'd taken him this much anguish just to realize he *could* be the male his mate needed.

Sian scratched his head. "I can't believe I asked how we would know her. I'd say one female is calling our attention."

"What *is* she?" Blace asked, staring at her.

"Half vampire, half phantom."

Sian whistled. "Those are rare."

"And powerful." Blace tore his gaze from Josephine. "If she's your mate, why is she attacking alone? And why do you smell like a nymph's bed at night's end?" Blace had always been amused by Rune's exploits; now he looked disappointed. "You're mated, and you're still with your tarts?"

Allixta sneered, "Once a whore, always a whore."

Rune growled at her—*hitting too close*. "I was going to sleep with a nymph in exchange for a way around the wraiths. Josephine's younger brother is trapped inside. She's been separated from him for more than half her life."

"I gather she wasn't on board with the nymph plan," Sian said. "Does she know she's your mate?"

Rune nodded. "I bungled this. I hurt her. I ended up stealing the prize I'd sought instead of bedding the nymph"—they raised their brows at that—"but it was already too late."

"What can we do?" Blace asked.

"If the Valkyries allow Josephine entry, she'll storm the lion's den without hesitation. I'll try to stop her, and in her present mood, she'll put me into the ground." He pictured her breaking his bow and planting it over his grave site. Rune dug into his pocket, taking out the fire-red feather. "I must be able to follow her inside." He needed his new arrow ready—*now*. Sweating, he split the feather with his claw.

Allixta said, "Is that what I think it is?"

"Phoenix feather. To take out the Scourge." He plucked another arrow from his quiver, one he'd refashion with the feather. *Must be straight and true.* "Val Hall is filled with what smells like an army of beings. I might need cover."

"Count us in," Sian said.

Not wanting to take his eyes from Josephine, Rune began to craft the new flights, his fingers working from muscle memory.

She targeted the cars next. She lifted them all with one raised palm. With her other hand, she flicked two fingers, and a yellow Lamborghini shot into the wraiths. The impact sounded like a missile hitting rock.

The Scourge warbled and wobbled, but returned to formation much more slowly this time. She was weakening them!

Another flick of Josephine's fingers. A Hummer hurtled toward the tempest.

Once he'd replaced the flights on his arrow, he used his blood to draw new runes on the shaft. Those symbols would connect his magicks with those of the feather.

As he worked, he could perceive the union—one power to direct the magicks and one to boost them.

He finished, taking one instant to gaze over his work before dropping the arrow into his quiver. He'd happily use this marvel to get his female back.

"This grows wearisome," Allixta said. "How long will she carry on?"

"Till she gets what she wants or drops," Rune answered, the awe in his voice undisguised. "My mate likes to keep things simple."

With another volley of cars, Josephine screamed, *"Come out and fight me, you bunch of pussies!"*

"And she loves a blunt tool," Rune added, his chest about to burst with pride.

SIXTY-FOUR

Her fury bubbling over, Jo traced to the cyclone, attacking the wraiths with her claws. Spectral matter sprayed! "I knew you could bleed!" She yelled with triumph, then called to Nïx, "You won't come out?"—she slashed the enraged wraiths over and over—"Then I'm coming in!"

The front door to Val Hall groaned open. Jo forced herself to let up, catching her breath as she floated back to wait. *Your move, Valkyries. . . .*

Someone unseen tossed a small bundle onto the porch. Jo squinted. A lock of hair. A key. So the rumor was true.

A wraith swooped in, snatching it up. The tempest parted like water around a rock.

They were letting Jo in. She dropped the rest of the cars—upside down, because she was a bitch. Then she floated toward the belly of the beast. *What wouldn't I do?*

"No, Josephine!"

Rune? When she spied him out of the corner of her eye, she waved her hand to pin him back.

"Gods damn it, don't go in there!"

Before Jo could reach Val Hall, pressure collared her throat. *How?* She was ghosting! The wraiths were still.

Comprehension. No one had intended to let her in; they'd used that key to let someone *out*.

A figure emerged from Val Hall.

Thad??

He strode past the wraiths, but his boots weren't touching the ground. Shadowy circles radiated around his eyes. His dark hair whipped over his pale face. His outline was faint.

Phantom faint. He looked as evil as they came. *Dear God, he is like me.* She reached for him. *"Tha . . . Tha . . ."*

His power slammed her to her knees, choking her. Her hands flew to her neck. She couldn't get air!

Rune bellowed, struggling against her telekinesis. He would hurt Thad to save his mate! She directed more force at Rune.

"Harder, kid!" some woman called from Val Hall. "Pop her bobble-head off!"

He was listening to her.

"Take her down, Thad! Come on, like we taught you."

The pressure increased, and Jo suddenly saw her future:

Thaddie's going to kill me.

As dizziness overtook her and black dots swirled her vision, memories of the past erupted in her mind. Thad's eyes were so like that woman's.

Like their . . . mother's. Jo had been with her right before her death!

Jo hadn't been her name then. She'd been . . . *Kierra.* A little girl. An eight-year-old halfling in Apparitia, the murky realm of the phantoms.

"It's worldend!" Kierra screamed. The sky was falling. Failing. *Wounded stars plummeted to their deaths, as bright as sparks from a flint.*

She clung to the edge of a vortex, her claws digging into the ground. All around her, more black holes hissed open, a wall of them, black upon black upon black.

Like spiders' eyes.

She had no idea where those sucking holes would lead—rifts had appeared in the ether as Apparitia had begun to die—but escaping through one was their only chance at survival. Mother had never teleported to another plane, couldn't evacuate them.

"Mother, come with me!" Some relentless force was crushing their dimension. A million screams had sounded with the first fires. Then the plains had jutted up into mountains. The nearby sea had risen, a pillar straight up into the sky. Flames had taken its place, blazing red for blue.

They'd heard rumors of a being who could crumble worlds using naught but his will.

With a pale hand raised to the night, her mother was fighting back. Between gritted teeth, she said, "No, I can't falter! Or we'll all be crushed!" If she teleported to Kierra, the dome she'd created above them might disappear.

She couldn't even crawl to her daughter. One of her hands emitted power; the other clung to her wailing newborn son. Her telekinesis was more powerful than most phantoms', but she was exhausted from delivering her baby just this morning.

Kierra's telekinesis was weak and unpracticed, but she had to fight like her mother. "Let me help you!" If only she were older!

"Nooo, Kierra! Save your power!"

The black holes grew hungrier, sucking at Kierra's legs. Her instinct clamored for her to become intangible. But she wasn't old enough yet. "Just try to reach a portal!"

Mother shook her head, her dark hair streaming all around her. "I need to keep yours open . . . as long as possible!" The sky plummeted lower, like the ceiling of a collapsing tunnel.

Mother's raised arm whipped in the howling gusts. "I'm going to let him go into the winds!" Her newborn? She wouldn't dare! "I'll direct him to you."

"Noooo, I might miss him! Please . . . chance any portal!"

"Catch him, Kierra! I know you can do it. And then don't ever let him go!"

With a cry, Mother released her precious baby to the winds. Just before he reached Kierra, huge spikes of crystal shot from the ground, sending him adrift by inches.

Kierra tensed her every muscle, readying to snare him. He was rising, heading for another vortex!

"Don't let him go!" Mother screamed.

"No, no!" Kierra stretched, her fingers splayed. An inch of space separated them. . . .

She managed a spurt of telekinesis . . . she snagged his swaddling! "Got him!" She cradled him with one arm. He was so tiny, his screams so loud. He didn't even have a name yet.

More explosions. Fire surged from the valley, racing toward them. Still holding up the sky, Mother went intangible. "You have to escape, dear one. You have to go." Lava seeped from the ground all around her.

"Come now!" Kierra screamed, tears streaming down her face. But she knew her mother would remain to defend this vortex entrance as long as possible.

"Keep him close. Protect him. I love you both so much." Flames towered around her ghostly form, about to swallow her. She mouthed, Dear one, please go.

Kierra mouthed back, We love you. *Past the flames, they met eyes.* I'll protect him.

Mother nodded and forced a watery smile. Just before she was engulfed, she saw Kierra release her hold and the vortex suck her children in—

Flying. Spinning. Weightless.

Kierra clutched the baby close as she zoomed down a tunnel of black, twirling over and over.

Vortex chutes crisscrossed. Waves of lava flooded in from other openings, speeding toward her and the baby. "Ah, gods, no!" She used her telekinesis to attempt a bubble around them. She hunched over her brother as lava coated the shield, heat and pressure grinding down on it.

Please hold, please hold, please hold.

That crushing force beat against her telekinesis. She clenched her eyes shut and prayed over and over. . . .

The heat gradually faded. She dared to glance up, blinking in confusion. Crystal? Her power had met lava under pressure, creating a transparent shell. It wrapped around her and the baby. A cocoon.

Time passed. Their momentum slowed. When the baby quieted, the total silence hit Kierra, and she sobbed for her mother. For her friends. For her world. She tucked her brother into the folds of her cloak, determined to protect him.

Eons eked by as they floated in their crystal cocoon, but they didn't age. Though she never felt hunger, she would cut her wrist and feed the baby.

Onward they floated.

Just when she'd decided they would be trapped in this existence forever, Kierra gazed up. Through the crystal, she witnessed . . . stars being born. She watched one planet learn how to spin. She could perceive the rotation of others. As if they danced for her.

Heaven.

She wept from the unutterable beauty. There's a curtain over the universe, but I'm seeing behind it. *Yet she wasn't to know these secrets. They weren't hers. No one child could bear that weight.*

Splendor broke her mind.

Her body was robbed of power, her abilities stunted. Her memories withered.

She and the baby continued on, floating as worlds bloomed and waned. Before her lids finally slid shut, she saw the universe reflected in an infant's half-closed eyes. . . .

Awakening. Can't feel my limbs!

After unending silence, she screamed, thrashing her legs. She jerked upright, banging her head against something. Crystal shattered all around her. Foreign sounds pained her sensitive ears. She hissed at the bright yellow light above.

Where am I? How have I come to be here? Ah, gods, *who* am I?

Movement in her arms. What was it? She opened her cloak to reveal a little infant just waking, blinking at her with hazel eyes, and all she knew was . . .

Love.

Her mother had given Thad to her! He and Jo had crossed the entire universe together. It couldn't end like this! She gasped out, "Thaddie." She reached for him, grasping, grasping—as she had fourteen years ago.

He stalked closer.

She couldn't maintain her telekinesis against Rune for much longer. He was fighting so hard! "Thaddie . . ."

"Us. Thad-de-us. That's my name."

Air. Need air. Rune was breaking free. *"Thad . . . pack."*

Thad's brows drew together, his outline flickering. "What did you say?" The chokehold eased.

"Brother! Here . . . to save you."

He released her with a yell. "Are you . . . *Jo?*" He traced to her, catching her just as her vision went dim.

SIXTY-FIVE

Freed from Josephine's telekinesis, Rune traced to Thaddeus. "Hand her over to me." He was all but begging with his bow shouldered and his palms up.

Thad ghosted with his unconscious sister in his arms, making her intangible as well. Rune couldn't snatch her away. He'd never wanted to fight so badly. Never had so many reasons why he couldn't.

The boy's eyes darted. "Who the hell are you?" As soon as Thad had figured out Josephine's identity, he'd gone from attacking to protecting her.

"I'm her mate," Rune rasped. "Give her to me."

When the other Møriør flanked Rune—in battle positions—Thad hissed.

Valkyries screamed from inside: "Bring her back to us!" "You won!" "You took that bitch down!"

Baring his fangs, Thad pulled Josephine closer to him.

Sounding as calm and reasonable as ever, Blace said, "We won't hurt you, boy. We mean no harm to you or your sister."

Allixta said telepathically, —*Speak for yourself. He bares his fangs at Møriør?*— An iridescent green light filled her palms.

—*Can you hold him?*— Rune asked her. —*Without* hurting *him? Please, witch! He could trace her anywhere in the universe.*—

She raised her hands, and slender tendrils of green slithered around Thad, through him, but he didn't seem to feel them, just gazed on warily.

—*Amazing,*— Allixta said. —*Even one of my power can't touch a shapeshifter like him.*—

The boy's mouth dropped open when Curses joined them. The creature wound between the Møriør, its movements predatory.

—*Control your beast, Allixta!*— Rune eased closer to Thad. "Brother, I need you to . . . just give her to me."

"Not a chance, mister. It looked like she was using telekinesis to keep you away."

"I need to explain some things to her. And she's injured. She must feed from me."

Thad was on the verge of tracing.

"Wait! Please! If you go, take this." Rune drew out his talisman. "Give it to her. I want her to have it."

Sian muttered aloud, "Hells."

The others understood the significance of the talisman. It had always reminded Rune to look toward the future; *Josephine is my future.* "She'll know what it means." He tossed it to Thad.

The boy caught it telekinetically, pulling it to his hand. Then he traced his sister away.

"Gods damn it!" Rune yelled. "I have no idea where he will take her." He leveled his gaze on Val Hall, on the wraiths that had resumed their guard. —*Nix will know.*— He unstrapped his bow, nocking the phoenix arrow.

—*There are more than just Valkyries inside,*— Sian said. —*Orion hasn't officially declared war on any of these factions yet.*—

—*Neutralize the wraiths, and then we'll reevaluate.*— Welcome counsel from Blace. —*After all, the arrow might not work.*—

—*Use the arrow to reach your target, then destroy her,*— Allixta said. —*As you told Orion you would do weeks ago. Have you forgotten your mission?*—

Rune drew the bowstring past his chin. No shot was more important than this one. He was as nervous as he'd been when first going to battle with a bow.

A flash memory of Orion: "Make your first shot count, archer. You'll remember it for the rest of your immortal life."

Rune had; Rune did.

—*Let your arrow fly,*— Blace murmured.

Rune relaxed his string fingers to loose the most perfect arrow he'd ever fired. On any other occasion, his heart would've soared at the precision of its flight.

Now he only wanted destruction. He got it.

The shockwave slammed into him, nearly laying him out. Sian shielded Allixta; Blace traced past the blast. Darach growled at it. Curses dug its claws into the ground.

The wraiths were scattered through the air! They lay dazed, hovering in different positions like a floating battlefield of dead. Val Hall's front door was wide open.

Nïx called in a cheery voice, "I'll be right with you, Møriør! Have to take my curlers out!"

Through the doorway, Rune could see legs jutting from under a couch. A woman wriggled out and popped to her feet.

Nïx?

Her hair looked as if she'd dust-mopped with her head, and her eyes were hazy. She told unseen beings, "I'll just be a moment. I'd like to talk with them privately. Enjoy the hors d'oeuvres that don't exist because Valkyries don't eat."

As she emerged from the hall, lightning shot toward her, bolts jagging down, seeming to plant inside her body. They projected all around her like the heads of a hydra. She wore a black leather skirt and boots—with a breastplate.

The design was olden, the metal heavily engraved. Lightning reflected in the glimmering surface. An anatomical heart had been etched into the center. Among the many shapes, he spied . . . a feather.

Has all this been planned? He nocked his last black arrow—one-and-done.

Nïx nodded at Rune, stopping a few dozen feet away. That bat of hers glided between lightning bolts to land on her shoulder. When a drift of dust settled on its fur, it sneezed.

Allixta arched a brow. —This *is the primordial Valkyrie?*—

"Greetings, Bringers of Doom. I'm Phenïx, soon to be the goddess of Accessions. I just have one little task left to kill."

—*Phenïx?*— Blace said. —*Is that her full name? And you had that feather?*—

Sian bared his fangs. —*We are not to be toyed with.*—

Allixta's magick deepened, steeping the air. —*Take her out, baneblood.*—

—*I need information first.*— And he doubted his arrow could breach the lightning.

—*You were* serious *about that?*— Allixta demanded. —*You have the shot; Orion ordered you to assassinate her.*—

Blace shook his head. —*We need to find Rune's mate. Nïx will know.*— The vampire was siding with him on this?

Though Darach revered matehood, he said, —*Shoot. Find mate later.*—

—*Find? So easily, then?*— Blace scowled. —*Says the male who's never lost anything.*—

—*Life.*—

—*Yes. You did lose your life, I suppose.*—

—*Sian, back me up!*— Allixta turned to the demon. —*Do we now complete only the convenient missions? Obey only the dictates with which we agree?*—

—*We* will *find your mate eventually, Rune,*— Sian said. —*But you'll never get a shot like this again.*—

—*Her lightning will burn my arrow. The bonedeath is my only option.*—

—*Then use it.*— Allixta said.

The Møriør had always been a unified front. Now they were at cross-purposes. And as they argued, other immortals filed out of Val Hall behind Nïx.

Two dozen Valkyries: one glowing, one carrying an extraordinary-looking bow, others with swords. A Fury among them had wings of fire.

When a contingent of fey archers followed, Rune said, —*Draiksulians.*— From the source dimension of all fey, the root of their slaving empire.

Ten Lykae emerged next, each one on the verge of turning. Their eyes were ice blue with aggression.

Darach said only, —*Descendants.*— He was half-turned himself, his body nine feet tall, his own eyes blue. His burgeoning muscles ripped his tunic in several places; he clawed it away.

Those Gaia Lykae scented the air, growling. Did they not recognize Darach Lyka, the alpha of their entire species?

Blace nodded at several vampires who'd suddenly appeared, joining the ranks. —*Forbearers, and a red-eyed natural-born. I recognize him. Lothaire. Powerful. Basically the primordial here. The female with him is vampire as well.*—

The clear-eyed vampires kept Lothaire in their lowering sights, muttering something about the "Gravewalker."

Nïx's Vertas alliance already had deep fractures within it.

Sian brandished his war ax when demons appeared, their horns sharp with hostility. The muscular males bared their fangs. —*Rage demons stand against us? Do they not comprehend what they guard in Rothkalina? And for whom?*—

Allixta's palms grew hotter when females exited the manor with their own hands alight. —*None of these witches have paid their taxes. None have permits. Yet they threaten hexes against their Overlady?*— Curses hissed, prowling back and forth.

—*So we're to draw battle lines?*— Blace slipped his sword free. —*This early?*—

Sian twirled his ax. —*What will it take to actually encounter a challenge?*—

—*They're not without their strengths,*— Allixta said. —*The witch with mirrors for eyes killed a Wiccae deity. I sense those divine magicks from here. She'll never be able to afford them.*—

—*We don't have time for this.*— Rune switched one-and-done for a bonedeath arrow, aiming at the ground near Val Hall.

Nïx canted her head, revealing her feylike ear. "Where are my manners? Can I offer you something to eat or drink? We have many nonexistent hors d'oeuvres."

"I want Josephine," Rune told the Valkyrie. "I know you see her even now."

"You *know* know? Ah, another psychic! Why should I tell you? She didn't even thank me before leaving. Rude phanpire."

"Thank you? For the punishment you meted out to her?"

The Valkyrie's eyes blazed silver. "I *taught* her."

"Don't play games with me, Nïx."

"Hmm? Something to drink or eat?"

"Tell me where Thaddeus took my mate."

"To a place you will *never* find," she said. "The District of the Gold, Purple, and Green Gardens."

Snickers sounded behind her.

—This is amusing to them?— Allixta was spoiling for a kill. *—How will those witchlings feel once I put a lien on their abilities? When all the spells they've ever cast boomerang back upon them? Their 'House of Witches' will crumble in a time of nightmares. The tax lady cometh.—*

Nïx gestured back at Val Hall. "Tsk tsk, Rune, you and your mate didn't leave this place as you found it."

The mighty oaks were strewn about like driftwood, the wraiths still dazed above. Upended cars crowded the property.

"But," Nïx said, "we remain."

Allixta conjured a larger beam of magick. *—Easily remedied.—* Addressing everyone, she said, "Trifling beings, you are presently beneath my boot heel; you just don't have the awareness to grasp your own doom. We are the bringers of it."

Lothaire, the red-eyed vampire, laughed. "Well, I like them already." At others' glares, he added, "What? That sounds like something I would have said. With, of course, a dash more verve." Then he asked Nïx, "Are we going to war or not? If we don't, this exercise is tedious enough to count as repayment, soothsayer."

Nïx absently told him, "Always with the payments, Enemy of Old."

Rune asked the Valkyrie, "You know what my arrow will do?"

She nodded happily. "It will pulverize all our bones, and nothing will ever heal us."

Lothaire said, "That sounds *unpleasant*. This is what we get for planning a fair fucking fight. We deserve nothing less." To his female, he said, "Trace the hell away from here. *Now*."

Rune drew his bowstring. "Tell me where Josephine is."

The lightning bolts around Nïx flared and expanded. "I'll never let that arrow hit the ground. I'll deflect it with my lightning—or my very body."

—*Can she do this?*— Blace asked.

Rune said, —*Yes.*—

"And if you kill me," Nïx continued, "your poor mate won't be a blood drinker anymore, will she?"

Blace stiffened beside Rune. —*What is she speaking of?*—

—*Josephine made a vow to the Lore not to drink if I went about the mission to kill Nïx without her.*—

Blace narrowed his eyes. —*Then you can't target this Valkyrie.*—

Sian said, —*I can.*—

Allixta added, —*As can I. The demon and I will wipe out this entire force.*—

Blace pointed out, —*Orion never commanded us to war here. Not yet.*—

One of the wraiths had begun to stir. It drifted over and materialized a massive braid of hair, as if pulling it from the ether, then dropped it at Nïx's feet. The braid was as long as Uthyr's tail. Locks of all different colors had been plaited into it.

The Valkyries' payments to the Scourge.

Nïx's hands flew to her cheeks in mock surprise. "But whatever could this be?" She toed the braid. "Are we starting our bar tab over? We did, after all, pay for *continuous* protection, and wraiths are levitating on the job right above us." She confided to Rune, "It is *so* hard to find good help these days." To the Scourge, she called, "Such a shame for you, when we were only one toll away from enslavement." She gave Rune a broad wink.

She might as well have booted him in the balls. —*She set all this up. The wraiths were about to exact their payment. She couldn't do anything to them, so she put me into play, a pawn.—*

For the first time, he wondered if this Valkyrie warlord had a shot at victory. If she ever grew coherent . . .

She stroked the bat on her shoulder, brushing away dust. "Rune, you're testing the limits of your mate's vow just by being here without her. Only one way to reverse this damage."

"How?" he grated.

"You vow to the Lore never to kill me. That would end your mission, nullifying her vow."

—She played me utterly.— He'd already lessened his utility to the Møriør this night. Now he would reduce it further? Would Nïx go down the line, neutralizing the Møriør one at a time until none were free to take her out?

He yearned to kill her just to rid his allies of her. His fingers tightened on his bow. Was he about to fail Orion for the first time?

"Before it's too late," Nïx said. "To sweeten the pot, everyone leaves in peace tonight."

Allixta's eyes flashed. "You presume to dictate terms—to *us*?"

"Yes, least-favorite-Wiccan-person. Until you return with the monsters you keep in Perdishian. Until you return with our *Undoing*. But my warlocks are working on a shield." Some of the Vertas immortals cast her questioning looks at that. Lothaire appeared amused. "I've heard it's challenging to take over a world—when you can't reach it."

This was a threat Rune would normally investigate and contain. For now, all he could do was pop his arrow off the string and slide it into his quiver.

"Chin up, Rune," Nïx said. "You don't really want to kill me. If you do, I will rise in memory and wallow in power. All the factions of Gaia will unite under my banner."

"Very well, soothsayer."

Allixta snapped, *—Don't you dare, baneblood!—*

"And no qualifiers, if you please," Nïx said. "This is for your mate's health and safety."

Gods damn it. "I vow to the Lore never to target you for death."

"Excellent." Nïx smiled. "That wasn't so hard, now, was it? Perhaps you'd like to go even further? Come, archer, step over to our side. Become one of the good guys."

"Good? Valkyrie, you have no idea what you're doing. You're far too young and confused to understand the ramifications of your actions. You spoke of the monsters we keep in Perdishian? They display more reason than you."

—Except for Kolossós,— Sian, Blace, and Allixta said as one. Darach grunted his agreement.

As if Rune hadn't spoken, Nïx said, "Join us, and I'll give you a signing bonus, tell you what the symbols on your talisman mean, what powers it doesn't hold. Maybe I could fill in the blanks of your mother's last letter to you."

Nïx knew? "I'm Møriør," Rune said simply. Orion might punish him for making that vow, but he still had Rune's loyalty.

"I understand," Nïx said, tucking her hair behind her pointed ear. "You can't blame me for trying. To win this war, I'll use every trick in my tricksy little bag of tricks." She faced Sian and mouthed, *Hold on to your ass, demon.*

He answered with a killing look.

Then she whispered to her bat, "Evac, Bertil." With a screech, it flew off.

Rune told Nïx, "Whatever your interest in Josephine is, *retire it.* She and Thaddeus are with us."

—Scent.— Darach sounded like he was on the very brink of a full turning. *—Mate.—*

Rune tensed. *—You have Josephine's scent?—*

He nodded. *—Close.—*

—We'll start in the city. I'll trace you all.— They clamped hands on his shoulders and forearms.

—We flee like cowards now?— Allixta said as Darach growled. But those two couldn't trace, had no choice but to come.

With one hand, Allixta grabbed Rune. With her other, she seized one of Curses' whiskers in her fist. —*Fine!*—

—*We'll return,*— Blace said. —*This fight is young yet. For tonight, we are done here.*—

Darach wasn't.

He inhaled a long breath, his immense lungs expanding.

—*Oh, fuck.*— Rune and the others braced.

With a gleam in her eyes, Allixta said, —*Huff and puff, primordial. Do it!*—

The wolf released his roar. A primal blast.

Nïx's lightning protected her, but beyond . . .

The gust scattered yelling immortals and swept the beleaguered wraiths across the night sky like flecks of dust. The force sent the manor's roof flying like a disk. Boards groaned, glass shattering. Walls collapsed.

Just as the deafening demolition quieted . . . the chimney crumpled.

Darach had flattened the manor. Val Hall was no more. The Valkyrie leader stood against a backdrop of destruction.

Rune nodded at her. "Good warring to you, Nïx."

She smiled blankly. "And a happy Accession to you, Rune."

SIXTY-SIX

A cool cloth bathed Jo's face. "Please wake up," said a muffled voice. "I didn't know it was you!"

Consciousness came by degrees, her head pounding. She blinked open her eyes. "Thaddie?" Her brain felt like jelly after her strangling.

After that memory.

Thad tossed away a washcloth, taking her hand. "I'm here. I'm so sorry! I didn't know you were Jo. I never would've hurt you." He helped her sit up on a couch.

She was in a living room with fancy décor and expensive-looking furniture. "Where've you taken me?" Her voice was scratchy.

"To my family's place in New Orleans. It's warded. You're totally safe."

New Orleans? He'd always lived in a suburban pad in Texas.

Except when he lived in a phantom realm for one day. *He and I crossed the universe, held in some kind of stasis.* They must be thousands of years old.

She hadn't unlocked everything from her childhood—only a few other dim snippets. Maybe she couldn't handle more than a peek at a time. "Thad, I've been trying to get to you in Val Hall for two weeks."

"Earlier, you said you were there to save me. From what?"

"Valkyries. I smelled your fear. I freaked out."

"Oh." He rubbed the back of his neck. "Actually, I was kinda scared of . . . you and that archer. You two were attacking, and I was inside. I didn't know who you were."

"You weren't a prisoner, were you?" He'd been in no danger, just as Rune had assured her.

"They're my allies. They've been helping me with my powers. Nïx told me a huge threat to the coven was coming, so I was there to protect Val Hall."

Nïx, getting the last laugh once again.

"She called for all hands on deck."

So that's why so many immortals had been there. Jo rubbed her throat. She hadn't thought things could possibly get shittier for her. Wrong.

She grieved for her mother. She already missed Rune, even though he was a cheating dickwad. Her neck was killing her.

But . . . *I'm talking to my little brother.* "What happened after I blacked out?"

"The Møriør came."

Rune had shown at Val Hall *after* he'd gotten through screwing a nymph. His allies had been there too? "Are Nïx and the others fighting the Møriør?" Not that Jo was worried about Rune.

"She said no one would die tonight; there'd just be a lot of redecorating or something. But I wasn't taking any chances with you when five freaking Bringers of Doom showed up with a big freaking cat! Before I ditched, your mate gave me this." Thad dug into his pocket, handed over Rune's talisman. "He said he wanted you to have it, that you'd know what it meant."

It meant he was falling for her. Which made his actions even worse! That prick could be in love with her, and he *still* would break her heart.

Jo reached for the talisman, half expecting her hand to veer. But then, he'd given it to her this time. She shoved it into her jeans pocket. Now she was going to have to see him just to return his belonging. "He say anything else?"

"That he needed to explain some things to you, and you needed to feed."

"Explain some things?" She'd bet. *Dove, you can't keep a dick like mine caged when it wants to be free.*

"Is he the dark fey I've heard about?" Thad asked. "Were your tears black because you've been drinking from him?"

"Yeah." She glanced at a mirror on one wall. Thad had washed the tracks from her face. "My blood'll be red soon enough." She turned back to him. "Do you remember me?"

He seemed embarrassed. "I'm sorry, but not much. I remember impressions. You singing to me under a bridge. Teaching me how to high-five. But I didn't know your face before."

"Then how?"

"All my life, I thought you were dead—until about a week or so ago when the crap hit the fan with my mom." He ran a hand over his mouth. "She found out what I am."

"You're not supposed to tell humans about our world."

"I *know*. She kind of caught me off guard."

Jo popped her neck. Thad could do a damn stranglehold like nobody's business. "Did MizB see you ghost? Go intangible? I do that involuntarily sometimes."

"Uh, not *ghosting* so much. More on the vamp side of things. Let's just say she discovered I drink blood." His cheeks flushed.

"How long you been drinking?"

"Only a few weeks. You?"

"Since I was eleven." He looked like he was about to ask more on that sore subject. *Not ready yet.* "MizB discovered you drink blood. And then . . . ?"

"I figured Mom would freak out to learn her son was a vampire."

Mom. Son. The words needled her.

"And she did. At first, my vampiness seemed to give her the wiggins."

Just as Jo's had done to Thaddie.

"But she mainly kept talking about you. When you came back after you were shot, she thought you were some kind of demon or spirit that was gonna drag me down to hell or something. She told you to go away.

After seeing me and hearing a whole 'nother world exists, she realized she'd banished an eleven-year-old girl from what should've been her new family. She had no idea where you were, or if you were safe. She's been overwhelmed with guilt."

Boo-hoo, MizB. Unlike Jo, the woman had gotten fourteen years of idyllic family life with Thad. Framed pictures of Thad milestones lined the fireplace mantel. *Screw her.*

But he appeared so worried about the woman. "I'm hoping . . . will you see her tonight? I know I'm asking a lot, and we don't deserve even a minute of your time. But I've never seen her cry before this—now she's always on the verge."

"Why would *you* not deserve my time?"

"Mom said I didn't want to go with you when you came back, didn't even recognize you. How could I not recognize the big sis who raised me?"

"Because I looked different. And you weren't exactly old enough to be a sleuth—I could stuff your ass into a backpack."

He seemed surprised by her crack, then his lips curled. "I heard about the Thadpack too." Seeing him smile began to erase the image of him trying to pop her "bobblehead" off.

She found herself grinning with him—

"Thaddeus?" MizB called from upstairs. "Is that you?"

"Jo, will you please talk to her? Just knowing you're okay would help her so much."

"I'm giving you fair warning: I'm not fit for social interaction on the best of days. And this has not been the best of days." Not to mention her exhaustion and thirst after all that telekinesis. "I was chucking cars not long ago, and I've got no love for your . . . mom." She massaged her temples against her growing headache.

"But you'll do it?" He blinked at her with those big hazel eyes, and she was putty.

Some things never changed. She shrugged.

His face lit up.

Why did he refuse to believe she was a bitch? "You'll end up regretting this, kid." She stood, readying for the showdown.

"No way! Lemme go and prepare her, okay?" He leapt up to rush toward the stairs. At the foot, he turned back. "You won't leave or anything?" He gazed upstairs, then to Jo, seeming torn. He traced to hug her, startling her. He was so tall. He had to hunch down just to rest his chin on her head.

Her surprise faded, and she hugged him back.

"Scared to let you out of my sight for even a minute." He eventually released her. "We'll be right down."

He disappeared, leaving Jo in this strange house—one more development to top off this epically weird night.

SIXTY-SEVEN

When Darach's tracking got Rune close enough to pick up Josephine's trail himself, he raced ahead of the other Møriør, following her meadowberry scent. His heart pounded, just as it had ages ago when he'd run headlong to that glen. . . .

He found her in an imposing mansion. His ears twitched when he heard her voice coming from inside. Conscious! She didn't sound afraid or too badly injured.

Her brother was within as well. Rune caught threads of Thad's scent, both new and old, and suspected the boy had taken her back to his home. Detecting no enemies nearby, Rune faced his allies. "I have it from here."

"You don't want us to storm this structure?" Sian asked.

Allixta reached up and scratched Darach under the chin. "Careful, or the wolf might blow it down."

Rune shook his head. "She's safe here with Thaddeus. I'm going to give her a couple of hours to cool off, then approach her."

"A couple of hours?" Allixta dropped her hand. "You told us she's waited half her life to reunite with her brother. Shouldn't they bond before you barge in, with all your nympho drama taking center stage?"

"She needs to know I didn't take that female."

Allixta rolled her eyes. "No, *you* need the halfling to know that. Selfish male! Let her have some bloody time for herself." To everyone, she said, "Sometimes the lot of you astound me."

Not to go to Josephine's side? At the thought, his desperate need to reach her redoubled.

Allixta said, "You might not have bedded the nymph, but you were *in* bed with her. You still reek of another female."

Rune turned to Darach, who nodded.

Damn it! This wasn't a simple misunderstanding that could be cleared up by his saying, "I didn't go through with it." He had been in bed with Meliai—the night after he'd claimed his mate. He struggled to recall what had happened with the nymph.

"We could see your mate's pain," Allixta said. "Naturally she'd just escaped *your* attentions."

"Watch yourself, witch."

"Were you ever unselfish with her? Do anything kind for her?"

He'd taken Josephine to a fey ball. In order to get laid. He'd romanced her. To secure her for the Møriør. He'd healed her from a fight. That she would've recovered from anyway.

Things would be different. Change? Now he only wanted the *chance* to.

"You forget," she added, "we've *witnessed* how you treat your 'tarts.'"

"It's not like that with Josephine," he snapped.

"Oh, really? Because fate says so?"

"Look into my mind." He gave them wide-open access to his thoughts.

One by one, they did. One by one, they paled.

"That's right," he said, sounding crazed. "I'm fucking gut-sick over her! Do you see why I'm maddened to be with her?"

Sian gave him a pitying glance. "I hope you're as good at apologies as you are at seduction."

In a marveling tone, Blace said, "You're seven thousand years old, and you have no idea how to handle this."

"Because it's that important!" Struggling to rein in his emotions—a blazing inferno—he turned to Allixta. "How long do I give her?"

"You're a spy. Spy on her. You'll know when the time is right to approach her."

Blace said, "We'll leave you to it, then."

Once they'd gone, Rune rolled up his sleeve to ink a concealment spell on his arm. He flinched when confronted with the contraceptive he'd painted.

Never again. Free.

He used his other arm. Hidden from sight, Rune stalked closer to the mansion, tracking her to a room downstairs.

He uncovered wards on the main house. He swiftly added his own runes to appropriate the protections, allowing him entry. He would step in if anything went sideways. The slightest hint of danger. Task complete, he peered in the window.

She stood alone in front of the fireplace, gazing at pictures on the mantel. Her eyes were stark, her outline flickering. The tear tracks were gone, but she remained shaken.

In the span of his life, he'd been with her for the blink of an eye.

He never wanted to open his eyes and not see her face.

Josephine had flung him to some place he'd never been before, and now he knew where.

Home.

He raised his hand to the glass, needing to touch her so badly he ached.

SIXTY-EIGHT

Jo turned toward the doorway of the sitting room when MizB and Thad walked in. Woman had some years on her—but she was still the same MizB, down to the boxy glasses and the lame type of pantsuit she always wore to the library.

Jo felt a hit of . . . something.

MizB adjusted her glasses. "Is it really you, Josephine?" She stepped forward as if they were going to hug.

Jo took a step back. "It's me." She'd checked out all the photos of Thad, resentful of the years she'd missed. She was fresh from her limited memories of her childhood in Apparitia, fresh from reliving the death of their real mother. Guilt weighed on Jo for not staying with Thaddie.

Keep him close. Protect him.

Jo hadn't. She hadn't been there with him.

"You're all grown up." MizB's tears welled. "And so beautiful."

"I brought her home directly," Thad said. "Haven't had much of a chance to talk to her."

"Please have a seat." MizB moved to a fancy chair with a stiff back. Thad crossed to the nearby couch, sitting as close to her as possible.

Awkward. Jo traced to the other end of the couch and sank down. She rubbed her nape and glanced at the window. She had the sense of being watched.

Would Thad's ward keep out Nïx? The Valkyrie might come with a bill for all the sports cars and trees Jo had trashed. Recalling that lightened her mood a touch.

"Oh!" MizB's eyes had widened. "You disappeared and reappeared. That's not something you see every day."

Jo frowned. "You had to have seen him do it."

"The only thing I saw was him drinking from his arm."

"Mom!"

Vampire masturbation. And MizB had just laid it out there. What an icebreaker.

Thad's face grew so crimson he'd probably get thirsty from it. He was such a teenage boy. Despite everything, Jo had to conceal a laugh behind a cough.

His mortified expression faded when he saw her face. He started to grin. "You think that's funny?"

She coughed again. "It's not *un*funny."

"I wasn't supposed to say that?" MizB blinked behind her glasses. "I'm just learning my way around all this."

Thad said, "It's fine, Mom."

MizB turned to her. "Well, tell me everything. Where did you two meet up?"

Thad looked at Jo to field this one. The Eagle Scout would have trouble lying. "Mutual acquaintances."

"That's so fortunate! How did you recognize each other?"

"You think I haven't kept up with my own brother? I can tell you his freaking baseball stats." Thanks to text-to-speech.

"Of course," MizB quickly said. "I should've expected that."

Thad leaned forward, resting his elbows on his knees. "You really can?"

Jo shrugged. "You can't steal bases for shit."

He gave a laughing groan. "*Tell* me about it. Hey, I bet I don't suck so bad since I started coming into my powers. But what about you—what do you do?"

Do? Besides slowly dying, desperate to see you every day? And getting my heart broken by Rune? "This and that."

"Are you married?" MizB asked.

"All by my lonesome." Jo propped her boots on the coffee table.

The woman wisely said nothing. "You never stayed with Mr. Chase?"

"Who?"

Thad shot Jo a wide-eyed look. So the Eagle Scout had told a lie after all?

Acting all casual, Jo said, "Nah, I do my own thing."

"We've never even met him—he just sent us the deed to his house, writing that he was Thad's long-lost uncle. It's all very mysterious." Her gazed flitted to Thad and back. "Have you unearthed any clues about where you two came from? About your parents?"

"Still sorting them out." Jo would tell Thad about her new, raw memory in private. And find about this Chase dude. "Our folks are gone though."

Sadness clouded Thad's eyes. Had he been holding out hope of meeting the parents? She didn't like to see him sad. She'd already gotten used to his easy grin, the one that said, *All is right in the world.*

"Thad's told me he could live to be very old." MizB took a tissue from her pocket. "I'm so glad you're back in his life. It's such a relief that he won't be alone after his grandmother and I are gone."

Jo narrowed her eyes. "Yeah, being alone for years and years is not something I'd wish on *anyone.*"

"I didn't know." Tears welled again. "I had n-no idea."

Thad rose and dragged a stool over beside her, patting her hand. "Mom, it's okay."

Clearly, Jo needed to make a not-so-graceful exit. "Look, I need to split—"

"I-I thought you'd died!" MizB cried. "I didn't know if you'd returned to take Thad to hell or to the grave. I didn't know this world existed!"

"I didn't either!" Jo rose to float/pace. The room's lights flickered eerily. "I woke up in a body bag! I thought I'd been resurrected. That I was some kind of ghost." Which, she supposed, was not far from the truth. "Then when I came for Thaddie, you were all get-thee-gone. I'm surprised you didn't douse me with holy water."

MizB dabbed at her eyes behind her glasses. "You were just a little girl—I told you that the day you were shot—but I didn't listen to my own words. I thought you weren't Jo anymore. I thought you would've wanted me to protect him from *any* threat."

Damn it, I would've.

"I'm the one who found your body behind the library. When I heard the gunshots, I left Thad with a colleague and ran out, but . . . there wasn't anything left of your . . ." She cleared her throat. "I wasn't prepared to see your face later that night. And you looked so different."

MizB had found her? Out of habit, Jo reached for her bullet necklace. Great, she'd left it at Rune's.

"I never would've let Thad go regardless," the woman continued. "I was terrified he was in danger from whoever shot you. I feared you two had witnessed something, and the gunman might come for Thad despite his young age."

So MizB would've been even more freaked out than Jo had allowed for? She slowed her pacing. All this new information screwed with her years of burning hatred. Plus, Thad had grown up so . . . good. Jo couldn't possibly have done better with him.

Because he couldn't possibly *be* better. "This isn't the best time to talk. I can come back another night."

As if she hadn't spoken, the woman murmured, "At Mr. B's wake, I saw you. You were at the window, sobbing in the rain as you watched Thad. I knew you were going to let him go, because I'd told you that's what a mother would do." Her tears started up again. "I thought you'd made the decision to pass on."

"I *did.*"

"I mean, to the beyond."

Jo's patience neared its limit. "Oh, for fuck's sake, woman. If Thad didn't love you, I'd pop you in the face."

Thad's shocked gaze darted from Jo to MizB and back. "Uh, maybe we shouldn't, um, talk to our elders like that?"

"Elders?" Jo was about to go hysterical. The two of them were millennia old!

But MizB smiled. "You used to say that to me all the time. Do you remember?"

Jo did.

"So I'm hopeful. I can't make up for all these years overnight. But having hope is enough for now."

Uncomfortable silence followed.

Then MizB rose. "I'll be right back." She paused at the doorway. "You won't go anywhere?"

Too tired to fight, Jo sank down on the couch again.

The woman hurried from the room.

"Thanks for covering about the uncle," Thad murmured. "It's a long story. I'll give you the lowdown later."

"I'm tanking this, kid. I'd say I'm not usually such a bitch, but it'd be a lie."

"You're doing awesome." Thad didn't seem discouraged at all, just the opposite. "Mom told me you were tough-talking and never sugar-coated things."

"I didn't know MizB saw my face looking like modern art." She pinched the bridge of her nose. "I don't want to say anything that's gonna hurt or embarrass you, so I think I should blaze. I was having a shit day before you and I ever mixed it up."

"What happened?" He leaned forward. "What made you cry? Tell me about it."

Confusion. "Like tell you . . . about my day?" Had anyone ever asked her to do this? "I broke up with my boyfriend. He's probably my mate— I'm definitely his."

"Is breaking up with a mate even possible?"

All things were possible in the Lore! "Yep. He couldn't keep it in his pants. So anyway, I should—"

"Were you with him long?"

"Two weeks," she answered. "So this isn't the best time to dig into the past with your"—she bit out the word—"*mom*."

"You can't go yet. Please stay a little longer." *No, not with the eyes.* "Please?"

Damn it! "Fine. I'll give this another fiver."

"Thanks, Jo!" His face lit up as if she'd promised the world(s).

"You look like you did when I gave you that Spidey doll. Best theft I ever committed."

"I still have it. It's on my bookshelf."

"No way!" *I'm with my little brother. Holy shit, we're talking.*

MizB returned, carrying a tray. "A little refreshment," she said, setting it on the coffee table. She'd brought three steaming drinks—a cup with a tea bag and two mugs of warmed blood. She even had a bowl of hot-chocolate marshmallows. "Fresh from the blood deliveryman."

They got delivery?

MizB looked like she was about to hurl; she must've heated it on the stove. So not only had the woman accepted Thad's changes, she was adapting to them.

What wouldn't MizB do for Thad? *We have that in common.* Two women who fiercely wanted what was best for him.

She offered Jo a mug with a weak smile. "Marshmallow, Josephine?"

Like luring a feral cat.

Jo exhaled, her anger deflating. As confident as she'd been at eleven, she hadn't been bulletproof, not enough at least. MizB had gotten Thaddie to safety after Jo had kicked her *first* ant mound.

All the woman had ever wanted was to be a good mom. She had been.

Jo took the blood, even accepting a marshmallow to be nice. "Smells good," she lied. Though dying of thirst, she'd been ruined for regular blood.

Still, both MizB and Thad looked overjoyed by her willingness to play ball.

For him, Jo supposed she could retract her claws every now and then.

He raised his mug. "To Jo's homecoming."

Better get used to the red stuff. She forced herself to choke it down. Like drinking sludge compared to Rune's high octane blood.

MizB said, "I guess you two didn't need to use utensils after all."

SIXTY-NINE

I really appreciate the effort you made in there," Thad said when he and Jo settled into chairs beside the pool. "I know it had to be strange."

Roger that. "I've done worse." The three of them had talked about the old library, and some of the wackier things Thad had done as a kid. He'd laughed so hard that Jo had even chuckled. Before she knew it, she'd finished her blood, and dawn had been approaching.

MizB had excused herself to go check on Gram, topping off their mugs again. "Why don't you go show Jo the pool? Just don't be too late."

Jo had stilled. "Late. You kidding me?"

MizB had blinked at her. "No."

Now Jo asked Thad, "What's this too late shit? Aren't you nocturnal?"

"I've been going to bed around four in the morning, and Mom and Gram have been getting up later. That way we can sit down for breakfast together."

"Your grandmother knows too?"

"I don't think so. She had a stroke, and they say she's got dementia. I don't know how much has registered, but I don't trace around the house or anything. She still cooks for me. Mom does too. Just in case."

"God, she could cook. Her chicken was like deep-fried crack."

He nodded emphatically. "Toughest thing for me to give up."

"So tell me about our mansion-buying uncle."

"He's a berserker named Declan Chase. He used to work for the Order, this human operation that studies immortals. He felt guilty 'cause he had me kidnapped and imprisoned on a detention island in the Pacific and all."

Jo's mug shattered in her fist, blood sloshing over the outdoor table. "The FUCK did you just say? Tell me how to find him, and I will put him in the goddamn ground."

"We're cool now, Jo. He paid for anything he did wrong. Trust me, he *paid.*"

"Someone did that to you, and you're good with him?!" She couldn't believe Thad had been in all this danger, and she hadn't known, hadn't been there to watch over him.

"DC ended up helping me escape before the island got bombed."

So much for his idyllic life. "What the hell happened?" She swiped her bloody hand down her jeans.

"I'd never encountered an immortal before I got imprisoned, definitely didn't know I *was* one. I never had any powers, but somehow the Order knew about me."

The Order's on my light-them-up list.

"I woke up in a cell, and I saw all these things that couldn't be right. I lost it, went comatose. I still would be, if not for Regin and Natalya."

Comatose? "What are they?"

"Regin is DC's wife now. She's the one who was kind of egging me on to attack you."

Jo *hated* that mouthy bitch—

"She saved my life on the island."

She's forgiven. "And Natalya?"

"She's one of my good friends. A dark fey assassin."

No kidding. "She lives in the city?"

"For now. I can't wait for you to meet her. She won't be pissed that you attacked Val Hall since she used to fight against the Valkyries on occasion." He sipped his blood. "She'd heard a dark fey male was in town, and she's been looking for one for a looong time. Your guy have a brother?"

"Not my guy anymore. You can tell her he's been looking for her too, was amped to have a lead on her. Cheers to the happy couple."

Rune flinched in his spot atop the property's brick wall. Why *wouldn't* she think he'd pursue that female?

Earlier Josephine had told the mortal MizB she was all by her lonesome—the same answer she'd given Rune two weeks ago.

Before they'd bonded. Before she'd become his, and he'd become hers. Before *them*.

Then tonight had happened, when he'd ridiculed her feelings for him and assured her he'd always be with others.

"Oh." Thad frowned. "I was kinda hoping Natalya and I might hook up. Maybe when I get fully transitioned."

Thad wanted Natalya? Rune found it heartening both siblings were attracted to dark fey. He could give the boy pointers.

Josephine shook her head. "Date a baneblood?" She had never called him that before, no matter how furious with him she'd been. "Do yourself a favor and forget it. Not worth the trouble."

Strike *heartening*. Waiting to approach Josephine had been the exact right call.

Thad seemed to consider that for a few moments, then said, "Nïx told me there was another phanpire—"

"Did you just say *phanpire*?"

"Yep. That's what she calls us."

Jo snorted. "Lame. Let's just call ourselves hybrids."

"But there are other kinds of hybrids."

"Yeah, but we're the best."

Thad nodded easily. "I knew there was another . . . hybrid, but Nïx told me the other one was mated to a dark fey, a Møriør."

"It's over. That's all in my rearview, kid." Josephine sounded disturbingly confident.

"The Møriør are bad, Jo."

He doesn't even know we leveled Val Hall.

"The Valkyries aren't? Your buddy Nïx wiped the pavement with my face. She crushed my skull and broke every bone in my body. I feared she'd do the same to you—that's why I was bent on saving you."

His jaw slackened. "She wouldn't do that. Are you sure it was Nïx?"

"She would, and she did. That Møriør was there to pick up the broken pieces." She seemed to be grinding her molars, and her outline flickered.

It is entirely *too soon to approach her.*

"Why didn't Nïx tell you I'm your sister?"

Thad's lips thinned. "Good question."

"Have you ever considered they're *all* bad? Maybe neither of us needs to be around any immortals. I mean, what does Nïx want with you anyway?"

"I think she and the others want me to fight the Møriør. But I just . . . I'm not sure I could take somebody down. I can't believe how bad I hurt you. Jo, I could've killed you."

Rune had had his doubts about the boy when he'd been hunched over Josephine with his fangs bared. No longer. Thaddeus Brayden was a good kid.

"It's cool," she said. "You jogged loose some memories for me, so no harm, no foul."

From her childhood?

"I was only using a fraction of my strength, sis. I'm wicked strong."

She grinned, and he matched her. They resembled each other much more when they smiled. Rune was noticing other similarities as well—the cadences of their speech, their humor, their mannerisms.

Because this boy had learned from Josephine, who'd been just a girl herself, taking care of a baby while living on the streets.

When Thad asked about the night she'd been shot and the months after, she admitted to meting out punishment, but he took it in stride.

She recounted that grim night and her struggles with her powers. Then she told him, "Leaving you was the hardest thing I've ever had to do. I'd gone to that wake intending to steal you and your new puppy, planning to ride off into the sunset together." She gave a humorless laugh, as if her idea had been idiotic.

"You ever think about coming back for me?"

"Every damn day. I wore those bullets strung around my neck to remind me I'd only hurt you. I kept up with your life as best as I could, and over the years it just seemed to get better and better."

Thad peered at her intently. "So what changed?"

"I saw you in this city. With Nïx. And then I learned about the Lore."

"You didn't know?"

"Two-week newbie here."

"Not much longer here," Thad said. "You mentioned you had some clues about where we came from. For the last few months, even before the island, I've been having these crazy dreams. I think they're connected to our past."

"What kind of dreams?"

"I see fires and earthquakes and portals sucking at my feet. I dreamed I was crossing the universe, and I was looking down at a baby."

"Thad"—she swallowed audibly—"you were looking down at yourself. You've been dreaming *my* memories. You must've harvested them when I fed you my blood on the journey."

"Journey?"

She took a deep breath. "We come from a place called Apparitia, the realm of phantoms. We're Apparitians. Or we were. You were born the day our world ended. . . ."

What the hells?

SEVENTY

Our mother was so brave and selfless," Thad finally said. He'd gone quiet once Jo had finished her story. "I've seen her face in your memories. You take after her."

Jo's brows drew together. "Thank you." She gauged his expression, wondering how he was doing with all this information.

"What about our dad?"

"I don't remember him well, just vague impressions—like you had of me. I get the sense he wanted to stay with us, but always got called away to go fight wars."

"I keep thinking maybe he could be alive," Thad said.

"After so many years, I don't know if you should hold out too much hope. I just want to remember more so I can make sense of things."

"We're Apparitians," he muttered. "How weird."

"Yeah, we're pretty much aliens." (Secretly, she'd always known it.)

"Should I call you Jo or Kierra?"

"I've been Jo longer than Kierra," she said with a shrug. "Was this too much for you? My brain felt like it was going to break from just this one memory."

"Nah, I'm good. Just have one question . . . Could I have been a cuter baby?"

She gave a surprised laugh. "No. Nor a louder one!" They were sharing a grin when fingers of light reached them. Sunrise. She'd been dreading it, wanting to talk with Thad for days more. "I should probably head out," she said, trying for a casual tone. "Maybe I'll drop by next week or something." *How am I gonna leave?*

"Next week?" His voice scaled an octave.

Her heart sank. "I mean, or whenever. I'm not going to intrude in your life. We can take it slow. Plan a visit here or there."

"Intrude? I thought . . ." He examined the armrest of his chair. "Thought you were gonna stay here with us."

"Oh! Ohh."

"We've got all this room. You'd have a wing to yourself."

"Thad, I've got to get back to my motel."

"Why?"

Because she needed to find other freaks? Nope. Been there, done that. Because she needed to maintain her Thad memorabilia? He was right here, holding his breath, hoping she'd move in!

Because she needed to be there in case Rune was looking for her?

Screw that. She would move out of her motel and find another one, refusing to look like she'd been waiting on him to show up.

"Being around MizB is weird," she told him honestly. "Case you haven't noticed, I don't play well with others."

"But you could," he quickly said. "It's like baseball. You just gotta learn the basics."

The basics of being domesticated? By the Braydens?

Jo supposed she couldn't lay into Rune for refusing to change when she wasn't willing to. Of course, she hadn't cheated on anyone. His talisman seemed to burn in her pocket.

She might want nothing to do with him, but she'd safeguard his cherished belonging until he returned for it.

"Come on, Jo. Just give it a try."

"What am I supposed to do here all day?" And in general. She was zoning in, but she'd found all her answers. Now what?

Start some kind of life after Rune.

"Spend time with me." Thad pulled his chair closer to hers, then took her hands. "We've got so much to talk about and see. I'll trace you to the places I've been, and you can trace me to all your places."

"But you've gotta have friends you want to hang out with. I'm not gonna be some big-sister bug interfering with your teenager plans."

"Since moving here, I've been going to Val Hall every day so Mom would think I was still in school. Now I don't have to hide what I am anymore. Plus, you're the closest Lorean to my age around. Come on, sis. Please? Just give us a week."

Enough with the eyes! She exhaled. "A week." She pinned his gaze. "You asked for it, kid."

Rune hurriedly worked to redirect the protections on this property to ward away Vertas creatures.

His mate was staying.

Josephine had launched an attack on Val Hall, and then the Møriør had destroyed it; this proximity to Nïx's army put Rune on edge.

From his spot outside the manor, he could see inside Josephine's new room. Thad was helping her get settled. She'd just returned from her apartment, carrying a small bag of clothes.

Rune had worried she was building up her reunion with her brother too much, that she was sure to be disappointed.

By the end of the night, Thad had all but begged Josephine to stay.

He was her number one. She seemed to be glowing with contentment as they cracked jokes.

Even recounting her memories of Apparitia hadn't hampered the siblings' happiness to have found each other.

Her tale had floored Rune. The two of them had barely escaped their home world—and only because of their mother's sacrifice. Then, floating in the ether, they'd seen behind the curtains of the universe.

Eventually, they'd gone into stasis—as the Møriør did. But that didn't negate their age.

Apparitia had died *thousands* of years ago. Josephine must be the oldest living of their hybrid species.

The primordial.

She'd told of a planet imploding? Of her screaming "worldend." Some in the Elserealms whispered *Orion* had destroyed Apparitia. Had Rune's liege obliterated it like a glass sphere? While Rune's terrified mate had fought to catch a newborn babe in the winds?

Rune had seldom questioned what his liege did, believing Orion had cause for all his actions. Now his first instinct was to confront Orion. But if the Undoing had targeted Apparitia, it must have been for a reason. What if he'd planned to assassinate two hybrid children?

If Rune alerted him, Orion might finish what he'd started. . . .

Josephine laughed and tossed a pillow at Thad. He caught it telekinetically and sent it right back at her.

Where did this night leave Rune? Was he to interrupt this bonding when all her dreams were coming true?

That mortal woman had described Josephine sobbing at the window as she'd given up Thad. Now Josephine had been embraced by this family. No longer was she gazing in from the outside. *Rune* was.

He burned to talk to her, to be with her. But she'd given Thad a week; shouldn't Rune give her the same? He told himself seven days was nothing in an immortal's life—even as he dreaded the prospect.

Yet that didn't mean he'd leave his mate and his brother here unprotected. Rune would take up residence in the carriage house by the pool, scent-and soundproofing it. From there he could watch over this family, contemplate what to do about Orion, and allow Josephine's temper to cool.

Unless she called for him, or wondered where he was. Or needed him for blood. Otherwise . . .

I'll give you one week, little mate.

SEVENTY-ONE

Jo lay in bed, head on her pillow, staring at the talisman on her night-stand.

Sleeping in this big bed without a towering dark fey still felt weird, even after so many days had passed.

At first, the excitement of seeing Thad—and her efforts to live in this household—had overshadowed her grief from losing Rune. She was still psyched to be with her brother, but now she pined for her ex.

Her first day here, Thad had gotten a call from Regin, detailing what had happened at Val Hall after he and Jo had vanished.

Jo had been blown away. Apparently so had Val Hall, thanks to a primordial werewolf.

And Rune had defeated the Scourge. "Somehow your archer scored a phoenix feather!" Thad had excitedly told her. "He used it for the flights on an arrow and shot the wraiths to kingdom come."

With a surge of nausea, Jo had realized the feather was the key he'd earned from Meliai in exchange for great sex.

Then Rune had threatened Nïx and all her immortals, the "Vertas MVPs" as Thad called them. But in the end, Rune had made a vow never to kill Nïx—so he could neutralize *Jo's* vow.

He'd done that in front of his allies. For her. . . .

Thad had also told Jo he wanted to help Regin and the others rebuild Val Hall, explaining, "The Vertas is more than just Nïx. Besides, she isn't even there. She told everyone she was taking a vacation for a while."

Jo had tried to make light. "Vertas, Møriør. Hey, let's let the freaks work this out in the schoolyard on their own."

"Regin and the others didn't know you're my sister. Nïx told them you're a hardcore Møriør here to unleash monsters and enslave us all."

Nïx, you bitch, that's how rumors get started. Then Jo had frowned. *I did have strong Møriør leanings.*

Because I fell in love with one.

After that day, she and Thad never talked about Rune specifically. She tried to hide how badly she yearned for the dark fey, but didn't know if she was fooling anyone.

Rune had once told her Darach Lyka could find anything in the worlds; Thad hadn't traced Jo too far from Val Hall. Rune had to know where she was. She'd thought nothing could keep a Lorean from his mate, yet he'd never contacted her.

She figured he must have returned to Tenebrous with the other Møriør. Even if he'd headed back to Earth directly, the journey would take a while.

Not that she would ever resume things with him. But it would be nice to return his talisman, get her bullet necklace back, and find some closure.

Was closure possible between mates?

Anything is possible in the Lore! she thought bitterly.

Hanging out with her brother was the only thing that could have kept her distracted. Over the last week, she and Thad had laughed. They'd watched movies. They'd swum. Jo had demonstrated how to ghost into shells and go fully invisible.

Soon she would show him how to delineate one's territory and protect it—and how to crush fight-stealing pimps.

If Jo had been a feral cat at the beginning of the week, the Braydens might have domesticated her a scoch. For Thad, Jo had been making the effort to get along.

The first day, he'd awakened her abruptly. "JOOOO!" he'd yelled from downstairs. "Breakfast is ready!"

She'd shot upright in bed, disoriented because she'd never had a wakeup call before and had barely slept. She'd dreaded dreams of Rune, hadn't wanted to see any more of his past when she couldn't handle his present.

Bleary-eyed, she'd gotten dressed, snagged the talisman she'd set on the nightstand, then stomped downstairs into the kitchen. "What the fuck is this, *Private Benjamin*?"

Gram had been there along with MizB and Thad. Oops.

MizB had told the woman, "Ma, I want you to meet—"

Gram had already shuffled over to Jo. Before Jo could hiss, the woman had kissed her forehead. "Hello, child." Then she'd shuffled back to the stove, all no-big-deal.

Over breakfast, MizB had asked if they had any plans.

Jo had rocked her chair back, balancing on two legs. "I was thinking about teaching ole Thad here how to roll drug dealers for coke-dusted cash. Maybe pummel some pimps. Don't they give Eagle Scout badges for shit like that?"

MizB had swallowed helplessly.

Hey, she'd invited Jo here. *Let the right one in, MizB.*

The woman had asked them to take out the freaking garbage first, then had the nerve to call, "Make good choices. . . ."

Day two, Gram had implemented a cuss jar. She'd tapped it while giving Jo a speaking glance.

Seriously?

When Jo brought over more clothes, MizB had mended all of them, even the ones that were supposed to be ripped. But Jo had bitten her tongue.

Both MizB and Gram continued to cook, MizB "just in case," so Jo pushed food around a plate when the family sat down for meals. She helped with dishes she'd never needed in the first place, wishing she had a rune for the chore.

Atop the mantel were two new framed pictures of Jo and Thad. Jo liked them because both had her giving the camera the bird, with her lips poised to say "Fuck off."

She went to bed at four, and never missed breakfast.

It isn't so bad here. She stared at Rune's talisman, sleep overtaking her. *Except for missing him. . . .*

At last, the week had come to a close.

As Rune had done each day, he traced from the carriage house into Josephine's room the moment she'd drifted off. But this time, he would remain until she woke.

The late night sky was thick with black clouds and thunder rumbled, but she slumbered on.

Sound sleeping was a vulnerability. He'd meant to help break her of that, but then he'd realized he'd always be there to watch over her.

He did so now, pulling up a chair beside her bed. He picked up the talisman from her bedstand, turning it in his hand over and over as his gaze lingered on her features. Her thick lashes, her finely-boned face. The gentle bow of her lips. The mouth that spoke so candidly and pressed against his flesh so ardently.

Though only seven days separated them and he'd always been close, Rune had missed her till his mind was wrong and his chest constantly pained him.

As Josephine had done as a ghost, he'd haunted the Braydens' home. No one from the Vertas had disturbed them. In fact, only one Lorean had tried to visit—Natalya, the dark fey.

Josephine likely wouldn't have welcomed her, so he'd traced to intercept the female.

Natalya was definitely of his species, with her plum-colored eyes, black claws, and the telltale pointed ears. She'd been yanking on a cap when he'd stopped her.

She'd raked her gaze over him. "You're the dark fey everyone's talking about, an assassin like me. Rune, right? I'm Natalya." Another long look. "Where have you been all my life, gorgeous?"

In the past, he would've deemed this female heavens-sent for him—before Josephine had claimed his heart, his mind, his body, his fucking dreams.

When Natalya had propositioned him—"A little secret between two banebloods"—he'd simply said, "Josephine is everything."

At that, Natalya had stopped eye-fucking him, and they'd spoken about the few others of their kind they'd met. She suspected he was the oldest living of them all. Not the firstborn, but still the oldest.

Was that why Orion had sought him out so long ago? Perhaps his liege hadn't thought Rune *less* because he was a halfling; perhaps Orion considered dark fey to be a species unto themselves.

With Rune as their primordial.

The idea had shocked him, but he'd still managed to talk up Thad, emphasizing how powerful the young man was becoming. Once fully transitioned, Rune had assured Natalya, Thad could withstand *any* poison. . . .

Rune was glad to have gotten that meeting out of the way. With an unknown out there, he never would've been able to convince Josephine he was hers alone.

Soon his mate would feel confident in him. Soon she would wake to find him here, and he was . . . nervous.

She hadn't spoken about him, and he still couldn't fathom what he'd say to her. When he needed his silver tongue most, it'd deserted him.

How to express his regret for the past? How could he tell her his hopes for the future when he didn't know what that future would entail? *My liege might have murdered your mother, your entire world.* Rune had come no closer to a decision regarding Orion and Apparitia.

She turned on her back, her hair tumbling over her pillow.

Her scent soothed his uneasiness, until it was replaced with a weary relaxation. He hadn't slept in eight or nine days.

Outside, the night darkened even more, but the room was warm and comfortable. Gods, he'd give his bow hand to be able to sleep next to her once again.

He watched the rise and fall of her chest and imagined lying with her in his glen as a breeze washed over them.

His lids grew heavier, and he leaned an elbow on the edge of the bed.

Even a Møriør needed to rest once in a while. Maybe he'd close his eyes for ten minutes. . . .

SEVENTY-TWO

*R*une was in Perdishian. He thought. Perhaps he dreamed?

If so, this reverie was the most lifelike he'd ever experienced.

He stood at the glass wall, gazing out. He breathed in air that smelled like cold stone and metal. His ears twitched with each of the stronghold's groans as it moved through space and time.

Orion joined his side. His eyes were obsidian, as obscure as usual, but Rune had never seen this visage before. The male stood only a few inches taller than Rune. His hair was as black as space. His face was pleasing with sharp cheekbones and even features.

Rune couldn't determine which species Orion imitated today.

They watched worlds pass in silence. Finally, Rune said, "I need to speak with you."

Without turning from the view, Orion intoned, "Speak."

"I failed to assassinate the Valkyrie. And now I can never kill her."

"Thousands have tried. None would have succeeded."

Rune faced him. "Then why dispatch me?"

Orion kept his gaze ahead, as if scanning for something. "We fail; we learn. Unless we fail to learn."

Should Rune tell him about Apparitia? Surely this was just a dream. Maybe his subconscious was rehearsing for this very conversation. In any case, Rune had trusted and believed in Orion for ages. By suspecting the worst, Rune would not only be doubting his liege; he'd be doubting his own judgment.

Rune would choose to believe . . . in himself. "My mate hailed from Apparitia."

Orion turned his head. "You want to know if I destroyed it. What do you think?"

"I think you didn't."

The black of Orion's eyes glimmered a strange, wondrous color. A hint of the being's satisfaction?

Good, then. Rune had been right, could feel the truth. Then he frowned. Was that color a clue to Orion's ancestry?

No, no, that couldn't be right.

"Ever loyal archer." Orion gave the subtlest nod. "You could have taken the hybrids and run."

"I trust in this. In you. In our mission." To save the worlds.

"In time, your mate will look into my gaze and know the answer for herself."

"But there's more. I can't harvest information as I have in the past—because I will never be untrue to her. Already threats arise that I can't contain." Nïx had said her warlocks were working to keep the Møriør out of Gaia. Warlocks were notorious for sacrificing nymphs to old gods. But Rune's informant pool was now gone.

Orion faced the star-shaped table. "How many wolves sit among us?"

Rune frowned again. "One."

"How many witches?"

"One."

"Archers?"

One.

Orion had never called him anything but archer, *even when Rune had possessed no skill. Rune had worked for millennia to become the best bowman in all the worlds—to be worthy of the name.*

Yet even after he'd become the best, he still hadn't become the *archer.*

Recognition overwhelmed Rune. "I sit at that table as the Møriør's archer." He had *become worthy of the name; he'd just never realized it.*

"Your arrows are far-reaching. Your arrows are silent. Archers fight from the front line and from the shadows, do they not?"

Assassin and front line. Those are my strengths. Those are my skills. *Before, Rune had taken on tasks he'd thought should fall to him, the former whore.*

Orion nodded as if Rune had spoken. "The archer's undoing was how he saw himself." Orion the Undoing saw weaknesses.

Rune had diminished himself, assigning his own skewed values.

He was about to ask if he was the primordial, then he realized it didn't matter.

Orion's lips curled. "Exactly."

A stray thought: He steers us as Nïx steers her army. *If Rune had been concerned about the Valkyrie's savvy, he was no longer. Orion couldn't be stopped—*

Rune jerked awake. Had Josephine moaned? She was twisting in the sheets, her brow furrowed, her outline flickering.

Nightmare? He'd burdened her with so many memories of torture and pain. . . .

She started to grow intangible. Then to *rise.* Sleep-ghosting—she'd warned him about this!

"Wake, Josie!" He dove for her hand. To tether her. She grasped his in sleep.

He began to disembody with her. "Whoa, you need to wake up, love!" His voice sounded faint and ghostly.

His heart thundered when they began to levitate. "You have to rouse yourself!"

Her eyes were squeezed closed, her body limp. They ascended past the ceiling. Past the roof. Into the night.

"Josephine!" he bellowed. They were drifting through the rain into the storm clouds. Higher. Higher. She wasn't going to wake!

Then so be it. "Josephine, understand me—wherever we're going . . . we're going to be together." He pulled her close and kissed her.

SEVENTY-THREE

J o blinked open her eyes. Rune was kissing her? When she stiffened against him, he drew his head back.

"Dream?" she asked.

His brows were drawn, eyes wild. "Not quite."

She frowned. She wasn't in bed? No, he was outside with her. The air felt really thin. And cold. She peered up. The stars burned bright.

Too bright.

She met his gaze—read their situation from the alarm in his expression. "I sleep-ghosted?"

"Yes, love." He swallowed. "Up."

She didn't want to look. "Wh-where are we?"

He gave a curt nod. In other words, *Yes, it's that bad.*

"Why are you with me?"

He grated, "Because that's where I bloody belong."

She peered down. Sucked in a breath. Panicked.

She started to embody, her stomach lurching as they plummeted.

As soon as she'd solidified enough, Rune coiled his arms around her and traced them to her bed.

"Ah, gods, Josephine." He tucked her into his lap, his lungs heaving.

"Wh-what happened?" Panting, she clung to him, savoring his heat and strength, inhaling his scent.

"We went for a trip." His heart pounded at her ear.

"I took you with me?"

With his chin on her head, he nodded. "You turned intangible and began to rise. I tried to wake you, barely catching your grip in time." He pressed his lips against her hair.

Catching her grip? "Why didn't you let me go? I know how scared of heights you are."

He drew back. "I will *never* let you go." He cradled her face in his hands. "Wherever you were headed—I don't give a fuck—that's where I want to be as well."

He'd been her anchor, refusing to release her. Just as she'd always wanted.

Then she remembered.

"I've missed you so much, Josie—"

She pushed at his chest until he eased his hold. "How did you know where I was?" She scrambled off the bed, standing to face him.

He stood as well. "I've known since that night at Val Hall." He was unshaven, with dark circles under his eyes. He'd lost weight, his jeans hanging looser than usual.

"You've been spying on me!"

He nodded shamelessly. "I've lived in the carriage house for the last week."

Then he'd overheard every conversation between her and Thad. "You need to go. Not doing this here. I'm not doing this with you."

"Please. Give me five minutes."

She glared, rubbing her arms. She was freezing in only a T-shirt—since it'd been chilly in the *stratosphere*.

"You're cold." He crossed to her, removing his coat. "Take my jacket."

Ignoring him, she traced to her closet for clothes. "I can't believe you've been right there all week," she called as she yanked on jeans. "Why not show yourself?"

"An ally pointed out I shouldn't barge in on your bonding with Thad. You'd waited more than half your life to reunite with him. I decided nothing should interrupt you two."

She snatched on a hoodie, her anger seething. She'd been in a good place with hating him. Then he had to go and follow her into space and all. "You were spying on me—except for when you went out to score?" She returned to her room. "The demon in you needs to get off multiple times a day, right?"

He closed the distance between them with two strides of his long legs. Standing too close, he gazed down at her. "The demon in me is mated. As is the fey. Both are quite happy about this."

Even now he could affect her. Luckily, all she had to do was recall . . . "That didn't stop you with Meliai."

"No, it didn't."

To hear it confirmed . . . Knife in gut. Her outline flickered.

"*I* stopped myself with Meliai."

"What does that mean?" *Please mean what I think it means!*

"I didn't have sex with her."

Wasn't the word *sex* a qualifier in this sense? "You two got off another way? A little slap and tickle for the nymph? Hey, as long as she was satisfied, right?"

"I was determined to breach the wraiths that night; I was in bed, naked with her."

Jo couldn't stifle her wince.

"No one got off in any way, and I guarantee she was anything but satisfied. But I don't really remember what I was doing—I get . . . detached. I go cold, and my mind grows hazy."

Flashes of a dream arose. A new one. Before Jo had sleep-ghosted, she must've seen another memory of his. She experienced that night on Ayers Rock from his point of view. When she'd admitted her phobia to him, he'd thought, *She fears floating away; I fear extinguishing my emotions forever. . . . Maybe we could be each other's anchors.*

Her lips parted. *I go cold.* He'd grown so detached that he'd feared staying that way forever.

She'd seen how unemotional he was with others. On that last night, he'd told her, "I want you to experience what it's like feeling utterly nothing."

But she'd experienced his emotions for her.

"I remember replaying every word of our fight," he said. "I was consumed with jealousy at the thought of you biting another."

His comment snapped her from her thoughts. "So I'm not the only one with jealousy issues?"

He gave her a look that said *You have no idea.* "I decided I never wanted another to know your bite. That it was *our* private act, only between us, to bond us. I realized that's how you view sex. And I realized I do too, with you. I abruptly stopped with Meliai, wanting only to get back to you."

Jo turned from him, putting space between them. "Well, good for you, Rune, you didn't sleep with her. You did assure me it wouldn't happen *every* night." In a fake cheery tone, she said, "Why, after the Accession, your cheating might taper off even more!"

He grimaced. "If I could take back those words—"

"I still won't tolerate it, and you still have to do it for your work."

"I resigned from that part of my job," he rushed to say. "Actually, I'd consider my new circumstances more of a promotion. I'm an archer only from now on."

She narrowed her eyes, refusing to get her hopes up. "Maybe there was some truth to the things you said. I don't see how this can work between us when you think I'm immature and childish."

"I believed you were trying to manipulate me because I never thought you'd choose to end this—even though you'd warned me."

"You were so adamant that night. It's hard for me to wrap my head around this turnaround."

"One of the reasons I was holding on to that life was because I didn't want to change again. Magh had forced me to so many times, and I think on some level, I equated change *with* her. So I resisted. Then I realized you were right—that transaction would have made me a whore. I recognized I'd never *stopped* being one."

"I was angry when I said that."

"You should've been. I was an ass. I'd continued to view myself as I'd been in the past. It didn't matter how much I'd accomplished or how far I'd climbed, I couldn't see my own worth." He rubbed a hand over his tired face. "Orion told me I was my own undoing."

Orion was still hitting all the right notes with Jo. "Where does that leave you now?"

"I hope starting anew with my beautiful mate. Those days are past for me, Josephine."

She almost ghosted through the floor with happiness. Wait . . . "You had a phoenix feather at Val Hall. Didn't you get it from Meliai?"

He closed in on her again. She craned her head up, meeting his eyes.

"I stole the feather, threatening her and the covey with a bonedeath arrow. Apparently, that's frowned upon. I'm banned from all coveys."

Jo's lips parted. He would do that for her? "But you're so admiring of them."

He laid his hands on her shoulders. "I admire *nothing* more than you." His words were silky smooth—but his voice was rough with emotion.

"You waited a week before approaching me? Weren't you dying to tell me you hadn't boned the nymph?"

"I was! But I wanted to put your needs before mine. I listened to you and Thad talking, and you were so happy. When you gave him a week, I promised you one as well."

She'd hoped he would live up to her memory of that groom; Rune was schooling the groom.

"I want . . . I *hope* you'll start drinking from me again—then you'll experience my feelings."

Her fangs sharpened for his skin so fast she gasped.

But then his brows drew together. "Unless my memories are hurting you. What were you dreaming of before? You have Thad with you, under the same roof—so why else would you float away?"

Her yearning had been sharp before she'd drifted off. "Because I didn't have you."

He swallowed thickly. "Did I hear you right?"

She laid her hand on his chest. Beneath her palm, his heart was *speeding up*. "I was thinking about you before I slept. Wanting you. Knowing I could never have you after that night."

"Can you forgive me? My actions were idiotic, my words to you hateful. I flinch to recall them. But I will atone if you give me the chance."

Could she? "What do you want from me?"

"Eternity. Everything. I want to start with marrying you. If you'll have me."

She was opening her mouth to say yes, then she recalled another obstacle. "You should know something before you commit to me. You'd talked about a promising lead on a dark fey female. She's here in the city. I think she's even an assassin—"

"I've met her."

If it took the rest of his immortal life, he'd erase that doubt from Josephine's eyes. "She came by to see Thaddeus. I thought her presence might upset you, so I intercepted her. Once I made it clear I was lost for you, we had a nice conversation."

Josephine nibbled her bottom lip. "Lost for me?"

"I told her you are everything." He rubbed his hands from Josephine's shoulders to her neck and back. How much he'd missed the luxury of simply touching her. "I also put in a few good words for Thaddeus."

Her hazel eyes widened. "Get the hell out."

"You don't have any reason to trust me, but I need to convince you

I've changed. I know a way you can feel confident in me." He gazed down at her beloved face, solemnly saying, "Josephine, I vow to the Lore I'll never—"

She slapped her palm over his mouth. "Ah-ah, Rune. When you're faithful to me, it won't be because a vow compels you to be. No more vows to the Lore for either of us, okay?"

She released him when he nodded. But he needed to make her *know*, as he knew. "You trust I'll be true to you?"

"Maybe you're not a *complete* idiot."

He grinned. "Then I vow *to you* I'll never be with another. I love you, Josie."

She sucked in a breath. "I love you too. Even when you're a dickwad."

"You said if we had sex, I'd be telling you things. That I wanted a commitment and a bond between only us, and I would never want another female as long as I lived. I was telling you that"—he ran his knuckles along her cheek—"I just didn't know it yet."

When she leaned into his caress, he knew she had truly forgiven him.

"And didn't *I* tell you that you loved me?" She reached up to twine her hands behind his neck. "I completely called that! When are you gonna realize I'm always right?"

"First step of matehood." The empty aching in his chest faded, warmed by a fire that would never die.

"You need to meet Thad."

He nodded. "I plan to apologize to him for our terse interaction."

She raised her brows, pleased. "What do we do about his Vertas preference?"

Rune tucked her hair behind her ear. "We do nothing."

"Huh?"

"He's a smart kid. If he's around us enough—and them enough—he'll make the right decision." Rune could tell she liked that answer.

"You gotta meet MizB and Gram too. Hey, you could actually eat all the food they insist on cooking."

"If I must," he said. "Over the last week, I might have contemplated sacking that kitchen for leftovers."

"I want to live with you, somewhere close to them."

With a thoughtful expression, he said, "I've got my eye on a condo in Trollton."

Dazzling smile. "I'm supposed to do breakfast in a couple of hours. I could tee up everybody, and you could show."

"I'll bring the ladies flowers. I'm smooth like that. Speaking of breakfast . . ."

Her gaze focused on his neck, on the pulse point that must be fluttering like mad. Her demeanor turned from cheery—to lusty. "My blood is red again. Black's more my color." She leaned up to graze his neck.

Just when he'd been thinking this day couldn't get better . . .

"Have me back in time—for now take me somewhere so I can bite you till you scream."

Like flipping a switch.

EPILOGUE

Jo's reading lessons had started today, and they'd just finished her first session.

Rune took this as seriously as her continuing rune studies. Their new place was covered with spelling Post-it notes. He'd rewarded each stride she made with kisses, making her a highly motivated student.

After Rune had deemed her brilliant, those kisses had landed him in bed. Well, what had he expected? When the first sentence he'd had her put together was *Rune loves Josie*, and he'd held her gaze? She'd been all over him.

Now they were lazing between the sheets, about to get ready for dinner at the Braydens'. Though their new crib (a badass ranch) was in Australia, Rune had used a spell to connect their side entrance to a closet in the carriage house. A knock on the door there was a knock here. They lived a nanosecond away.

He'd also tricked out their new bedroom. Directly above their bed was a barrier spell to prevent sleep-ghosting. It matched the one on the floor. Nobody was going anywhere with Rune on watch. Not that she could when he held her tight, even as he slept. . . .

After Jo and Rune had reunited that first morning—again and again—she'd taken Thad aside. She'd eloquently explained her and Rune's previous relationship issues: "Thought he'd boned this nymph. He didn't. My guy's solid again. Gonna marry him when his people get here."

Thad had looked as happy about that development as Rune had about Mount Hua.

"Just give him a chance, kid. He's funny and smart. You'll like him."

Thad hadn't been disappointed so much by Rune's Møriørness; he'd been bummed Jo was moving out: "I just got you back."

"You're not losing me—you're gaining him. He's already protective of you. Since I'm his mate, you're his brother by fate."

"Brother." Oh, she could tell Thad had dug that. "Huh. Two siblings in a week?"

When the guys in her life had met, Rune had told Thad, "I want to apologize for being so brusque with you last week. I was panicked over my mate's well-being, and I reacted badly. My name is Rune Darklight, and I'm very pleased to meet you." He'd offered his hand.

Thad had taken it. "Thaddeus Brayden. And I totally get it. I could've listened better, but I was freaking out because I'd just been strangling my big sister and all."

Rune had nodded thoughtfully. "I doubt she'll let *that* happen twice, no?"

Thad had grinned. And Jo had known *all is right in the world.*

Since then Rune had traced her and Thad to new dimensions, showing them wonders. The guys got along great, despite Thad's Vertas leanings. Today, he'd gone to meet with some of them to plan Val Hall's rebuild.

But that was okay. With Nïx missing and Orion still a universe away, the war had hit the snooze button. . . .

Now Rune pressed a kiss to her head. "I hope we're having fried chicken tonight."

"Based on your reaction the first time, I think a repeat is guaranteed." No matter how far afield they traveled, Jo, Thad, and Rune convened with MizB and Gram for at least two meals a day. Rune had been the delighted recipient of home-cooked dinners; the women were overjoyed to have someone to cook for.

Jo now had tons of people in her life, interacting.

And there would only be more. Rune wanted her and Thad to meet his allies.

When Rune had heard her talking about Apparitia, he'd feared his liege had destroyed her world. But Rune had chosen to, well, have faith in his faith. "I was right to," he'd told her. "Orion strikes hard at his enemies, but he had nothing to do with Apparitia."

Rune's fellow Møriør, Blace, had once lived on the periphery of the Elserealms where her home world had been located. The vampire might be able to help uncover more information about her parents.

She would ask Blace once she visited Tenebrous. Not anytime soon, though. She didn't want to leave her brother behind for the days it'd take to get there and back. When she'd invited Thad to go with them, he hadn't wanted to leave MizB and Gram. Not yet . . .

Rune stroked her hair and exhaled with satisfaction. "Meadowberry."

She grinned against his chest. She'd dreamed his memories of those fields, of the bliss he'd felt lying among them, with sugar from the berries on his lips and breezes rustling the leaves.

When she'd recounted her dream, he'd cradled her face. "Every day with you is like that now. I'll know that bliss forever. And I'm determined you will too."

The future was so bright. . . .

She'd thought there was no greater connection than destiny decreeing them joined. But there was—the *choice* they'd made to love each other.

Rune shifted her in bed so he could rise above her. "I want you to learn one last word today."

"*Another* one?" she grumbled, acting put-out.

"Uh-huh." Rune pierced his finger for blood, and her eyes went heavy-lidded.

He drew four letters over her chest. Over her heart.

In a breathless voice, she asked, "What does it say?"

His eyes darkened as he rasped, *"Mine."*